Hawthorne: Hazed Hooked Hammered & Hijacked

Hawthorne: Hazed Hooked Hammered & Hijacked

By
Jay Dubya

Published by
Bookstand Publishing
Pasadena, CA 91101
4324_2

ISBN 978-1-63498-200-9

For Sierra and Lindsey

Other Books by Jay Dubya

Adult Fiction

Black Leather and Blue Denim, A '50s Novel
The Great Teen Fruit War, A 1960' Novel
Ron Coyote, Man of La Mangia
Frat' Brats, A '60s Novel
Pieces of Eight
Pieces of Eight, Part II
Pieces of Eight, Part III
Pieces of Eight, Part IV
The Wholly Book of Genesis
The Wholly Book of Exodus
The Wholly Book of Doo-Doo-Rot-on-Me
Thirteen Sick Tasteless Classics
Thirteen Sick Tasteless Classics, Part II
Thirteen Sick Tasteless Classics, Part III
Thirteen Sick Tasteless Classics, Part IV
Thirteen Sick Tasteless Classics, Part V
So Ya' Wanna' Be A Teacher!
Mauled Maimed Mangled Mutilated Mythology
Fractured Frazzled Folk Fables & Fairy Farces
FFFF & FF, Part II
Nine New Novellas
Nine New Novellas, Part II
Nine New Novellas, Part III
Nine New Novellas, Part IV
One Baker's Dozen
Two Baker's Dozen
RAM: Random Articles and Manuscripts
Time Travel Tales
Modern Mythology
UFO: Utterly Fantastic Occurrences
Prime-Time Crime Time
Snake Eyes and Boxcars
Snake Eyes and Boxcars, Part II
The Psychic Dimension
The Psychic Dimension, Part II
Shakespeare: Slammed, Smeared, Savaged and Slaughtered
Shakespeare: S, S, S & S, Part II
First Person Stories

The Arcane Arcade
Thirteen Tantalizing Tales
PLOTS
PLOTS, Part II
THEMES
Hawthorne: Hacked, Shakespeare: Sacked, & Thurber: Thwacked
Suite 16
The FBI Inspector
Poe: Pelted, Pounded, Pummeled and Pulverized
Twain: Tattered, Trounced, Tortured and Traumatized
London: Lashed, Lacerated, Lampooned and Lambasted
O. Henry: Obscenely and Outrageously Obliterated
Homer's Odd Sea Odyssey
HOMER'S ILL Iliad
The Timeless Time Machine
War of the Worlds
The Invisible Man

Young Adult Fantasy Novels and Stories

Pot of Gold
Enchanta
Space Bugs, Earth Invasion
The Eighteen Story Gingerbread House

Contents

"Nathaniel Hawthorne" (1804-1864)

For many years Nathaniel Hawthorne had attempted to become an established popular fiction writer. After a decent New England college education, Hawthorne soon returned to familiar Salem, Massachusetts where the aspiring author lived with his mother and sisters for twelve years, staying secluded in a lonely room writing short stories and novel manuscripts. In 1837, his first work titled *Twice-Told Tales* was successfully published.

Hawthorne was chummy with some of the more famous New England literary writers of his time including Herman Melville, Henry Wadsworth Longfellow, and Ralph Waldo Emerson.

Two of Hawthorne's better-known works are novels *The Scarlet Letter* and *The House of the Seven Gables.* "Young Goodman Brown," "The Great Stone Face" and "Rappaccini's Daughter" are three of the author's best known short stories.

Most of Hawthorne's retelling of classic stories from mythology had been published in his work *Tanglewood Tales*. Another famous Nathaniel Hawthorne short story collection is *Twice-Told Tales,* which includes the selections "The Minister's Black Veil", "Dr. Heidegger's Experiment" and "The Great Carbuncle".

"Young Goodman Brown"

Young Goodman Brown was a good man who stridently stepped forth at sunset into the main cobblestone street at Salem Village. After crossing the threshold, the gentleman put his head back and exchanged a parting kiss with his young wife. And Faith, as the wife was aptly named, thrust her own pretty head into the street, letting the wind play with the pink ribbons of her cap, while she whispered an imperative instruction to Goodman Brown. "When you're away on 'husband's night out', don't you dare try screwing my promiscuous, nymphomaniac sisters Hope and Charity!" Faith sternly commanded. "After all Goodman, we're prudish Puritans through-and-through. Don't ya' get it!"

"I'm not going into the forest to get laid," Goodman replied. "I just want to get some orange marmalade poison ivy instead!"

"Dearest Heart," the newly-married wife again whispered, softly and rather sadly, when her warm lips were quite close to his cauliflower ear, "Please put-off your journey until sunrise, and sleep in your own bed tonight. A lone woman is troubled with such dreams of infidelity, and such filthy thoughts of group sex that she's afraid of herself sometimes. Pray tarry with me this night, dear Husband, of all nights in the year. I'm hornier than Hell; and I'm now over having my bloody period! And Goodman, you can play your guitar, and be my personal minstrel after my annoying menstrual!"

"My love and my Faith," young Goodman Brown replied, "of all nights in the year, this one night I must tarry away south in the direction of Tarrytown from thee. My journey, as thou callest it, forth and back again, needs to be occurring 'twixt now and sunrise. What now? My sweet, pretty wife doubts my integrity already, and we being but three-months married? I mean, I've only cheated on you ninety-seven times!"

"Then, God bless you, and safeguard your admirable penis and testicles!" Faith prayed, with the pink ribbons of her black bonnet blowing directly into Goodman's face. "And may you find all well when you come back to Salem Village and discover your three naughty younger brothers in the fuckin' sack with me."

"Amen, my 'fairly pretty' one!" Goodman Brown answered. "Say thy prayers this evening, dear Faith, and go to bed at dusk, and I'm pretty certain no harm will come to thee with my three strong, post-pubescent, punk brothers playing doctor under the linen bedcovers with you."

So, the newlyweds parted; and the young man pursued his way until, being about to turn the corner by the meeting-house where souls were cured, right next to the meat-house where meat was cured, Goodman Brown looked back and noticed the head of Faith, still peeping after his departure, with a melancholy expression evident upon her rosy countenance, in spite of her pink ribbons and hidden wet pink pussy.

"Poor, little Faith!" the traveler thought, for his heavy heart smote his sensibilities like the sword of Perseus had decapitated Medusa. "What a wretch I am to leave her, just to embark on such a dumb-ass errand as mine is! She talks of dreams, too. I thought as Faith spoke there was trouble upon her face, as if a premonition had warned her of what oddball work is to be performed tonight. But no, no; it would kill my dear wife to even contemplate it. Well," the ambler uttered to himself' as was his bad public habit, "she's a blessed angel on Earth, who just has to wing-it for this evening; and after this one night, I'll cling to her skirts and follow her from the outskirts of Salem Village all the way to Heaven's Gate, or to Hell's Door if need be."

With *that* excellent resolve for the anticipated future marital reunion, Goodman felt himself compelled and justified in making more haste on his present 'evil force purpose' before his erratic bowels completely emptied fecal matter into his clean pants. The fearful fellow had taken a rather dreary road, darkened by all the gloomiest trees of the expansive New England forest, which barely stood aside to let the narrow path creep through its very ominous interior.

'Ah, yes,' Goodman reckoned. 'Whenever I see tall evergreen trees in the forest, I fully realize how my lonely heart pines for my wonderful Faith!'

And then, young Brown hastened his pace and ambitiously accelerated his chubby rear-end into a mild trot. The meandering trail was as lonely as could be, and a distinct peculiarity prevailed in such a quiet dark solitude, a weird silence that the paranoid traveler knows not who or what might be concealed by the innumerable trunks and by the thick tree boughs precariously suspended overhead. With measured lonely footsteps, the wary trekker may yet be passing through an unseen multitude of hidden dangers that would make Goodman Brown more than an endangered species.

"There may be a devilish Indian, maybe a Brave from Atlanta, or perhaps a Black-hawk from Chicago, lurking behind every tree," Goodman Brown stammered to himself. And then, the nervous asshole glanced fearfully behind and added, "What if the Devil himself should be at my very elbow! I'm a strong son-of-a-bitch, but certainly no match for that barbaric supernatural fuck-head, ubiquitous Satan!"

Goodman's head, now being turned back south again, Mr. Brown passed a crook of the road, and with his keen eyes looking forward again for potential human crooks, beheld the figure of a man, clad in grave-but-decent attire, comfortably seated at the foot of an old oak tree. The waiting eight-foot-tall giant arose at Goodman Brown's rapid approach, and then walked onward side by side with him.

"You're late for our secret rendezvous, Goodman Brown," the tall fellow observed and recognized. "The clock of the Old South was striking incessantly as I came through Boston, and that was a full three hundred-and-fifteen-minutes and eighteen-and-a-half-seconds-ago."

"Faith kept me back a while," metaphorically replied the young romantic, with a tremor denoted in his voice, caused by the sudden appearance of his obscure companion, though not wholly unexpected. 'If I had gotten laid like I had wished, I'd be less nervous now after releasing all of that pent-up energy during hot, lengthy sex!' Goodman speculated as the unlikely pair entered deeper into the dark woods.

It was then late dusk inside the deciduous forest, and deepest yet in that part of the woods where those two simpleton, fuck-heads were journeying. As nearly as could be discerned by Goodman, the companion traveler was about fifty-to-sixty years of age, apparently in the same social rank of life as Goodman Brown; another lowly lowlife, nondescript, unhappy asshole, and the odd fellow 'bearing' a considerable resemblance to *him,* both weirdos looking somewhat like discontented black and white pandas.

Still the two, having nothing better to do at midnight than to saunter and bull-shit in the dark forest, the pair might have been mistaken for tall father and short son. And yet, though the elder person was as simply clad as the younger, and as simple in manner, including speech and idiocy too, the older jerk-off had an indescribable air of one who knew plenty about the world, and who now thought the world of Goodman Brown, the young man possibly collaborating in a gay relationship, which might be started during an unexpected nocturnal eclipse brownout on that ominous Salem, Massachusetts night.

The fairly well-dressed forest stranger (not ranger) would not have felt abashed at the governor's dinner table, or in King William's Court playing basketball, tennis, badminton, or lawyer, were it possible that his bisexual affairs should call him thither. But the only thing about the anonymous tall asshole that could be fixed-upon as remarkable was his fabulous, magical walking-staff, which could marvelously walk-around without him ever holding the object.

The long thick stick, longer and thicker than Zeus's fabled dick, bore the likeness of a great and curiously wrought black snake. The viper might almost be seen to twist and wriggle itself like a living serpent, even when neither Goodman Brown, nor any other male (including transgender ones), could see *his* own limp pecker when taking a long half-hour piss. That viper stick animation, of course, must have been an ocular deception, possibly assisted by the uncertain New Moon's light.

"Come, Goodman Brown," insisted his fellow-traveler. "This is a dull pace for the beginning of an arduous forest journey. Take my staff, the long serpent I am holding, and not the short erect one between my legs, if you are so soon weary."

"Friend," Goodman replied, exchanging his slow pace for a full stop. "Having kept my covenant by meeting thee here, it is my purpose now to return from where I came. I have scruples touching the matter thou are currently bullshitting, for by reputation, I am a mere Salem dumb-ass, and you're an important Salem smart-ass!"

"Sayest thou, so?" the keeper of the serpent acknowledged, smiling apart from his monologue. "I'm presently only a keeper of the serpent, and not a full-fledged keeper of all reptiles in the Salem Zoo House. Let us walk-on, Goodman, for we have no horses, mules, or donkeys to transport our tender asses. Nevertheless," the dark stranger continued his verbal rambling, "reasoning and discussing as we go, all about morality, immorality, and other religious Puritanical nonsense, too. And if I convince thee not about my horse crap ideas, thou shalt in good judgment turn back toward Salem at your' discretion. We are but a little way into the forest yet, so naturally Goodman, I maintain that you can't see the fuckin' forest for the trees."

"Too far! Too damned far into the dark interior! I wish I had *four balls!*" exclaimed the young good man, unconsciously resuming his gait because he had been afraid of 'striking out'. "My cowardly father never ambled at midnight into the woods on such an obscure errand, nor did his craven father before him. We've been a race of honest Puritan men and good Christians, ever since the days of the New Testament martyrs, and the years of the Koran's suicide bombers; and shall I be the first of the name of Brown that ever took this path and kept it, for I've no special peripheral desire to ever become a fucked-up path toll collector!"

"Such company, thou wouldst say," observed and stated the elder hooded trekker, interpreting his current pause. "Well said, Goodman Brown! I've been as well-acquainted with your family as with ever a one amongst the impure and pure Puritans; and that's no trifle for me to say. I had helped your grandfather, the constipated chronically constable, when he had lashed the adulterous Quaker woman for wearing fake eyelashes. And it was I that brought your father a pitch-pine knot, kindled at my own hearth, to set fire to an Indian village, in King Philip's War," the phantom stranger reminded Goodman. "I had taught your old man how to be a constructive, destructive arsonist."

"Yes, pop and grand-pop always remarked how you liked to start fires, and that you had evolved into an excellent pyro-manic," young Brown attested. "You really know how to turn the heat up a notch, that's for damned sure."

"Your pop and old grand-dad really loved moonshine whiskey," the dark stranger disclosed to his prospective new disciple. "Both undistinguished snot-noses were my good friends; and many a pleasant walks did we have along this same familiar path, and returned merrily back to Salem like gay homosexuals after midnight. I would fain be friends with you for *their* sake. Let's now take a long stroll in the dark down Memory Lane!"

"I'm only trying to distill the truth. If it be as thou sayest," replied Goodman Brown. "I marvel that pop and old grand-dad never spoke of these moonshine or forest trek matters; or, verily, I marvel not, seeing that the least rumor of the sort would've driven them from New England all the way to Tim Buck-Tooth's house back in downtown Salem. We are a people of prayer, and good works to boot, and abide by no such immoral wickedness such as committing mortal sin and evil debauchery."

"Wickedness or not," evaluated and emphasized the dark traveler with the twisted snake staff, "I have a very general acquaintance here in New England. The deacons of many a church have drunk the communion wine laced with delicious moonshine liquor with me; the selectmen of diverse towns proudly have made me their swimming instructor and chairman; and a majority of the Great and General Court are firm supporters of my deviant interests also," the dark-shadowed phantom ambler bragged. "The governor, and I too, play canasta and blackjack together, and when we get it on, we play stud strip poker. But these are state secrets I'm now sharing with you, that is, Goodman Brown, I'm confidentially advising you that if you play your cards right, beginning tonight, you'll quickly advance to a high level in Salem society."

"Can this be done so outside a sinful casino?" Goodman Brown questioned, with a stare of amazement directed toward his unperturbed companion. "Howbeit, that presently, I have nothing to do with the powerful governor and council, and now you suddenly want me to play strip poker with them, possibly in the nude; those faggots that run Salem politics have their own naked ways, and the connivers are no rule of example for a simple, straight, ordinary husband like me. But, were I to go on with thee, Stubborn Stranger, who had been a close intimate friend with pop and with old grand-dad, how should I meet the eye of that good old man, our suspected faggot minister at Salem Village?" Goodman rhetorically asked the sinister tall phantom. "Oh, his high-pitched staccato voice would make me tremble both on Sabbath Day, and on Saturday lecture day. The son-of-a-bitch sounds like a Castrati choir boy when the gay shit-head talks. Thank goodness, I've never heard the ugly faggot cocksucker sing!"

Thus far, the down-to-earth elder traveler had patiently listened to his fledgling associate with due gravity. But now, the phantom companion burst into a fit of irrepressible mirth, shaking himself worse than a Quaker, quivering so violently that his snake-like staff actually seemed to wriggle in sympathy.

"Ha! ha! ha!" the mysterious fuck-head shouted again and again; and then composing himself declared, "Well, go on, Goodman Brown; go on; but, please, don't kill me with your naïve humor, or else I might die laughing from it, ha, ha, ha!"

"Well then, for me to end the matter abruptly at once," flustered Goodman Brown reacted, considerably nettled. "There is the salient issue of my wife, Faith. It would break her dear little heart if I were to leave her for a gay male partner; and I'd rather break my own balls with a sledgehammer if I were forced to abandon her and her magnificent furry pleasure garden."

"Nay, if that be the sole case for objection," the other forest trekker objected and commented, "then I insist that you go thy separate way, Goodman Brown. I would not for twenty old women substitute the elderly bitch my eyes detect hobbling before us. I promise you that your Faith back in Salem will not be coming to any risk or harm."

As the peculiar-minded stranger spoke, the garrulous asshole pointed his irregular-shaped staff at the aged female figure ahead on the dusky path, of whom Goodman Brown recognized to be a very pious and exemplary-looking dame, who had in his youth taught him his catechism and his breast-sucking, and who was still his moral and spiritual adviser, jointly with the Salem Minister and Deacon Gookin, who also was taught serious breast-sucking by "the popular tit woman".

"A marvel, truly, that Goody Cloyse should be so far into the wilderness, sharing her bountiful goodies at nightfall," Goodman determined and remarked. "But with your leave, Anonymous Guide, I shall take a long-cut through the woods until we have left this promiscuous Christian woman and her nice firm behind, behind. Being a stranger to you," young Brown vociferated and then cleared his throat, "the hoary bitch might ask whom I was consorting with, and where, I was going. I don't need that jealous old hag biting my dick off while giving me intense fellatio. I heard it from the vineyard's grapevine, yes, from another sinister gay stranger just like yourself named Marvin, that Goody Cloyse's sharp teeth had once administered a vicious bite to the minister's limp erection!"

"Be it so, young Goodman," the confused path-stroller's fellow-traveler opined. "That sort of S and M dandy dick bite you've just mentioned sounds quite goody-goody to me. Betake you to the woods, and let me keep the path clear."

Accordingly, the young man turned aside, but took care to suspiciously watch his new-found companion, who advanced softly along the road until the itinerant pervert had come within a staff's length of the old expert dame proficient at administering fellatio to both ministers and to non-ministers alike.

Goody Cloyse, meanwhile, was making the best of her way, with singular speed for so aged a wrinkled woman, and mumbling some indistinct and indiscernible words, sounding something like a Neo-Christian Satanic prayer reciter, doubtless, as she demonstratively wiggled her firm ass to-and-fro along the shadowy path. The phantom traveler, dressed in black, just like local Puritan Reverend Jonathan Cache, put forth his staff and touched her withered neck with what seemed to be the serpent's tail.

"The Devil!" the pious old lady screamed. "That diabolical viper's tail is a replica of the Devil's red dick!"

"Then, Goody Cloyse knows her old Friend, doesn't she?" observed and spoke the dark traveler, directly confronting the old harlot's countenance, and leaning on his writhing stick while admiring the open-mouthed woman's sharp incisors. "Old Bitch; let's just not have verbal intercourse!"

"Ah, forsooth, and is it your worship indeed I'm confronting?" the good old Irish dame from Notre Dame spoke. "Yea, truly it is, and in the very image of my old gossip, Goodman Brown, the youth's grandfather who was my first dead victim. But would your worship ever believe it? My magical flying broomstick hath strangely disappeared, stolen as I suspect, by that unhanged witch, Goody Cory. And all *that* stealthy pilfering shit happened when my face and mouth were being anointed with the minister's hot sperm juice, and with his favorite pet's wolf's bane! It's really hard being a sex-crazed vampire nowadays, yes, it is, especially at my advanced age!"

"Mingled with fine wheat and the fat of a new-born babe," cryptically replied the dark shape of old Goodman Brown, the queer, scary ventriloquist voice originating from the mouth of the obscure forest stranger. "Goody Cloyse, your terrific fellatio therapy just blew me away, right into the fuckin' afterlife!"

"Ah, your worship knows the secret sperm juice and wolf's bane recipe," the delighted old lady shrieked, cackling aloud. "So, as I was saying, being all ready for the slated spiritual revival meeting, and having no horse or zebra to ride upon, I made up my mind to hoof it by foot into the woods; for the Salem big-butted scuttle-butters tell me there is a nice young man to be taken into unholy communion tonight. First, I presume, pantheistic communion with nature, as that numb-nuts philosopher Thoreau thoroughly suggests, and then, communion with me, ha, ha, ha!

But now," Goody Cloyse closed her eloquent oratory while still wearing her black clothes, "your good worship will kindly lend me your arm, and we shall be there at the tent-less, demonic soul revival in a twinkling of an eye, or in the sparkle of a night star."

"That can hardly be," her sinister and mysterious Friend argued. "I may not spare you my arm, Goody Cloyse; but here is my staff if you wish to expedite your journey by flying non-stop, first class to your scheduled revival destination, if you will."

So, saying those pathetic prophetic words, the sinister stranger threw his snake-decorated staff down at Goody Cloyse's swollen feet, where, perhaps, the object assumed life, being one of the rods which its owner had formerly lent to the Egyptian magi before, according to the Old Testament Bible, the wise advisers to the Pharoah had quickly died of advanced "staff-infections".

Of this suspect fact, however, Goodman Brown's pea-sized brain could not fathom sufficient cognizance. The one-night forest trekker (looking for a one-nighter) had cast-up his eyes in astonishment, and then peering-down again, beheld neither Goody Cloyse, nor the abominable serpentine staff, but his pupils only perceived his fellow-eerie traveler standing there alone, who had prudently waited for *his* attention as calmly as if nothing had ever happened to Goody Cloyse, who incidentally was not wearing vanishing cream, but only a little minister's sperm juice upon her disappearing wrinkled face.

"That old woman taught me my catechism and my breast-sucking exercises, and her chest flesh was colder than a witch's tit!" the young married man indicated to his fellow forest ambler; and there was indeed a world of relevant meaning in the mere utterance of *that* simple comment.

"Yes, Goody Cloyse isn't exactly a Miss Goody-Goody Two-slippers," the mysterious phantom stranger informed Goodman. "She sort of reminds me of the flying aviator wife of the Wizard of Og, featured in the Old Testament Book V, *The Wholly Book of Doo-Doo-Rot-on-Me.*"

* * * * * * * * * * * *

The oddball forest pair continued walking onward along the Path of Ignorance towards an undisclosed important destination, while the provocative elder traveler exhorted his callow shallow companion to make good speed and persevere along the darkened trail, discoursing so aptly that *his* infallible arguments seemed rather to spring-up like ideological jack-rabbits into the bosom of his eloquent oration, rather than to be actually suggested by *his* own thinking.

As the duo ambled-on into the darkened interior, the Grimy Reaper in minister's attire plucked a maple tree branch to now serve as Goodman's convenient walking stick, and the morbid personage began to strip it of the twigs and little boughs, which were wet with evening dew, and with some wild animal's doo-doo, too.

The moment that Mr. Goodman Brown's fingers touched the improvised "Moses staff", the pole became strangely withered and dried-up, as if being exposed to a summer week's heated sunshine. Thus, the disparate pair proceeded southward, at a good free pace, until suddenly, in a gloomy sleepy hollow of the road, Goodman Brown sat himself down upon an enormous tree stump and refused to go any further, because his addled brain had then become especially stumped.

"Friend," young Goodman Brown addressed, stubbornly giving his non-political stump speech. "My Puritan mind is made up. Not another step will I budge on this eccentric errand into the dense wilderness. What if a wretched old hag with a dried-up, lice-infested love-tunnel does choose to go visit the Devil when I thought she was instead going to Heaven to be on Cloud Nine, making-out with a horny rebellious archangel? Is that any reason why I should quit my dear Faith and go after *her,* the raunchy disappearing old witch bitch with the dried-up, lice-infested crotchola trying to hustle my ass?"

"You'll definitely think better of this recent phenomenon you had just witnessed by and by," Goodman's alter-ego acquaintance predicted rather composedly. "Sit here and rest yourself a while; and when you feel like moving your ass forward again, I suggest that you take a goddamned hike, Goodman! There is always my trusty staff to help you along the Path of Knowledge, er, I mean along the Path of Escaping Puritanical Ignorance."

Without any more words being enunciated, the foreboding dark trekker threw his vernal companion the aforementioned maple stick, and soon the phantom was as speedily out of sight (no, he was not blind), as if the bizarre asshole had supernaturally vanished directly into the deepening gloom through some mystical, occult sort of environmental osmosis, amazingly duplicating the quite instant disappearance of old retired hooker, Goody Cloyse.

The young man sat a few moments by the dismal roadside, praising himself greatly, and thinking with how clear a conscience Mr. Brown should meet the gay LBGT minister in his morning walk, nor shrink from the eye of good old Deacon Gookin, whom Goodman had theorized the dusky stranger was (or had been) impersonating.

And what calm sleep would be his own that very night, which was to have been spent so wickedly, but so purely and sweetly now, in the arms of Wife Faith; or perhaps Sister Hope, or maybe even Mother Superior Charity! Amidst those particular pleasant and praiseworthy meditations, Goodman Brown's ears heard the distant tramp of horses' hoofs pounding along the road, and the neurotic dumb fuck deemed it advisable to conceal himself within the verge of the forest, conscious of the guilt-laden curious purpose that had brought him thither, though now so happily turned-away from baneful temptation, and equally baneful Puritanical sin.

On came the hoof tramps and the voices of the militant riders, two grave old voices, conversing soberly as their powerful steeds drew near. Those mingled sounds appeared to pass along the road, within a few yards of the young man's makeshift hiding-place; but owing doubtless to the depth of the gloom at that specific forest spot, neither the travelers nor their steeds identities were identifiable to Goodman's inferior eyesight.

The on-a-mission figures' dangling legs brushed against the small boughs along the wayside, and it could not be seen that the riders had intercepted, even for a moment, the faint gleam from the strip of the dull sky's brief opening through the trees, a view which the jockeys must have just passed by *their* hiding observer's location.

Goodman Brown alternately crouched, as if taking a healthy crap, and then stood on tiptoes as if taking a short piss, pulling aside the camouflaging branches and thrusting forth his head as far as he could without discerning so much as a fleeting shadow.

The new forest encounter vexed Mr. Brown the more, because unemployed Goodman could have sworn, were such an honest thing possible, that he had recognized the unique voices of the faggot minister and the preacher's loyal associate, believed-to-be-gay Deacon Gookin, trotting along quietly upon their stallions, as the unscrupulous pair was wont to do, when bound as companions by necessity in the direction of some obscure sacramental ordination, or of some irrelevant ecclesiastical council. While yet within hearing distance, one of the religious riders stopped to pluck a birch switch.

"Of the two events, Reverend Sir," the voice sounding like that of the theoretically gay church deacon spoke. "I'd rather miss an ordination dinner than miss tonight's hastily-scheduled impromptu revival meeting. Rebel churchgoers tell me that some members of our LBGT community are to be assembled here from Falmouth; from Foul Mouth, and beyond, and others from Connecticut (Cunt Etiquette), and also a few radical Biblical scholars from Rhode Island, besides several adherents of the local Indian powwows, who, after their fashion, know almost as much deviltry as the best of us demented LBGT Rebel Puritan Christians do. Moreover, there is a goodly young woman to be taken into wicked communion during tonight's imaginative, newly-written, contemporary group sex sacrament."

"Mighty well, Deacon Gookin!" the solemn old tones of the influential faggot minister agreed. "Spur-up my Aide, or we shall be late for our spurious activities, ha, ha, ha. Nothing can be done, you know, until I get on the ground and get attacked by devout, aroused LBGT followers in my new shadow congregation."

The horses' hoofs clattered again against the forest ground and the voices, talking so strangely in the night's empty air, passed-on through the thick vegetation, where no church had ever before been gathered, or solitary Christian prayer ever practiced. Where then, could these totally fucked-up, sanctimonious, formerly holy men be journeying so deep into the heathen wilderness?

Young Goodman Brown caught hold of a tree for support while finally taking a long healthy piss, making the ground so soggy that his feet were ready to sink-down into the wet earth. Feeling faint and dizzy, Goodman's bloodshot eyes stared-up to the night sky's constellations, doubting whether there really was an inspirational Divine Heaven existing above him. Yet, there was the deep blue Arch of Paradise, and the surrounding stars brightening around it.

"With Heaven above, and with Faith below, I will yet stand firm against the Devil's trickery!" Goodman Brown maintained. "I'm fuckin' straight, and I refuse to be gay! I'm definitely not a fellow fellatio to either the faggot minister or the supposedly gay deacon!"

While Young Mr. Brown still gazed-upward into the deep Arch of the Firmament, and then lifted his hands to pray to his Biblical Deity, though no apparent wind was stirring, a low cloud hurried across the zenith and ominously obscured the brightening stars. The vanishing dark blue sky was still visible, except directly overhead, where a black mass (here: not a religious ceremony for African Americans) of clouds was sweeping swiftly northward. Aloft in the air, as if from the depths of the inexplicable cloud, came a confused and doubtful tone of gibberish-sounding voices.

Once the avid, astute listener fancied that his ears could distinguish the accents of towns-people of his own place and time, presumably, fucked-up Salem Village men and women, both pious and ungodly, many of whom Goodman had met both at the communion and ex-communication tables, and had seen in the past other rowdy revelers possessing similar voices, rioting for free beer and liquor at the raucous town tavern.

The next hallucinating moment, so indistinct were the queer sounds, Goodman doubted whether he had heard nothing except the murmur of the old forest, whispering softly without a wind, conversing with the nearby babbling brook.

Then, blasting through the eerie air wafted a stronger swell of those same familiar Sunday Puritan church tones. The myriad choir altos and sopranos, along with the male bass and baritones, were akin to the musical notes and octaves heard daily among the faithful at Salem Village; but never until now originating from a dark forest.

There was one special voice of a young woman, uttering sorrowful lamentations, yet saturated with an uncertain sadness, and entreating for some favor, sexual in desire of course, which perhaps, it would grieve her to obtain any satisfaction in fucked-up Puritan pre-colonial days, where inflexible Taliban-type rules prevailed. And then, all of the vague and nebulous two-dimensional multitude, both saints and sinners' alike, all producing prolific shouts and shrieks, all alien-outlandish voices seeming to encourage and invoke the disturbed girl's excessive spirit-consuming lust for sex to heighten.

"Faith!" Goodman Brown exclaimed, in a voice of agony and desperation. "I wanted to get laid, too, before our wedding!" And the echoes of the enchanted forest egregiously mocked the lost young fellow, his voice again crying, "Faith! Faith!" as if the gathered bewildered wretches were seeking his virgin wife's frightened attention, all through the entire anti-Puritan ceremony.

The cry of grief, rage, and terror was yet piercing the night air, when the unhappy husband held his breath in order to organize a satisfactory response to what Goodman had been witnessing. There was a definite scream emitted, drowned immediately in a louder murmur of quarreling fucked-up dissonant voices, fading into far-off fucked-up laughter, as the dark cloud slowly swept away, leaving the clear and silent sky doming above Goodman Brown's vulnerable, easily-influenced head.

But then, something fluttered lightly down through the air, and caught upon the branch of a tree. The young man seized the cotton material, and his eyes beheld a pink ribbon, which Young Mr. Brown intelligently and sagaciously conjectured symbolized Faith's luscious wet pink snatcheroo.

"My Faith is gone!" the puzzled idiot ascertained, after enduring one stupefied moment of reflection without the aid of a hand-held pocket mirror. "There is no good man on Earth; and sin is but a lousy immaterial name. Come, Devil; for to thee is this world given. I would prefer to live forever in Hell in pleasurable sin than for all eternity in Heaven being denied all the things that bring me primitive biological satisfaction and gratification. Why is mortal life such a fucked-up travesty? Am I witnessing some perverted Devil Cult ceremony?"

And, maddened with despair, so that *the spectator* laughed loud and long at his moral and immoral folly, did Goodman Brown grasp his staff and set forth again, at such a rate of speed that his movement seemed to fly effortlessly along the dark forest path, rather than to walk or run its length. The road grew wilder and drearier, and more faintly traced, and soon vanished at a distance, leaving the petrified staff-flyer in the heart of the dark wilderness, still rushing onward with the base instinct that guides mortal men to voluntarily perform evil.

"I can now understand how Goody Cloyse uses her flying broomstick to sweep a good man like me off his feet!" Young Brown realized and muttered to the various trees his airborne progress had been speeding by. "Wow! This experience is truly me owning a really neat fly-by-night business operation! And now Goodman," the tragic fool commenced singing to himself, "so ya' met someone and now you know how it feels, Goody, Goody!"

The whole forest was currently abundant with frightful sounds such as the creaking of the tall trees; the howling of wild beasts, and the yells of fanatical drunken Indians. Sometimes, the swirling wind tolled like a distant church bell, and sometimes the intense breeze gave a broad roar circulating around the swift-moving, flying traveler, as if all Nature was personally laughing and scornfully mocking aviator Brown and his fast forest passage.

But now, Goodman comprehended that he himself was the chief horror of the dangerous scene, and the moral high-velocity traffic violator shrank not from its other enveloping horrors in total terror.

"Ha! ha! ha!" exhilarated Goodman Brown roared when the sarcastic wind seemingly had been laughing at him. "Ventilate my balls, but don't break them! I still must orgasm with my lawful wife Faith to further dispel this horrendous immoral experience! Let us hear which Asshole, either supernatural or human, will laugh loudest," the makeshift broomstick rider yelled to the blurring forest like an obsessed maniac. "Think not to frighten me with your pretentious deviltry. Come witch; come wizard; come drunken Indian powwow participants; come Devil himself; and come ya-hoo asshole forest voices, here comes dependable Goodman Brown to the rescue. You may as well fear me as I fear you, anonymous asshole supernatural voices!"

In truth, all through that section of the haunted forest, there could be nothing more frightful than the figure of Goodman Brown going absolutely berserk upon the converted flying staff. Onward the fearless navigator flew among the majestic tall pines, brandishing his new-found black magical staff with frenzied gestures, now giving vent to an inspiration of horrid blasphemy, and now again shouting forth such laughter as to set all the moral and immoral echoes of the forest laughing like hyperactive demons gathered all around him.

Thus, sped the demoniac upon his extravagant, esoteric course, until, quivering in sheer excitement among the trees, the merry huge stick jockey noticed a red light beaming before him, a glow similar to when the felled trunks and branches of a clearing have been set on fire and then chillingly, the flames throw-up their lurid blaze against the sky at the precise hour of midnight.

Goodman paused with his euphoria, in a lull of the tempting tempest that had driven him onward, and his ears then heard the swell of what seemed a contemptible hymn, weird-sounding lyrics rolling solemnly from a distance with the weight of many fucked-up voices. Young Brown knew the tune well; it was a familiar one often sung in the choir of the gay village people's meeting-house.

The verse soon died heavily away, and the reprise was quickly lengthened by a boisterous chorus' ascension, not of human voices, but of all the sounds of the benighted wilderness, pealing together in awful pantheistic harmony. Goodman Brown cried-out, and his plea was lost to his own ear.

"I never 'met-a physical' straight woman I didn't like," Goodman lowly declared to himself'. "I need to read the Koran more often in order to learn how the hell I should treat Good Faith more tenderly!"

In the interval of silence that ensued, now-psychotic Mr. Goodman Brown stole forward until the light glared fully upon his disbelieving eyes. At one extremity of an open space vista, hemmed-in by the dark wall of the formidable forest, arose a rock, bearing some rude, natural resemblance either to an altar or a pulpit. The huge rock (which slightly resembled St. Peter) was surrounded by four blazing pines, their tops all aflame; their stems untouched, relentlessly flickering like colossal lit votive candles at an evening prayer meeting. The mass of foliage that had overgrown the boulder's summit was all on fire, blazing high into the night sky, and the immense conflagration was seen as fitfully illuminating, flamed, and enveloping the whole field.

Each pendent twig and leafy festoon was aglow in a red blaze. As the intense light arose and then fell in rhythmic yo-yo fashion, a combination straight and gay, all-inclusive church congregation alternately shone forth, then disappeared in shadow, and again grew, as it were, out of the utter darkness, populating the entire heart of the solitary woods all at once.

"Grave and dark-clad Rebel Salem Village residents has indeed mustered," Goodman Brown stuttered. "Where the hell is the Singing Nun anxiously intoning the melodic lyrics of 'Stairway to Heaven'?"

Among the corralled chorus, quivering to-and-fro between gloom and splendor, appeared the frowning faces that would be seen next day at the province council board, and others which, Sabbath after Sabbath, including the eerie members of Black Sabbath Apostates, looked devoutly heavenward, and benignly over the imagined crowded pews, where an abundance of farts from kneeling, repentant sinners were rising in putrid succession, and thus, permeating and neutralizing the heavily-incensed unholy air.

Some tale-tellers affirm that the governor's kinky mistress was in attendance at the forest fiasco, masturbating like crazy. At least there were high society lesbian dames, well-known to *her* there, too, and bisexual wives of honored husbands also, along with a bevy of widows, but no representation of African black widows.

Either the sudden gleams of light flashing over the obscure open field bedazzled Goodman Brown, or the naïve trespasser perceptively recognized a score of familiar Salem Village church members, all famous for their especial phony sanctity.

Deacon Gookin had arrived on the scene, and the pompous asshole waited at the skirts of that venerable comrade in sin, his revered openly out-of-the-cupboard fat gay pastor. But, irreverently consorting with those grave, disreputable, and impious people, those holier-than-thou elders of the Puritan Church; those chaste dames and dewy virgins, there also were vile men of dissolute lives, along with prostitute women of spotted fame, desirable attractive wretches given over to all mean and filthy vices, and suspected even of committing horrid Puritan immorality like kissing, touching, and showing their ankles in public.

It was strange to see that the good shrank not from the wicked, nor were the dumb-ass sinners abashed by the dumb-ass future saints. Scattered also among their pale-faced enemies were the drunken Indian shamans, or "powwows", all barbaric savages who had often scared their native forest settlers with more hideous incantations than any fucked-up chants known to imported English witchcraft.

"But where is Faith?" Goodman Brown whispered to himself. And as the memory of numerous sexual encounters with Hope and Charity vividly came into his overburdened heart, the penitent fellow trembled, his mind finally fathoming the true fact that dead saints and living sinners alike were all fucked-up assholes. "Lord, give me sanctuary from all of this Hell on Earth!"

Verse after verse was crudely sung by the heterogeneous chorus (which obviously included homos' and lesbians, as well); and still the collective chorus's voices swelled between the deepest tone of a central mighty organ, a twelve-foot-high, massive, thick, circumcised erection, shaped exactly in the fashion of an Iroquois totem-pole.

And with the final peal of that dreadful forest anthem, there was a thunderous sound, as if the roaring wind had suddenly gone amok. Then, the loud noise of rushing streams; the howling of wild beasts, along with every other voice of the un-concerted devil-may-care hinterland was religiously mingling, and according with the voice of guilty and not-guilty man, the erratic articulations were together participating in spiritual homage to either the Prince of Peace or the Prince of Darkness.

The four blazing pines threw-up loftier flames, and obscurely discovered shapes and visages of horror upon the smoke-wreaths floating above the impious assembly. At the same moment, the fire on the rock shot redly forth, and formed a glowing arch above its base, where now appeared a self-appointed figure. With reverence be it spoken, the two-dimensional human form bore no slight similitude, both in garb and manner, to some grave divine and prestigious personage belonging to the Salem, New England church.

"Bring forth the converts!" a deep voice bellowed, echoing through the field and rolling into the forest. "Bring them forth!"

At that stern command, Goodman Brown stepped forth from the shadow of the trees and approached the queer-sounding Tower of Babel congregation, with whom the visitor felt a loathsome brotherhood by virtue of the sympathy of all that was understood as being humanly and immorally wicked inside his grieving heart.

The ceremony intruder could have well-nigh sworn that the shape of his own dead father was sternly beckoning him to advance forward, austerely looking-downward from an overhead drifting smoke wreath, while a beckoning woman, with dim features of despair, threw out her hand to warn the forest revival guest to move back.

'Is this Mother?' Goodman wondered in awe. 'It could be Mother. She was always a very supportive woman, just like this disturbing manifestation seems!'

But young Goodman Brown had no power within his being to retreat one step, nor to resist, even in thought, when the grim-faced Minister along with old Deacon Gookin seized his arms and led the encroacher directly to the blazing rock.

'Holy shit!' Young Goodman imagined. 'I hope I'm not being sacrificed for the sake of this fucked-up forest congregation! And I don't see any trace of my fuckin' psychiatrist or guidance counselor anywhere in the whole dumb-shit crowd to give me sage advice!'

Thither came also the slender form of a veiled female, led between Goody Cloyse, that pious breast-milk giving teacher of the catechism, and Martha Carrier, the popular Salem hooker who had often arrogantly claimed that she had received the Devil's Promise to be the exclusive Prom Queen of Hell. A rampant hag was she, but a good ten-minute fuck nevertheless. And there stood the proselytes, and the accompanying acolytes, soon approaching the bizarre satanic altar beneath the canopy of raging fire.

"Welcome, my Children," the mysterious phantom dark figure announced. "Yes, welcome to the joyful communion of your human race.

Ye confused mortals have found thus young your nature, along with your individual abstract destinies. My Children, alertly turn your fat and skinny asses and look right behind you!"

The obedient assembled worshipers rotated their indoctrinated heads around like a tame flock of complying, herded sheep. And flashing forth, as it were, in a sheet of roaring flames, the fiend devil worshipers were astonishingly seen mingling with the pious moral churchgoers in attendance; the smile of mutually accepted welcome gleamed darkly upon every fucked-up visage.

"There," the anonymous sable form resumed his sermon at the makeshift podium. "Are all whom ye have reverenced and despised from youth. Ye, deemed them either holier or less desirable than yourselves, and then shrank from your own sin, contrasting *that* human-created criterion with *their* separate lives of righteousness and of prayerful aspirations. Yet here are they, all gathered together as one mankind, yes, one splendid, harmonious, compatible humanity, all present inside *my* worshiping assembly."

The ominous figure paused for a moment, so that all present mentally and emotionally connected with *his* extended litany. "This night it shall be granted you to know their wholly, unholy secret deeds: how hoary-bearded church elders have whispered wanton words to the young maids of their households before screwing the innocent virgins into soft mattresses; how many a woman, eager for widows' weeds, has given her husband a foul drink at bedtime, and let him sleep with the poison in his stomach upon his deathbed; how beardless brazen youths have made haste to inherit their fathers' wealth by poisoning their mothers after their aberrant mothers had successfully poisoned their fathers; and how fair damsels, blush not, sweet ones too, have dug little graves in the garden, and bidden me, the sole guest to an infant's funeral, because the rest of you stupid assholes would instinctively stone her to death if the teen mother revealed that she had become pregnant before entering blessed sacred wedlock. Rejoice now brethren, for all the world's mortals, both good and bad, are now one splendid unified chorus!"

* * * * * * * * * * * * *

The assholes, both straight and LBGT, did so unite, holding hands. And by the blaze of the hell-kindled torches, the wretched, newly converted man beheld his Faith, and the liberated wife her husband, both afflicted mortal souls trembling before that unhallowed altar.

"Lo, there ye stand, my Children," preached the tall alien figure, in a deep and solemn tone, almost melancholy with its despairing awfulness, as if the speaker's once angelic nature could yet mourn for *our* entire miserable race. "Depending upon one another's hearts, ye had still hoped that virtue was not all a gullible poet's abstract dream. Now are ye undeceived by virtue of my enlightening sermon. Evil is the nature of mankind. The words 'sacred', 'holy', and 'religion' are simply hollow language terms grotesquely contrived by ancient, greedy scholars. Evil along with pleasure must be your only happiness. For good and evil are tonight and forever but one entity! Welcome again, my Salem Children, to the essential communion of your inferior race."

"Welcome Brethren," the fiend worshipers repeated, in one contrasting cry of bitter despair and sweet triumph. "Welcome!" the disingenuous assembled shit-heads reiterated.

'This is positively great news!' Goodman pragmatically reckoned. 'Now, I can screw every straight and bisexual doll in Salem without the anchor of guilt shackled around my non-existent soul, and thus, slowing-down my gratifying sexual prowess!'

The next morning, young Goodman Brown approached slowly into the main street of Salem Village, staring-around like a still-befuddled and addled man. The old gay Minister was taking a pleasant walk along the town graveyard to develop an appetite for breakfast, and to also meditate upon his impending sermon, and the self-righteous asshole casually bestowed a blessing upon Goodman Brown as *he* nonchalantly passed.

Unemployed Brown, who was aspiring to found a profitable local parcel delivery service, shrank from the venerable passing faggot as if to avoid an anathema. The perplexed fellow had never before dealt with the self-defeating plague known as "internal conflict". Goodman's very sustenance was being ferociously challenged by everyday Salem reality. Mental turmoil (along with emotional chaos) was now negatively dominating his rapidly disintegrating spirit.

Later that morning, old out-of-the-closet Deacon Gookin was present at domestic church worship, and the holy words of his lethargic hypocritical prayer were heard through the side open window. 'To what God does the wizard pray?' Goodman Brown pensively conjectured. 'It doesn't really matter if one is straight, bisexual, gay or trans-gender! Priest, minister, rabbi, bishop, pope, imam or deacon! Fucked-up charlatans all! Providence does not reside in Providence, or in Heaven, or in any place else. The Minister, the Deacon, the shrewd politician, and the corrupt judge, they are the true heretics and the real agnostics, who daily deluge and manipulate *us* daily with their dumb-ass propaganda!'

Goody Cloyse, that most excellent old Christian whore, stood in the early sunshine at her own lattice fence, catechizing a little girl who had kindly brought the wench a pint of fresh morning moonshine. Goodman Brown snatched away the child as if she had been in the grasp of the heinous Minister Fiend himself.

18

Turning the corner by the Salem meeting-house, the resident apostate spied the head of Faith, with her pink bonnet ribbons blowing in the breeze, gazing anxiously forth, and bursting into such joy at the sight of Goodman that the happy wife skipped along the street and almost kissed her husband before the whole insane village could ever criticize her display of public affection.

But recently converted Goodman Brown looked sternly and sadly into her loving and caring face, and beheld Faith's smile, and then the louse of a spouse passed-on without even offering either a polite hand wave or a sarcastic oral greeting.

Had Goodman Brown fallen asleep in the forest and only dreamed a wild nightmare of a spooky witch and Lucifer meeting? Which bitch was a true witch: Goody Goody Two-Slippers Goody Cloyse, or voluptuous Faith Brown?

Be it so if you will, but alas, it indeed was a most necessary forest dream of evil omen for young Goodman Brown to experience. A distraught, a sad, a darkly meditative, a distrustful, if not a desperate old man did the troubled fellow eventually become, ever since the night of *that* dreadful forest clearing encounter.

On the Sabbath day, when the fake solemn congregation was indulgently singing a holy psalm, Goodman could not listen because a contradictory anthem of venial and mortal sin was rushing loudly upon his ears, and drowning-out all the blessed vocal strains. And when the gay Minister spoke from the bully pulpit with power and fervid eloquence, and, with his right hand pressed upon the open Bible, made fraudulent and invalid proclamations affirming the sacred truths of Puritan religion and of Puritan sin; and of saint-like Salem lives; and of triumphant Salem moral deaths; and of future bliss, or misery unutterable, then did Goodman Brown turn pale and vomit upon the faggot Deacon's expensive, lost big-wig, which had been inexplicably left lying in the church's side-bushes.

And in his marital bed, often waking suddenly, precisely at midnight, harrowed Goodman Brown shrank from Faith's embrace and desperately wished for a quenching sample of Goody Cloyse's rich mother's breast-milk. And at morning or dusk, the converted disbeliever scowled and muttered to himself, and Mr. Brown gazed sternly at his appalled wife, and instantly turned-away from her pretty face, from her enticing tits, and also from her firm ass.

And when Goodman had lived and further suffered long over a century's time, and right before the Forest Victim had been borne by pallbearers to his churchyard grave as a corpse, outliving Faith by nearly three decades, on his deathbed old Brown lustily craved for the wrinkled body of the retired and buried, whorey Goody Cloyse.

"The Great Stone Face"

One afternoon, when the brilliant sun was descending in the western sky, a mother and her bratty boy were closely sitting at the termite-infested front porch door of their diminutive, ramshackle cottage, chatting incessantly about a legendary local mountain feature having the rather distinct appellation, "The Great Stone Face". The pair had but to lift their gullible eyes to notice right there and then that the phenomenal attraction was plainly visible to be witnessed, although situated several miles away. All the while, radiant setting sunshine was brightening every aspect of the mammoth mountain's remarkable, exaggerated features.

And precisely what was *that* outstanding native marvel, the Great Stone Face?

Picturesquely positioned amongst a cluster of lofty New England high hills, there exited a pristine valley so spacious that the geography contained many thousands of fucked-up, unappreciative, indolent inhabitants. Some of these lackluster assholes dwelt in poorly-constructed log-huts shaped like primitive igloos, with the black forest (recently imported from Germany) enveloping all around *their* shanty domiciles. Also, dense brambles and thick vegetation cluttered and encroached-upon their vulnerable asses, all along the steep and difficult hill-sides. Other more fortunate idiots enjoyed comfortable farm-houses as their dwellings, and those lucky misfit families profitably cultivated the rich soil that flourished upon the gentle slopes, or upon level surface patches of the truly spectacular valley.

Other mediocre, less-motivated jerk-offs were congregated into populous villages that seemingly never advocated birth control or abortions. Those colonial Puritan settlements were places where a wild, highland river stream, tumbling-down from its mysterious origin somewhere in the upper mountain region, had been caught and tamed by human cunning. During the commencement of the great American Industrial Revolution, the swift water flow compelled machinery inside and outside mills to turn. Capitalism then resulted from this huge transformation from farming to small fabric mills and factories, the aforementioned mills and factories not being made of fabrics at all. The exploited employees laboring inside the newly-constructed facilities never availed themselves of either learning, or knowing about, the writings of that insane German bull-shitter, Karl Marx.

The myriad inhabitants of that lazy, tranquil valley were quite numerous, and of many modes of life. But all of the region's folks, both grown derelict adults and juvenile delinquent children alike, had a kind of familiarity with the landmark Great Stone Face. Some quixotic observers, having maintained chaste hearts and souls, and who practiced

Puritan sexual abstinence, and prudishly shunned basic anatomy show-and-tell experiences, surprisingly possessed the gift of distinguishing this grand natural wonder (the weirdo mountain facsimile) more perfectly than many of their baneful, sinning, adulterous neighbors.

The extraordinary Great Stone Face was a true creative work of Mother Nature, a genuine product of the almost-worshiped Majestic Force, being engaged in *her* perpetual, fickle playful mood. The alluded-to visual sensation had been formed on the perpendicular side of a landmark mountain by some immense rocks, which had been structured-together in such a position as, when viewed at a proper distance, the composition's appearance precisely resembled the general features of a gender-bias "human male countenance".

It seemed as if an enormous giant (or perhaps a contemporary eccentric Titan) who had been more enamored with his face than with his penis or testicles, had crudely sculptured his own likeness upon the front of the enormous precipice. Obviously, there was the broad arch of the forehead, which ascended a fantastic hundred-feet in height; included was the formation's extensive nose, with its long twenty-five-meter bridge. And also discernible to the viewer's eyes were the vast lips, which, if the pair could have spoken, would have rolled their thunder-accents from one end of the impressive valley to the other, repeatedly bellowing-out understandable exclamations' such as "Fuck you!" and "Shit!", along with other noteworthy expletives.

True, it is that if the unwary spectator approached the spectacle to achieve a position too near, he or she would unintentionally lose the outline of the gigantic visage, and the intrigued witness could only detect a heap of ponderous and mammoth rocks, all clumsily piled into chaotic ruin, one upon another. Retracing his or her steps backwards, however, the fabulous human-like features would again be seen; and the farther he or she withdrew from the boulders without tripping, falling, or rupturing a testicle or tit, the more that a bold likeness of a human face would be evident, naturally, with all its original divinity and accompanying enigma intact.

The magnificent male image appears constant until each evening when it progressively becomes dim in the vague twilight distance, with the low-lying clouds and associated glorified vapor of the mountains clustering about it. At that magical moment, the Great Stone Face positively seems to be alive and ready to devour several nearby sleepy villages as a pre-midnight snack.

The quiet hamlets indeed constituted a very happy environment for mischievous children to grow-up to manhood or womanhood, with the Great Stone Face peering-off in the distance directly before their enchanted eyes. All the visage's features were indeed noble, and the overall expression was at once grand and sweet, as if it were the glow of a vast, warm heart; yes, a loving organ that truly embraced all mankind in its straight, gay, and lesbian affections. And the general community's daily observation even had room to include LBGTQRSTUVW protest demonstrations, too. It was an "all-inclusive education" throughout the whole vicinity to simply look at and admire the fascinating Great Stone Face.

According to the belief of many unreliable, area know-it-all, self-appointed historian shit-heads, the valley owed much of its fertility to *this* colossal "benign male facial anomaly" that was continually beaming its artificial blessing over the neighboring hamlets, illuminating the clouds, and infusing its bland tenderness into the gentle sunshine, inspiring all kinds of fantastic straight and LBGTQRSTUVW sex each and every night.

* * * * * * * * * * * *

We had awkwardly begun this non-adventurous tale with an apathetic mother and her obnoxious young boy non-ambitiously sitting before their cottage-door. The listless duo was gazing at the Great Stone Face with nothing better to do, or pursue, and the lethargic twosome had been casually talking about the all-too-familiar mountain spectacle.

"Mother," doted-upon Ernest said, while the Titanic visage gently smiled upon the lame-brained lad as if the crag had been a hostile nefarious pedophile. "I wish that the distant face could speak, for I think it looks so very kindly at me that its voice must need to be pleasant and gay, just like our faggot church minister's sermons. If I were to see a man in real life sporting such a handsome effeminate face, I should love him dearly and allow him to wildly molest me."

"Look, Ernest," the mother imperatively corrected. "A face cannot speak; only a person's mouth and lips can perform *that* complex function! Now, Son, if an old prophecy should come to pass," continued his somewhat-concerned parent, "we may in the village occasionally see a man with exactly such a greedy, shit-eating, faggot-like face as that one we watch every lousy morning, noon, and evening, out of complete and utter boredom."

"What half-assed prophecy do you mean, dear Mother?" Ernest eagerly inquired. "Pray, tell me about it before I have to barf for the fifth time today! I seldom believe any of that quasi-religious, sentimental bull-shit stuff, you know!"

So, the slow-learner's dumb-shit mother told the inquisitive kid a bizarre story that her own mother had told to her, when she herself was just a tad younger than little Ernest. It was a crackpot fantasy story, not of things that were past, but of events yet to come; an absolutely illogical tale, nevertheless, so very old that even the fire-water drinking Indians, the true chronic alcoholics who had formerly inhabited this *lush* valley, had heard the bull-shit from their lying, hallucinating forefathers a thousand times. The freakish legend had been originally murmured by the polluted mountain streams to an inebriated shaman, and later the babble was related to the clan's Chief by a babbling brook, and next finally the droll nonsense was whispered to the entire tribe by the prevaricating north wind, which had been swirling among the forest tree-tops.

The principal, outlandish, irrational notion was that at some future fictitious day, a gifted child should be born hereabouts, a progeny-prodigy who was destined to become the greatest and noblest personage of his time, and a most-vital individual whose mature countenance, in manhood, should bear an exact resemblance to the Great Stone Face.

Only a few insane, old-fashioned people, along with several naïve young ones, likewise, in the ardor of their unrealistic fanciful hopes, still cherished an enduring faith in this old unrealistic prophecy. But others, who had seen more of the world, had impatiently watched and waited until the assholes were weary with fatigue. Those apostates had beheld no man with such a singular face, nor any man that proved to be much greater or nobler than his or her neighbors. The naysayers concluded the flimsy account to be nothing but an idle, ancient, fucked-up tale, with almost everyone insisting, "We can't have archaic and eat it too!". At all village events, the fictional great man of the revered prophecy had not yet appeared.

"Oh Mother, dear Mother!" Ernest earnestly cried, clapping his hands above his head. "I do hope that I shall live to see this forecasted freak-of-nature come onto the local scene, even before I enter puberty at age ninety-four and then soon thereafter lose my miserable virginity at age ninety-five!"

The tot's prostitute mother was an affectionate and thoughtful woman, who felt that it was wisest not to discourage the generous hopes of her little out-of-wedlock boy. So, the mom only stated to Ernest in reply to his inquisitive nature, "Perhaps you may have a surprise ejaculation before you reach puberty, something akin to a prudish girl experiencing a virgin birth!"

And Ernest never forgot the weird story that his whoring mother had told him about the general distant mountain phenomena, just to shut the young annoying pest up. It was always in the tyke's curious mind, surfacing from his subconscious, whenever the pesky nuisance looked-upon the Great Stone Face, which was quite apparent upon the faraway mountain. The little prick had spent his entire childhood in the dilapidated log-cottage where he had been born, and the kid was dutiful to his 'Cathouse mother', and helpful to her in many responsibilities, like escorting horny men into her bedroom, and also by assisting her with his little hands by stitching-together cotton sock condoms that Ernest thought were her imitation slippers. But all throughout his unique enterprise, the youngster's loving heart desired escaping the drudgery of his monotonous, futile life.

In that manner, from being a happy yet often pensive child, Ernest grew-up to be a mild, quiet, unobtrusive, punk teenager, and during the summer months, the little fink became sun-browned while feigning decent labor in the crop fields. But with more intelligence brightening his personality than is seen in many lads who have been taught at famous schools such as Yale, Harvard, Princeton, and Sing-Sing, Ernest was often edified by his fawning mother while speaking to other village prostitutes, who often defiantly muttered under their breaths, "Who gives a ram or sheep's shit?"

Yet Ernest had had no formal schoolteacher, save only that the Great Stone Face became the acne-faced imbecile's exclusive tutor. When the toil of the day was over, the disillusioned miniature nutcase would gaze-up at the nondescript rock formation for hours, until the whimsical dreamer began imagining that those vast facial features actually, in reciprocation, recognized him.

And the Great Stone Face deemed to give the out-of-touch lad a big smile of kindness and encouragement, in response to the dumb-shit lazy kid's own look of veneration. But the ostensible, esoteric secret of the oddball telepathic communication was that the boy's tender and confiding simplicity discerned what other village assholes could not perceive or see; and thus the "Stone Face's" love, which had been benevolently meant for all, became Ernest's rather lion's share portion.

About this totally dull period in American history, there spread a rumor throughout the immense valley, which repeated the bizarre claims that the prevaricating hamlet liars had foretold from ages long ago. And decades later, a newly-arrived sage, who had been predicted to bear a special physical resemblance to the Great Stone Face, had appeared at last.

It seems that, many years before, a dashing young man (who always refrained from sprinting) had migrated from the lonely valley and settled at a distant seaport. After getting together a tidy sum of pilfered money, the skillful crook had set-up a more legitimate business, functioning as a respectable shopkeeper. His name, but I could never learn whether it was the tricky fellow's real one, or possibly a nickname that had grown out of his suspicious insular habits and success in life, was Gathergold, and not "Gladstone" as often believed, even though the village newcomer had only one massive testicle that he used when indulgently screwing Ernest's overprotective prostitute mother.

Being shrewd, active, and endowed by Providence with that inscrutable faculty which develops itself into what the ignorant world calls "good luck", on-a-mission Mr. "Gladstone" Gathergold became an exceedingly rich merchant, and soon an owner of a whole fleet of bulky-bottomed ships that had safely transported newly invented ribbed condoms along with smuggled multi-colored dildos from the precarious Barbary Coast to the New World. Ironically, all the so-called civilized countries of the globe appeared to join hands for the mere purpose of adding heap after heap to the monstrous accumulation of this one covetous entrepreneur's tremendous, ever-proliferating wealth.

The cold regions of the north, almost-located within the gloom and shadow of the Arctic Circle, with all of its frigid Eskimo women huddled together in primitive igloos, sent Gathergold their tribute in the shape of furs fabricated out of shaven pussy pubes. And then, hot African natives sifted for "Gladstone' the golden sands of that continent's crocodile-infested rivers, and the sweating laborers obediently gathered-up the ivory tusks of countries' great elephants that had been killed out of the dense jungles. The Eastern Orient maritime traders came, bringing Gathergold the rich shawls, and the spices, and the teas, and the treasure troves of diamonds and rubies, and only to briefly mention the gleaming purity of large pearls that most genuinely looked exactly like enlarged erect clits.

The ocean, not to be behindhand with the relative earth's bounty, yielded-up her mighty whales' vast sperm ejaculations, that Mr. Gathergold might sell the sea mammals' reproductive fluids to a plethora of impotent human assholes, and thus make a sizable profit of his "indispensable whale oil fertility medicine". Be the original commodity what it might provide, it was accessible gold within Mr. Gathergold's avaricious grasp. It might be said of Gladstone, er, that is, Gathergold, as of Midas in the classic mythology fable, that whatever the lucky bastard touched with his finger, with his toe, or with his flaccid, tiny dick, immediately glistened, and next grew yellow, and then mystically had been changed at once into either sterling silver, or lustrous gold. The abundance of wealth suited the lucky bastard still better, as the happy possessor eagerly sorted and stacked high piles of excellent coins, personal treasures that had been acquired mostly from his string of brothels and bordellos extending from Shanghai all the way to Shangri-La. The lucrative syndicate of international whorehouses was appropriately known throughout the sinful world as Gladstone Gals Galleries, LLC.

And, when Mr. "Gladstone" Gathergold had become so very rich that it would have taken the bastard a hundred-years to simply count his burgeoning wealth, the mogul bethought himself of his native valley, and after great meditation, the wealthy bumpkin resolved to perhaps end his last days where he had been born. With this understandable nostalgic purpose in mind, the successful importer commissioned a skillful architect to design the tycoon such a typhoon-proof palace in which to live, as should be fit for a proud baron of industry having *his* vast fortune and importance.

As almost-redundantly mentioned, it had already been rumored in the isolated valley that Mr. Gathergold had turned-out to be the prophetic personage who the weak-minded public had so long and vainly looked for, and that his visage was the perfect and undeniable similitude to the remarkable countenance of the Great Stone Face. People (Ignoramuses) were ready to speculate and believe that this comparison must need to be the legitimate fact, and even illegitimate Ernest had placed maximum credence in the visual relationship between Gathergold and the amazing Great Stone Face.

When the doltish citizens beheld the splendid edifice that rose (as if by magical enchantment) upon the site of his (Gladstone Gathergold's) former weather-beaten farm-house, everyone within shouting distance coincidentally commented, "Ain't that some crazy shit going on here! Ernest's daddy's erection is even greater than the largest penis on the whole continent! That house looks like a damned New York City Museum!"

The mansion's exterior was of marble, so dazzling white that it seemed as though the whole magnificent structure might melt-away into butter in the shimmering sunshine, or possibly change into gold coins, not like the bronze pennies of Mr. "Gladstone" Gathergold's younger days, when the parsimonious skinflint used to pay for Ernest's mother's sexual favors. The newly-constructed, opulent edifice had a fine ornamented portico that was supported by tall Corinthian pillars, beneath which was a lofty, huge mahogany door, studded with silver knobs, and made of variegated Amazon wood that had been brought from various South American river swamps. The windows, rising from the floor to the ceiling of each stately suite, were each composed of but one enormous pane of glass, installed solely for the demanding, reclusive, pain in the ass, Mr. Gathergold.

Hardly anybody in the village had been permitted to see the interior of this superb palace. But it was reported, and with good semblance of truth, to be far more gorgeous than the palatial outside, in-so-much that whatever was common iron or brass in other houses, was now fabricated from ornate silver or gold in this one.

And Mr. Gathergold's elaborate bedchamber made such a glittering appearance that no ordinary man would have been able to close his eyes there, let alone from distraction, ever achieve an ordinary erect dick for too long. But conversely, on the other hand, Mr. Gathergold was now so inured to wealth that perhaps the rich codger could not have closed his eyes unless he had felt perfectly secure with his vast possessions, and it was heavy village scuttlebutt that purported, "Mr. Gladstone's frequent white dreams were really Mr. Gathergold's golden dreams come true, instead."

In due time, the inimitable mansion was externally finished. Next came the upholsterers, with magnificent imported furniture from Italy and France; then, a whole troop of black and white servants followed, all of them two-toned; these newly-hired attendants represented the loyal harbingers of Mr. Gathergold, who, in his own aristocratic person, as had been reported in the village gazette, was expected to ceremoniously arrive by rented carriage at sunset.

Our unsophisticated friend, Ernest, meanwhile, had been deeply stirred by the idea that the great man, the noble man, the man of prophecy, after so many ages of frustrating delay, was at length to be made manifest to appear in *his* native valley. The boy's imagination comprehended that there were a thousand ways in which Mr. Gathergold, with his vast wealth, might transform himself into an angel of wonderful generosity, and then supernaturally assume control and practice charitable philanthropy over human affairs as wide and benign as the prodigious smile of the Great Stone Face.

Full of faith, hope, and shit, Ernest never doubted what the gossipy people orally maintained was true, and now the simple-minded lad was to behold the living likeness of those wondrous features exhibited upon the nearby mountain-side. While the psychologically-disturbed adolescent's eyes were still gazing up the valley, and fancying, as he always did, that the Great Stone Face was cooperatively returning his gaze, and then magically looking kindly at him, the rumbling of wheels was heard, with the discernible sound approaching swiftly along the winding road.

"Here he comes!" cried a group of people who were assembled to witness the happy arrival. "Here comes the great Mr. Gathergold! Prepare to be disowned and disinherited, callow illegitimate fool, Ernie!"

The imperial-looking carriage, drawn by four white Arabian horses prancing-around the turn (and failing to bend the bend), rumbled into full view. Inside the well-appointed coach, thrust partly out of the window, appeared the physical appearance of the old jaundiced "Gladstone". The passenger's skin was grotesquely yellow as if the rich gent's own Midas-hand had somehow transmuted his entire epidermis, including his often-gossiped "only Chinese testicle". The distinguished Mr. Gathergold had a low forehead; small sharp eyes, which were sunken with innumerable wrinkles and visible facial craters; and finally, very large gold teeth embedded behind very thin lips, that the bearer made still thinner by obsessively pressing them together as if the pair were vibrating female genitalia.

"The very image of the Great Stone Face!" shouted the excited townspeople. "Sure enough, the old prophecy is true; and here we have the great man come at last! But we wonder if his dick is rock hard like his yellow-skinned ugly mug and bald skull!"

"The creep looks like old King George III of England!" shouted a blind idiot in the crowd. "But I'm sure that King George had two golden nuggets, and not just one like one-stone Gladstone does!"

"I think he looks more like that Greek asshole Julius Seizure!" a second uneducated buffoon with 20/20 vision falsely reckoned. "Or maybe more like that other ancient Greek brute, Brutus."

And, what greatly perplexed Ernest was that the dumb-fuck townspeople seemed actually to believe that here was the likeness of which the shit-heads often spoke. By the roadside, there chanced to be an old beggar-woman, along with two little beggar-children, stragglers from some far-off region northwest of Salem. As the custom-made carriage rolled onward, those vagrants held out their hands and lifted up their doleful voices, most piteously beseeching charity from the rich philanderer.

A yellow claw, the very same one that had clawed together so much incredible wealth, now resembling a lobster's appendage, poked itself out of the coach-window, and soon the golden hand arrogantly dropped some cheap copper coins upon the ground. Although the great man's name had been Gathergold, the carriage rider might just as suitably have been nicknamed Scattercopper, a decrepit jerk-off having massive brass balls instead of a single tiny golden one. Still, nevertheless, with a hardy shout, and evidently with as much good faith as ever, the mesmerized people bellowed, "He is the very image of the Great Stone Face! Throw us non-counterfeit silver and gold coins this time and not cheap copper, you conceited, tightwad Asshole!"

But melancholy Ernest turned his head sadly from the wrinkled shrewdness of that sordid, speedily-passing visage seated inside the coach, and the youth gazed further-up the valley. Amid a gathering mist, gilded by the last sunbeams and rays of warm hope, the innocent-minded urchin's pupils could still identify and determine those glorious features, which had impressed and branded their images into his disillusioned soul. But what did the benign stone lips seem to say?

'He will come! Fear not, Ernest! The great leader/philosopher will come and enlighten you!' the dumb-shit kid imagined.

The years went on, and Ernest eventually ceased to be a fucked-up idealistic teenager. The deranged dreamer had then grown to be an idle young man. He attracted little notice from the other more astute valley inhabitants; for those non-perceptive hicks saw nothing extraordinary in *his* way of life save that, when *their* day's labor was over, Ernest still loved to go apart from their company and stare and meditate upon the Great Stone Face, an inanimate figure that couldn't give a flying smelly finger-lick about anything around the vicinity, including wet, pink, pussy perfume!

According to the residents' idea of the farce-like legend, the silly anecdote was a total folly, indeed, but pardonable. Ernest was courteous, kind, and neighborly, and the young man neglected all duty for the sake of indulging in that idle habit in which he persisted daily. The local dumb-dicks never suspected that the Great Stone Face had become a wise teacher to the "irresponsible juvenile", and that the sentiment which was expressed in paying homage to a stone face on the mountain would enlarge the young man's heart, filling it with wider and deeper sympathies, and perhaps also causing a massive coronary to occur. The local gentry knew not that thence would come to Ernest a better wisdom than could be learned from slutty pornography books, and a better life achieved than could be molded mimicking the defaced example of other more tragic human lives like Blackbeard the Pirate, and the not-so-gay Attila the Hun.

Neither did Ernest know that the thoughts and affections which came to him so naturally, jerking-off, and pumping splendid pussy in the cornfields and atop the local farms' haystacks, and also inside his bisexual girlfriend's grimy bed, and wherever the dreg communed with himself and had telepathic intercourse with the Great Stone Face, the last-mentioned experience undoubtedly being of a higher tone than those which area men shared with *him,* gay homos or otherwise.

The born-again-asshole was indeed a simple soul, simple as when his mother first taught him the old suspect Great Stone Face prophecy. Regardless, Ernest loyally continued to behold the marvelous features beaming and being reflected and shadowed down the valley, and the foolish dolt still wondered why the gargantuan rock formation's human counterpart was so long in making *his* grand appearance.

By that time years later, poor Mr. Gathergold had been dead and buried, falling victim to a new incurable disease generally referred to as "yellow psoriasis". And the oddest part of the entire matter was, that the mogul's disproportionate wealth, which was the body and spirit of the importer's essential existence, had mysteriously disappeared before his death, leaving nothing of "Mr. Gladstone" except a skinny skeleton, covered-over with a pathetic and horrible-looking wrinkled, withered, yellow skin.

Since the melting-away of his extensive gold supply, it had been very basically conceded that there was no such striking resemblance of Gathergold to the element known as aurum on the schoolhouse's chemistry class's periodic table. So naturally, the indecisive, ever-vacillating 'village people' did not recognize Mr. "Gladstone" Gathergold as a true-blue Macho Man, not even in his so-called "yellow belly golden years". The mercurial-minded citizens collectively ceased to honor the formerly rich "impostor", and the residents quietly consigned Mr. Gathergold to forgetfulness after his swift demise, bankruptcy, and deceased existence.

Once in a while, it is true, that the dead Mr. Gathergold's memory had been brought-up in connection with the magnificent palace which he had built, and which had long ago been turned into a cheap affordable "brothel hotel" for the accommodation of traveling strangers in need of instant sexual relief. And the versatile building was also utilized for the satisfaction of the sex-starved multitudes that came every summer for "hot female favors", and some frivolous new arrivals even dared to coincidentally visit that famous natural curiosity upon the high mountain, the Great Stone Face.

Thus, over the course of several decadent decades, the ill-starred Mr. Gathergold has been discredited, renounced, and his noteworthy biography was symbolically thrown into the gloomy shade of the Great Stone Face; according to developing public conjecture, the legendary man of area prophecy and renown was yet to arrive upon the serene village scene.

* * * * * * * * * * * *

It so happened that a disoriented native-born son of the remote valley, many years before Ernest ever achieved adulthood, had enlisted in the Army as an ordinary soldier, and, after a great deal of hard fighting and wildly screwing generals' wives' and daughters' asses directly into bed mattress springs, the war hero had then rose in rank to become an illustrious commando commander. Whatever the proud military officer may be called in war (whore) history, his identity was known in base camps and on the numerous battle-fields under the queer-yet-poetic nickname of Old Blood-and-Thunder.

This war-worn veteran, being now infirmed with age, possessing myriad scars and wounds, and being weary of the turmoil associated with an active career with the military, along with a licentious and promiscuous sex life, had signified his sincere intent of returning to his native valley. The heroic Commander was hoping to find repose and serenity where the out-of-semen Old Fart every now and then, remembered leaving the fertile region in his youth.

The inhabitants, many of them now OBAT's geriatric neighbors, and other being past casual acquaintances, along with their grown-up bisexual and trans-gender children, were resolved to welcome the renowned and revered warrior back to the small community. The folks had planned a canon salute, along with a public vegan dinner to boot; and all the more enthusiastically, it being affirmed that at last, the likeness of the Great Stone Face had actually finally appeared, being celebrated in the public square. Naturally, expectations were mounting. An aide-de-camp of Old Blood-and-Thunder, travelling at midnight through the off-the-beaten-path valley on his rented donkey cart, was reputed to have been moonstruck with noticing the astonishing resemblance.

Moreover, the schoolmates and early summer school contacts of the guest General were ready to testify on oath that, to the best of their nebulous recollection, the aforesaid Commando Commander had been, in facial countenance, exceedingly similar to the majestic mountain image. And when OBAT was a petulant boy, the idea of similarity had never occurred to *them* at that placid period, because the Great Stone Face had never been a boy, let alone an obnoxious, drooling toddler.

Great therefore, was the *general* excitement that had spread throughout the somnolent valley. And many people, most in need of an optometrist, had for years never once thought of glancing at the visage Great Stone Face, now spent their entire time gazing at the pleasant phenomenon, even sitting in their outhouses peering through the opened door, just for the sake of knowing exactly how sensational and dynamic General Blood-and-Thunder might look.

On the day of the scheduled festival, Ernest, with all the other mentally-challenged people of the almost-forgotten valley, abandoned their trivial work assignments. Like programmed robots, the crowd proceeded to the very spot where the sylvan banquet had been assiduously prepared.

As Ernest and the other dumb-shits approached the food-laden picnic tables, the loud voice of the Reverend Dr. Battleblast was heard, beseeching a blessing upon "the especially good things" like plagues, famines, and pestilences that had been set before them, and extoling the eminent friend of peace through warfare, in whose honor the patriotic citizens were mutually assembled.

The picnic tables were arranged in a cleared space of woods, shut-in by the surrounding trees, and tangled poison ivy and poison oak growths. A vista opened eastward, and the wide space afforded a distant view of the Great Stone Face. Over the General's high-chair, which was a highchair relic from the home of George Washington, there was an arch of verdant boughs bending overhead, with wild laurel growths profusely intermixed. The speaker's platform had been surmounted by his country's Stars and Stripes' banner, beneath which "OBAT" had won two decisive victories while also fighting dangerous deer ticks and Lyme Disease in the dense woods surrounding the great notorious mountain.

Curious Ernest raised himself on his tiptoes, in hopes to obtain a glimpse of the celebrated guest, but there was a mighty crowd congregated about the many tables, all anxious to hear the toasts and speeches, but most definitely, to catch any word that might fall from the "Great General" in reply to embarrassing questions of marital infidelity. And soon, a volunteer company, doing civic duty as impromptu bodyguards, pricked ruthlessly with their bayonets at any particularly quiet person harassing no one among the raucous throng.

So Ernest, not realizing that Old Blood-and-Thunder might be his true biological father rather than Mr. "Gladstone" Gathergold, the lad, being of an unobtrusive character, was involuntarily and roughly thrust quite into the background, where the fickle fool could see no more of the "Old Benedict Arnold" wannabe'.

To console himself, the distraught young fellow automatically turned towards the Great Stone Face, which, like a faithful and long remembered friend, looked-down and smiled upon Ernest through the forest vista. Meantime, however, the vulnerable viewer could overhear the remarks of various neurotic psychopaths, who were verbally preoccupied subjectively comparing the similar features of the ruddy, florid-faced, decrepit war hero, with the stone countenance positioned upon the distant mountain-side.

"Let's face it Bro'! 'Tis the same face, to a hair!" one crazed buffoon hollered, showing extreme joy. "Pimples, pores, blemishes and blackheads, the details being all positively identical, too!"

"Wonderfully alike, that's an unmistakable fact!" responded another authoritative imbecile in the crowd. "They look like two peas in a pod, even though the face on the mountain is twenty-times bigger than Old Blood-and-Thunder's entire fuckin' anatomy!"

"Like wow, Neighbor! I call the face upon the ridge Old Blood-and-Thunder himself, as if the bastard's deliberately showing-off his total excellence in a monstrous looking-glass!" boomed a third village cretin, his intoxicated brain totally removed from reality. "And why not? He's the greatest resident of this or another age, way beyond a doubt. OBAT is greater than Moses, Genghis Khan, Buddha, and George Washington all melded together! Yes, yes! Genghis, Genghis, he's our man, if he can't do it, either Kublai or OBAT can! Ha, ha, ha! Where's my damned pom-poms?"

And then all three hoarse speakers standing in the throng gave resounding ear-shattering shouts, which communicated an electricity wave to the crowd, and a strong community roar quickly generated from the now-shocked-but-ecstatic thousand or so participants. The incredible sound volume amplified to a boisterous response that went reverberating for miles among the mountains, until an astute listener might have supposed that the Great Stone Face had poured its contaminating, contagious halitosis into the wicked cry.

All of those manifold comments, along with all of the vast, ridiculous, unanimous enthusiasm, together found merit in the totally thrilled audience's behavior. But dear Ernest, the unmotivated idler, reluctantly considered that the permanent all-too-familiar mountain-visage had finally found its identical human counterpart.

Ernest had imagined that this long-looked-for personage would appear in the character of a dynamic promoter of peace, and not one of fanatical war, possibly a military fluke uttering abundant wisdom, and doing unprecedented good; and making people happy having multiple orgasms during and after his speech. But callow Ernie's moral-driven conscience contended that Providence should choose its own method of blessing mankind. A triumphant warrior and a bloody sword did not qualify 'the war criminal' as being the personal savior of the rural rustic community.

"The General! The General!" was on that occasion the standard cry. "Hush! Silence! Old Blood-and-Thunder's going to make a vital speech. Let the absurd Old Fuck enlighten us!"

Even so; for the esteemed commander's cloak being removed, the General's health and coordination had been drunk with bourbon. Amid boisterous shouts of exaggerated applause, the military crusader stood upon his feet to thank the gathered company for their euphoric indulgence. Ernest managed to see the intoxicated war hero, and immediately thought, 'This drunken asshole looks like shit!'

And there too, visible in the same glance, through the vista in the evergreen forest, to Ernest's perceptive eyes, appeared the Great Stone Face! And was there over yonder, such a resemblance as the crowd had imagined and testified? Alas, the distraught fellow could not recognize any similarity, and Ernest rationally realized that the personages in the crowd gathered all around *his* presence were all full of shit, just like Old Blood-and-Thunder was!

Ernest's eyes beheld a war-worn and weather-beaten, morbid-looking countenance, full of false energy, and expressive of a contrived iron will. And indeed, the expected gentle wisdom, along with the deep, broad, tender sympathies, were altogether lacking in Old Blood-and-Thunder's fucked-up visage and demeanor. And even if the Great Stone Face had assumed *his* normal look of stern command, despite the fake rhetoric, the visiting General still appeared to be weak, wimpy, feckless, and totally full of shit.

"This is not the man of wonderful prophecy, as legend has specifically depicted and described," sighed Ernest to himself, as the local young fellow made his way out of the yelling and clapping throng. "And must the world wait longer yet? I mean in truth, this elderly jerk-off cavorting before my suspect eyes isn't even capable of jerking-off! OBAT has not an ounce of sticky semen left inside his miniature testicles!"

The mists had united about the distant mountain-side, and the grand and awful features of the Great Stone Face could again be perceived, awful-but-benign, as if a mighty angel were sitting atop the rolling hills, and the colossal form now appeared to be enrobing himself' in a cloud-vesture of gold and purple. As the disappointed observer looked more intensely in the same direction, disconsolate Ernest could hardly believe that a broad smile beamed over the whole granite visage, with a radiance quite brightening, although without motion of the lips or any bird-flip from a non-existent middle finger.

The spectacular visual manifestation was probably the effect of the western sunshine, melting through the thinly-diffused vapors that had swept between Ernest and the solid mountain object at which the young fool had been gazing. But *that* aspect of *his* ancient mineral friend made Ernest hopeful, as if he had never ever wished in vain.

'Fear not, my one and only Disciple,' seemingly said the rock's usually non-garrulous heart. 'Fear not Ernest; he will come, and as you can plainly observe, Old Blood-and-Thunder's coming and popping a heavy load-days have been over, since about a quarter of a century ago!"

More years sped swiftly by, and tranquilly inside the believer's heart also drifted away. Ernest still dwelt in his native valley, and was now an impractical dumb-shit, middle-aged, unemployed derelict. By imperceptible degrees, the juvenile-minded flake had gradually become known among the people, who had accurately regarded the lackluster lotus-eater as being basically "fucked-up".

Now, as heretofore related, utopian Ernest occasionally labored for his daily bread, and even this day was the same simple-hearted dumb fuck that he had always been. But the nonchalant fellow had thought and felt so much, and had given so many of the best hours of his life to contemplating unworldly hopes. The dreamer's hollow desire for accomplishing some great noble good for mankind was not reaching any satisfactory result, and now it seemed as though the simpleton-asshole had been talking with non-existent angels, the transient heavenly spirits being unaware of, or apathetic about, all the concurrent "Stone Face bull-shit" still going on.

Not a blessed or condemned day passed by, suggesting that the world was not the better because that unselfish middle-aged man, humble as he was, had quietly lived without accomplishment or great happiness. Indeed, Ernest had never stepped aside from his own mediocre path, yet out of a sense of charity, would always extend a favor or a kindness to his myriad apathetic-and-unappreciative wise-ass, shit-head, dumb-fuck neighbors. Almost involuntarily too, Ernest had finally realized his true aspiration, and the late-bloomer became an avid traveling church preacher, claiming out loud, "There's a Methodist to my madness!"

The recently out-of-the-closet minister uttered erudite truths that when wrought upon, ineffectually molded and feebly improved the lives of those living in the hamlet who had heard Ernest utter his religious holier-than-thou daily bull-shit. Most-remarkably, the new parson's moral lectures, along with his futile "fire and brimstone eternal punishment sermons", had miraculously cured and converted a total of three lesbians, five male homosexuals, and seventeen trans-gender fuck-heads, all falsely vowing to pursue a chaste and celibate Puritan lifestyle.

* * * * * * * * * * * *

When the hot-headed citizens' minds had had a little time to cool, the folks were ready enough to acknowledge their blatant blunder in imagining any special similarity between General Blood-and-Thunder's truculent, austere sourpuss, and the benign visage occupying yonder mountain-side. But now again, there existed talking-points, gossip reports, and many written paragraphs in the various valley newspapers, each account affirming that the likeness of the Great Stone Face had appeared upon the broad shoulders of a certain eminent statesman.

This emerging prominent politician, like Mr. "Gladstone" Gathergold and Old Blood-and-Thunder, had once been an obscure native of the valley, but had left the vicinity in his early days, and then conscientiously taken-up the bureaucratic and parasitic bull-shit trades of law and politics.

Instead of the rich man's wealth and the warrior's sword, this new philandering asshole had a vibrant tongue, originally used to perform cunnilingus on Ernest's prostitute mother, and the infected mouth organ was in many respects mightier than both mammon and a sharp military weapon together. So wonderfully eloquent was he (this newly-arrived verbose dip-shit) that whatever the equivocating orator might choose to say, his audiences had no choice but to believe his ever-prattling horse-crap; wrong looked like right, and right like wrong; for when it pleased the powerful orator, the opinionated fuck-head could make a kind of illuminated mint-green fog extend from his foul breath, and the glowing vapor competently concealed the natural daylight with its entrancing power. The gifted speaker's tongue, indeed, was a kind of magical riveting and rotating instrument: sometimes it rumbled like peals of thunder; sometimes it warbled like the sweetest classical music, but most of the time, it abused men's ears and grossly contaminated woman's snatcheroos, too.

The untrustworthy statesman's mouth was both the blast of war and the song of peace; and it seemed to have a heart of its own, although the jerk-off's auricle was nowhere like *him* being an American oracle. In good truth, the talkative charlatan was a perceptible, wondrous itinerant. And when his persuasive tongue had acquired the maniac all other imaginable success, and after his speeches had been heard and accepted in different marble halls of state, and also expertly utilized in filthy whorehouse corridors, "the orator", became well-known for sucking-up to powerful rulers all over the world. Old Stony Phiz finally convinced his fellow shallow-minded countrymen to select the "weirdo weasel" to run for the nation's Presidency.

Before *that* historic time, as soon as the political hack began becoming famous, his raunchy staunch admirers had noticed the close resemblance between himself and the fabled Great Stone Face; and so many voters were struck by the stellar parallels. In fact, it was a popular rumor that Old Stony Phiz's dick would "phiz" every time the contemporary Demosthenes urinated into an empty soda pop bottle. The creative phrase "Whiz Phiz" was considered giving a highly-favorable aspect to Old Stony's political prospects; for, as is likewise the case with the eminent Popedom living a king's life in Rome's Vatican, nobody ever becomes President without taking a nickname other than his own.

While his phony friends and cohorts were doing their best to make his Presidential nomination, Old Stony Phiz set-out on a visit to the precise valley where he had been born to evaluate whether its feeble-minded inhabitants were truly "born-yesterday Democrats". Of course, the talented speechmaker had no other objective than to shake hands with his fellow-citizens, and Phiz neither thought nor cared about any effect which his progress through the New England countryside might have upon the impending national election.

Magnificent preparations were made to receive the illustrious statesman. A cavalcade of well-disciplined horsemen set forth to meet the ambitious politician at the State's nearby boundary line, and all the area voters left their separate businesses and homes and gathered along the wayside to witness the famous bozo pass, and gladly listen to the dolt pronounce his oral excrement.

Ernest was among those aforementioned enthralled bystanders. Although more than once disappointed by two earlier "Great Stone Face masqueraders", the idealistic moron had such a hopeful and confiding nature, an invalid, wimpy self-concept, which indicated the naïve fool was always-ready to believe in whatever seemed beautiful and good, even while peering into another person's asshole with the aid of a lit candle. Ernest's peculiar habit was to examine every available female nook and cranny, desperately searching for a particular likeness of the Great Stone Face.

The political cavalcade came prancing along the road leading into the tiny village, with a great clattering of hoofs and a mighty cloud of dust, which rose-up so dense and so high that the visage of the mountain-side "Great Stone Face" was then completely hidden from Ernest's eyes. All the great yeomen of the neighborhood were there riding on horseback; militia and police officers were in uniform; the representative member of Congress; the sheriff of the county; the editors of two almost-defunct newspapers; and many local farmers and wanted criminals were in compulsory attendance, too.

If the pictures and portraits carried in the long parade were to be trusted, then Old Stony Phiz's resemblance to the exquisite mountain face, it must be confessed, was exotically amazing. We must not forget to mention that there was abundant marching in the lengthy procession. Several marching bands made the echoes of the mountains ring and reverberate with the loud triumph of their glorious musical strains. The airy, soul-thrilling melodies harmoniously broke-out among all the surrounding heights and accompanying hollows, as if every crevice and precipice of that native valley had found a distinct voice to admirably welcome the bullshitting politician.

But the grandest effect of all was when the far-off mountain peaks echoed back the invigorating music; for then the Great Stone Face itself seemed to be substantially swelling and savoring the lyrics of the triumphant chorus, in acknowledgment that the garrulous man of prophetic destiny had finally arrived.

All of that distracting cow-manure was occurring while the ecstatic people were throwing-up their hats (and their meals), and shouting with a glee so contagious that the susceptible heart of Ernest reactively kindled-up, and the nearby dupe likewise threw-up his hat and shouted, screaming as loudly as the loudest one present, "Huzza for the great man! Huzza for Old Stony Phiz! May his phiz dick whiz forever phiz abundant semen and urine!" But as yet, gullible Ernest had not yet seen the disingenuous bull-shitter in the flesh.

"Here he is, now!" cried those easily-influenced assholes who stood there smoking strong sweet marijuana alongside Ernest. "There! There!

Look at Old Stony Phiz, and then at the Old Man of the Mountain, and see if *their* appearances are like identical twin-brothers, one of cold lifeless stone, and the other of warm mortal blood, sweat and tears!"

In the midst of all this gallant array of raw emotion came an open barouche, drawn by four impeccable white horses; and inside the magnificent barouche, with his massive head uncovered, sat the notorious national statesman, Old Stony Phiz himself.

"Confess it," said one of Ernest's shoulder-to-shoulder fascinated neighbors to the mesmerized observer. "The Great Stone Face has met its match! Hail to our glorious village hero! May the poco loco hombre enjoy many a heroine, and mucho quality heroin pussy, too!"

Now, it must be fully acknowledged that, at his first glimpse of the countenance which was bowing and smiling at the crowd from inside the opulent barouche, Ernest did fancy that there was a firm resemblance between Old Stony Phiz and the very familiar boulder face situated upon the landmark mountain-side. The politician's brow, with its massive depth and loftiness, and all the other exceptional facial features, indeed were boldly and strongly hewn, as if in bold emulation of a more-than-heroic Olympian model. But the sublimity and stateliness, the grand expression of a divine sympathy that illuminated the mountain visage, and emphasizing its ponderous granite substance into inspirational spirit, in retrospect, might here be sought in vain.

Something most-relevant had been originally left-out of the visual equation, or had instantly departed into oblivion. And therefore, the marvelously gifted statesman had always a weary gloom evident and reflected in the deep caverns of his eyes, as of a child that has outgrown its playthings, or of a man of mighty faculties and little aims, whose dismal dreary life, with all its high performances, was both vague and empty. Apparently, to Ernest's fathoming of the ongoing situation, no high principles had endowed Old Stony Phiz's political ambitions with perceived "moral reality."

Still, Ernest's boisterous neighbor, standing nearby, was thrusting his elbow into *his* side, and pressing him for an affirmative answer.

"Confess! Confess Young Man!" the elderly coot remarked. "Is not he inside the sleek carriage the very picture of your Old Man of the Mountain?"

"No!" Ernest bluntly exclaimed. "I see little or no likeness. In truth, Old Stony Phiz's facial cheeks look like those flabby ones upon mayor's fat assed wife!"

"Then, so much the worse for the Great Stone Face!" his unaffected neighbor replied. And again, the indoctrinated, hoodwinked pinhead sent-up a vociferous shout for Old Stony Phiz passing by.

But Ernest turned-away, melancholy, and almost despondent: for this was the saddest of his disappointments, to behold a haughty man who might have fulfilled the prophecy, and had not the moral authority to do so. Meantime, the raucous cavalcade, the banners, the music, and the series of barouches swept past, with the vociferous crowd in the rear, leaving the dust to settle-down, and the Great Stone Face to be revealed again in the distance, with the grandeur that it had worn for untold centuries.

'Lo, here I am, Ernest!' the benign stone lips seemed to say to the perpetual dreamer. 'Don't be lugubrious! I've waited longer than thou, and am not yet weary. Fear not; the anticipated authentic ninny will come some-day, without a fizzled-out hard-on.'

* * * * * * * * * * * *

The years hurried onward, treading in their haste on the previous one's heels. And now, the annual calendars began to bring an abundance of white hairs on *his* hollow head. And with the scattered snow-like growths appearing upon Ernest's scalp, the passage of time had made "reverend wrinkles" (not an area priest or minister) across his forehead, and age had plowed furrows into the frustrated fellow's collapsing cheeks.

But not in vain had the lethargic dumb-ass grown old: more than the white hairs on his head, the depressed sage's insignificant thoughts were frenetically swimming-around inside *his* still-juvenile mind. Ernest's facial wrinkles and furrows were inscriptions that Mother Nature, and her relentless spouse, Father Time, had meticulously engraved, and in which stubborn Ernest had written legends of "asinine knowledge" that had been tested by the *tenor* of an unproductive life, many decades long-before the Sopranos ever became popular entertainment sensations.

And Ernest had ceased to be obscure among the insecure, psychotic mountain folk. Although unsought for and undesired, the fame which so many ingrates desperately seek, had now claimed to discover the true "Old Savant", and notoriety had made the new sensation known throughout the great world, beyond the limits of the secluded valley in which the "Junior Socrates" had once dwelt so quietly.

Left wing uber-liberal college professors, and even the active influential men of cities, journeyed from afar to see and converse with Ernest, as if the village knucklehead was a human social magnet; for the report had gone abroad that this simple recluse had flawed reckless ideas unlike those of other more-pragmatic men. Ernest possessed enviable knowledge not gained from books, but "wisdom" originating from "a higher divine order". The widespread discussion was as if venerable

Ernest had been communicating with the angels and saints, those entities being described as *his* inspired personal friends. Whether it were a sage or statesman; or philanthropist, pimp, thief, or trans-gender mortician, Ernest amiably received those unique visitors with the suave sincerity that had characterized his general attitude from boyhood; that is, his propensity for persistently-demonstrating preposterous naivete.

While the socially established and accomplished guests attempted imitating *his* stupid drivel, Ernest's face would kindle and shine upon them, as if radiating a mild evening light. Pensive with the fullness of such bullshit-type discourse, the disillusioned, bashful preacher's drunken and drug-addicted visitors took leave, and soon went their way; and the departing, inebriated trekkers, while passing up the isolated valley, momentarily paused to stare at the Great Stone Face, imagining that they had seen its likeness in a human countenance, but the egotistical shit-heads could not remember where the fuck their recent encounter with the comparable visage had been noticed.

While Ernest had been growing-up and later growing old, a bountiful Providence had granted a new poet to bless and traverse this baneful Earth. A traveling poet, likewise to *his* three renowned predecessors, was a native of the valley, but had spent the greater part of his life at a secret distance from that romantic region, pouring-out his sweet musical words amid the bustle and din of pathetic cities.

Often however, did the mountains, which had been familiar to "the bard" (in his childhood), lift their snowy peaks metaphorically into the clear atmosphere of the insane poet's poorly-organized rhyming verses. Neither was the Great Stone Face forgotten in *his* astute memory, for the wandering poet had celebrated the legend in an creative ode, which was grand enough to have been uttered to Ernest by *its* own majestic stone lips.

This newly-arrived, demented man of verbal genius, we may say, apparently had descended from heaven with wonderful endowments. If the bard sang of a mountain, the eyes of all mankind beheld a mightier grandeur reposing upon its breast, or soaring to its lofty summit, than had before been inadequately seen. If the poet's theme were a lovely lake, a celestial smile had now been thrown over it, to gleam forever upon its glittering surface. Besides a need to escape the sins of urban life, the wanderlust poet trekked back into his native valley to interpret the work of the Creator, before deleterious environmentalists ever discovered the insular area, and besieged the reticent population with their inane insane rhetoric.

The songs of this itinerant poet gradually found their way to Ernest, who read the distorted verses after his customary daily toil, which was defined as aimlessly sitting on the bench before his ramshackle cottage-door, where for such a length of time, the idealistic dreamer had filled his repose with suicidal thoughts, by intensely and hypnotically gazing at the Great Stone Face. Indeed, the brainless crag' couldn't give a healthy or unhealthy shit about its most devoted admirer. And now as the "Aged Swami" read his poetic stanzas that caused his essential soul to thrill and swell within, psychotic, senile Ernest lifted his eyes to the vast countenance beaming on him so benignly.

"Oh, majestic friend," the Old Codger murmured in a trance while stupidly addressing the mindless Great Stone Face. "Is not this strange mendicant poet standing before your scrutiny worthy to resemble thine excellence?"

The Eternal Stone Face seemed to favorably smile, but conversely answered not a word or syllable.

Now, it so happened that the fucked-up hobo poet, though the lunatic had in his past dwelt so far away, had not only heard of Ernest, but had meditated much upon *his* famed character, until the nutcase "man of nomenclature" deemed nothing so desirable as to meet this rather uncommon, pure-hearted human.

One summer morning, therefore, the bewildered portly poet took passage by means of a certain New England railroad, and, in the decline of the afternoon, alighted from the dusty cars at no great distance from Ernest's modest, in-need-of-repair cottage. The great hotel, which had formerly been Mr. Gathergold's stellar palatial mansion, was close at hand, but the castrated impotent poet, Mr. Knowstones, with his carpet-bag tucked upon his arm, inquired at once where "Preacher Ernest dwelt", and was resolved to be introduced and accepted as the shy laconic parson's guest.

Approaching the door, Poet Knowstones immediately found the good old fellow, holding a volume of *Dantes Inferno* in his hands, which alternately, the parson silently read while not speaking. And then, with a finger placed between the medieval text's pages as an improvised bookmarker, Ernest disregarded the presence of the corpulent poet, and instead looked lovingly at the Great Stone Face.

"Good evening," announced the impotent bard. "Can you give a weary traveler a decent night's lodging? You don't have to worry about being sodomized. Like most poets and idle dreamers, I have no balls!"

"Willingly," Ernest answered. And then the accommodating host added, broadly smiling, "Methinks I never saw the Great Stone Face look so hospitably at a stranger to this almost-unknown mountain community. In fact, I'm the only fucked-up resident of this fucked-up village who gives a freakin' shit!"

The exhausted poet sat-down upon the splintery bench beside the inspired preacher, and the mentally-warped pair shared verbal intercourse, because gay physical intercourse was physically impossible on the castrated no-nut poet's end. Often, the hoary poet had held intercourse with the wittiest and the wisest leaders of different communities, but never before with a basically-retarded individual such as reticent Ernest, whose thoughts and feelings had suddenly gushed-up with such a natural freedom.

The host/minister made great meaningless and immaterial truths seem so familiar to the sagacious poet, by virtue of *his* simple, pure uncanny utterances. Angels, as had been so often pontificated, seemed to have wrought with the self-proclaimed preacher, seemingly endorsing Ernest's unique oratorical propaganda.

As Ernest in return reciprocated and listened to the poet, the parson imagined that the Great Stone Face was bending forward to eavesdrop on the bard's noteworthy monologue. The fanciful preacher gazed admirably into the poet's glowing eyes. Of course, obviously these two New England fuck-heads were having intense intercourse without having intense intercourse.

"Who the hell are you, my strangely-gifted, bullshitting guest?" Earnest asked. "I hope the fuck you aren't the fabled Grim Reaper on patrol in disguise!"

The poet then laid his finger upon the newest volume that Ernest had been avariciously reading. "Forget this ludicrous *Dantes Inferno* bull-shit! You have to read these poems, my poems," the wandering rhymer commanded. "You must know me, for I'm the cowardly asshole who had authored them."

Again, and still more earnestly than before, Ernest's eyes closely examined the poet's facial features. Then, the potential asylum patient turned towards the Great Stone Face; then back, with an uncertain expression being reflected, with *his* beady eyes thoroughly scrutinizing his oddball guest. But then, the elderly resident's countenance fell; Ernest shook his head, and grievously sighed.

"Why are you so fuckin' sad?" inquired the mediocre poet. "Are your hemorrhoids acting up? Do you' require an enema?"

"I'm deeply sorrowed because," replied Ernest, negatively shaking his aching head from side to side, "all through life, I've awaited the fulfillment of a totally fanciful prophecy; until I read these illogical poems; your disgraceful dumb-shit poems, I had hoped that the language and truth I had been seeking all my life might be fulfilled in your ingenious verses. But truly, your work is astoundingly fucked-up, a complete travesty, and it's unworthy of ever revealing the infinite majesty of the Great Stone Face!"

"You had hoped," declared the un-rattled poet, faintly smiling, "to find in me the bona-fide likeness of the Great Stone Face. And you are justified in being disappointed, as formerly you had been with Mr. "Gladstone" Gathergold; with Old Blood-and-Thunder, and then later with fraudulent Old Stony Phiz. All three of whom could have been *your* biological father. Yes, Ernest, it is my imminent doom that you have brilliantly deciphered. You must add my anonymous name to the illustrious three aforementioned impersonators, and thus record another dismal failure of your lofty aspirations and hopes. For dear Ernest, in shame and in sadness, do I now speak these' humble words. Parson Ernest, I am not worthy to be typified by yonder benign Promethean image. If the face on that huge mountain were an asshole instead, then possibly it could be me!"

"And why?" asked Ernest while pointing to the worthless volume of poems. "Why are not these convoluted thoughts of yours divine like those authored in the Holy Bible?"

"They do have a minor strain of the Divinity," replied the somewhat proud-but-insulted, unsuccessful wordsmith. "You can hear in their message the far-off echo of a heavenly song. But my wasted wandering life, just like yours, dear Ernest, has not corresponded with my nomadic thoughts. I have had grand dreams in my pristine youth that always resulted in white dreams on my already-stained bed sheets. Damn it! Why must mundane biology always trump intellectual and spiritual pursuit?"

"Holy shit, Professor Knowballs, er, I mean Knowstones!" Ernest exclaimed. "You're just as fucked-up as I am!"

At the hour of sunset, as had long been his frequent custom, Ernest was to discourse an outdoor parable to an assemblage of the listless, apathetic neighbors. The preacher and the poet, arm in arm, still talking together and fantasizing a wonderful same-sex romance, ventured to the familiar community spot. The location was a small nook nestled among the hills, with a gray sturdy precipice behind, the stern front of which was relieved by the pleasant foliage of many creeping plants that formed a dull tapestry for the overhead naked rock. The vegetation was hanging there like celebratory festoons sagging from the cliff's rugged facade. In another direction was seen the Great Stone Face, with the same natural cheer displayed, being combined with the same transcendent solemnity.

"This dumb-ass poet and I are getting married!" Ernest announced to the now-shocked Christian crowd amassed on the scene. "Since I'm a self-appointed preacher, I'll adroitly perform the wedding!"

The poet, as he intently listened, felt that the integrated being and character of Ernest constituted a nobler strain of poetry greater than any *he* had ever written. His eyes glistening with tears, and soon the enthralled bard gazed reverentially at his new-found partner, the venerable parson, and said within himself under the shade-tree canopy

44

that never was there an aspect so worthy of a prophet and a sage as that mild, sweet, thoughtful countenance, with the glory of magnificent white hair diffused among dense, white dandruff flakes.

"You've put the homo' back into the designation 'Homo sapiens'," the rejuvenated poet gushed, much to the detriment and astonishment of the stunned, narrow-minded, Protestant crowd. "Too bad we're two fagged-out faggots! Holy fried shit, Ernie! I do feel a wonderful pulsation happening somewhere in my genitalia zone!"

At a distance, but distinctly to be seen by all, high-up in the golden setting sun, there appeared the Great Stone Face, with hoary mists shrouding it, like the white hairs around Ernest's brow and ears.

At that specific moment, in sympathy with a thought which he preacher was about to utter, emaciated Ernest's face assumed a special expression of celestial grandeur, so imbued with benevolence and love that its appearance inspired the chubby, fat-assed poet to impulsively and irresistibly shout, "Behold! Behold! Ernest is himself the likeness of the Great Stone Face! Ernest is not only a sight to behold, but also a sight to be held! Kiss me preacher man!"

Then, all the distraught village people, even those that had just exited the town YMCA, each person looked and fathomed that which the deep-sighted poet had claimed had actually been genuinely true. The ancient prophecy had finally been fulfilled.

But Ernest, having finished what he had to state, aggressively took the poet's arm, and the pair together walked slowly homeward, still hoping that some wiser and better man than either himself or the fucked-up poet would by-and-by appear, the anonymous newcomer bearing an *exact* resemblance to the GREAT STONE FACE.

"The Three Golden Apples"

A hero in Greek mythology was a lesser god whose father was an Olympian deity, and whose mother was a mere gorgeously-stacked, horny mortal. One such legendary hero was Hercules, whose pappy was king-god Zeus, and whose mom was a vivacious, stunning princess named Alcmene. That particular genealogy resulted because the divine king of the gods nonsensically (don't ask me why) preferred human juicy pussy to heavenly juicy pussy.

Hercules was doomed (or fated) to live a life of struggle, unhappiness, and strife. Hera, the jealous queen of the gods and Zeus's spiteful wife, despised Hercules since *he* was the offspring of her husband's infidelity, while having an intense affair with a mere mortal woman with a nice juicy pink pussy. Hera used her supernatural powers and compelled Hercules to temporarily become insane by burning-down his own house, and then killing his wife and children, and after the blaze had subsided, *he* then discovered that *their* bodies hadn't been barbecued.

Since there were no psychiatrists, psychologists, social workers, or guidance counselors around to fuck-up people's minds in ancient times, Hercules trekked to Delphi to consult the *Oracle,* which in this case was not a chamber of the heart, even though *she* often gave advice about love. The lady prophet instructed Hercules that to atone for his egregious crimes against his family, he had to perform twelve labors for *his* cousin Eurystheus, King of Argos. For his eleventh labor, Hercules needed to journey to northern Africa, and then select three golden apples from an enchanted tree that grew in the Garden of Hesperides, which was monitored by four beautiful dancing sisters having alluring, hairy, golden-blonde beavers.

Before the Garden of Hesperides had been overrun with weeds and crabgrass having really sharp claws, people all around the world were skeptical about the story of a glorious tree that bore gigantic golden apples. Many young boys, eager to see the world, desired to visit the legendary garden, and bring back a golden apple to give to their girlfriends in exchange for a deluxe piece of ass at an Argos hotel, featuring Spartan accommodations.

Many of the bold adventurers had never returned from their expeditions, preferring to munch on the pussies of the four Daughters of the Evening Star for the rest of their mortal lives. And the worst part about the whole ordeal was that a nasty dragon with a hundred heads (fifty slept while the other fifty kept watch guarding the Golden Apple Tree) would unexpectedly devour the would-be hero right when *he* began licking the pink inners of the first sister's golden blonde snatcheroo.

Hercules had just finished wandering through the land of Italy, looking to buy a Sicilian pizza with anchovies, but the mortal champion couldn't find any such commodity because he had been trekking on the Italian peninsula, and not ambling about in Sicily. The roaming hero wore a lion's skin, which had been given to him along with his heavy 'club' by the generous King Eurysthesus at an Argos *Lions Club* Meeting attended by all two members.

At every cave or village Hercules visited, the rover inquired about how he could locate the famous Garden of Hesperides. Many of the Italian residents said they had heard of the notorious garden and of the fabled Golden Apple Tree, but none knew exactly where to find those two references. "I think it's not far from where you can buy Sicilian pizza with anchovies!" one senile village elder living beneath Mt. Etna explained to the rambling hero.

"Where's that?" Hercules demanded, raising his club with his right hand, while intensively scratching his balls with his left appendage.

"If I knew that important bull-shit," the demented, hoary-bearded codger replied, "I'd be eating Sicilian pizza with anchovies right now, rather than talkin' to a lost asshole like you!"

At last, Hercules arrived at the brink of a pristine river, where he first took a lengthy piss, and then spotted beautiful young blonde damsels twining flower wreaths, and incessantly gossiping while intermittently checking-out each other's hairy golden beavers through the sheer transparent white gowns the blonde chicks were wearing. The muscle-bound demigod instantly thought that he was at *Bush Gardens* rather than at the Garden of the Hesperides.

"Please confirm to me, you dazzling young sexy maidens," the powerful-looking stranger began in an uncharacteristic cordial voice. "Is this the right way to the Golden Apple Tree? I'm temporarily blinded by your beauty, and can only see and appreciate Bush Gardens at the moment."

"The Garden of the Hesperides, indeed!" one of the Daughters of the Evening Star amazingly shrieked. "That is what you're seeking?"

"We thought that mortals stopped searching for the wonder after so many failures and aborted missions to steal golden apples from the ancient gnarled tree," the second fair damsel with the hairiest bush chimed-in. "What a pity all of those young, well-endowed studs have stupidly died!"

"And pray tell, wandering hero," the third voluptuous virgin said, "what business brings you in quest of the great tree from antiquity? Tell us all about your exploit if you will."

"A certain king with a long fucked-up name too difficult to pronounce has ordered me to pilfer three of the finest golden apples growing on the mythical tree," Hercules confided as the muscular trekker started to achieve an enviable erection, which was *hard* for him to conceal.

The damsels saw the hero's tool rising and pulsating beneath his loosely fitting lion's skin, and started giggling as if they had feathers rubbing against their armpits. "And I must tell you, well-endowed traveler," the fourth maiden piped-in, "that most young men with average-sized peckers go in quest of the apples to retrieve one for their girlfriends, or for their mistresses in the name of love. But I can plainly see from your throbbing glory that you're not an ordinary tiny-dicked man. Do you love this retarded king so much that you would risk your life for him? Are you fuckin' gay, or are you some sort of demented, sidetracked pedophile?"

Hercules felt very uncomfortable being interrogated in such an unfamiliar manner by the fourth *damsel in this dress*. "Where do you nice pussies, er, I mean golden-haired maidens live? Where is your home?" the brute of a man inquired as the famous Greek deftly changed the controversial subject from himself to the four horny virgin bitches.

"Oh, we don't live in a house or a ghetto!" the first maiden replied.

"And we don't live in a cave," the second maiden with the fluffiest blonde beaver added.

"We just hang-out in this garden and dance around the Golden Apple Tree over yonder when we aren't doing cunnilingus or sixty-nine on each other. As our father always told us when we were youngsters, 'Eat' out more often'!"

"I see," answered Hercules in an admiring fashion. "I'm glad to hear that you fair young ladies don't live in a house, because I do have a certain propensity for pyromania when it comes to family dwellings. But I've approached you in friendship," the champion of great deeds continued, "and after I successfully obtain the three golden apples, I'll allow all four of you to suck on my humungous tool, all at the same time. It sounds like you four pretty bitches need a little diversion to your limited sex life, besides all of that dull lesbian bull-shit you've alluded to!"

"That sounds like an appropriate diversion all right," the first damsel readily admitted. "If we suck you off, we can retain our virginity, and still dance around the Golden Apple Tree, just like Lord Zeus wants us to do!"

"Your mission sounds more like a *Herculean* labor than an ordinary Promethean task!" the broad with the hairiest blonde bush contributed. "Who are you stranger?"

"I see that you've already heard of me," the hero with the massive club chuckled. "My name *is* Hercules."

"That's just great!" the third attractive blonde acknowledged. "And after you pop your massive load, and shrink your marvelous apparatus, you can then use that wooden club as a dildo and shove it repeatedly up each of our assholes!"

"Oh Hercules, your magnificent accomplishments are famous all over the known world," the first maiden melodramatically complimented. "We don't think it extraordinary any longer that you're in quest of the Golden Apple Tree and its divine fruit."

"My dear 'comely' maidens," Hercules answered as the searcher almost prematurely ejaculated all over the damned place. "Now that you know my name and have examined my exposed long thick male equipment, can you tell me which way it is to the singular Garden of Hesperides? I'm near-sighted, and can only see 'bushes' that are close by. Since eyeglasses haven't been invented yet, I can't see shit far away. I can only smell it!"

"We shall provide you with the best directions we can," assured the four damsels all together. "But as you know," the third maiden continued, "in Greek Mythology, nothing for mere mortals is easily achieved. You must first go to the seashore's beach and locate the Old One. Then, your big challenge is that you must convince or force the wily fuck-head to inform you precisely where the prized Golden Apples are to be found."

"Look ladies," Hercules objected. "I'm definitely near-sighted, and can't see this damned tree you're alluding to that I know is somewhere close by. Just tell me where it is, and that'll save me a lot of valuable time and wasted effort with interrogating the Old One, whoever the hell he is!"

"How's this for incentive for doing things *our* way?" the second maiden insisted. And with her preface being completed, all four damsels lifted-up their transparent white gowns, got-down on the ground lying on their backs, and then simultaneously opened their luscious blonde beavers and pink slits for Hercules' much-appreciated inspection and approval.

"Okay, okay you win!" Hercules exclaimed before the traveling admirer popped a huge load that knocked the loose lion's skin garment right off his body. "Sorry about that!" the famous champion apologized as he embarrassingly picked-up his lion' skin, and awkwardly reentered it as his four female fans giggled and laughed in astonishment at the white sticky wetness all over their bodies. "I'll return for that blowjob I promised you'll all be administering after I finish the three golden apples' assignment," Hercules vowed. "By then, my tool should be reloaded, and quite ready to explode another wicked jet of sticky semen into your lucky faces!"

"Remember, Hercules," the third damsel emphasized. "The Old One is really the Old Man of the Sea. He possesses remarkable abilities that you'll soon discover."

"Yes," the fourth maiden agreed. "And whatever the talented asshole attempts, be sure to latch onto him and hold tight, until he gives you the information that you seek. Until then," she proceeded, "we'll just hang-out here next to the Golden Apple Tree you've sought, and we'll simply dance around, and then twine flower wreaths while gossiping about your fantastic manhood. Too bad you're so damned near-sighted and have to go through all this additional bull-shit to get the golden apples, but unfortunately, that's the way fucked-up mythology works!"

Trekking to the north, the on-a-mission champion heard the sea roaring in the distance, so the wanderer increased his pace and arrived at a hard-sanded beach, having loud surf and great waves. Some green shrubbery was situated on a hillside next to a cave, so Hercules decided he'd investigate the area to see if any edible fruit grew there. The journeyman clambered-up the steep, treacherous ridge, and then cautiously ambled-across a lush green carpet of wild grass that was blended-in with thick clover.

An old man (or what appeared to be an old man) was sleeping at the cave's entrance. As Hercules more closely examined the snoring figure, the observer determined that *it* was a combination of human being and sea creature, having fish scales on its extremities, and also being web-footed, much like a mallard or a goose worthy of taking a *gander* at. The Old One's beard was more like a seaweed tuft than an actual accumulation of gray or black whiskers.

The hero grabbed the resting Old One's arm with one hand, and the old coot's dick with the other, and the disturbed creature awoke from its deep sleep in a very startled-but-belligerent frame of mind. The Old One instantly transformed into a stag with long antlers, but Hercules maintained a strong grip on its front leg and aching pecker. Then, the Old One converted into a tremendous female eagle without *a bird,* so Hercules had to move his left arm and latch onto one of the ferocious animal's razor-sharp talons, and hold as tightly as he could. Immediately afterward, the Old Man changed into a fierce, barking three-headed dog baring six-inch-long fangs in each of its mouths, which were desperately attempting to bite the hero's cock off. But Hercules was so determined in capturing the talented shape-shifter that he held on with all his great might. Next, the incredible Old Man of the Sea switched into Geryon, a savage six-legged man-monster that instantaneously pissed into Hercules' face with all half-dozen of its dingles.

The Old One was now becoming both exhausted and frustrated from fruitlessly expending so much energy, and as a last resort, became a huge viper, which vainly tried coiling its body around the champion's chest, and futilely constricting the air out of his lungs. But the brave hero squeezed the enormous serpent's head so tightly that the viper hissed in agony. The Old Man's power to change into anything else had been effectively neutralized by the visitor's steadfast resolve. Its magic was no longer a surprise, or a deterrent to Hercules's superhuman mettle.

Finally, the Old Man realized that it was absolutely fruitless to battle and to resist the formidable strength of his new-found adversary, so *he* voluntarily relinquished *his* stubborn opposition, and reappeared in *his* natural, geriatric-looking form.

"Pray powerful mortal, what do you want with me?" the very fatigued Old Man of the Sea panted. "You almost squeezed the breath out of my gills, and the shit out of my ass! If you don't let go of me, I shall evaluate you to be a very uncouth and uncivil member of your moronic species!"

Unfazed, the Greek hero retained his disabling grasp. "My name is Hercules," the stranger to that seashore proudly and loudly announced. "And I shall never release you from my death-grip until you reveal the nearest and quickest route to the Garden of the Hesperides. If you fail to surrender those directions, I guarantee I'll turn you inside-out, and then squeeze the breath *into* your gills and the shit back *into* your intestines! So just cooperate and stop givin' me a lot of your stupid, evasive ever-changing bull-shit! And don't dare try turning into a damned bull, either!"

"Okay, I concede defeat," the Old One begrudgingly answered. "You should go south and at the division of the road, turn left, and follow that path to where you shall encounter a very colossal giant that holds the world upon his big brawny shoulders. And if the Titan should be in good spirits, the Goliath shall tell you where the Golden Apple Tree is situated. And," the Old One shrewdly added, "I don't think you'll be able to subdue the Titan like you had so easily done with me. Now, I suggest that you get your diabolical hands off my arm and my dick, and use some seaweed over there to wipe the three gallons of disgusting yellow piss off your face and beard."

"You stupid shit!" Hercules chided. "You should've turned into the colossal ogre you had alluded to!" Hercules then thanked the Old Man of the Sea for *his* accurate instructions, and resumed his itinerary proceeding in the aforementioned direction, and then, obediently taking the appropriate referred-to branch in the road. After several hours of exhaustive walking, the burly muscular fellow approached a peninsula with a tremendous mountain in its center, but upon closer examination, what the hero thought had been a volcano was really the figure of a huge giant holding the sky upon his mammoth shoulders. It was indeed a very exceptional and spectacular sight to behold.

Stationary cottony clouds around the Titan's waist looked-like an immense white girdle, and those formations resting under his chin made the fearsome, gargantuan hulk appear to have an old man's light-gray goatee. A breeze slowly moved the cumuli from around the Titan's prodigious face, and Hercules finally beheld the behemoth's full countenance. The monster had eyes as big as ponds, and a mouth as wide as a lake. A very lugubrious expression was evident upon the giant's visage, giving the impression that the Titan was completely bored and depressed about his monotonous burden of holding up the azure sky while standing on the Earth.

An active forest was growing and spreading between the Titan's sizable toes, and each had *a corn,* just like every one of the tall oak trees had when each had originated from 'a corny' *acorn.* The towering, despondent Titan finally looked-down from his high elevation, and spotted Hercules standing below, impatiently waiting to be recognized.

"Who are you loitering and dawdling down there near my toenails?" the frightful figure thundered.

"I am Hercules!" The hero bravely bellowed back in a vibrant voice that almost-rivaled the volume of the giant's awesome bass. "I'm seeking the Garden of Hesperides."

"Well, I'm Atlas, the mightiest Titan the world has ever known," the formerly lackadaisical brute communicated. "I've been assigned by Zeus to act like a bandit, and *hold-up* the damned sky!"

"I understand now why you appear to be in such a miserable quandary," Hercules sympathized. "But dear Atlas, can you show me in which direction is the Garden of Hesperides? I've already visited Bush Gardens and enjoyed it very much!"

"What do you want there?" Atlas challenged. "You must want to get killed! Ha, ha, ha!" the immortal phenomenon boomed as his mood oscillated from gloomy to buoyant in five short seconds.

"I need three of the golden apples," Hercules explained, "to give to my fuck-head cousin, the lunatic King of Argos. If I don't bring them back to the King, he'll tell me to 'Ar-go fuck yourself'!' I'm sick and tired of hearing that fucked-up joke over and over from him!"

"Good one, ha, ha, ha!" the Titan cackled and then coughed, as the Earth beneath his feet quaked. "Good one indeed! But let me tell you that there is no one except me who can trek to the garden and snatch those three golden apples for you. If it weren't for this stupid bull-shit of me having to hold up the sky for Zeus," the giant indicated, "I would make six long steps across the Mediterranean Sea and secure the three bitchin' objects for you."

"But I thought the Golden Apple Tree was in northern Africa near where the Daughters of the Evening Star dance, twine floral wreaths, masturbate, and eat each other out!" the muscular mortal revealed.

"Their imitation apple tree is just a fuckin' decoy for the real one," Atlas readily clarified. "I can execute your errand in a jiffy."

"But can't you just place the sky onto one of the nearby mountains?" Hercules cleverly inquired. "That seems like a relatively easy solution."

"None of them are quite high enough to be effectively utilized," the melancholy giant bitterly lamented. "But noble Hercules, if you stand on yonder mountain over there, your head would be on a level with mine. You could temporarily relieve me of my eternal penalty while I could venture and fetch your gleaming golden apples, and deliver them to King Ar-go fuck yourself! Ho, ho, holy shit! I made a funny! Ha, ha, ha! I made a fuckin' hilarious funny!"

The hero was puzzled for a moment, and then he advanced a rather relevant question to the ponderous figure before him. "Atlas," the punished on a quest fellow inquired, "is the sky exceptionally heavy? I am but a mere mortal, and perhaps not equal to performing such a *titanic* undertaking!"

"Not at first, Hercules," the Titan boomed as thunder echoed through the neighboring mountain valleys. "But after a millennium or so, it gets to be a pain in the neck, not to mention being a royal pain in the ass. I desperately need to take a lengthy break so that I could relieve my full kidneys, and flood and fertilize the entire *Sahara Desert* with my piss!"

Hercules was still dubious of the giant's motives. "And just how long, Atlas, will it take you to acquire the three golden apples, and then return to repossess the sky from my humble, mortal shoulders?"

"That minor task can be accomplished in only a few minutes," the Titan promised. "I shall take giant steps of fifteen or twenty-miles at a stride, and be at the garden and back before your balls ever develop a double hernia. How do ya' like those friggin' apples, Hercules?" the enormous fellow indulgently laughed, causing tremendous destructive earthquakes that comprehensively obliterated seven LBGT villages and eighty-seven brothels in the immediate vicinity.

"I have limited options, Atlas," Hercules admitted, "so I shall climb the mountain behind your back, and then you can transfer the sky onto my unworthy shoulders. I always wanted to stand head and shoulders above other men, so I suppose here's my opportunity to distinguish myself' from the cowardly masses. I mean to say, Atlas," the garrulous fellow proceeded, "I want to do something great in my lifetime, and not just kill a hundred-headed dragon, or wrestle and destroy a family of irate gorgons, all possessing huge hemorrhoids. When I get to the mountain peak, then hand me the fuckin' clear blue sky! That deed will be my contribution to posterity!"

Soon, the sky was shifted from Atlas onto Hercules, who immediately discerned that the overwhelming weight was more than unpleasant to bear. 'What if Atlas skips town and never returns?' Hercules pondered. 'Oh well, it's too late to do anything about it, as long as he has his freedom to ramble all over goddamned creation looking for virgins' cherries to bust!'

The giant's first instinct was to stretch in order to expand his many contracted muscles. The Titan certainly was an impressive and sensational sight, and the merry behemoth then happily abounded about, capering and prancing all over the area, causing three major cities on the northern coast of Africa to crumble and then catastrophically tumble into the Mediterranean Sea.

Then Atlas bellowed out, "Ho! Ho! Ho!" so loudly that Zeus heard *his* exclamations resonating on top of *Mt. Olympus*, hundreds of miles away from the rather horrifying sound's source. The giant finally remembered his pledge to Hercules, and stepped into the wine-dark Mediterranean Sea. Ten-miles out into the continental basin, the water came up to the giant's knees, and twenty-miles out (the greatest depth), the water rose to Atlas's chest.

'I just hope he remembers the three golden apples,' Hercules prayed. 'If the Titan decides to start swimming and churning his arms, Atlas will surely drown the entire population of the whole fucked-up Earth!' the sky-holder realized. 'Maybe that's not such a bad fuckin' idea after all! But I really pity poor Atlas. If this weight seems irksome to me after only five-minutes, how horribly irritating it must be for him after three millennia of such monotonous bull-shit? The lofty giant's only satisfaction is that he could be a voyeur, watching from *this* height thousands of unwary people simultaneously getting their freakin' rocks off on three separately-viewed continents!'

Fifteen-minutes later, Hercules's heart began palpitating wildly when the strongman observed Atlas returning from *his* incredible trek across the sea. In his right hand were three fabulous golden apples that were three-times the size of cantaloupes. When the giant emerged from the sea and stepped onto the shore, Hercules politely commended the Titan for his promptness, and for his diligence.

"I'm happy to see you've safely returned," the hero sincerely related. "And I'm thrilled that you've absconded with the three golden apples I had requested!"

"Without a doubt! Without a fuckin' doubt, Hercules!" the mighty Titan summarized. "I helped myself to the most beautiful apples growing on the enchanted tree. And the fucked-up hundred-headed dragon was quite a spectacle to behold. He was rather defensive and hostile at first, but then the stupid shit finally realized that he didn't want to fuck with me! It's too bad *you* had to miss all of the wonderful bull-shit I got to witness first hand!"

"You had a most splendid ramble indeed," Hercules concluded and complimented, "and you've completed the project just as easily as I could've done myself'. And now since I have to complete the labor that you've so graciously assisted me in doing," Hercules elucidated, "I have to transport those fabulous apples to my cousin, the asshole King of Argos. It's now time for me to give you back your unlucky burden. Here Atlas; let's exchange the rare-aired' atmosphere for the coveted three golden apples. To tell you the truth, I'm getting a bit dizzy and giddy from a lack of oxygen way up here!"

"Why as to your recollection of recent events," the imposing Titan roared as Atlas deftly juggled the three huge golden apples into the air with his right hand, sending each one twenty-miles or so into the stratosphere, and then repeating the process, "I consider you Hercules to be a little too illogical. I can deliver your precious apples to your cousin, the King, possessing the fucked-up name, much quicker than you can," Atlas pragmatically declared. "I'll take my longest strides, even if I occasionally devastate a fragile city or two along the way. Now that I have liberties to enjoy and pursue," the Titan indicated, "I have no interest in obeying Zeus's unjust edict any longer."

Hercules shifted his body around on top of the adjacent mountain peak, becoming uncomfortable with both the weight of the sky and with Atlas's new-found independence. Two stars in the night firmament tumbled from horizon to horizon, and everyone on Earth thought that the end of the world was certainly imminent.

"Oh Hercules, you need more practice at your new art!" the Titan criticized with abundant laughter. "Believe me when I say I've not lost as many stars in the last ten-centuries. Patience and fortitude will be the virtues that'll enable you to perfect your craft! Ha, ha, ho, ho, ho! Hercules, you don't know an outhouse from your asshole!"

"What the fuck!" Hercules exclaimed in astonishment. "Do you plan to make me perform your shit-eatin' responsibility forever? Zeus will punish your ass worse next time, after *he* finds out about your blatant insubordination to *his* divine authority!"

"Fuck that despotic asshole, Zeus!" Atlas disrespectfully yelled, causing a tremendous sonic boom that leveled stone houses and wrecked gay marriages on three continents. "Zeus only does shit *to* you and never *for* you. Hercules, I might return to this place in a hundred-years, or maybe in half a millennium, to relieve you of your inhumane encumbrance," the giant considered and offered. "Well then, if in a thousand-years I happen to become bored with the world's wondrous variety, I might return and switch places with you. If you can prove you can do the work of a Titan," Atlas amply chuckled, "then history will honor and revere your name, dear Hercules. You'll receive many well-deserved accolades!"

"Stop bustin' my balls with your haughty bull-crap, and quit breakin' my back with this agonizing sacrifice I'm enduring!" the hero adamantly complained. "I'll gladly hold up the sky until you return if you'll promise to do me just one small favor!"

"And what exactly is that?" Atlas asked, as the huge character continued to adroitly juggle the three golden apples with his right hand, while looking at and negotiating a favor with Hercules.

"This great sky weight is chafing my sensitive shoulders," Hercules squawked. "And I'd like to use my lion's skin as a cushion to protect my delicate mortal skin. I cannot endure standing here for countless centuries without having any skin on my shoulder bones. I need fuckin' protection!"

"Bend over, and the friction will certainly chafe your ass in addition to lacerating your shoulders," the giant laughed while totally amusing himself. "But your request is certainly a legitimate one. I shall take back the sky for just five-minutes to give you a brief breather, so that you can adjust your lion's skin and make it into a soft blanket," the Titan agreed. "Next, I shall be off to Argos to deliver your apples, and then roam the Earth, and even descend down into the dark Pit of Tartarus in hope of reuniting with, and emancipating, my fellow Titans, who've been sentenced and punished by Zeus."

The jolly (non-green) giant tossed-down the three golden apples, and cheerfully took back the sky from Hercules's supposedly chafed shoulders, and then transferred it onto his own. The Greek hero wasted little time in sprinting down the mountain, picking-up the three treasured apples three times the size of cantaloupes, and then heading for the nearest road leading back to the Daughters of the Hesperides.

"Hey, where the fuck do ya' think you're goin'!" the victimized Titan bellowed at the clever mortal trickster.

"I'm gonna' get the blowjob of my life from the four *comely* sisters with the terrific blonde bushes!" Hercules smartly answered. "And as for my cousin the king, he can wait and twiddle his thumbs for his three golden apples. I might just hang-around the Daughters of the Evening Star for a few decades, and really get my reproductive pipes cleaned-out!"

"But you're breaking your goddamned promise!" the aggravated Titan boomed, causing a hundred-foot-high tidal wave to disintegrate the coastal city of Argos, and in the process, drowning its crazy King along with most of his subjects and predicates. "I've been fuckin' hoodwinked!"

"You shouldn't vehemently protest and be so extremely jealous, just because I'm going to get the ideal blowjob of the millennium from the four *comely* sisters with the terrific blonde bushes!" Hercules ridiculed and reiterated. "After all Atlas; look at it this way! You've been really royally *fucked* by this most-recent development! You oughta' feel greatly satisfied!"

"I hope you become impotent, and that your sperm-worm never again becomes firm!" Atlas futilely bawled.

"Not a tiny bug's chance caught in a thick spider's web," Hercules insisted. "You can enviously watch the whole damned blowjob thing from a distance, you arrogant, unscrupulous, perverted voyeur!"

Eventually, Atlas became fatigued of his grueling chore, and over centuries of toil, converted into a solid mountain, and to this very day, those high summits in northern Africa are still benignly referred to as the *Atlas Mountains*. And when thunder is heard in the local valleys, some superstitious asshole natives still believe that the loud booms are the sounds of the pathetic giant Atlas yelling and pleading for Hercules to return to complete *his* long-neglected promise.

"The Minister's Black Veil"

Taking-out his sexual frustrations on an inanimate object, the Sexton stood in the porch of Milford meeting-house, pulling lustily like a hyperactive chimpanzee at the bell-rope. The hunch-backed, elderly village people came wobbling along the cobblestone street. The feeble elders were hobbling about with their rickety canes and their makeshift wooden walkers.

Children with bright faces tripped merrily beside their parents, or mimicked a graver gait in the conscious indignity of ruining their soiled and tarnished, faded Sunday clothes. Spruce bachelors, all spruced-up, looked sidelong at the promenading pretty maidens, and sporting semi-erections, the horny assholes fancied that the Sabbath sunshine had curiously made the strutting Puritan dolls prettier than on week-days.

When the throng had mostly streamed into the rector's porch, the sexton again began tolling the bell, keeping his keen eye upon the Reverend Mr. Hooper's door. The first glimpse of the clergyman's figure was the correct signal for the bell-ringer to cease the metal object's clanging, noisy summons.

"But what has good Parson Hooper got upon his face?" the Sexton shouted in astonishment. "It's certainly not one gigantic zit-type blackhead!"

All those hearing the Sexton's exclamation immediately turned about and beheld the semblance of Reverend Mr. Hooper, pacing slowly (in his normal meditative manner) toward the town meeting-house. With one accord, the startled witnesses began expressing more wonder than if some strange, newly-arrived, morbid minister were coming to dust the cushions of Mr. Hooper's germ-infested pulpit seat. Soon, a brief conversation ensued.

"Are you sure it is our parsimonious parson?" inquired Goodman Gray, the Sexton's assistant. "This is definitely a black day in our village's undistinguished history!"

Goodman Gray was a good man, and also the Sexton's younger sibling. Together, the Sexton and Goodman had played musical instruments in a Puritan underground gay sextet, along with their brothers "Jammin'" Benjamin, Dorian, and a certain distant French cousin having the unique surname appellation, "Poupon".

"Of a certainty it is indeed good Mr. Hooper, without his gym trunks and basketball," replied the appalled Sexton. "He was to have exchanged pulpits with Parson Shute of Westbury, but Parson Shute sent a note to excuse himself' yesterday, being asked to preach a funeral sermon over in Westbury. And so, disappointed Reverend Mr. Hooper can't today shoot hoops with Parson Shute!"

The cause of so much amazement may appear sufficiently slight. Mr. Hooper, a gentlemanly personage of about thirty-years of age, although still a bachelor lacking a minimal college degree, was dressed with due clerical neatness, as if a careful wife had starched his band, and had dutifully brushed the weekly dust and cake crumbs from his impeccable Sunday garb.

One thing, however, was remarkable in Reverend Hooper's no-overalls overall appearance. Swathed about the reverend's forehead and hanging-down over his face, so low as to be shaken by his dragon's breath, Mr. Hooper had been sporting a macabre-looking black veil. On a nearer view, the strange apparel seemed to consist of two folds of black crepe, which entirely concealed his features except for his exposed mouth and chin, but probably did not intercept his sight further than to give a darkened aspect to all living and inanimate visible things: animal, vegetable or mineral.

With this gloomy and mysterious black shade suspended-down before most of his face, good Mr. Hooper walked onward at a slow and quiet pace, stooping somewhat during his saunter, and then looking on the ground for small litter wrappers, as is customary with abstracted men in deep contemplation. In the process of his mania, the minister took time to nod kindly to those of his startled parishioners, who still impatiently waited on the meeting-house steps. But so wonder-struck were the stunned spectators that the preacher's amiable greetings and gestures hardly met with any return salutations.

"I can't really feel as if good Mr. Hooper's face was behind that piece of black cloth," muttered the anonymous Sexton to his brother, Goodman Gray. "This whole friggin' village is loaded with crepe hangers and wannabe' crepe hangers! Looks like a whole lot of crappy crape bull-shit going on to me!"

"I don't like it one iota," muttered an old woman as the hag wobbled her fat ass into the meeting-house. "He has changed himself into something awful, only accomplished by hiding his face. What the hell is the fucked-up charlatan trying to prove? Does Mr. Hooper have some kind of foreign venereal disease on his face?"

"Our parson has gone stark raving mad!" insisted Goodman Gray, following his older brother across the small church's threshold. "Mr. Hooper's choice of wardrobe is quite bizarre. I'll talk with the town constable in private. In truth, I think that our unpredictable minister definitely needs his bell rung!"

A vicious rumor of some unaccountable legitimacy had preceded Mr. Hooper into the combination church/meeting-house, and had previously set the volatile congregation all astir. Few could refrain from twisting their heads toward the opened door; many stood upright and turned directly about, while several rather bored, rambunctious, neurotic, little boys clambered-upon the seats, and simultaneously crashed-down again, causing a terrible racket.

There was a general bustle that pervaded the large room's hectic atmosphere; a discernible rustling of the women's gowns, and a perceptible shuffling of the men's feet, accompanied in the background by erratic and spontaneous loud, nervous farting in the pews. The hubbub greatly was in contrast with (and in opposition to) the traditional hushed repose, which should ordinarily prevail with the grand entrance of the village minister.

But Mr. Hooper appeared not to notice the widespread perturbation of his gossipy, paranoid congregation. The preacher entered the church with an almost-noiseless step, bent his head mildly toward the horizontal pews situated on each side, which abundantly stunk from the volume of nervous farting going on. The Reverend Hooper politely bowed as he passed-by his eldest parishioner, a century-old, white-haired curmudgeon, who was occupying an arm-chair positioned in the center of the aisle, a distinct honor reserved for comatose old farts.

It was rather strange for one to observe how slowly this venerable, partially blind, palsied, old coot became conscious of something singular in the crazy appearance of his pastor. The feeble codger seemed not fully to partake of the in-progress prevailing wonder until Mr. Hooper had ascended the stairs and showed himself' in the pulpit, all the while imagining that he was Captain Ahab, searching the vast ocean for Moby Dick. Soon, the whaling ship captain impersonator came face to face with his astonished congregation, that is, except for the parson's eyes and nose occupying the space behind the hideous black veil.

That mysterious emblem was never once withdrawn during the entire service. The veil's material shook with *his* measured breath, as the lecturer calmly narrated the morning psalm, the text temporarily throwing its obscurity between the sinister minister and the Holy Scripture passage the reverend was methodically reading. And while the enigmatic pastor diligently prayed to (and for) his almost-delirious attendees, the suspect veil-of-interest lay heavily upon his uplifted countenance, fully suggesting a black funereal appearance. 'Does Mr. Hooper seek hiding his face from the dreadful Bible text that specifically pertained to the value of death's role in efficiently eliminating any instinctive male erection and then swiftly initiating Resurrection?' one church member considered.

Such was the negative effect of that simple piece of folded black crepe. More than one woman of delicate nerves felt compelled to leave the meeting-house to quickly cross the street, and visit the general store to confidentially purchase *their* own black veil hairy pussy covering. Yet perhaps the 'pale-faced' congregation (no Indians allowed) was almost as fearful a sight to the wily minister as was his black veil happened to be to those astounded, seated assholes.

Mr. Hooper had the distinguished reputation of being an eloquent preacher, but certainly not an energetic or ambitious one: the strange fellow strove to win his people heavenward by vocally implementing mild, persuasive influences, rather than to drive the folks thither by the tremendous thunders of fire and brimstone speeches that would emphasize furious, burning-hot flames shooting-down from Heaven, and then having the lethal electric bolts zooming straight-up *their* tender assholes.

The sermon, which the oddball orator then delivered, was marked by the same characteristics of style and manner as the general tone of his standard pulpit oratory, the dramatic theme being "Death is wonderful! Be happy, accept it, and let it happen! Death is your only passport to Heaven!"

But there was something either in the sentiment of the parson's discourse, or in the wild imaginations of the audience, which somehow cobbled together, making the obnoxious monologue the most powerful effort that the Puritan congregation had ever heard from their unpredictable pastor's lips. The sermon was tinged rather more darkly than usual with the gentle gloom of Mr. Hooper's outlandish "Enjoy dying" temperament, which the minister seemed to relish. "Die with one venial sin on your soul, and Lucifer will cauterize your asshole for all eternity; that is, instead of having the merciful Lord performing that same kind of simple punishment only occasionally during your earthly existence; that is, brethren, as long as *you* mortal sinners remain mere mortals!"

The additional subject of venial sin in the preacher's sermon had reference to secret desires, such as the wish to masturbate, besides those sad mysteries which we skillfully hide from our nearest and dearest acquaintances; for example, an event in a dream like having group sex at a terrific orgy. And according to Reverend Hooper's stern pulpit rhetoric, the Omniscient and Ubiquitous Lord can detect (and is always aware of) any immoral bull-shit that an errant mortal could ever consider committing, including either minor venial or major mortal sin.

'Reverend Hooper is taking all the fun out of life,' thought one farmer in the third pew, church right. 'He who is without sin, let him roll the first boulder!'

'Who needs to hear this irrelevant shit?' pondered a pensive hussy sitting directly across the aisle from the irritated farmer. 'Take my dildo away from me, and I'll have to have sex with my fucked-up husband more often! Who needs to listen to this threatening hell-fire horse crap? I wonder if Reverend Hooper has an extra-big salami dangling between his skinny legs, or does he possess a tiny pussy penetrator instead?'

A subtle power was breathed into the minister's ominous words, representing a force that generated both fear and contempt among the members of the congregation, who all unanimously loathed the idea of having their delicate assholes cauterized by Satan, or by any other supernatural nutcase demon. The most innocent girl, and also the most-horny man, felt as if the renegade preacher had crept upon them behind his awful veil, and ingeniously discovered their hoarded iniquity of both deed and thought. The preacher's intrusion into their innermost lusts seemed just as horrible as supernatural lightning and hellfire shooting-up their delicate assholes.

Many parish listeners spread their clasped hands upon their bosoms, and upon their crotches, to protect those anatomical areas from sudden violent supernatural attack. There was nothing terrible in what Mr. Hooper said, at least no permanent destruction or bodily termination, even though some of the horny women and kinky girls were licking their lips and imagining the thrill of being romantically seduced by the alluring man hiding behind the black veil. And yet, many decades before the invention of the seismograph, with every tremor evident in *his* melancholy voice, the hearers quaked inside their stinking, fart-ridden pews, all of which smelled even worse when everyone was obediently kneeling-down.

'I need to plow into my wife's sister's snatcheroo after I plow the cornfield,' the naughty haughty farmer was thinking. 'If Mr. Hooper got laid more often, he wouldn't have pounds of backed-up semen clogging-up his fuckin' brain!'

'The farmer sitting across from me enjoys humping and pumping pussy,' the across the aisle hussy considered. 'I understand that he has a frigid wife whose body is colder than a witch's tit. I think it's time to lift my black dress and show my ankle in his direction, after we exit to the street. I've concluded that Reverend Hooper's crummy Puritan morality bull-shit really sucks!'

A terribly potent, unsought pathos came hand-in-hand with the listeners' responsive awe. The townspeople longed for a breath of wind to blow aside the hideous back veil, almost believing that a stranger's visage (rather than Reverend Hooper's) would be discovered, though despite the familiar form, the essential gestures and voice were indeed those of Mr. Hooper, and not those of some kinky male stripper, or some homosexual couch dancer.

At the close of the weird service, the frustrated churchgoers hurried-out of the mass with mass confusion, everyone being eager to communicate his or her pent-up amazement, and everyone quite eager to share his or her accumulated body fluids with complete strangers. Temporarily, the village's population was concerned about sexual gratification, and also physical relief of anxiety, more so than the attendees were contemplating about the minister's loathsome black veil. Some folks gathered in little circles, huddled closely together, with their busy-body mouths all whispering about how Mr. Hooper needed to get laid, and that the "fucked-up Reverend" should immediately forget about the emotionally disturbing, awesome, and monotonous fire and brimstone punishment theme.

Some neurotic church members went home to pleasurably play with their privates in private. Others talked loudly and profaned about the strange Sabbath-day, while also persistently criticizing Mr. Hooper's "prudish Puritanism" with bursts of ostentatious laughter. A few church apostles shook their sagacious heads, intimating that they could penetrate the black veil mystery by paying for Mr. Hooper's scheduled libido evaluation from the county's award-winning Advanced Psychiatric Sexual Abnormalities Team.

One or two concerned citizens who had hastily evacuated the church affirmed that there was no particular mystery at all to the surreptitious minister and his now-trademark black veil, but only that Mr. Hooper's eyes were so weakened from continuously reading smutty pornography magazines by the midnight lamp as to require necessary shade during daylight and early evening hours.

After a brief interval of deep meditation, Mr. Hooper also exited the church, vigorously scratching his testicles while walking in the rear of his rebellious flock. Turning his veiled face from one gossiping group to another, the Gospel lecturer paid due reverence to the assembled 'hoary whore-heads'; then next, the suave parson saluted the middle-aged villagers, demonstrating bland dignity with extended middle fingers shoved deep inside his black pants pockets.

As their assumed friend and deft spiritual guide, the preacher greeted the young females with mingled authority and love, and next laid his hands upon the little children's heads to bless *their'* souls, while seriously contemplating gentle pedophilia.

Such deportment was always Reverend Hooper's predictable custom on the Holy Sabbath Day. But indeed, uncommon and bewildered looks repaid Mr. Hooper for his phony courtesy and his fucked-up general appearance. Unlike on former, more rational occasions, on *that* day no one aspired to the honor of walking by their pastor's side, for his new black veil had scared the blessed shit out of everyone.

Old Squire Saunders, doubtless disabled by an accidental lapse of memory, had neglected to invite Mr. Hooper to his dinner table to say "feast your eyes" on the delicious turkey being served that evening.

'Instead of blessing the turkey, Mr. Hooper should bless the inactive red rooster between my rickety legs!' the miserable old coot thought. 'That grotesque-looking black veil is enough to make any woman's tits sag, and cause my flaccid dick to shrivel-up into a tiny insignificant flesh-ball! I do mean,' Old Squire Saunders managed to ponder, 'when I piss, I pretend that the yellow urine is white semen, and I nearly have an enormous coronary attack every single time. Thanks to the reverend's reprehensible black veil, I'll honestly not know whether I'm fuckin' coming or going!'

Reverend Hooper then turned his frail body in the direction of the parsonage, and at the moment of his closing the door, the enigmatic preacher was observed looking back upon the still shell-shocked people, all of whom had their eyes fixed upon the "masquerading moron minister". A sad-but-brief smile gleamed faintly from beneath the black veil, and flickered about his mouth, glimmering in sheer delight as the cleric disappeared into his abode's sanctuary to read another volume of smutty pornography.

"How strange," an upset lady uttered, "that a simple black veil, such as any woman might wear on her church-issued bonnet, should become such a terrible thing when adorning upon Mr. Hooper's pocked face! Holy shit, Horace! I have a bee in my bonnet! You're always bragging about being a goddamned WASP! Chase the son-of-a-bitchin' insect the hell away from me!"

"Something must surely be amiss with Mr. Hooper's intellect," observed ad declared her wise husband, as Horace (the geriatric senile village physician) licked and sucked on his recently-acquired flying insect bee sting. "But the strangest part of the whole affair, Martha, is the effect of that black veil, even on a sober-minded man like me. Though it covers only our pastor's face, the contemptible object throws its influence over his entire person, and makes Mr. Hooper ghost-like from head to foot. Do you not feel it so?"

"Truly, I do," Martha replied, adjusting a bulky undergarment rubbing her chaffed chest beneath her Sunday black dress. "And I would not be alone with him for the whole world. What woman wants to be molested by a madman minister wearing a ghoulish black veil? I wonder if he is not afraid to be alone with himself. Mr. Hooper must spend limited time sitting on his hopper!"

"Important, impotent men sometimes are so egocentric," commented Horace, her husband. "That's why I'm a freakin' born again alcoholic, who is constantly in and out of rehab'. Too bad our Mr. Hooper is a devout tea temperance idiot. The sober asshole doesn't know that being on the wagon is a lot happier experience than being off of it! Have I ever told you, Martha? The demented son-of-a-bitch actually wants me and my drinking pals to form the AAAA: Asshole Alcoholics Anonymous of America!"

The afternoon service that Sunday was attended with similar circumstances as the morning's extraordinary debacle. At its conclusion, the church-bell tolled for the funeral of a young lady who had recently died after suffering from a very complicated combination herpes/gonorrhea condition. The mournful relatives and saddened friends were assembled inside the prayer-house, and the more distant acquaintances stood about the door, speaking of the myriad good qualities of the deceased slut. Suddenly, their idle chatter was interrupted by the appearance of Mr. Hooper, his face still covered with his black veil, which was now during a formal funeral interpreted as an appropriate emblem.

The unorthodox (here: non-Greek Puritan) clergyman stepped into the viewing room where the young lady's corpse had been laid, when just three days before, the young lady had been laid in a neighbor's high haystack. The Reverend bent-over the coffin to bid a last farewell prayer of his now-deceased, venereal-infected parishioner. As the odd Church Official stooped, his morose veil hung straight-down from his oversized forehead, so that if the dead woman's eye-lids had not been closed forever, the lifeless maiden might have seen his actual face, and loudly screamed with understandable fright.

'Could Mr. Hooper be fearful of her possible otherworld glance, so intimidated that he so hastily caught back the wicked, vile secret that the black veil had been concealing?' old Squire Saunders speculated. Another person who had watched the strange non-verbal interview transpire between the dead girl and the living minister scrupled not to affirm that at the very instant, when the clergyman's features were momentarily disclosed, the corpse had slightly shuddered, consequently rustling the shroud and muslin cap, with the dead girl seemingly pleasurably exclaiming, 'Don't! Stop! Don't! Stop! Don't stop! Don't stop! Don't stop! Yes! Yes! Oh Yesssss!'

From the dreaded coffin, Mr. Hooper then slowly passed-into the main chamber of the gathered mourners, and soon stepped to the head of the staircase to recite the selected funeral prayer. It was a tender and heart-dissolving oration, quite full of sorrow and false testimony, yet so imbued with celestial hopes that the dead whore's soul would certainly be adequately redeemed, and subsequently transported by angel courier directly to Heaven's Pearly Gate.

The entire congregation trembled in response to the reverend's demeanor (misdemeanor), their putrid-smelling armpits displaying ample perspiration from all the dark-themed linguistic inspiration their offended ears had heard. An hour later, the expected funeral procession to the cemetery had formed on the main village street, with the dead girl's black wooden coffin, moving in a hearse pulled by two black horses, and Mr. Hooper wearing his black veil walking behind.

"Why do you look back?" a gentleman ambling in the somber procession asked his worried partner. "It's only a dead girl's body, and certainly not the little harlot's ghost that's being buried. That sex-starved teen bitch isn't going to give guys any more quality blowjobs, or have any more 'Yes! Yes! Yessss' type multiple orgasms, that's for damned sure!"

"I had a fancy," the wife replied, "that the minister and the maiden's spirit were actually walking hand in hand. I think in my odd hallucination, Mr. Hooper had been screwing the young hussy many multiple times, indeed many more times than her reputed multiple orgasms!"

"And so had I dreamt likewise," answered the agreeable husband. "I theorize that the minister's black veil symbolizes Mr. Hooper having a secret love affair with the dead hussy, who has been speculated and labeled by the Church Council of Celibate Elders to be the Devil's devious daughter!"

"And don't forget," added the opinionated gossipy spouse. "It's been rumored all over town that Reverend Hooper's wife over in Salem had also died last week. Maybe the minister is turning into a spider, starting with his ugly pocked face. Yes, that's it, my Husband! Our sinful, philandering, conniving church minister is wearing the black veil because he's gradually transforming into a black widower!"

"Truer words were never spoken, My Dear!" the amenable husband concurred. "It all makes perfect sense in my mind right now, with the minister's reported first wife, living over there in Salem. Now confidentially, I hear from hearsay that Mr. Hooper is going to be a key judge, brashly officiating at the upcoming, narrow-minded Salem witch trials!"

That night the most handsome couple in Milford Village was to be joined in holy wedlock. Although generally reckoned to be a melancholy man, that evening Mr. Hooper had planned to exhibit a placid cheerfulness in his demeanor, a manner which the church official reluctantly reserved for such happy occasions. The company at the wedding awaited his tardy arrival with impatience, trusting that the palpable awe which had gathered over him throughout the day would now be temporarily dispelled. But much to everyone's apprehension, such was not the result.

When Mr. Hooper arrived at the sacramental ceremony, the first thing that the residents' eyes rested upon was the same horrible black veil which had added deeper gloom to the aforementioned funeral, but conversely, could portend nothing but evil to the anticipated wedding. Such was the object's immediate effect upon the guests that a cloud seemed to have rolled duskily from beneath the black crepe, and soon, the vision ominously appeared to dim the light of the flickering church candles.

'I wonder if Parson Hooper is wearing black underwear,' hypothesized the frightened bride. 'How totally horrid can an experience be! It's Sunday night, and I'm getting married during a Black Sabbath!'

'I wonder if he uses black condoms and black dildos,' the well-groomed groom conjectured. 'I can't wait for the local underground sextet to play during the reception feast.'

The bridal pair stood-up before the all-too-solemn minister, but the bride's cold fingers quivered in the tremulous hand of the wiggling bridegroom. And the girl's death-like paleness caused a whisper that the maiden, who had been buried a few hours before, was truly being reincarnated from her fresh grave to be first-time married, and to be later laid again.

'This arcane minister ought to be blackballed if his testicles and scrotum haven't ben already,' thought the non-virgin bride.

'I can't wait to get this black wedding over with,' evaluated the virgin groom. 'I've waited twenty-one years for this biological opportunity. I'd even screw my new wife in the hotel ballroom, if no bridal suite is available over at the dilapidated village hotel.'

After performing the inordinate ceremony, Mr. Hooper raised a glass of imported red wine to his lips, wishing happiness to the newly-married couple. The preacher's gay-sounding staccato intonation had been delivered in a strain of mild pleasantry that ought to have brightened the facial features of the concerned guests, beaming wonderfully upon their sanctimonious asses like a cheerful gleam from a blazing hearth.

At a later instant, catching a glimpse of his abnormal facial appearance in the church vestibule's looking-glass, the black veil involved the capture of the minister's own spirit, and the morbid mask also engendered the horror with which it had wickedly overwhelmed all others attending the oddball matrimony.

Mr. Hooper's frame instantly shuddered, his lips grew white, and next, the quivering preacher spilled the untasted wine upon the rugged carpet. The petrified fellow swiftly reconfigured his addled senses, and quickly exited the building. The Reverend's shadowy form rushed forth into the evening's darkness, for the Earth too had on her black veil, that only *his* erudite scrutiny could then perceive and appreciate.

* * * * * * * * * * * *

The next morning, the entire village of Milford talked (it was a talking village) of little else other than Parson Hooper's non-sexy black veil. That, along with the intrigue concealed behind the black veil, supplied a popular topic for discussion between community acquaintances meeting in the street along with good, healthy menstruating women, gossiping periodically at their open windows.

The black veil saga was the first item of news that the talkative tavern keeper told his dumb-fuck traveling guests. The impudent children babbled of "the evil mask" on their way to school. In the village schoolhouse, one imitative little imp covered his face with an old black handkerchief, scaring the shit out of the victimized schoolmaster, as well as the other little imps not having the modern luxury of owning black handkerchiefs.

It was remarkable that of all the busy-bodies and impertinent loiterers in the parish proper, not one ever ventured putting the plain question to Mr. Hooper, wherefore the dumb-shits had insisted on doing such a stupid-ass stunt. Whenever there appeared the slightest necessity for such logical, mature, adult interrogation, Mr. Hooper would effectively discourage any impending questions by telling the parishioners to "shut the fuck up, or else you'll together suffer excruciating asshole cauterization for all eternity."

A feeling of dread descended upon and formidably plagued the New England community. No one dared to challenge Mr. Hooper, and then risk the need of cutting a second asshole. But soon thereafter, some anonymous source had the bravery to report the minister's black veil aberration to the local bishop, who promptly deputized a delegate to visit the petty New England village, and investigate the particular lunatic scenario, before the parson's quirky behavior accidentally mushroomed into a scandal of major proportions.

The minister received the spiritual envoy with friendly courtesy, but became silent after the bishop's hit-man prosecutor was quickly seated, leaving to his visitor the whole burden of introducing *their* important business.

The county ambassador stared incredulously at Mr. Hooper wearing his weird, occult veil, thinking, 'It's almost winter time, and the temperature seldom goes above freezing. What the hell is this stupid shit doing still wearing a freakin' black mosquito net around his giant-sized forehead and across most of the dumb-fuck's infamous pocked face. And that distasteful hanging thin black crepe gives me the creeps, too!'

Being so astounded from viewing the extraordinary sight, the bishop's deputy refused demanding from Reverend Hooper a valid confession. In fact, no reference to the minister's black veil was ever initiated or pursued during the entire ten-hour general conversation.

Finally, the befuddled, politically-correct deputy returned in an abashed state of mind to the gullible, politically-correct bishop, expeditiously pronouncing the complex matter, "too weighty to be handled except by a strict cowardly council of the state churches", if, indeed, the issue might not ultimately require a General Synod to convene in order to sufficiently interrogate the suspect rebel minister.

But there was one village vicinity person named Winnie Winkle, who was unappalled by the awe with which the black veil had impressed everyone else besides her. When the oral news circulated that the church deputy had returned to the sitting bishop without any plausible explanation, Winnie's involvement in the drama became activated. As being the minister's plighted fourth and current wife, the former Winnie Winkle reckoned that it should be her exclusive privilege to know exactly what the black veil concealed. 'If he doesn't tell me a feasible story, I'll cut both his nose and dick off, and then sew his dick where his nose should be, and next then, let the cheating bastard bleed to death from having his pecker severed from his wounded abdomen!' the vitriolic, vindictive fourth wife thought, amusing herself fully.

At the minister's first visit, therefore, the former Winnie Winkle entered upon the sensitive subject with a direct simplicity which made the task much easier to discuss, both for her seventh-husband and herself. After the queer-but-not-gay parson had seated himself upon the home's most comfortable hard black-leather chair, the wife fixed her eyes steadfastly upon the dismal-looking veil, but could discern nothing of the dreadful gloom that had so over-awed the ignorant multitude; it was but a double fold of black ,crepe hanging-down from her estranged husband's forehead to his mouth, and the thin black barrier slightly stirred with the exhaling of his powerful hurricane bad breath.

"No," said Winnie, and then shrewdly smiling at her beleaguered spouse. "There is nothing terrible in this piece of crappy material you're wearing, except the fact that it hides a wonderful pocked face, which I'm always fairly glad to look upon. Come now, good Sir; let the sun shine from behind the filtering cloud, whatever the hell *that* stupid-shit metaphor means. First, lay aside your baneful black veil, and then fluently and concisely tell me why the hell you've put that asinine thing on in the first place."

Mr. Hooper's smile glimmered faintly, before the penitent husband offered his ridiculous reply. "There is an hour to come," declared he, "when all of us shall cast aside our vile veils. Take it not amiss, beloved wife, Winnie, if I proudly wear this piece of crappy black cloth until then. Before that imaginary time arrives, this idiotic veil avails me! Do you fuckin' fathom my infallible bull-shit?"

70

"Your veiled words are a mystery, too," returned the attractive-but-humble young lady. "I demand that you take away the toxic-looking black veil, at least for the moment. I hate conundrums more than I've always despised giving you oral sex! And don't you ever again tell the gossip-mongering congregation from the elevated pulpit, 'I never had sex with that woman'! Your shallow deceitful words are gross, outright lies!"

"Winnie, I promise I'll someday remove the black veil," Minister Hooper stated, "so far as my personal vow to myself may suffer me. Know then, Woman; this veil is a type of inexplicable symbol, and I am bound to wear it ever, both in light and darkness, in solitude and also before the gaze of the low-intelligence attendance in my dwindling congregation. No mortal eye will ever see the veil withdrawn, or else, I proclaim that they'll get their fat and skinny asses horrendously cauterized morning, noon and night. I presently announce to you, Winnie, that this dismal, eerie shade must separate me from the corrupt baneful world; and even you, Winnie, can never come behind it, or else the divine black veil draped over my pocked face will be curtains foretelling severe reprimand for your belligerent disobedience."

"What grievous affliction hath befallen you?" the estranged fourth wife earnestly inquired. "That you should thus darken your big beautiful shit-brown eyes forever? I mean, if you want two black eyes, I'll fuckin' merrily give them to you!"

"If it be a sign of mourning, or a sign of mourning sickness," Reverend Hooper obtusely answered, "I, perhaps, like most other mere mortals, have sorrows dark and deep enough to be typified by a dreadful black veil. Basically, the honest-to-goodness truth is that I just enjoy scaring the living shit out of every other doltish asshole meandering around in the village square!"

"But what if the unapologetic world will not believe that it is a type of innocent sorrow you are deliberately projecting?" uttered and urged Winnie. "Beloved and respected as you are by a very small minority of the congregation, there may be whispers that you hide your face under the consciousness of secret, guilty mortal sin. For the sake of your holy office, do away with this fucked-up black veil scandal, or put your lackluster religious career in certain jeopardy!"

The color crimson rose into the pissed-off wife's cheeks as Winnie Winkle intimated the nature of the rumors that were already abounding throughout the whole village, and now throughout the entire countryside. But Mr. Hooper's delusional mildness did not forsake him. The clever minister even smiled again, that same lugubrious, defeated smile which always appeared, showing like a faint glimmer of light, especially exhibited in the past when the Reverend Mr. Hooper had failed climaxing and thus ejaculating, after strenuously performing heavy-duty masturbation.

"If I hide my face for sorrow, there is cause enough to keep for tomorrow," the romantic fool amateurishly rhymed. "And if I cover my visage for secret sin, what mortal might not do the same fuckin' thing in a frenzied monkey-see, monkey-do imitation?" And with that gentle-but-unconquerable bit of obstinacy, the obdurate minister resisted his wife's further entreaties, and impulsive sexual come-ons.

At length, Winnie sat silent and readjusted her floppy tits inside her restrictive black undergarments. For a few moments, Mrs. Hooper appeared lost in thought, probably considering what new erotic methods might be administered to the minister to entice her former lover, and have him withdraw from participating in so dark a "dumb-shit fantasy black veil folly".

'Is my seventh husband mentally ill?' Winnie sincerely asked herself. 'Surely, a mental asylum should trump this personal asylum my husband's erratic mind has awkwardly created.' And then, crying like a woman drowning in emotional agony, Winnie Winkle arose from her chair and stood trembling before Reverend Hooper.

"And do you feel or conceive it, then, at last?" said he, stating his mind mournfully. "All the blood always rushes from my dick to my head. I can no longer achieve an adequate erection. I might as well be dead, Winnie! I might as well be fuckin' dead!"

The wife made no reply, but instead covered her eyes with her hand and speedily turned to leave the room. Reverend Hooper rushed forward and caught her arm, impulsively placing her right hand upon his limp reproductive gland.

"Have patience with me, Winnie!" the parson passionately requested. "In church you used to play the organ, but now my organ refuses to provide you any adult play-time! I'm now an immensely confused jerk-off, who is no longer capable of jerking-off. I believe I'll soon have to visit the grist mill and ask Mr. Winthrop if I could have a hand job!"

"Lift the veil but once and look me straight in the face," insisted the horny woman, desperately desiring to get laid in the nearest bed or haystack. "I want to determine if you still have a goddamned dick, er, I mean face!"

"Never Winnie! It cannot be!" Mr. Hooper adamantly replied. "My pocked face must remain covered, or else my ass is grass, and your ass is cauterized!"

"Then, I say farewell, you' unscrupulous, self-centered, narcissistic asshole!" Winnie nastily articulated. "I strongly suggest that you carefully look inside your dingy outhouse and get your shit together!"

"One final thing, Winnie," remarked the Reverend Mr. Hooper. "Being a parasitic minister was indeed an easy life for me. I didn't have to labor and toil with callused hands to make a living as the village tallow chandler; as the neighborhood blacksmith, or as the town cooper must do six very arduous and difficult days a week!"

Winnie then violently withdrew her arm from his firm grasp and slowly departed the room, pausing at the door to give one long, shuddering gaze that seemed almost coyly to penetrate the dumb-shit mystery of the very vexing and perplexing black veil. 'I must now hurry and go shack-up with the cooper tonight, without the tallow chandler and the blacksmith ever knowing my whereabouts!'

But even amid his accumulative grief, Mr. Hooper smiled, thinking that only a trite material emblem had successfully separated him from worldly happiness, though the horrors which it shadowed forth must be drawn as a matter of huge dispute between the fondest of cheating, unfaithful lovers.

* * * * * * * * * * * *

From that inconvenient time, no decided attempts had been made to remove Mr. Hooper's black veil, or by a direct appeal, to conscientiously discover the great secret which *it* was supposed to hide. Most everyone in the village strongly desired to protect and preserve his or her vulnerable asshole from Satan's rectum-busting sodomy by means of the Devil utilizing blazing fire and brimstone. But in regard to the weak-minded and feeble-hearted multitude, good Mr. Hooper was irreparably both a liability and a controversy. The gentleman minister could not stroll the street with any credible peace of mind, and so cognizant was the veiled parson that the gentle and timid would turn aside to avoid his approach, and that other feckless sidewalk pedestrians (including the hookers and the fifty cent a trick street walkers) would make it a point to maneuver themselves directly in his path, as to futilely offer free sex, just to obtain a brief glimpse under his fluttering black veil.

In truth, the Reverend's own antipathy to the veil was known to be so great that Mr. Hooper never willingly passed before a mirror, nor stooped to drink at a still water fountain, or at a nearby horse bucket. This particular mystique was what gave plausibility to the egregious whispers which purported that Mr. Hooper's conscience had been torturing him for his guilty enactment of some great unknown crime or sin, too horrible in nature to be either debated or discussed. 'He's a witch devoid of female genitalia! He's a dick-head who pisses out of his nose!' were common familiar community sentiments in relation to poor Mr. Hooper's black disguise.

Thus, from beneath the black veil there rolled a cloud into the sunshine, an ambiguity of either sin or sorrow, which enveloped the poor minister wherever the hell Parson Hooper roamed, so that love or sympathy could never reach him, or ever impact or affect his defunct libido. It was gossiped that both ghost and fiend consorted with him, and the obstinate abstinent minister surrendered to neither of the tempting entities, never offering for gratis his sexual favors.

With his spine shuddering, but giving no indication of outward trepidation, Mr. Hooper ambled continually in perpetual shadow, either groping darkly within the depths of his own soul, or gazing through a spiritual lens that saddened the whole world, which accentuated the public's tendency for worshiping sensationalism over religious piety. Even the lawless wind, it was believed, respected his dreadful secret, and never once dared ruffle the fuzz growing upon Mr. Hooper's scrotum sac. But still, despite these devastating adverse circumstances, good Mr. Hooper sadly smiled at the pale visages of the worldly throng, as the pathetic preacher passed by their idle afternoon prattle.

Among all its bad influences, the black veil had the one desirable effect of making its wearer a very efficient clergyman. Yes, Mr. Hooper's fearful appearance, combined with his angry sermons, scared the damned hot hell out of everyone. By the aid of his mysterious emblem, for there was no other apparent cause, "the man of the black cloth" became a man of awful power over souls that were in extreme agony for having to avoid sin, and now everyone in Reverend Hooper's pissed-off congregation had their bowels in an uproar, because the hypocrites could no longer commit evil, and were forced to choose Heaven after death as an alternative to the Devil's Lustful Heaven-on-Earth.

The few remaining village sinners about to die cried aloud for Mr. Hooper to console their doomed state, and the obdurate assholes would not yield their final breaths until the Rev' appeared at their deathbeds an hour before the Milford undertaker would put the hysterical souls on cemetery lay-away. And yes, much to the art of dying, the awesome black veil indeed scared the dying person right out of life, and directly into adamant death's gruesome grasp.

Strangers came long distances to attend services at the Rev's church, with most of the pilgrims having the mere idle purpose of gazing at his black covered "neck-down figure", because it was forbidden for the visiting hillbilly red-necks to behold the minister's "cloaked black neck". But many of the visiting hicks were made to quake prior to their departing, even though the perverted assholes were dysfunctional Puritans, and not psychotic Quakers.

Once, during the end of Governor Belcher's administration, Mr. Hooper was appointed to preach the election sermon. Covered with his black veil, the now-famed speaker stood before the chief magistrate, the county council, and the state representatives, and the revved-up Reverend wrought so deep an impression that the legislative measures caused all attending nauseous government officials in the State Assembly to chronically burp, especially the bureaucratic Honorable Governor Belcher.

In that ass-kissing manner, Mr. Hooper spent a long, unproductive, hollow life, irreproachable in outward interaction, yet shrouded in dismal suspicions; the personage at the parsonage was kind and loving, though unloved and dimly feared; a despised man apart from men, Mr. Hooper was understandably shunned in sharing both *their* health and their joy.

As years wore on and evolved into history, the deplored minister acquired a novel name throughout the New England churches, and the people throughout the region now called him "Father Hooper", because the gloomy fellow had changed his Puritan religion to the Episcopalian faith in order to piss-away the remainder of his dim life. Nearly all his parishioners were of mature age when the Reverend had initially settled in the New England village, and over the years, had been borne-away by *their* many funerals.

Mr. Hooper now had a congregation of three misguided misfits sitting inside his wooden Episcopalian Church, and ironically, a more crowded one of three-thousand-cadavers interred inside the old Puritan churchyard. And having wrought so late into the evening and done his daily work so well, it was now good and grave Father Hooper's turn to finally experience eternal rest.

* * * * * * * * * * * *

Several persons were visible by the shaded candlelight in the death-chamber of the old clergyman's rectory. Natural connections to any immediate family, Reverend Hooper had none. But there was the grave-though-unmoved newly-arrived village physician, seeking only to mitigate the last pangs of his first patient whom he could not save; the rookie doctor telling Reverend Hooper on *his* deathbed, "Hoops, you Episcopal devil, you! You're enough for someone like me to change their goddamned religion!"

Then, there were the deacons, and other eminently pious members of his former Puritan church, who had ostracized Reverend Hooper in life, and now-ignored his community impact in death. There also, not boycotting the minister's death and burial, was the Reverend Mr. Clark of Westbury, a young and zealous zealot who had ridden his mule all the way to Milford in haste for the purpose of exorcising evil "Catholic and Episcopalian" demons, along with other baneful spirits that might be swirling-around the rectory of the expiring minister. And there also present was the village nurse, no hired handmaiden of Death, but she had once been seriously targeted to be Mr. Hooper's wife number five.

And devoted Winnie was the sole female mourner courageous enough to attend Mr. Hooper's discredited wake, hoping with intense conviction that the erratic bastard would never wake again! And there lay the hoary head of good Father Hooper, lying upon the black death-pillow with the black veil still swathed about his brow, and eerily reaching-down over his ruddy pocked face, so that each more difficult gasp of his faint breath caused the facial cover to stir and flutter-around, much like a sailing kite still firmly attached to his rock-hard, very stubborn forehead.

Winnie suddenly became more intrepid and soon felt compelled to approach the coffin and remove the black veil that still shrouded her dying husband's countenance. The woman became shocked out of her mind when the seemingly dead corpse bellowed-out, "Look Bitch; if you have the unmitigated audacity to dare touch this fuckin' black veil, then I'll diabolically haunt your ass for the remainder of your doomed earthly tenure!"

At length, the death-stricken, decrepit, Episcopalian priest lay quietly in the torpor of mental and bodily exhaustion, with an imperceptible pulse and subtle breath, which grew fainter and fainter; that is, except when a long, deep and irregular inspiration seemed to prelude the imminent flight of his meandering spirit. "Dare touch this fuckin' black veil, Bitch, and I'll come alive from the dead, and savagely scare the accumulated feces out of your obese ass, and every accursed day hence will be a ghostly Hallow's Eve for you!"

The minister of Westbury, who after two divorces secretly had converted to Catholicism, entered the almost-empty church and timidly approached the dismal bedside. "Venerable Father Hooper," the vicar prefaced, almost vicariously. "The moment of your soul's ejaculation, er, I mean ejection from the body is at hand. Are you ready for the lifting of the black?"

Father Hooper at first replied merely by a feeble motion of his head; then apprehensive, perhaps, that *his* meaning might be doubtful, the dying minister exerted himself to speak.

"Yea, yea," said he, in faint accents. "My soul hath a patient weariness until that versatile veil be lifted. I desperately want to escape this reprehensible, mundane reality, the sooner, the better. Take the pernicious black veil off my ruddy pocked face, so that I can finally get my tired ass propelled out of here!"

"And is it fitting, my dear disciple," resumed the Reverend Mr. Clark, "that a man so given to prayer, of such a blameless example, holy in deed and thought, so far as mortal judgment may pronounce; is it therefore fitting that a father in the Episcopalian Church should leave a shadow on his memory that may seem to blacken a life so pure? I pray you my venerable brother," continued Mr. Clark, "let not this thing be! Suffer us to be gladdened by your triumphant aspect as you go to your eternal reward. Before the veil of eternity is adroitly lifted by yonder Whore Winnie Winkle, please allow me, a licensed cowardly disciple of God, cast aside this baneful black veil from your ruddy pocked face; now Angel of Death, I request thee to escort this fucked-up soul the hell out of here, as Mr. Hooper has so imperatively decided." And thus speaking, the Reverend Mr. Clark bent forward to reveal the mystery of so many years.

But, exerting a sudden energy that made Reverend Mr. Clark stand aghast, Father Hooper snatched both his fellow clergyman's hands from beneath the coffin burial blanket, and then pressed his palms strongly upon the apocalyptic black veil, resolute to wickedly struggle if the converted Catholic Minister of Westbury wished to contend with a restless dying Episcopalian priest.

"Never!" the insanely delirious dying clergyman cried. "Never on Earth should I yield this precious prize. Never!"

"Dark old Clergyman," exclaimed the affrighted Reverend Clark. "With what horrible crime upon your soul are you now passing to the final judgment?"

Father Hooper's breath heaved: it rattled-about in his raspy throat; but then, with a mighty effort grasping forward with his arthritic hands, the obstinate Episcopal Priest caught hold of life, and held death back until he should barely speak.

The dying phenomenon even raised himself' to a lying position, and there he sat semi-erect, shivering with the arms of Death wrapped around him, while the black veil, still being draped over his face, fully hung-down, appearing so awful at that last dreadful moment in the gathered terrors.

And yet a faint, sad smile seemed to glimmer from an internal obscurity, and the force lingered-upon Father Hooper's lips. Then, the dying man uttered his last words to wrinkled Winnie Winkle and to craven Reverend Mr. Clark.

"I'll see you two troublesome assholes in the next world, if there is a fucked-up next world to see you in!"

"Rappaccini's Daughter"

A young man, named Giovanni Guasconti, came, very long ago, from the more southern region of Italy, after the novice had graduated last in his class from Mafia Regional High School. The greenhorn's principal aim was to pursue his important studies at the prestigious University of Padua. Giovanni, who had but a scant supply of gold ducats inside his shallow, ripped pocket, took lodging in a high and gloomy chamber of an old edifice, which certainly wasn't the palace (or even the servant's quarters) of a Paduan nobleman.

The dust-laden dump exhibited atop its single entrance the armorial bearings of a fucked-up, rather indigent family long since extinct. The youthful impressionable stranger, who was not unstudied in the abundant pornography poems of his antiquated country, recollected that one of the ancestors of *that* loser family, and perhaps once an occupant of that very inferior domicile, had been pictured by Dante as a partaker of the immortal agonies of the Italian author's rather legendary, diabolical Inferno.

These reminiscences and associations, together combining with the tendency to experience heartbreak, being natural to a young man alone for the first time, venturing-out of his familiar native sphere, caused Giovanni to sigh heavily, and inadvertently inhale three huge green headed flies. After nearly coughing and choking his lungs out onto the rickety floor, the distraught young traveler sneezed convulsively a dozen times to clear his nostrils, and then with bloodshot eyes, sadly looked around the rather desolate and ill-furnished apartment.

"Just what I don't need for inspiration!" the new big city arrival exclaimed to the apathetic, drab blue ceiling, with both his arms extended upwards. "A primitive, pathetic piss-poor pad in Padua!"

"Holy Virgin, Signor!" cried old Dame Lisabetta, who had been readily won by the youth's remarkable beauty and obvious bulge in his leotards; the hag kindly endeavoring to give the chamber a habitable air. "Your evaluation of this nasty apartment was wrong. This abominable rat-hole is nothing to sneeze about! Now Giovanni, do you find this old fleabag room gloomy? For the love of platonic intercourse being enjoyed in Heaven, then, just stick your grease-ball head out the window, and you'll see as bright a sunshine as you've ever witnessed since you had left Nipples, er, I meant to say, Naples."

Young callow-minded Guasconti mechanically did as the old promiscuous retired whore had advised, but could not quite agree with Lisabetta that the Paduan sunshine was as cheerful as that of southern Italy, where sultry nudist camps and hot sex farms abounded. Such as it was, however, the sun's radiant rays fell-upon a lush garden situated beneath the window, and expended its fostering warm energy upon a variety of healthy plants, which seemed to have been carefully cultivated with exceeding care.

"Does this garden below belong to the house?" Giovanni asked. "Where I come from, there are plenty of naked girls and nude women in gazebos and in spas, sunbathing in places just like the one below. In Naples, we jokingly call an area such as that one beneath this window Bush Gardens!"

"Heaven should forbid such vulgarity occurring, Signor. Unless the garden you've mentioned is fruitful and contains better pot herbs than any that grow below us now," answered old Lisabetta, slowly rubbing her enlarged clit, "I'd say you're trying to bull-shit me. No;" resumed the old lowlife bitch. "That garden you've observed below is cultivated by the hands of eccentric Signor Giacomo Rappaccini, the famous plant doctor, whose reputation has been heard of as far away as your native erect Nipples, er, I mean Naples. It is said that the doctor distills these plants into medicines that are as potent as a charmed aphrodisiac. Oftentimes, you may see Signor Rappaccini diligently at work, and perchance the signora, his virgin daughter, too, meticulously gathering the strange flowers that grow and thrive inside the gorgeous garden."

The old kinky hag had now done what she could for the drab presentation of the less-than-mediocre chamber, and then after commending the young man to the protection of the saints, along with the horny Roman and Greek goddesses Venus and Aphrodite, the hoary, no-teeth, former hooker took her departure.

Bored Giovanni still found no better occupation than to curiously look-down into the garden beneath his one and only window. From its general appearance, the student judged the setting to be one of those unique botanical gardens which were of an earlier date in Padua than currently present elsewhere in Italy, or in the whole wide world, including famous and risqué Bush Gardens in Naples.

'Perhaps it might once have been the pleasure-place of an opulent family that valued sex and more sex; for down there is the ruin of a marble fountain in the center, sculptured with rare artistic flair,' Giovanni speculated. 'But the fountain is so woefully shattered that it's impossible to trace the original design. Even the cherub on top has had his marble balls busted. The flowing water, however, continues to gush and sparkle from the Roman boy's erect penis, and then arching high into the sunbeams. God, that's exactly how I piss!'

A low gurgling sound ascended-up to the young man's window, and the sensation made Giovanni feel as if the fountain were an immortal spirit that was echoing its dissonant song unceasingly, and without heeding the myriad vicissitudes (obviously caused by humans) around it.

All about the pool into which the water subsided grew various plants, all of which seemed to require a plentiful supply of moisture for the nourishment of gigantic leaves, the necessary liquid being provided by the accommodating pissing cherub.

In some instances, banks of flowers gorgeously grew in magnificent arrays near the side stone walls. One shrub in particular, set in a marble vase inside the pool located next to the residence's cesspool, bore a nice profusion of purple blossoms, each of which had the luster and royalty of a splendid gem. Every portion of the rich, fertile soil was populated with a variety of plants and herbs, which, if less beautiful, still showed tokens of assiduous care. 'The lucky son-of-a-bitch who owns this nifty-garden could start a floral delivery service with the god Mercury as its emblem logo,' Giovanni mused and considered. 'That kind of flourishing business could make my imaginary partner Hermes and me quite wealthy!'

Some flowers had been placed in urns, rich with old carvings, and others in common garden pots, some of them growing cannabis; several thick vines crept serpent-like along the ground, or climbed high upon faded bricks, using whatever means of ascent was offered them, reaching right up to the roof of the garden's solidly-built outdoor shithouse. One plant had wreathed itself around a statue of Lesbos, which was thus quite veiled and shrouded in a drapery of hanging foliage, which covered her exaggerated tits and shaved crotch, so happily arranged that the figure might have served as a sculptor's LBGTQRS art study.

'That hard-looking cold statue down there can't be Venus de Milo, because it's not disarming enough. Oh, I see now!' Giovanni then realized. 'That tough-looking lady upon the pedestal is the sexually-disoriented dyke Sappho, supposedly the first lesbian living on the Greek Isle of Lesbos. Her crack seems all it's been cracked-up to be,' evaluated the lad, as his devious imagination mentally separated from the abundant greenery, while his perceptive eyes closely examined the statue's twat from the overhead window. 'It's too bad that frowning Greek bitch was a goddamned lesbian! I mean, at least she could've been a kinky bisexual instead!'

The knowledgeable student paused while still peering-down from his elevated vantage point. Then, the aspiring medical doctor keenly noticed three white round balls lying upon the verdant lawn. 'I never learned in any of my art texts back in Naples that Sappho was constipated, and only shit perfectly circular hard marbles!'

While Giovanni stood at the window, his ears heard a rustling originating from behind a screen of dense green tree leaves, and the viewer soon became aware that a person was busy at work 'fucking-around' in the north end of the huge garden. His noticed figure soon emerged into full view, and the previous phantom showed himself to be a tall, emaciated, sallow and sickly-looking man, who incidentally had been dressed in a black academic scholar's robe, the same type of ridiculous black garb that professors wear at ridiculous kindergarten and college graduations.

The laborer was beyond the middle term of life, actually being an old fart with long, gray, curly hair; a thin gray beard, and a classic face singularly marked with age marks and wrinkles. But in truth, the codger inside the garden possessed a singular countenance, which could never, even in his more youthful days, have expressed much warmth of heart. Basically, the old coot looked apathetic, selfish and totally fucked-up.

Nothing could exceed the intentness with which this scientific gardener examined every shrub which grew in his path: it seemed as if the old asshole had been looking into the plants' innermost nature, making salient observations in regard to their creative essence, and discovering why one 'Who gives a shit?' leaf grew in *this* shape, and another developing in *that* 'Who gives a shit?' form.

On the contrary, the garden proprietor avoided their actual touch, or the direct inhaling of their odors, with a certain caution that impressed Giovanni most disagreeably; for the old man's demeanor was that of one walking among malignant influences, such as savage beasts, or deadly snakes, or evil spirits, which, should *he* allow them one moment of license, would wreak upon him some terrible fatality.

All this bull-shit was strangely frightful to the young man's imagination, to witness that air of insecurity in a person cultivating a garden; that most simple and innocent of human toils, and which had been like the joy and labor of the unfallen Biblical parents of the race. Was this garden, then, the Eden of the contemporary world? And this maniacal man, with such a perception of harm in what his own hands had caused to grow; was he the modern Adam?

The distrustful gardener, while either plucking-away the dead leaves, or busily pruning the two most-luxuriant shrubs (without also wearing a tu-tu), protected his hands with a pair of thick gloves that in the past, the garden fanatic had probably used to participate in senior citizen boxing matches at the nearby Montague Rectangular Sports Garden.

When ambling in his current walk through his botanical paradise, the crazed experimenter eventually came to the magnificent plant that hung its purple gems beside the about-to-crumble marble fountain. The determined geezer then placed a kind of mask over his wrinkled mouth and nostrils, as if all the environmental beauty surrounding his skinny ass concealed a deadlier malice than himself. But then, finding his started task still-too-dangerous to perform, the potential geriatric hospital patient drew back, removed the mask, and called loudly, but yelling with a horribly hoarse voice that even a miniature pony wouldn't recognize.

"Beatrice! Beatrice!" the diseased throat vociferated. "Shit! Because of my malignant cancer, I can't even mutter a fuckin' utter, even though I'm a Leo wearing leotards!"

"Here I am, my ice-cold parent. What would you need?" cried a youthful feminine voice from the window of the opposite house. Yes, a delicate girl's voice as rich as a tropical sunset, and such a sweet intonation that quickly made Giovanni think of deep penis penetration into a wet pink love tunnel. "Are you screwing-around again in the garden, Father? Why the hell do I call you Father? You're a freakin' mad scientist, and not a lost pedophile priest just aimlessly walking-around down there!"

"Yes, Beatrice," the apparently frustrated gardener answered. "And I need your help right this minute. I've forgotten how to use the scissors, and can't find my heavy-duty cutting shears."

Soon, there emerged from under a sculptured portal the figure of a youthful, voluptuous, big-breasted girl, whose tits were too damned large for even the most expansive double-breasted woman's suit to accommodate. Beatrice looked stunningly vivacious, and her blithe spirit seemed filled with life, health, and energy. And most all of her physical female attributes were tensely girdled inside the damsel's tight-fitting azure-blue dress, which beautifully covered her most-alluring, virgin pleasure hole.

Yet Giovanni's fancy must have grown morbid, as his engorged-with-blood reproductive snake began throbbing, and then slowly uncoiling, inside his tarnished brown leotards, which instantly needed major mending. The powerful impression which the fair maiden made upon his erect pecker was as if here was an extraordinarily special flower, the human sister of those vegetable ones thriving over yonder; more beautiful than the richest red roses, or the finest yellow tulips, which then automatically made Giovanni Guasconti think about two lips; not the ones upon the luscious girl's mouth, but the pair of hairy ones between her lank legs.

'Who needs to masturbate when I could get laid in the shade!' the new university student excitedly concluded. 'I'd like to deflower that hot-looking doll right this instant! Oh no! I'm having a goddamned premature ejaculation! It's not a nocturnal wet dream! It's a damned daytime nightmare!'

As comely Beatrice descended the garden's four stone steps, and soon sauntered-down the familiar flagstone path, it was observable that the knockout teen honey had been inhaling the perfumed scents of several of the plants of which her boxing legend father had most carefully avoided contact.

"Here, Beatrice," the apparent parent indicated. "See how many needful clips require to be done to our chief purple treasure. Yet, shattered as I am, my vulnerable life might pay the penalty of approaching our prize, me standing dangerously close as this most difficult circumstance demands. Henceforth, my true-blue assistant, I fear that this precarious plant must be consigned to your sole charge. Oh shit, Beatrice! You again forgot to bring your office clipboard to record the clippings!"

"And gladly will I undertake the cutting," the splendid young lady answered, as the daughter bent towards the magnificent purple flowered plant, and opened her arms as if to lovingly embrace it. "Yes, Father. I promise to use cutting-edge technology! The shears will be sheer pleasure!"

As Beatrice ardently and gingerly clipped-away, in fact much better than a Yankee clipper (New England barber), Giovanni, positioned at his lofty window, rubbed his eyes, and next removed with a convenient frayed cloth, the sticky semen that had just filtered through his retarded leotards.

'She speaks to the flowers as if they are her human sisters,' the now non-aroused onlooker marveled. 'I wish I could play an instrument like the guitar or mandolin. Then, I could be the flower of the music world, and easily win over dear Beatrice's affections in a Roman minute.'

The interactive scene below soon terminated. Whether Dr. Rappaccini had finished his labors in the garden, or that his watchful eye had caught the young stranger's covetous face observing above, the old curmudgeon now took his daughter's arm, and swiftly retired into their residence. Night was already closing-in; but oppressive oxygen exhalations seemed to proceed from the plants, and steal upward past the apartment's open window. And Giovanni, closing the lattice, experienced cold shudders while maneuvering the shutters.

Immediately, the romantic fool paced to his couch and dreamed of a rich flower, and of a beautiful girl, amazingly both one and the same integrated species. The nouns flower and maiden were quite different, and yet the same entity, and fraught with some strange peril in either shape. Beatrice's more-than-scary aged father, Professor Giacomo Rappaccini, might get pissed-off at the adolescent's flirtation with his treasured daughter, and quickly and violently 'pistil whip' vulnerable Giovanni to death.

But there is an influence in the light of morning that tends to rectify whatever errors exist in a young jerk-off's quixotic love fancy, or even in his exercise of poor social judgment. We may have observed during the sun's decline, the naïve adolescent dreaming and fantasizing about intrepidly giving Beatrice a full-moon on that night, which was to reveal only a half-moon.

Giovanni's first movement that evening was a lengthy bowel movement. Then, gaining essential intestinal fortitude, the university student rose from his tawdry couch, advanced to the window, opened the shutters, and gazed-down into the garden which his dreams (and not his gushing semen) had made so fertile. Young Guasconti was surprised (and a trifle ashamed) to discover how real his vicarious, fucked-up, voyeur love affair had proved to be.

The young idealist rejoiced that, in the heart of the barren, now-tranquil city, the new arrival had the privilege of overlooking that sacred spot of lovely and luxuriant vegetation. The garden scene would keep horny Guasconti in communion with Nature before jealous Dr. Rappaccini would savagely excommunicate Giovanni from the enthralling 'Garden of Eden' for avariciously pumping both the hard and soft poop out of his virgin daughter's ass.

Neither the sickly, thought-worn, very decrepit Dr. Giacomo Rappaccini, nor his brilliant enticing daughter, was now visible (or for that matter, invisible). Giovanni could not determine how accurate were his observations about 'obsessive and compulsive' Dr. Rappaccini, and the botany scientist's hot-looking daughter, indeed without obsessive and compulsive Guasconti ever being introduced to either garden visitor.

'I got to somehow meet and shack-up with that Beatrice babe,' the sex-starved eighteen-year-old thought. 'Maybe, I'll successfully steal some money, take her on a Grand Canal gondola ride over in Venice, and then plow my erect fadorkenbender straight into *her* grand canal!'

* * * * * * * * * * * *

In the course of the next day, Giovanni paid his respects to Signor Pietro Baglioni, distinguished professor of medieval medicine at the university, and without dispute, a physician of eminent repute. Giovanni had brought a fine letter of introduction to the elderly professor, who apparently was a genial, out-of-touch, out-of-the-loop academic suffering from Lupus disease. The erudite scholar invited the young man for dinner, and then the medical pedagogue made himself' very agreeable by the freedom and liveliness of his bull-shit conversation, especially when warmed by a flask or two of Florentine Tuscan wine, which had been prepared by Dr. Baglioni's eighteen- year-old girlfriend, Florence.

Believing that men of learning in and around Padua knew about each other's reputations and myriad contributions to art and science, Giovanni took the opportunity to mention the name of Dr. Giacomo Rappaccini.

But the renowned professor did not respond with so much cordiality as young Guasconti had anticipated.

"Unfortunately, ill evil would become a teacher of the divine art of medicine," Professor Pietro Baglioni criticized, in answer to the impertinent dumb-ass question of the brash student. "I wish to withhold due and well-considered praise of a physician so eminently skilled as Giacomo Rappaccini, but on the other hand," the medical guru aptly qualified, "I should answer your stupid-shit inquiry carefully, because in my irresponsible youth, I used to be a fraternity drinking buddy of *your* old man over at the Palermo Spaghetti Institute, so I don't want to have you interpret any erroneous ideas originating from my loquacious commentary. The truth is that our worshipful Dr. Rappaccini possesses as much science as any member of the revered Padua faculty, where most of the instructional staff members have lost their faculties. Now then, Giovanni. Despite Dr. Rappaccini's myriad eccentricities, I must confess that there are certain grave objections concerning his professional character."

"And what are those disturbing challenges to which you allude?" the inquisitive young man audaciously asked. "Is he a Lotus Eater? Has he invented giant-sized carnivorous man-eating lilacs? I promise you, Professor Baglioni. Whatever you disclose to me about the baneful botanist, mum's the word!"

"Has my new-found friend Giovanni any life-threatening disease of body or heart, that he requires the services of an accomplished physician?" the medical professor oddly asked, with a forced smile. "My advice is to stay away from the Padua horse and mule cart carriage station, or else you might get a terminal illness! Ha, ha, ha!"

"Very funny, Professor!" the extremely interested student acknowledged. "But please Signor, divulge to my ears more about this perverse Dr. Rappaccini."

Dr. Baglioni paused for a minute to awkwardly organize his disheveled, fleeting thoughts. "It is said of him, and I, who know the man fairly-well," the distinguished physician prefaced. "I can attest and answer, for it's quite true that the demented fanatic cares infinitely more for *his* plant science than the same insane asshole does for mankind. I must speak frankly here Giacomo, er, I mean Giovanni. Dr. Giacomo Rappaccini doesn't give a mouse's shit about either you, or me, or mankind. He only cares about his cherished plants," Baglioni orally continued, shaking his bald head in a negative fashion. "When I say the word 'plants', I'm not speaking of factories or manufacturing facilities. I'm referring specifically to flowers and vegetation, and also to other fucked-up products of nature like that. Rappaccini's half-dead patients are interesting to him, only as subjects tailored for some new botanical experiment of some peculiar and dangerous sort."

"Methinks he is an awful man indeed to detest humanity so obnoxiously," visiting Guasconti remarked, mentally recalling the cold and purely intellectual aspect the student had evaluated of conniving Rappaccini fucking-around in the family garden. "And yet, my worshipful Medical Professor, is it not a noble spirit to be so dedicated to the study of tropical and non-tropical topical vegetation? Are there other scientists capable of so spiritual a love of Botany? Is Dr. Rappaccini an avowed vegetarian; an avid vegan?"

"God forbid," the palsied professor, somewhat-testily answered. "Have you lost your cognitive thinking, Young Man? I don't believe that you're a gay fruit, but are you instead an incompetent brain-dead vegetable? I insist that your atrocious rhetoric makes no fuckin' common sense whatsoever!" Dr. Baglioni vehemently asserted. "Listen carefully, you aspiring asshole! It is better for me to heal a baby's illness in a nursery than for Rappaccini to save a dumb-ass flower or shrub in *his* nursery. Giovanni, I find your excessive curiosity to be more academically honest. You're a facetious, shallow-minded asshole, just like your old man was back at the glorious Palermo Spaghetti Institute. Do I make myself fuckin' perfectly clear?"

"Thanks for giving me the worthless rap on Dr. Rappaccini," the vernal dinner guest half-apologized. "Only tell me more damaging gossip, if you desire to do so!"

"It is *his* absurd theory, which hypothesizes that all medicinal virtues are comprised within those substances which we term and catalog as vegetable poisons," Dr. Baglioni very angrily related. "These miscellaneous toxic plants the totally-insane maniac mischievously cultivates with his own diabolical hands. And mendacious Rappaccini is believed even to have produced new varieties of poison; yes, new toxins more horribly deleterious than any other chemical compounds normally prevalent in Nature."

"Holy shit, Professor!" Giovanni exclaimed. "Your descriptive account of Dr, Rappaccini's bizarre, radical experiments not only defines the colossal problem; it fuckin' *compounds* it!"

"Yes, Giovanni. It's an absolute miracle that the deranged Signor Doctor does less mischief than might be expected," Dr. Baglioni maintained. "Now and then, it must be considered by the educational establishment that the zealous charlatan has effected, or seemed to have effected, a marvelous cure for shingles by ingeniously using hay from British thatched roofs and straw from African huts, amazingly combining the melted-down ingredients' mixture to create a viable vegetable compound, that evidently, fully alleviates the disease's symptoms."

"I see," the university student comprehended and declared. "Dr. Rappaccini probably contemplated that shingles on roofs might be the key clue to solving the shingles condition in asshole humans. And so, the botanist had wondrously invented a fantastic compound consisting of boiled straw and hay!"

"Exactly!" the pissed-off, envious Medical Professor verified. "Now, the lousy son-of-a-bitch is trying to create an intelligent, thinking, problem-solving cucumber, and then transfer his results to increasing the intelligence of mentally-challenged humans. Tell me Signor Giovanni, is *that* fucked-up idea of his insanity, or genius?"

"I don't know, Professor, for you see," conveyed young Guasconti, "I'm not too much smarter than a radish, let alone a sophisticated cucumber earning a doctorate degree!"

The youth might have taken Dr. Baglioni's opinions with many grains of allowance had the teenager known that there was a history of academic warfare of long continuance, the rivalry occurring between the Medical Professor and the oddball Dr. Rappaccini, in which the latter was generally thought to have gained the professional advantage because of the much-heralded shingles cure discovery.

"I honestly know next to nothing about the important information you've just explained," Giovanni admitted, after musing on what had been said of Dr. Rappaccini's exclusive zeal for plant and vegetable science. "I know not how dearly this strange scientist may love his art; but surely, there is one mortal object that is dearer to him than botany, a certain gender item that might fascinate and motivate him. The narrow-minded asshole does have a beautiful daughter."

"A-ha!" the Medical Professor exclaimed with an indulgent, hardy laugh. "So, now my friend Giovanni's sexual-desire secret is out and exposed. You *have* heard of this pulchritudinous daughter, whom all the semen-shooting young straight men in Padua are positively wild about, although not half-a-dozen of the immature idiots have ever had the good chance to ever inspect her flawless face."

"So, tell me, Professor. What the hell do you know about lovely Beatrice! I'm rather anxious to learn all the horny details!"

"I detect that you wish to make Rappaccini's Daughter into Giacomo's Rape-accini's Daughter," naughtily jested and laughed the university's chief surgery lecturer. "Even before I had developed my bad case of Parkinson's disease, and had to abandon my practice of lobotomy neurosurgery for the sake of performing basic autopsies," Dr. Baglioni elaborated, "I've learned little of the Signora Beatrice, save that Rappaccini is said to have instructed her deeply in his clandestine plant science, and that, young and beautiful as local fame reports her, she is already-qualified to fill a professor's chair at the university. Perchance her influential father destines her to occupy *my* faculty seat, the dirty, envious bastard! So now, with those confidential opinions being shared, Signor Giovanni, drink-off your fifth glass of cabernet, so that you can get the hell out of here, and begin studying your easy-to-read, large print medical textbooks!"

"Anything else to tell me Professor?" the very annoying first-year anatomy student asked.

"Yes, Giovanni! Cease being a fucked-up gullible dickhead. Start thoroughly thinking with your' human brain, instead of with your goddamned reproductive fadorkenbender!"

* * * * * * * * * * * *

Young Giovanni Guasconti decided to return to his modest lodging, somewhat-heated with the wine he had voraciously quaffed, and which now caused his tender brain to swim with strange fantasies in reference to Dr. Rappaccini and the beautiful, big-titted Beatrice. On his way to his apartment, happening to pass by a florist's stall, the drunken romantic purchased a fresh bouquet of flowers.

'After I had bought the cheap bouquet of daisies, several gay pansies (or perhaps petunias) had strolled by my staggered gait, the inordinate queers walking hand-in-hand,' the inebriated student remembered. 'Holy crap! A faggot is another designation for an effeminate homo', and a *fagot* is a bundle of gathered sticks. I hope that Beatrice doesn't prefer having intercourse with LBGTQ-plus faggots, because of the unique tree fagot reference.'

Ascending the creaky steps up to his lofty dismal chamber, the dizzy occupant soon seated himself near the room's single window, but his body was within the shadow thrown by the depth of the wall, so that the junior spy could look-down into the garden below with little risk of being easily-discovered by potentially antagonistic, possessive Dr. Giacomo Rappaccini. All observable objects beneath his eyes existed in a totally serene solitude. The random strange plants were basking in the early evening sunshine, and now and then, nodding gently to one another in the weak breeze, as if in acknowledgment of mutual sympathy and kindred fraternity.

In the midst, situated alongside the shattered marble fountain, grew the magnificent shrub, with its purple gems clustering all over it; botanical jewels glowing in the evening air, and gleaming back again out of the depths of the adjacent water fountain pool. Soon, as half-intoxicated Giovanni had half-hoped, and half-feared, a fabulous female form majestically appeared beneath the antique sculptured portal, and casually ambled through the central path of the now moonlit garden.

On again beholding the sight of magnificent Beatrice, the young man was startled to perceive how much her beauty exceeded his recollection of it; so brilliant, so vivid, and so desirable was her tantalizing hourglass figure.

'Beatrice could easily be Miss Italy in any national beauty contest,' assessed the greedy-hearted medical student. 'She makes Juliet Capulet look like the ugly Mother Superior at the now-defunct Lasagna School for Orphaned Girls over in Bologna!'

Approaching the central shrub, Beatrice threw open her arms, as with a passionate ardor, and drew the bush's branches into an intimate embrace, indeed administering a firm hug so personal that her features were hidden inside its leafy bosom, and her glistening ringlets all intermingled with the aromatic flowers, as if the exotic broad had been erotically initiating an abnormal sexual encounter.

"Give me thy breath and all thy energy, my dear sister," Beatrice weirdly exclaimed. "For I am faint with common air. And give me this purple flower of thine, which I separate with gentlest fingers from the short stem, and am placing the bloom close beside my most-appreciative heart."

'Jesus Christ!' Giovanni imagined. "Not only is Beatrice a lesbian like Sappho of Lesbos was, but the crazy chick thinks that the shrub is another female to adore and caress. If this post-medieval Renaissance world isn't completely fucked-up, then I don't know what the hell is!'

With those most-peculiar words spoken, Giacomo Rappaccini's beautiful daughter plucked one of the richest purple blossoms off the shrub, and was about to fasten the petal onto her bosom. Just the thought of the girl wanting to make love to a stupid-assed shrub flower made the eager voyeur's dick shrink and shrivel-down inside his tight brown leotards.

'What utter bull-shit!' the light-headed, hiccupping viewer critically thought. 'I wonder if they're about to rub bushes.'

But now, unless Giovanni's five hefty draughts of red wine had bewildered his senses, a singular incident next occurred. A small, orange-colored reptile, of the lizard or chameleon species, creeped (crept) along the path and jumped forward, just at the feet of Beatrice, also giving Giovanni the creeps. Beatrice had observed the remarkable phenomenon transpire, and the girl crossed herself in the traditional Christian sign. Sadly, but without surprise, did she act; nor did Rappaccini's daughter, therefore, hesitate to arrange the fatal flower situated upon her bosom.

"Leaping lizards! Am I awake? Have I lost my reliable senses?" the student protagonist whispered to himself. "What is this odd-behaving being up to now? 'Beautiful', I shall warmly call her, or inexpressibly 'terrible', a complete, psychologically disturbed, sexually confused, Italian princess goddess? That's what the hell this virgin vixen is!"

Beatrice now strayed carelessly through the colorful garden, approaching closer beneath Giovanni's window, so near that the whimsical jackass was compelled to thrust his head quite out of its concealment in order to gratify the intense and painful curiosity which she had involuntarily excited. At that dramatic moment. a huge two-toned insect happened to crawl over the side garden wall, and the aggressive creature truly-frightened the bug-eyed, drunken, horny university student.

Beatrice gazed at the speedy insect with childish delight, and in an instant, the animated spider grew faint and fell at her feet, the thing becoming quite dead from no reasonable cause, unless the queer event was a result of the atmosphere exhaled from her faint breath. Again, Beatrice crossed herself in the standard Holy Trinity Christian sign, and sighed heavily as she bent over to thoroughly examine the motionless dead insect.

An impulsive shocked movement of Giovanni's arms and head immediately drew Beatrice's eyes to the overhead window. There, Rappaccini's Daughter beheld the skull and face of the young fellow, rather possessing a Grecian urn cranium shape than an Italian head, with fair, regular features, and a glistening of gold among his recently acquired fake yellow earrings. Not knowing exactly what else to do, Giovanni instinctively threw-down the inferior bouquet which he had hitherto held in his hand.

"Signora," the idiot said. "Those are pure and healthful uncostly flowers for you to smell and savor. Wear them in your fluffy tresses for the sake of me, Giovanni Guasconti of Downtown Naples."

"Thank you, Signor," a somewhat-alarmed Beatrice replied, with her rich melodic voice that came forth as if it were magical music. And then, with a mirthful expression, half-childish and half-woman-like, the smiling girl announced, "I accept your gift of cheap withering daisies, and would fain recompense it with this precious purple flower. But if I toss it into the air, it will not reach you. Som Signor, I strongly suggest that you get your ass out of here before my old man shows-up and summons the constable for you to spend the whole night sobering-up in the nearest jail."

Beatrice lifted the frail bouquet from the ground, and then, as if inwardly ashamed at having stepped aside from her maidenly reserve in order to respond to a stranger's unexpected surprise greeting, the fair damsel passed swiftly homeward through the bountiful garden. But few as the moments were, it seemed to Giovanni, when the beauty was on the point of vanishing beneath the sculptured portal, that *his* beautiful bouquet was already beginning to uncannily wilt within her loose grasp.

"I just blew my golden opportunity to plant my erect pickle smack in the center of Beatrice's weedy garden," Giovanni sobbed and lamented. "God! When am I ever going to get laid in Padua!"

* * * * * * * * * * * * *

For many days after that daisy bouquet incident, the young man avoided the window that looked into Dr. Rappaccini's garden, thinking that the mad scientist would incessantly endeavor to decapitate Guasconti with his hand shears, or viciously and repeatedly stab him with his sharp scissor blades.

'Maybe I should evacuate Padua, along with this rat-trap apartment, and forget about the bewitching Beatrice and her positively lunatic old man,' Giovanni surmised. 'Sometimes rank cowardice is a better option than fucked-up valor. Oh well, maybe tomorrow I can catch a glimpse of Beatrice sunbathing nude upon the cesspool lid.'

Sometimes, the greenhorn university student attempted to assuage his fever spirit by initiating a rapid stroll through the streets of Padua, or by ambitiously taking his gait beyond the city's gate: his measured footsteps kept time with the throbbing of his brain, and the pulsing of his excitable dick, so that the brisk saunter was apt to accelerate itself soon into a mild sprint. One day, the trekker found himself arrested, but not by the police; his arm had been seized by a portly personage.

"Signor Giovanni! Fat chance of meeting you on the piazza!" the corpulent, baldheaded gentleman commenced his narrative. "Stay calm, my' young friend. Have you already forgotten me? I'm the guy who had beaten the shit out of your wimpy old man on fraternity pledge night."

Yes, it was envious Professor Baglioni, whom Giovanni had deliberately avoided ever since their first meeting, honoring a gut feeling that the medical instructor's shrewd sagacity would look too deeply into the callow student's secret love desires concerning Beatrice Rappaccini. Endeavoring to recover his composure, Guasconti stared forth wildly from his inner world, into the outer one, and spoke like a romantic fool lost in a passionate dream.

"Yes, I am Giovanni Guasconti. You are Professor Pietro Baglioni. Now leave me the fuck alone! Let me pass!"

"Not yet, not yet, Signor Giovanni Guasconti," brashly answered the perceptive, smiling Medical Professor, but at the same time, scrutinizing the youth with an earnest-but-suspicious glance. "I did grow-up side by side with your delusional father, and knew all of his peculiar proclivities. And shall his son, an incredible ditto of *your* dumb-ass parent, in both appearance and behavior, pass me like a complete stranger in these archaic streets of metropolitan downtown Padua? Stand still, Signor Giovanni; for we must have a word or two before we part."

"Speedily, then, most worshipful Professor, speedily," Giovanni nervously responded with feverish impatience. "Does not Your Worship see that I am in serious haste? Must I now have to tell you that I'm suffering from a bad case of advanced diarrhea?"

While the two acquaintances were speaking, a sinister-looking man in black approached along the street, stopping and moving feebly like a person in deleterious health. The pedestrian's face was marked with a most sickly and sallow hue, but yet so pervaded, with an expression of piercing and active intellect that a casual observer might have easily overlooked.

As the infirmed old fogey passed, the afflicted person exchanged a cold and distant salutation with Dr. Baglioni, but then the feeble walker fixed his frightful eyes upon Giovanni with an intentness that seemed to bring-out whatever negative emotion that was within him to absolute contempt. Nevertheless, there was an extremely weird quietness represented in the stern evil look, as if taking merely a speculative, scientific acknowledgement of the lad's presence, and then concurrently not exhibiting any particular human interest in the young man whatsoever.

"It is Dr. Rappaccini!" the Medical Professor whispered to his student when the sickly, pallid-faced stranger had finally passed. "Has he ever seen your face before? Don't be surprised if he wants to vilely poison your ass tomorrow."

"Not that I better know his identity," Giovanni affirmed. "All I wish to do is screw his daughter into total euphoria. What the hell's wrong with that?"

"He has seen you now! He must have seen you before! Using relevant botanical terminology, your delicate ass is grass!" Baglioni emphatically claimed. "For some purpose or other, this demented man of science is making a case study of you. Be prepared to be squeezed into a test tube for future analysis. I know *that* nefarious look of his quite well! It's the same blank expression that coldly illuminates his face as he bends over a bird; a mouse, or a butterfly, which in pursuance of some obscure experiment, the cruel investigator then kills his targeted subject by administering the noxious perfume of an innocent-looking flower. That Botany pedagogue possesses a hideous stare as deep as Hell's Nature itself, but certainly, indeed without Nature's kind warmth of propagating love. Signor Giovanni, I will stake my life upon it! You're the subject of one of Rappaccini's major experiments! If I were you, I'd get the fuck out of Padua right this instant, or else risk being emulsified, or possibly wholly vaporized right into oblivion."

"Will you make a fool of me?" Giovanni passionately asked. "Listen Signor Professor Baglioni; you've maliciously described an untoward experiment in speculative detail. On the contrary, I believe I should implicitly trust Dr. Rappaccini. He looks about as harmless as a pet boa constrictor."

"Doomful naivete! If you exhibit cooperative patience, you shall be promptly executed and delivered to the afterlife; that is, if you believe in the hereafter, then you gotta' understand what Dr. Rappaccini is *here after*. Get my general gist, Asshole!"

"And the Signora Beatrice; what role does she have in this unfolding mystery play?"

"Don't be surprised if she winds-up being the alluring bait, and you the captured hooked fish," the grim-faced medical teacher declared. "Beware of my dire prediction coming to fruition, er, I mean coming to vegetation! If the charming bitch you have the hots for looks too good to be true, then the charming bitch *is* too good to be true!"

But impetuous Guasconti, finding sanctimonious Baglioni's pertinacity excessively intolerable, forcefully broke-away from the bothersome conversation. Soon, Giovanni was fast gone into the darkness of night before the well-intentioned, gossipy professor could again roughly seize his arm. The very aware medical instructor looked after the young man's departure with worried eyes, and then the honest trouble-warner shook his head in absolute disgust.

"This must not be," greatly disappointed Dr. Baglioni said to himself. "This fucked-up youth is the son of my old fucked-up friend Antonio, and I vow that Giovanni shall not come to any harm from the crazed lunatic's planned botanical destruction. And besides," Pietro continued his personal mumble, "I'll not permit this fanatical madman Rappaccini to 'snatch' the lad out of my own hands, just because Giovanni desires entrance into beautiful Beatrice's snatch. And besides, I have yet to collect Giovanni's medical school tuition. Perchance, most learned Giacomo Rappaccini, I may intelligently foil your nefarious scheme precisely where you least dream of being checkmated! I shall not allow my friend's son to be a lousy pawn on your scurrilous botanical chessboard!"

* * * * * * * * * * * *

Meanwhile Giovanni, intrigued with the geometric concept of circumference, had pursued a circuitous route home, and at length found himself staggering at the door of his inferior lodging. As Master

Guasconti crossed the dilapidated threshold, the resident was met by old Lisabetta, who smirked and smiled, and the ugly wench was evidently desirous to attract his attention onto her lackluster, sagging tits, and flabby wrinkled ass. After ignoring the old witch's puckered lips, the seasoned dame laid her grasp upon his cloak.

"Signor! Signor!" the housekeeper whispered, still with a hungry smile dominating over the whole breadth of her grotesque, wart-faced visage. "Listen Signor! Stop being a fuck-headed Neapolitan! There is a private entrance into the garden you don't know about!"

"What did you say?" Giovanni returned, reeling quickly about. "Did you say that there is a private entrance into Dr. Rappaccini's exclusive garden?"

"Hush! Hush! Not so damned loud!" Lisabetta softly spoke, putting her age-spot, mole-laden hand over his mouth. "Yes; it wends into the worshipful doctor's garden, where you may see and admire all his fine shrubbery. Many a young man in Padua would give a year's gold simply to be admitted among those most-excellent, rare flowers."

Giovanni put a piece of gold into her trembling greedy hand. "This coin is for your espionage information, and not for sex. You'd have to work a lifetime to earn enough money for me to even consider having any kind of regular or oral sex with you. Even if I was blind, I would vomit at the mere thought. Now Lisabetta, I demand that you show me the fuckin' secret way. And you better not be involved in a goddamned conspiracy with Dr. Rappaccini against me. If so, I promise I'll hastily shove a watermelon up your plump ass, and a saguaro cactus up your raunchy cunt, both objects simultaneously!"

Giovanni's withered, haggish guide soon led the distraught young man along several remote passages, and finally undid an obscure door, through which, as it was opened, there came the sight and sound of rustling leaves, with the broken sunshine rays glimmering among them. Giovanni stepped forth, and forcing himself through the entanglement of a shrub that wreathed its prickly tendrils over most of the hidden entrance, and amazingly, soon stood beneath his own window inside the open area of Dr. Rappaccini's exotic garden.

Giovanni recognized but two or three separate plants in the collection, one a gigantic watermelon, and the second being a large saguaro cactus. "See the melon and the cactus, Lisabetta," the medical student pointed-out and verbally indicated. "Now get the fuck out of here before I decide to sodomize you with the two unorthodox dildos."

Several moments later, while busy with those contemplations and garden observations, the intruder heard soft rustling, and turning rapidly, his eyes beheld Beatrice emerging from beneath the sculptured portal.

After Lisabetta had scampered out of the forbidden garden into a side portal, Giovanni searched-around and suspected that several plants in his immediate vicinity were indeed poisonous. Suddenly, Beatrice approached the then-discovered lad, and the sweet doll's quiet, placid demeanor immediately put his apprehension at ease. There was a look of surprise expressed upon Rappaccini's daughter's impeccable face, but her overall grace seemed vastly brightened by a simple and kind engenderment of endearing pleasure.

"You are an accomplished connoisseur in rare flowers, Signor," Beatrice commenced with a smile, specifically alluding to the cheap daisy bouquet that her new amorous neighbor had flung from the high window. "It is no marvel, therefore, if the sight of my Father's special collection has tempted you to take a closer inspection. If he were here right now," elegant Beatrice eloquently stated, "Father could tell you many strange and interesting facts as to the nature and habits of these most stellar shrubs; for he has spent a lifetime engaged in such studies, and this garden is truly *his* small world."

"And as for yourself, fair Lady," Giovanni replied, "fame says true that you likewise are deeply skilled in the virtues indicated by these rich blossoms and by these spicy erotic effervescent plant perfumes. Would you deign to be my instructress? I should prove to be an eager beaver scholar studying your eager beaver, er, I meant to say, I would be an eager beaver if personally taught by the famous Signor Rappaccini himself."

"Are there such idle rumors circulating about me?" Beatrice asked, with the musical tone of a pleasant laugh. "Do people in the outside world beyond these high walls actually say that I'm skilled in my father's science of plants? What a jest is *that* erroneous hearsay! No; although I've grown-up among these splendid flowers, I know no more of them than their hues and perfume; and sometimes methinks I would fain rid myself of even that same small knowledge," the auburn-haired, silk-dressed goddess articulated. "There are many flower varieties represented here, and those not the least brilliant, neither shock nor offend me when the blooms meet my curious eyes. But pray tell, Signor, do not believe those radical stories about my science achievements. Believe nothing of me save what you see with your own eyes. Have you visited an optometrist lately? You hardly seem a man of vision!"

"And must I believe all that I have seen with my own eyes?" Giovanni pointedly asked, while the recollection of recent former snooping scenes made him fully recollect. "No, Signora; the pupils in my eyes are really your pupils to learn and master Botany, along with other impertinent academic bull-shit. You demand too little of me. Bid me to believe nothing, save what comes from your own divine crotch lips. Er, I mean from your own divine mouth lips."

It would appear that Beatrice vaguely understood the impulsive university student in a fantasy sort of manner. There came a deep flush to her cheeks, although her ass was fully covered; but the *"human deity"* looked directly into Giovanni's eyes, and responded to his gaze of uneasy suspicion with a queen-like haughtiness.

"I do so bid you, Signor, although I am not running an Italian or Dutch auction here," Giacomo Rappaccini's Daughter oddly replied. "Forget whatever you may have fancied in regard to me. If true to the outward senses, still it may be false in its internal essence; but the words of Beatrice Rappaccini's lips are true from the depths of my vulnerable heart, and then extending outward. Those truths you may believe, although I have yet to say anything especially pertinent or significant."

Beatrice's voice and attitude suddenly became gay, and the daughter appeared to derive a pure delight from her incidental communion with the horny youth, a meeting not unlike what the maiden of a lonely island might have felt conversing for the first time with a voyager from the civilized world. Evidently, the girl's experience of life had been confined within the limits of that isolated garden.

Rappaccini's Daughter talked now about matters as simple as the daylight; and about common summer clouds, and now the strange maiden asked elementary questions in reference to the city, and then inquired about Giovanni's distant home; his friends; his mother; and his sisters, with each of the odd questions indicating an incredible lifelong seclusion.

Then, the maiden picked-up a purple flower and gently held the stem and petals to her pallid nose. Immediately, Giovanni realized that the rare purple flower and Beatrice's fragrant breath amazingly smelled identical.

"For the first time in my restricted life," Rappaccini's lonely daughter murmured while eerily addressing the purple flower, "I had forgotten thee while conversing with this young man."

"I remember, Signora," Giovanni accurately recalled, "that you once promised to reward me with one of these living gems in return for the bouquet which I had the happy boldness to fling toward your bare feet. Permit me now to pluck it as a memorial of this most fortuitous meeting."

The callow romantic briskly made a step towards the aforementioned shrub with extended hand, but Beatrice darted forward, uttering a shriek that pierced through his heart like a dagger. The concerned girl anxiously caught his hand, and drew it back with the whole force of her slender figure. Giovanni felt her mere touch, the sensation instantly thrilling his throbbing testicles.

"Touch it not!" the maiden exclaimed in an agonized voice. "Not for thy life! It is fatal, and will be lethal to your body, including your hyperactive genitals!"

Then, hiding her very embarrassed face, the upset girl fled from her suitor's company, and quickly vanished beneath the dull sculptured portal. As Giovanni followed her escape with his melancholy eyes, the youth beheld the emaciated figure and pale intelligence of Dr. Rappaccini, who had been warily watching the recent garden encounter. Master Guasconti knew not how long the crazed botanist had been spying on his ass from within the eerie shadows of the secret garden entrance.

* * * * * * * * * * * *

No sooner was Giovanni Guasconti alone in his gas chamber (lots of farting being done) that the image of Beatrice came back to haunt his passionate musings, her mental manifestation invested with all the witchery that had been gathering around her form, ever since his first dynamic glimpse of her fantastic body. Whatever formerly had looked ugly (including Lisabetta's scuzzy face and horrendous body) was now beautiful; or, if incapable of such a change, half-decent anyway. Thus, surrendering to the need-to-get-laid, the class-cutting university student spent the night, neither falling asleep nor dropping-out of bed, until the kiss of dawn had begun awakening the slumbering flowers flourishing inside Dr. Rappaccini's fucked-up botanical garden.

When thoroughly aroused in a none sexual manner, Giovanni suddenly became aware of a burning and tingling agony in his right hand, the very one which Beatrice had grasped in her own palm when the naïve dumb-shit was at the point of plucking one of the gemlike flowers. On the back of that swollen hand was now a purple print showing an explicit design of four small fingers, and the likeness of a slender thumb upon the young fool's aching wrist.

"What the fuck's this shit?" the afflicted youth shouted to no one but himself. "I think I'm turning into a goddamned purple pansy or lavender petunia! Perhaps I'm even changing into a shrinking violet violet! If so, I hope I'll be a straight pansy or petunia, and not a gay faggot shrinking violet that had fallen off a Sicilian shrub!"

Giovanni rambunctiously wrapped an unkempt handkerchief about his color-changing hand, and wondered what evil creature had mysteriously stung him, but the chronic dreamer soon forgot his pain with his mind in a tranquil reverie of Beatrice; the dumb-fuck romantic wondering if she was really a Purple People Eater.

After the first encounter with the inimitable beauty, a second was in the inevitable course of what is generally called "fate or destiny". A third; a fourth; and next, another intentional meeting with Beatrice in the garden was no longer an occasional incident in Giovanni's daily life, but within that whole green open space. in which the lover might be compelled to live a monotonous. insular existence as a shunned purple human.

Being accustomed to Giovanni's predictable return each morning, Beatrice expectantly watched for the youth's appearance, and the damsel flew to his side with confidence, even though the girl lacked the luxury of wings upon her angelic back. If, by any oddball chance, the smitten-by-Cupid's-arrow dumb-fuck suitor failed to come at the appointed moment, Rappaccini's Daughter faithfully stood beneath the now-familiar apartment window, and sent-up the rich sweetness and flagrant fragrance of her thick flowery breath, the strong aroma floating around the medical student in the middle of his personal *gas chamber,* and the emitted warmth would then metaphorically echo and reverberate throughout the four chambers situated inside the young fellow's captivated heart.

"Giovanni! Giovanni! Why tarry thou? Calm-down and come down!" And down the wooden steps the already turning-purple asshole hastened, with the infatuated dumbbell descended into that seemingly magnetized Eden trap of very poisonous purple flowers.

On the few occasions when Giovanni had seemed tempted to overstep the social limits and grab Beatrice's firm tits, or reach for her hairy bush, Rappaccini's Daughter instantly grew so sad, and so stern, that the pristine doll wore such a look, scaring the accumulated feces out of Giovanni's increasingly purple rectum. At such times, the suitor was so startled at the horrible suspicions inhabiting his addled mind that his love grew thin and faint, and soon Master Guasconti's once potent sex organ shrunk-down to thimble-size in the gloomy morning mist.

A considerable time had passed since Giovanni's last confrontational meeting with eminent Dr. Baglioni. One morning in late October, however, the lazy dunce was disagreeably surprised by a prompt visit from the ax-to-grind professor, whom the concerned lad had scarcely thought of for several whole weeks, deliberately playing hooky, and being absent from the esteemed university.

The visitor chatted carelessly for a few moments about the unreliable gossip abounding in the city and around the university, and then after his small-talk subsided, Dr. Baglioni took-up what the revered college lecturer considered to be a pertinent topic.

"I've been reading a work written by an old classic author," the somewhat-literate medical man revealed, "and my weary eyes met with a story that strangely interested me. Possibly you may remember the sage tale. It is of an Indian prince, who sent a beautiful woman as a present to Alexander the Raisin, er, sorry Giovanni, I had meant to say Alexander the Great. The gift princess I've just mentioned was as lovely as the dawn, and as gorgeous as the spectacular sunset. But what especially distinguished her was a certain rich perfume evident in her breath; a hypnotic scent richer than a garden of Persian roses," the professor impressively described, all the while curiously staring at Giovanni's peculiar purplish skin. "Alexander the Grape, er, I mean to say *Great,* as was natural to a youthful conqueror with an oversized ego and comparable penis, fell in love at first sight with this magnificent female; but a certain sage physician, happened to be present, causing much trouble and chaos, discovered a terrible secret in regard to her."

"And what was that terrible secret?" Giovanni asked, turning his eyes downward to avoid those of the garrulous professor. "Would the Indian princess be crushed like a soft grape in a wine press because of Alexander's obvious crush on her? Did Alexander buy her a grape jelly sandwich at a new deli in India?"

"That this lovely woman," continued Professor Baglioni with austere emphasis, intentionally ignoring Giovanni's stupid drivel, "had slowly-but-surely been nourished with poisons from her birth upward, until her whole nature was so imbued with toxins that she herself became toxic to other humans. Poison was her dominant element of life. With that rich perfume saturating her breath, the lethal princess blasted the very air around her with noxious gas, more horrible than a bull elephant's two-minute-long reverberating fart. Her love would've definitely been poison; her embrace certain death. Is not this a marvelous tale parallels your horse-shit infatuation with Beatrice Rappaccini?"

"A childish fable, and nothing more," Giovanni maintained, nervously squirming in his chair as if to expel from his own asshole a bull elephant sized lengthy fart. "I marvel how Your Worship finds time to read such nonsensical fiction, scattered among your more-important medical studies."

"By the by," the wily professor added, looking uneasily about the dingy, dismal apartment so as not to stare at his absent-to-class student's purple-hued epidermis. "What singular fragrance is this odor that drenches the air within your apartment? Is it the perfume of your grimy gloves? It is faint, but positively delicious; and yet, after all, by no means, is it one iota agreeable. If I were to breathe it for long, methinks it would rot my lungs and make me ill. It is like the breath of a condemned, contaminated flower; but despite my poor vision, I see no *fuckin' flowers* anywhere in this repulsive chamber."

100

"Nor are there any," Giovanni verified, "and besides, flowers don't have sex like humans do, so there can't be any damned *'fuckin' flowers'*. Now Professor, I urge you to leave the practice of medicine, and then become an expert in agriculture, because in my acute judgment, I think you're ready for the fuckin' funny farm!"

"Yes, Lad; but in truth, my sober imagination does not often play such wicked tricks as yours does," Dr. Pietro Baglioni sarcastically declared. "And were I to fancy any kind of putrid odor, it would be that of some vile apothecary drug, and not a fucked-up artificial flower fragrance, just like the one depicted in the popular Italian love song *Arrivederci Aroma*. Now, in regard to our worshipful friend, Dr. Rappaccini," the university medical teacher lucidly elucidated, "as I have heard from hearsay, there are tincture formulas with foreign alien odors richer than those of Alibaba's Araby. Doubtless then, my dumb-ass medical disciple, the fair and learned Signora Beatrice would administer to her patients with draughts as sweet as an Indian maiden's breath; but extreme woe to him that sips or smells the highly potent intoxicant!"

Giovanni's face soon evinced many contending emotions. The tone in which the mentally-feeble and physically-frail Professor Baglioni had alluded to in regard to the pure and lovely daughter of Dr. Giacomo Rappaccini was an overwhelming torture to the student's sensitive soul; and yet the intimation of an adverse view of her character, an evaluation opposite to the student's own perception, gave instantaneous distinctness to a thousand dark demonic suspicions to inhabit Giovanni's mind.

"Signor Professor," the aggravated purple-skinned lover stated. "You were my father's friend; perchance too, it is your purpose to act in a similar friendly disposition towards his now-perplexed son. I would fain feel nothing towards you, save respect and deference. But I pray you to observe, Signor, that there is one subject on which we must not speak a fuckin' vowel or consonant. What you know or hypothesize," distressed Giovanni editorialized, "is not the true virtue, or the pure character of Signora Beatrice. You cannot, therefore, estimate the wrong, the blasphemy, the false witness, and the verbal injustice that your toxic words have regrettably characterized about the Indian princess's, er, I mean to say, about Beatrice's benign attributes."

"Giovanni! My poor ignorant hollow-minded Giovanni!" the worried medical professor exclaimed with a dire expression of pity. "I know this wretched girl far better than you do, for obviously I am *not* turning purple and you evidently are. You shall hear the truth in respect to the malicious poisoner Dr. Rappaccini, and his equally poisonous not-so-innocent daughter; yes," Baglioni proceeded with his rambling piercing discourse. "The young bitch is just as poisonous as she is beautiful. Listen carefully, you' human purple mushroom; even if you should clobber me on the head with a violin to do violence to my gray hairs, it shall not silence me one iota. That old fable of the Indian princess has become a veritable truth performed by the deep and deadly science of Dr. Rappaccini, and also evident in the alluring person of lovely Beatrice. Be aware and wary of her distinct detrimental odors Giovanni, especially the enticing one being emitted by the girl's wonderful hot love tunnel!"

Mixing humiliation with mortification, shocked Giovanni groaned and defensively hid his violet-toned purple face.

"Her crazed and incensed father loved the smell of incense," Baglioni continued, "and the compulsive lunatic was not restrained by natural affection from offering-up his only child in this horrible manner; yes, offered as the sacrifice of his insane zeal for science. The botanical alchemist who Beatrice admires is indeed a medical fraud, a most dangerous medical fraud at that! And the nut-job will offer his daughter on his botanical altar of contempt, just to vindicate his diabolical theories in addition to his mendacious pursuits."

"It is a horrid, dreadful dream," Giovanni muttered. "And surely, it's a veritable nightmare you're presently dictating to my dubious, disbelieving ears."

"But heed my prosthetic, er, I mean 'my prophetic' words, my callow juvenile Asshole," the obdurate professor resumed, "and attempt to be of good cheer, son of my illustrious former college fraternity drinking friend. It is not yet too late for your rescue and to salvage your endangered life. Possibly we may even succeed in bringing back this miserable flower child before she winds-up in San Francisco protesting constructive things like war and capitalism."

"You're a chemist besides being a medical doctor," Giovanni complimented his talkative guest. "What's your solution Professor?"

"Behold this little silver vase I've removed from my pocket! It was inspirationally wrought by the creative hands of the renowned Benvenuto Cellini, and the vessel is quite worthy to be a love gift to the fairest dame in Italy," Baglioni optimistically explained. "But its fabulous contents are invaluable. One little sip of this antidote would've rendered the most virulent poisons of the Borgias innocuous. Doubt not that it'll be as efficacious medicine against those wretched mixtures of the scurrilous Giacomo Rappaccini. Bestow the vase, and the precious liquid within it, upon your fair Beatrice, and hopefully await the beneficial result."

Dr. Baglioni laid a small, exquisitely-wrought silver vial upon the table, and soon withdrew his hands, leaving what he had said to produce its effectiveness upon the young man's mind.

"Holy hallelujah!" the instantly-relieved student yelled without farting. "First, I listen to your ridiculous Indian princess anecdote, and now I've learned about your fantastic Beatrice antidote! How dually remarkable can a solution get!"

"We will yet thwart Rappaccini and his formidable insanity," the adamant Medical Professor promised, as the ancient scholar decided to finally descend the squeaky stairs.

* * * * * * * * * * * **

Throughout Giovanni's whole acquaintance with Beatrice, the suitor had occasionally been haunted by dark surmises as to the beauty's dark-side character; yet so thoroughly had Rappaccini's Daughter made herself appear as a simple, natural, most-affectionate and guileless creature, that the negative image of her now, espoused by Professor Baglioni, seemed so strange, uncanny, and incredible.

"I gotta' institute some decisive test," Giovanni attested, as the infatuated fellow incredulously peered at his purple image being reflected from his grubby apartment's sole mirror. "The lizard, the insect, and the flowers have continued to bug me about Beatrice's chameleon nature, and about her flagrant perfumed breath that makes me' fume inside with purple rage. I know what the fuck I'll do!" the love-struck student decided. "If I can witness one purple flower instantly wither within Beatrice's elegant hand, that'll prove Professor Baglioni's outlandish theory to be true. I'll venture-out to the florist shop, avoid the pedestrian pansies and petunias sauntering by, and purchase another bouquet of daisies to give my precious doll-baby buttercup. Otherwise," Giovanni enunciated to his purple hourglass image, "I'll have to be a lonely purple wallflower at the upcoming freshman hop!"

After purchasing the rather ordinary daisies with his last gold ducat, the romantic fool comprehended that it was now the customary hour of his daily secret rendezvous with Beatrice Rappaccini. Before descending the steps leading to the secret portal that gave access into the precarious botanical garden, Giovanni mumbled, "At least her poison has not yet insinuated itself into *my* system. I'm not yet a blooming idiot; a victimized purple flower in the process of being perilously perished within her witchy grasp."

After returning to the stranger-than-fiction garden, and after recovering from his most recent fantasy stupor, the besieged boyfriend began watching with curious eyes a spider that had been busily at work artfully hanging its networked web. Giovanni bent towards the insect, and soon emitted a deep, long breath. The spider suddenly ceased its toil, and the web vibrated with a tremor originating within the body of the black arachnid. Again, Giovanni sent forth a breath, deeper, longer, and imbued with a venomous feeling, seemingly emitted out of *his* now-viperous heart: the experimenting novice knew not whether he was a wicked wizard, or perhaps only a clumsy nincompoop desperately in love. The affected spider made a convulsive grip with its limp limbs, and soon hung dead upon its intricate web.

"Accursed! Fuckin' accursed!" Giovanni lividly cursed and muttered. "Have thou grown so poisonous that this deadly insect perishes by thy own lethal breath?"

At that moment, a rich, sweet voice came floating-up from the opposite end of the evilly-enchanted garden. "Giovanni! Giovanni! It is past the hour! Why tarry so tardily thou? Come to me! Come in your wonderful, filthy, white-stained leotards!"

"Yes," Giovanni courteously replied. 'She is the only being whom my breath may not slay! Would that it might!' the gallant, infatuated jerk-off silently concluded.

After meeting and briefly greeting, the unlikely pair ambled-on together, sad and reticent, and came thus to the marble fountain and to its accompanying pool of water, recently deposited by the night rain, still, several puddles remaining on the ground. Nearby grew the shrub that bore the incomparable, gemlike, outstanding purple blossoms. Giovanni was affrighted at the eager enjoyment, the sensational appetite so to speak, with which the youth presently found himself inhaling the fragrance of the "condemned flowers", so as had exactly been esoterically depicted by sagacious Professor Pietro Baglioni.

"Beatrice," the university freshman abruptly asked. "Whence came this shrub?"

"My Father had created it," the girl responded with untainted simplicity. "My Father thinks and believes *he* is the Creator!"

"Created it! Created it!" Giovanni indignantly repeated. "What do you mean, Beatrice? Stop worshiping your reprehensible old man as if he's God Almighty!"

"He is only a wise, dedicated little man fearfully acquainted with the secrets of Nature," Beatrice expressed. "And at the hour when I first drew my initial breath into my infant lungs, this peculiar plant sprung from the soil, the offspring of his weird science, and of his extraordinary scientific intellect."

"Tell me more malignant malarkey," the befuddled suitor implored. "My insufficient, hapless brain now requires less-cerebellum and more-cerebrum!"

"While I was but *his* earthly child," Rappaccini's curvaceous daughter continued her singular narrative, now alertly observing with terror that Giovanni had been drawing nearer to the shrub. "Approach not that plant!" Beatrice imperatively commanded. "It has supernatural qualities that you can little dream of. But dearest Giovanni, I eventually grew-up and blossomed with the remarkable plant, and was later mystically nourished with its potent breath. I soon comprehended that *it* was my twin sister, and I loved it with a human affection; for, alas! Hast thou not suspected it; an enveloping awful doom that looms in the gloom from womb to tomb?"

Here Giovanni became overly vexed, and the exotic garden visitor frowned so darkly upon Beatrice that she paused from her unusual pronunciation and trembled. But her faith in *his* almost-tangible tenderness reassured her, and made her blush, regretting that she had doubted his sincere veracity for even an instant.

"There was indeed an awful doom," the girl continued her recollection, "that is, upon the effect of my father's fatal love of science, which coincidentally estranged me from all society of my kind. Until Heaven sent thee, dearest Giovanni, oh, how lonely I was. I now implore you! Plant your purple plum inside my purple pussy garden right now!"

"Was it a hard doom?" Giovanni asked, fixing his eyes upon her while rearranging his hard, swelling, purple erection, which was pulsing-around inside his only pair of brown, white-stained leotards.

"Only of late have I known how hard it truly was," the puzzled daughter commented, tenderly glancing at his hyperactive boner. "Oh, yes, but my heart was torpid, and therefore quiet about excessive emotional excitement."

"Accursed one!" the boyfriend shrieked, with venomous scorn and heightened anger prevalent in his tone of voice. "And finding thy solitude, thy wearisome, thou hast severed me likewise from all the warmth of life, and hast enticed me into thy dangerous region of unspeakable horror! I don't need a piece of ass so badly as to die for it! Hell no! Fuck that shit!"

"Giovanni!" Beatrice exclaimed, turning her large bright brown eyes upon his purple face. But the force of his honest words had not found its way into her impregnable mind; Rappaccini's Daughter was merely thunderstruck six-full-hours after the day's heavy rain had fallen.

"Yes, poisonous thing!" repeated Giovanni, beside himself with passion. "Thou hast vilely done it! Thou hast blasted me! Thou hast filled my veins with toxins before I could die from lustily filling your crotch with purple semen! Thou hast made me as hateful, as ugly, as loathsome, and as deadly a creature as thyself; a world's great wonder of hideous monstrosity! An emotional freak without a frivolous circus sideshow! Now, if our breaths be happily as fatal to ourselves as to all others, let us join our lips in one lethal kiss of unutterable hatred, and so die together!"

"What has befallen me?" Beatrice murmured, alarmed with a low moan generating out of her hurting heart. "Holy Virgin; pity me, a poor heart-broken child about to get laid by a bouncing, hard, throbbing purple pickle!"

"Thou-dost you pray?" Giovanni bellowed, still with the same fiendish scorn being expressed upon his countenance and in his voice. "Thy very prayers, as the strange words come from thy celestial lips, taint and corrode the atmosphere with shades of death. Yes, yes; let us pray!" yelled the hysterical suitor. "Let us go to the local church and dip our fingers in the holy water at the portal, and then together perform the Sign of the Cross! The insane fanatics who will come after us will perish, being plagued by a predatory purple pestilence! Let us jointly sign crosses and articulate our inconsequential prayers into the apathetic air! The contaminated atmosphere will be scattering curses abroad in the likeness of holy symbols! According to our fucked-up Christian customs and traditions," the lad argued, "all this stupid religious shit must first happen before we can acceptably get laid, and then mutually and simultaneously die!"

"Giovanni," Beatrice nervously answered, for her grief was ascending far beyond common passion. "Why join thyself with me in communicating and enacting those terrible sinful words you've mentioned? It is quite true that I am the horrible thing thou hast named me. But what hast thou to do, save to only shudder at my hideous misery; to go forth out of this garden and mingle with the remainder of thy lackluster race, and forget that there ever crawled on Earth such a monster as poor diseased Beatrice? Have you never screwed a Gorgon before?"

"Do you pretend or feign ignorance?" Giovanni interrogated, scowling upon her as if she was Medusa reincarnated. "Behold! This strength, this incredible power called love I have gained from the pure and pristine daughter of Dr. Rappaccini. Blessed is the fruit of thy womb, and I can't wait to lick it after you diligently suck upon my throbbing grande banana!"

A swarm of summer insects began flitting through the air in search of the food promised by the fragrant floral odor emissions of the fatal garden shrubs. The hungry bugs circled around Giovanni's head, and the creatures were evidently attracted towards his presence by the same influence which had drawn the bugs from the sphere of several of the aromatic shrubs. The suitor issued forth a purple-tinted breath among their flying colony, and Guasconti smiled bitterly at Beatrice when a score of the besieged insects fell dead upon the wet turf.

"I see it! I see it now!" Beatrice shouted. "It is my father's fatal science at work here! No, no, Giovanni; it was not I! Never! Never! I had dreamed only to love thee and be with thee for a little time, and so to let thee gradually pass-away into my past, leaving but thine image in mine heart, and the splendid memory of your throbbing erection in my firm hand; for, Giovanni," Rappaccini's Daughter convincingly added, "believe it or not, though my body be nourished with poison, my spirit is God's adventurous creature. And my famished soul craves love as its daily food. But my avaricious and cynical father has ironically united us in sharing this fearful sympathy. Yes; spurn me; tread upon me; kill me, if need be, but first screw me into high ecstasy before either or both of us die! Oh, what is death after such eloquent words as thine have spoken? But it was not I. Not for a world of bliss would I have ever killed, even a tiny ant, either deliberately or by accident."

Giovanni's passion had virtually exhausted itself in its most recent outburst from his purple lips. There now came across him an odd sense, mournful, but not without tenderness; his comprehension was a valid and true interpretation of the intimate relationship between Beatrice and himself.

"Dear Beatrice," Giovanni addressed the gorgeous girl while she shrank-away as always at his erection's waving approach. "Oh, my dearest Beatrice; our fate is not yet so desperate. Behold! There is a medicine, a very potent mixture of profound ingredients, as a wise physician has persuasively assured me, and the magical formula is almost divine in its efficacy."

"Well, what the hell is this miracle cure?" the frustrated girl demanded knowing. "We can sell it at the piazza mart and make ourselves a propitious fortune!"

"The compound is composed of elements and benign drugs that are the most opposite to those by which thy awful-awesome Father has brought this insidious calamity upon thee and me. It is distilled of blessed herbs, blended with life-giving vitamins, fruits, and special minerals, all the items hardly available at the corner Health Apothecary Shop, let alone at the discount piazza mart. Shall we not quaff the elixir together, and thus be mutually purified from evil?"

"Give it to me before you give it to me!" Beatrice demanded, first pointing to her boyfriend's bouncing erection, and next extending her hand to receive the little silver vial which handsome Giovanni had taken from his bosom, while thinking about Beatrice's bosom. "I'll drink this miracle antidote, but do thou await the result."

The anxious girl put Baglioni's antidote to her lips, but at the same moment, the figure of Dr. Giacomo Rappaccini emerged from the side garden portal and maneuvered slowly towards the deteriorated marble fountain. As the vile villain drew near, the pale man of science seemed to gaze with a triumphant facial expression at both Giovanni and the pristine virgin maiden, as might an artist, who should spend his life in achieving a magnificent statue, finally becoming fully satisfied with his success.

The gaunt-faced botanist stopped and paused; and next, the mad experimenter's bent form grew erect with conscious power. Dr. Rappaccini spread-out his ancient hands over the lovebirds in the attitude of a benevolent gracious Patriarch imploring a blessing upon his cherished children; but indeed, those were the same vile hands that had thrown poison into the stream of *their* lives. Giovanni trembled and Beatrice shuddered nervously, and the petrified girl instinctively pressed her hand upon her heart.

"My daughter," Dr. Rappaccini announced. "Thou art no longer lonely in the world. Pluck one of those precious gems from thy sister shrub, and bid thy bridegroom wear it in his bosom. I promise you that it'll not harm him now. My science and the sympathy between thee and him have so wrought within his system that he now stands apart from common men, as thou dost, daughter of my pride and triumph, apart from ordinary women. Pass on, then, through *this* world, with your new-found love becoming most dear to one another! The young man's purple semen shall turn to white sperm juice once more!"

"My Father," Beatrice courageously answered, with her demeanor feeble-and still, as the daughter spoke with her quivering hand upon her heart. "Wherefore didst thou inflict *this* miserable doom upon thy only child?"

"Miserable!" Giacomo Rappaccini's voice boomed. "What mean you, foolish girl? Do you deem it misery to be endowed with marvelous gifts against which no human power or any mortal strength could rival or conquer; to be able to quell the mightiest opponent with a single potent breath; to be as delightfully terrible as thou art beautiful? Wouldst thou, then Daughter, have preferred the condition of a weak woman, exposed to all evil and capable of none yourself?"

"I would fain have been loved, not feared by quixotic purple lovers," Beatrice sadly stated, sinking her desirable body down upon the garden's ground. "But now it matters not. I am going into eternity, Father; departing to where the evil which thou hast striven to mingle with my being will pass-away like a fleeting dream; yes, like the fragrance of these poisonous purple flowers, which will no longer taint my breath among the flowers of your accursed Eden. Farewell, Giovanni! Thy words of hatred are like toxic lead within my heart; but they too, will fall away as my soul either ascends into glorious Heaven, or descends into diabolical Hell."

And thus, the poor victim of man's ingenuity, and also the innocent product of thwarted nature, a sweet girl needlessly sacrificed for the cause of perverted scientific knowledge, had fatefully perished there, at the feet of her father and of her dearest love, Giovanni.

Just at that moment Professor Pietro Baglioni appeared inside his medical student's overhead apartment window. The agitated university pedagogue called-down loudly, in a tone of triumph mixed with accompanying horror.

"Rappaccini! Rappaccini! Is *this* tragic result my eyes are witnessing the upshot of your evil experiment gone fatally wrong! You perverted monster!" the incensed medical professor loudly exclaimed. "You've selfishly sacrificed your own flesh and blood daughter upon your contemptible altar of botanical science!"

"Feathertop"

"Dickon," Mother Rigby yelled. "Bring a coal for my pipe so that I can finish putting the scarecrow's dick on!"

The pipe was in the old dame's mouth when the hag spoke those imperative words. The witch had thrust the object between her lips after filling it with tobacco, but without stooping to light it at the hearth, where indeed there was no appearance of a fire having been kindled that morning. As soon as the order was given, an intense red glow was emitted out of the pipe's bowl, and a whiff of heavy smoke escaped from Mother Rigby's pallid lips. From where the coal came, and how it had been brought by an invisible hand, I have never been able to either fathom or discover *that* principal principle.

"Good shit!" Mother Rigby commended, with a nod of her hideous head. "Thank ye, Deacon Dickon! Ha, ha, ha! And now all I have to do is make some testicles and an acceptable epididymis for this better-than-average scarecrow, and my vital task will be done. Be on call, Dickon, in case I soon need your obedient services again."

The on-a-mission old hussy had risen thus early (for as yet it was scarcely sunrise) in order to set about manufacturing a unique scarecrow *from scratch,* since the old bitch-witch had a myriad of venereal warts both inside and outside her stench-laden, putrid-smelling snatcheroo.

'At first I had planned putting this nice bird frightener in the middle of my corn-patch,' Mother Rigby recalled. 'But it's now the latter week of May, 1770, and the crows and blackbirds have already detected the little, green, rolled-up leaves of Indian corn just peeping out of the soil. Maybe I should visit my sister Eleanor, or consult my harlot cousin, Lady Madonna, to obtain some sage advice from those two politically-disoriented whoring Tories! Now I hope my assembled scarecrow will be able to also scare-away all the fucked-up politicians, priests, rabbis, ministers, and pedophile imams around these parts, and then make the parasitic bastards eat crow every G. D. morning, noon and night!'

But on that unprecedented occasion, fickle Mother Rigby had awakened in an uncommonly pleasant humor, and was further pacified by her aromatic pipe tobacco. Contrary to her disreputable nature, the moronic witch now resolved to creatively produce something especially fine, beautiful, and splendid, rather than a creation being hideous, horrendous and horrible.

"I don't want to set up a hob-knobbing hobgoblin in my own corn-patch, and then almost scaring the crap out of black-birds and turkey buzzards patrolling at my own doorstep," Mother Rigby mumbled to herself, puffing-away, and then choking and coughing out a whiff of dense smoke. "I could do it if I pleased, but I'm tired of engaging in marvelous black arts things, so I'll play it safe and keep within the bounds of everyday common magic business, just for variety and society's sake. I'll reform and conform, that's what the fuck I'll do. Besides," the wily witch reckoned, "there's no use in scaring the balls and tits off of little annoying children within a mile roundabout, although it's true that I really love seeing the little bastards and crying bitches run-away in a panic stampede, crapping their pants in their haste to get the hell home."

It was settled, therefore, in the old cunning cunt's own mind, that the scarecrow should represent a fine gentleman of the colonial period, so far as the available materials at hand would allow. Perhaps it may be as well to enumerate the chief articles that had gone into the composition of that developing remarkable figure.

The most important item of all, probably, although it made so little show, was a certain black magic broomstick, upon which Mother Rigby had taken many airy atmospheric gallops at midnight, and the versatile item was also used as a functional five-foot-long narrow dildo. The magical broomstick now would serve the scarecrow (Feathertop) as a functional spinal column, or, as the often-unlearned Massachusetts' local assholes politely phrase it, "A utilitarian non-vertebrae backbone".

One of Feathertop's arms was a disabled flail which used to be wielded by Goodman Rigby, the town's rugby coach, before his spouse had made him jerk-off without stopping for seven consecutive weeks, and then poor Goodman experienced a fatal, massive ejaculation of his spirit right out of his about-to-die body. The scarecrow's left arm and right appendage, if I am not mistaken, was composed of two kitchen pudding sticks and a pair of broken chair rungs, and putting it mildly (the pudding sticks), the disparate items had been neatly-but-loosely tethered together at the elbow.

As for "Feathertop's" skinny, emaciated-looking legs, the right one was a hoe handle stolen from a still-practicing, fully-licensed New England "hoe", and the left leg had been composed of an undistinguished and miscellaneous stick pilfered from the Salem dump's community woodpile.

The scarecrow's lungs, stomach, liver, and other "internal affairs" of that "invented anatomy" were nothing better than a meal bag stuffed with ordinary straw, and with strawberries, blackberries, blueberries, raspberries, and with numerous assorted dingle-berries inside. Thus, we have made-out (without even kissing) and described the skeleton and entire physical being of the improvised scarecrow, with the exception of its defective head; and so, that rotund cranium had been admirably supplied by a somewhat-withered and shriveled huge orange pumpkin, in which Mother Rigby had cut two holes for the eyes, and a slit for the

112

mouth, leaving a bluish-colored knob in the middle to adequately pass for an experimental nose.

The last organ to be operated upon was the cutting of a viable hole in the scarecrow's scrawny ass, allowing "Feathertop" to pass gas in the same manner as all human assholes do.

"I've seen worse heads on mortal shoulders, at any rate," observed and muttered Mother Rigby to herself. "And many a fine gentleman has a pumpkin head in addition to a dumpy ass, indeed, just as well as my magnificent dumb-ass scarecrow does."

But the "imaginative invention's" clothes, in this case, were to be the ultimate complimentary complement of the aristocratic, hay-headed straw-man in order for "Feathertop" to make hay when the sun shines, and to distill illegal whiskey at night when it would be moon-shine time. So, the mischievous old hag took-down from a wall peg an ancient British plum-colored coat that had been sewn together during a London fog, and with relics of fine imitation embroidery woven on its seams, cuffs, pocket-flaps, and button-holes. But lamentably, the coat was worn and faded, just like Julius Caesar's Roman military uniform presently looks. The queer-in-appearance outfit was patched at the elbows, tattered at the skirts, and quite threadbare all over. On the left buttocks was a round hole that Mother Rigby had opened in the thin drab material, where a former wearer, thinking he was hot shit, had partially seared-away the cloth while experimenting with one of his half-assed ideas.

To match the much-to-be desired plum-coat, a velvet waistcoat of very ample size was also to be worn, and the colorful apparel, had been formally decorated with autumnal red, yellow, orange, and brown maple leaves. Next came a pair of scarlet breeches, once worn by the French governor of Louisbourg, and the knees of which had touched the lower step of the elevated throne that had formerly been situated inside the rum-drinking Bourbon king's gold-gilded outhouse. The gregarious aforementioned Frenchman had given these small-clothes to an Indian powwow, where the tribal chief used the items to keep his "wig-wam" during the height of winter. After several cold Februarys had passed, the disgruntled Indian chief parted with the colorful garb, bartering the ridiculous articles to the old witch for several fish gills and deer antlers at one of the major spring Iroquois forest dance tribal shindigs.

Furthermore, Mother Rigby produced a pair of silk stockings and dressed them on the odd figure's legs, where the knickers showed their visual stupidity by covering the two wooden sticks miserably protruding through the sock holes. Lastly, the crafty sorceress ingeniously placed the wig of her dead husband (who as a teenage political wizard had ascended from the rank of small wig to big wig in the Whig Party) on the bare scalp of the pumpkin, and next the haggard-looking hag surmounted the whole eclectic haberdashery ensemble with a dusty three-cornered hat, in which was stuck the longest tail feather obtained from a dominant henhouse rooster.

'This feather from the 'capon' pierced inside the scarecrow's cap will truly be a feather in his cap when Feathertop clumsily puts his cape-on and boldly ventures-out upon his first worldly caper!'

Then, the coy old dame stood the preposterous figure up in a cobweb-cluttered corner of her cottage, and chuckled to behold its yellow semblance of a jaundiced visage, with its knobby little nose thrust-up like a fucked-up snobbish semi-circle. The assembled scarecrow had a strangely self-satisfied aspect, and seemed to say, "Come take a gander at me, Asshole! I'm as fucked-up looking as you are, and if you're lucky, I'll maliciously goose your lucky ass over near Swan Lake."

"And you truly are well-worth admiring, that's an observable fact!" Mother Rigby opined, in recognition of her own skillful handiwork. "I've made many a puppet since I've been a devious witch, but methinks this is the finest production of them all." And then thinking to herself about her new artifact, the warty-faced conjurer objectively assessed, 'It's almost too good a wardrobe for a commonplace cornfield scarecrow to possess. And, by the by, I'll just fill a fresh pipe of tobacco, and then transfer the manikin out to the rear corn-patch. I only hope his sewn-on scrotum sac doesn't fall-off during the short trek!'

While filling her essential magical pipe, Mother Rigby continued gazing with almost maternal affection at the inanimate figure conveniently placed in the cruddy corner. To say the truth, whether it were chance, or skill, or downright witchcraft, there was something wonderfully human in the fabrication of *that* ludicrous shape, majestically bedazzling with its tattered, inelegant finery; and as for the scarecrow's jaundiced round countenance, the simulated jack o' lantern appeared to humorously shrivel its yellow surface into a genuine grin; a funny kind of expression existing betwixt scorn and merriment, as if the creation inexplicably understood itself to be a mocking jest at mankind. The more Mother Rigby proudly stared at her inimitable specimen, the better she was pleased.

"Dickon," she demanded sharply. "Another blazing coal for my failing pipe! And make it anthracite and not bituminous!"

Hardly had she spoken, then just as before, there was a red-glowing coal ember mystically glowing on the top of the inserted tobacco. The hideous-looking hag ceased her cackling, and drew-in a long whiff, puffing the nicotine forth again into the morning air, where the fumes struggled their way through the one dusty cracked pane of her ramshackle cottage's small window.

Superstitious Mother Rigby always liked to flavor her pipe with a "coal-of-fire" obtained from the particular left chimney corner. But who had brought the coal from it, none-other person than the invisible messenger who seemed to urgently respond to the name 'Dickon'. And furthermore, the old raunchy bitch really didn't know *that* specific detail either, or for that matter, the sorceress in fact didn't care a New England healthy shit about the magical servant, either.

"That puppet yonder," thought and spoke Mother Rigby, still with her eyes fixed upon the attractive scarecrow, "is too good a piece of work to stand all summer in a corn-patch, simply frightening-away the crows and blackbirds. He's capable of better things like attempting a long row to hoe in human high society. Why, I've danced with a worse manikin at last fall's Salem Witch Trials Cotillion, when handsome male partners happened to be scarce and in short supply, mostly because of the numerous "Indian scalping festivals" that had been occurring in the nearby area. What if I should let this remarkable Feathertop gamble his chances among the other men of straw, along with the empty-headed rich human assholes who go bustling about the insane world?"

The old witch took three or four more whiffs of her addictive pipe, and then prodigiously smiled. "He'll meet plenty of his straw-brained, incompetent brethren at every street corner and tavern!" the gabby hag continued as she indulgently puffed-away. "Well, I didn't mean to dabble in rudimentary witchcraft to-day, that is, venturing further than the lighting of my indispensable pipe. But a bona-fide witch I am, and a witch I'm likely to always be, and there's no use trying to shirk that fuckin' responsibility. I'll make a reliable man of my scarecrow, were it only for the joke's sake! Feathertop will take a brave gambol into human affairs to intrepidly gamble his chance at fame and success!"

While muttering those peculiar-but-ambitious words, Mother Rigby removed the magical pipe from her own mouth, and thrust it into the scarecrow's facsimile crevice, which represented the same facial feature of the amusing manikin's pumpkin-faced mouth.

"Puff, darling, puff!" the sorceress ordered. "Puff-away, my fine fellow! Your life depends on it! But don't puff so strenuously that you'll turn into a fucked-up magic dragon!"

That ludicrous command represented being an absolutely strange exhortation, undoubtedly, designed and orally expressed to be addressed to a mere concoction of sticks, straw, and old clothes, with nothing better than a shriveled pumpkin for a head, and a maple tree twig for an erect prosthetic dick. Nevertheless, we must carefully hold in remembrance all of this rather wholly, impertinent bull-shit.

Indeed, Mother Rigby was an accomplished witch of singular power and dexterity; and, keeping this fact duly before our skeptical and cynical minds, we shall see nothing beyond credibility in the extraordinary sequence of amazing incidents. When the old dame bade Feathertop to puff, there came a billowing whiff of smoke, wafting-up to the decaying ceiling, the source of the fumes originating from the scarecrow's mouth. Each successive puff upon the arcane pipe became more powerful and robust.

"Puff-away, my magnificent pet! Puff-away like there's no tomorrow, my pretty one!" Mother Rigby kept repeating, with her pleasantest frightful smile. "It is the breath of life to ye; and that you may take my word for. Just puff thick smoke into the air, and not any sweet delectable, sweet baked cream puffs, either! I fuckin' have too much acne on my ugly puss already!"

Beyond all question, the pipe was undoubtedly bewitched, way beyond any of Mother Rigby's former pipedreams. There must have been a spell released either in the potent pilfered tobacco; or in the fiercely-glowing coal that so mysteriously burned on top of it, or in the pungent-but-aromatic smoke which seemed to exhale from the kindled fuel. The straw-filled figure, after a few dubious attempts, at length blew forth a volley of smoke traveling all the way from the obscure fireplace corner, and then up into the (nailed-to-the-ceiling-rafters') stuffed raccoon's open mouth.

The mystical cottage fog soon eddied and melted-away among the thousands of swirling overhead dust particles. For the two or three whiffs that were next enacted, the coal curiously still glowed, and the enchanted pipe's tobacco emitted a radiant gleam over the scarecrow's orange-colored visage. The old witch vigorously clapped her bony hands together in glee, and immediately, three moles, four warts, and five large wens fell from her arms upon the grimy, wood-planked floor.

Mother Rigby smiled encouragingly upon appreciating the unique quality of her phenomenal handiwork. The nefarious witch had comprehended that the experimental charm she had initiated had worked rather well. The scarecrow's shriveled yellow face, which heretofore had been no identifiable countenance at all, had already produced a thin, fantastic haze, as if it were now of human likeness, shifting its attention to-and-fro repeatedly, and its neck from left to right across the shoulders. The whole absurd figure, in like manner, assumed an excellent show of vitality, such as depictions we mortals often impart to ill-defined shapes among the clouds, sometimes idiotically saying, "That cloud looks like a tit," or "That one appears to be an erect donkey's dick," or perhaps, "Those three kinky clouds are having non-stop group LBGT sex!"

If we must need to pry closely and further into the whole matter, it may be doubted whether there had been manifested any real change in the scarecrow whatsoever. Perhaps the entire demonstration had been merely a type of spectral illusion, or maybe a cunning effect of light and shade, so colored and contrived as to delude the eyes with smoke but no mirrors. The miracles associated with witchcraft seem always to have a very shallow subtlety about them; and at least, if the above explanation does not hit the truth about the miraculous event, then my lousy, exaggerated bull-shit can suggest no better hypothesis.

"Well puffed, my pretty lad!" hoary Mother Rigby deliriously shrieked. "Come; inhale another good stout whiff, and let it be with might and main, all the way to Bang Whore Maine, ha, ha, ha! Puff for thy life, I tell thee! Puff-out of the very bottom of thy imitation heart, if any heart thou hast, or for that matter, any inexplicable supernatural bottom to it! Well done, again!" redundantly praised the old bitch. "Truly, this whole fantastic business of pipe smoke inhaling and exhaling really does suck! Thou didst suck in that mouthful as if for the pure love of it. Suck Feathertop, suck! And when you finally do achieve sustained life, my special Scarecrow, you can drop the goddamned pipe and begin non-stop *raven*ously sucking my flabby, sagging tits! Remember always, Feathertop. Life itself sucks!"

* * * * * * * * * * * *

And then the ingenuous witch beckoned to the minimally-energized lethargic scarecrow, throwing so much magnetic potency into her gesture that it seemed as if the hag's imperative directive must inevitably be obeyed, just like the hypnotic call of the wild when it summons the Alaskan wolves.

"Feathertop, you aren't dumb-ass Little Jack Horner! Why lurkest thou in the corner, lazy one?" the curious hag asked. "Rise and shine! Step forth I command! You shall become most charismatic! Thou hast the whole wide world before thee!"

Upon my suspect word, if this poppycock legend I'm now sharing were not one which I had heard on my grandmother's knee, and which had established its place among things credible before my childish judgment could objectively analyze its probability, I question whether I should have either the face or the balls to now continue telling this nonsensical, incredible tale.

In obedience to Mother Rigby's demanding word (words), and extending its artificial arm as if to reach her outstretched wart-less hand, the manufactured figure rose, and in a cumbersome attempt, made an awkward step forward; a kind of hitch and jerk performed by an inebriated jerk-off, and then Feathertop tottered and wobbled, almost losing his vertical balance. What could the roguish witch expect? It was nothing, after all, except an uncoordinated, hapless fucked-up scarecrow stuck upon two flimsy sticks.

But the strong-willed, despotic bitch, for a full half-hour, incessantly scowled, and also relentlessly beckoned, and next Mother Rigby flung the energy of her purpose so forcibly at this poor combination of rotten wood fragments, and musty straw, and ragged garments, that Feathertop soon became inspired and compelled to then show himself as a superior breed of culture, in spite of the reality of immaterial things such as scientific logic and non-fiction literature.

So, the animated manikin amazingly stepped into the dilapidated cottage's sole beam of windowpane sunshine. There, "Feathertop" awkwardly and ungracefully stood, poor devil of a contrivance that the dumb-shit was, with only the thinnest, frail vesture of human similitude about it, through which was evident the stiff, rickety, incongruous, faded, tattered, good-for-nothing patchwork of its fucked-up, mediocre existence, which was nearly ready to sink into a pathetic heap of rubbish upon the filthy floor.

Shall I confess and express the truth? At this present point of authorial self-analysis, the foolish-looking scarecrow reminds this writer of some of the lukewarm pedestrian literary characters prevalent mostly in romance novels, superficially composed of basic heterogeneous, nondescript elements, used for the thousandth monotonous time, and never worth using again, with which romance writers (and myself, no doubt, among the rest of the moronic fanciful assholes) have so overpopulated the wacky world of fiction.

But suddenly, the fierce old hag began to get antagonistic, and Mother Rigby demonstrated a glimpse of her diabolical nature (like a viperous snake's head, peeping with a hiss out of her evil-hearted bosom), at the pusillanimous, feckless behavior of the very thing which the rather bored witch had taken the trouble to assemble.

"Puff-away, wretched wretch!" she wrathfully commanded. "Puff, puff, puff, thou futile, unsophisticated creation composed of flammable straw and infinite emptiness! Thou art a male rag unable to menstruate! Thou mealy meal bag! Thou pumpkin head is not even good enough to make ordinary pie! Thou ambitious nothing! Where shall I find a name vile enough to call thee by? Puff, I say, and suck in thy fantastic life with the rich smoke of the Devil's black creation! For if you neglect to comply with my stern instruction," the dictatorial witch theorized and stated, "I shall snatch the pipe, using my rancid lice-infested snatch, straight from thy mimicking mouth, and then I'll mercilessly hurl thy paltry form to where that sizzling red hot coal came from. If that fate doesn't burn you up, then I don't know what the fuck will!"

Thus, threatened and warned, the unhappy scarecrow had no viable alternative other than for him to strenuously puff-away upon the pipe for dear life. As his need for survival prescribed, Feathertop applied his little lips lustily to the pipe stem, and his strong repetitious effort sent forth such abundant volleys of tobacco smoke that the small cottage kitchen seemed to become entirely vaporous. However, taking into account her great intensity, Mother Rigby was not fuming, despite her involuntary, deeply-prolonged coughing and sneezing episode.

Indeed, enduring great fear and incessant trembling did this poor scarecrow puff-away like a hyperactive chimney, suddenly feeling addicted to tobacco. But his valiant efforts, it must be fully acknowledged, served an excellent purpose; for with each successive whiff, the determined contrived figure lost more and more of his dizzy and most perplexing 'misdemeanor', and the more oxygen Feathertop would *miss* inhaling, *the meaner* his puffing became.

With the increased puffing, the weird scarecrow's very shabby garments, moreover, now stunningly partook of the magical change from shoddy rags to regal riches, and the tawdry buttons upon its uniform now shone and glistened with the brilliant gloss of pure-illuminated gold. And, half revealed amongst the eddying smoke, an alert yellow visage bent its lusterless eyes upon gasping and choking Mother Rigby.

At last, the old witch clinched her fist and shook it at the innocent, knowledge-starved figure. Not that the sinus-congested bitch had been positively over-the-top angry, but the old hussy was merely acting on the established code of unpatented medieval black magic principles. But here was the essential crisis that had to be resolved. Should Mother Rigby fail in what she now had initiated, the witch would become the international laughingstock of tarot card readers, astrologers, gypsies, and palm interpreters (along with evil-minded third-degree witch practitioners everywhere).

"Thou definitely hast a man's aspect," she noted, speaking sternly to her speechless creation. "Should I therefore detect in your minute oral sounds the echo and imitation of you producing a contrived human voice, your extremely weak endeavors being poorly duplicated and ineffectively employed! I bid thee speak! Speak if you may even utter complete jabberwocky like any asshole pontificating priest or politician! And please don't sound too gay or effeminate, either!"

The very nervous scarecrow gasped, struggled, and at length emitted a slight murmur, which was so incorporated with its smoky breath that the impatient witch could scarcely tell whether the hardly-audible sound was indeed a voice, or only a cursory whiff of errant tobacco. Some narrators of this legend hold the opinion that Mother Rigby's conjurations, along with the fierceness of her indomitable will, had compelled a familiar replica human spirit to be aroused into the figure, and that the voice was indeed actually *his,* but who in this fucked-up world really gives a shit about such random speculation?

"Mother," mumbled the weak stifled voice. "Be not so awful with me! I would fain speak; but being without necessary wits, I'm at wits end! What can I say without sounding like a commonplace, pitiful priest, or a commonplace pathetic politician?"

"Thou can speak logically and clearly, darling, canst thou!" the witch gleefully exclaimed, relaxing her grim countenance into a broad smile. "And what shalt thou say except the honest truth, that verity being that you presently sound like an asshole priest, or dumb-shit politician! Say, indeed!" implored the haughty hag. "Art thou of the brotherhood of the empty skull, and you now demand of me to listen to, and heed, what inadequate bull-shit thou shalt say? Thou shalt think and say a thousand things, just like the lackluster run-of-the-mill priest or mediocre politician, and saying those phrases and sentences a thousand dumb-ass times over, and predictably, thou shalt still sound exactly like those stupid-shit cretins, and have said absolutely nothing of merit! What a silly circus the world of mankind truly is!"

Noticing that the scarecrow seemed somewhat-addled and bewildered by her most recent rant, Mother Rigby managed to regain her composure, and somberly addressed her creation in a more rational and suave tone of voice. "Be not afraid, Feathertop, I tell thee! When thou came into the world (whither I purposely send thee forthwith), I had promised myself that thou shalt not lack the wherewithal to talk like all the other superficial assholes babbling-away out there. Talk! Why, thou shall articulate like a mill-stream, if thou will. Thou hast brains enough for *that* enterprise, I trust! If you think mightily, and then say something fairly significant, just using regular hollow rhetoric, you possibly could end-up with your own church or governor's mansion."

"At your service, Mother," anxiously responded the quick-read manikin. "But not at your sanctimonious religious service!"

"Wonderful! Wonderful!" reiterated and praised the now-proud witch. "And that last bit of pertinent nomenclature out of your mouth was indeed well said, my pretty one," Mother Rigby emphasized. "Then, thou speak like thyself, and your words meant nothing, just like those of the mentally-challenged Pope in Rome; just like the retarded Archbishop of Canterbury, and just like the equally thick-headed, slow-learner King of England. Now Feathertop, thou shalt have a thousand such-set irrelevant phrases in your thinking and speech repertoire, and five-hundred additional silly-assed phrases in ready reserve to boot. And now, darling Feathertop," the old bag continued her comprehensive understanding of insignificant human matters, "I've taken so much pains with thee and thou art so beautiful, that, by my troth, I love thee better than any witch's puppet in the entire world; and in the past, I've made them of all sorts: clay, wax, straw, sticks, night fog, morning mist, sea foam, whale sperm, chicken eggs, and chimney smoke, just to name a few. But thou art the very best concoction produced thus far," evaluated and revealed the old hag. "I mean, I don't even have a fuckin' laboratory in which to labor, nor can I afford the luxury of one, either. So now, my Adam, give heed to what the hell I have to say, in order to find and get your Eve."

"Yes, kind Mother," the constructed figure answered in a more confident baritone. "With all my heart!"

"With all thy heart!" confirmed the old witch, setting her palsied hands to her sides, and laughing loudly like an obsessed insane maniac. "Thou hast such a pretty and sincere way of speaking that I honestly feel like shacking-up with you and ecstatically working your maple pleasure stick. And thou didst put thy hand to the left side of thy waistcoat as if thou really had a real one to utilize! Oh, my beloved Feathertop. I do believe that you're ready to take a seat in Parliament, or possibly on the throne inside the Massachusetts' governor's marble outhouse, ha, ha, ha!"

"Is there anything else to disclose to me Mommy Dearest? I want to find my Eve and get laid!"

"These idiotic mortals ambling-around and living large out there, especially the wealthy ones with fat wallets, having plenty of ego issues that you will conscientiously exploit, in order to advance yourself and improve your current dismal lot," the Lady Conjurer loquaciously related. "Nowadays, everybody has issues, and no one has problems like dumb-fucks used to have in the good old days. Anyway," resumed the old woman, "the humans you'll encounter all have the same dumb-ass vanities, and I'm not referring to the cabinets under their bathroom sinks, either!"

"How did you learn all of this secret psychology and sociology stuff?" the fascinated puppet asked. "Somehow, my hungry brain needs to know this trite, trivial shit!"

"After Harvard College, I had a trans-gender operation performed, and went from being male to female," informed the testosterone-lacking Spellbinder. "Then, after my bad-luck bisexual Whig husband had accidentally died from inhaling too much snuff two decadent decades ago, I voraciously studied medieval witchcraft techniques and now, here I am, twenty-years later, with my own revolutionary black magic experimental methods to use. Actually, I'm lonely Mother Rigby, without even a goddamned bankrupt nun convent to administer and run!"

So now, in high good humor with this fantastic contrivance of her own machination, Mother Rigby anxiously informed the eager-to-learn scarecrow that Feathertop must go and play his leading role upon the great world stage, where "not one man in a thousand," she affirmed, was ever gifted with more real substance or ability than the stupid-shit scarecrow now possessed.

For her amusement, the bemused witch comically endowed her new-found disciple with a gold mine in El Dorado, and of ten-thousand shares in a gigantic soap bubble company; and of half a million acres of vineyard at the North Pole; and of a dark cloud castle floating high in the sky; and of a brothel complex in the Vatican, and also of a bordello chateau in Spain; of an arid desert whorehouse in Arabia, together with all the rents and income therefrom accruing.

Resuming with verbalizing the litany of her lucrative gifts to Feathertop, the self-pleasing hag further made over to him the cargo of a certain ship, laden with valuable salt of Cadiz, which she herself, by her necromantic arts, had caused ten-years before to founder off the coast of Bermuda, in perhaps the deepest part of the Atlantic. If the salt were not totally dissolved into the already-saline ocean, the salvaged commodity could be brought to market, and it would fetch a pretty penny for the scarecrow from the international "Maritime Fishermen's Association", who had a bad reputation of "not going for salt" when Old Salt personal debt obligations are involved.

So that Feathertop might not lack readily-available money, the notorious lady cauldron-stirrer gave the scarecrow a bag of copper farthings of Birmingham manufacture, being the only coins she had managed to save, and likewise, the wench afforded her heir a great deal of brass, which the witch immediately applied to his testicles, thus granting her creation a pair of highly coveted brass balls to successfully enact his impending chicanery.

"With that brass alone," Mother Rigby maintained, "thou canst pay thy way all over the Earth. Kiss me, pretty darling! I have done my best for thee."

"Kiss my ass!" the now independent scarecrow exclaimed. "You can lick my dry rectum hole too, while you're at it down there!"

Furthermore, that the novice adventurer might lack no possible advantage towards a fair start in pursuing life, the somewhat-excellent old dame provided Feathertop a token by which he was to introduce himself to a certain Magistrate; to a respected member of the city council; to a prosperous merchant, and last but not least, to a revered elder of the local church (the four distinct capacities constituting but one superlative special man), who haughtily stood and executed his obnoxious bull-shit at the head of the gullible "Liberal Arts Society" quite active in the neighboring metropolis.

The witch's spoken token was neither more nor less than a thousand words, which Mother Rigby lowly whispered to the talented and gifted scarecrow, and which the scarecrow was to later whisper and repeat to

the very impressed merchant, who positively loved the extraneous bull-
shit of so-called "important people" as much as the garrulous human dolt
cherished his own bizarre nomenclature.

"Gouty as the old fellow is, judging by the magnitude of his oversized
big toe, the pompous fool will gladly perform thy specified errands for
thee, when once thou hast judiciously given him those vital directions
you have warranted in his legal-minded ear," explained the perspicacious
old witch. "Mother Rigby knows well the ordinary proclivities of
worshipful local Magistrate Jeremiah Gookin, and the Worshipful Justice
is indeed well-acquainted with invincible Mother Rigby as well! For you
see, Feathertop, we were once fraternity brothers at Harvard, you know!
Your pop and I had mastered how to make Yale locks right there on
campus."

At that juncture the irascible witch thrust her wrinkled face close to
the puppet's mandible, which was agape, and now the perceptive hag,
chuckling irrepressibly, and simultaneously fidgeting all through her
mortal being, all the while euphorically expressing and experiencing
excessive delight with her extraordinary creation. The wily bitch was
busily contemplating the quite novel idea which the jaded jezebel now
meant to enthusiastically communicate to her most-novel Feathertop.

* * * * * * * * * * * *

"The Worshipful Master Gookin," whispered the occult-skilled
wench to her' precocious, new-found apprentice, "hath a comely maiden,
his pretty daughter. And hark ye, my inquisitive pet! Thou hast a fairly
handsome outside appearance, and a pretty wit operating inside your
vegetable skull, too. Yes, a pretty wit to match your noble plagiarized
face! Thou will think better of my statements regarding the intelligence
of the masses, once thou hast seen more of the dimwits' wits that abound
in the neighboring city. Now then," seriously lectured Mother Rigby,
"with thy perfect physical outside, and with thy keen quality attributes
inside, thou art the very facsimile man to easily win a young girl's heart.
Never doubt your audacity or your magnetic sex appeal! I tell thee it shall
be so, and in short order, pretty Polly Gookin is soon thine own wife to
have and to eagerly screw! Pinocchio's wood pecker has nothing on
you!"

All that terrific preliminary education was occurring while the new
creature had been sucking in and exhaling the vapory fragrance of his
corncob pipe, and the delighted scarecrow seemed now to continue that
pleasurable occupation, as much for the enjoyment it afforded, and also,
because the pipe was an essential condition of his very existence.
Feathertop was indeed a "quick read," and it was plainly wonderful to see

how exceedingly similar to a masculine human being the fellow greedily learned, adapted, and behaved.

His eyes (for the scarecrow appeared to possess a sparkling pair), ears, and mind were bent on fathoming the recommendations of Mother Rigby, and at suitable junctures, the creation nodded or shook his head in agreement. Neither did Feathertop lack the appropriate words that were proper and warranted for the particular situation or occasion: "Really! Indeed! Go to hell! Pray tell me! Is it possible? Fuck-off! Upon my word! By no means! What's the time? Oh! Ah! Shit! What the fuck?" and other such weighty utterances as to imply astute attention, adequate inquiry, acquiescence, or persuasive dissent on the part of the enamored, pretentious listener.

Even had you stood by and seen the scarecrow constructed, you could scarcely have resisted the conviction that the jovial jerk-off perfectly understood the incredibly cunning counsels which the old witch had prodigiously poured into his counterfeit ears. The more earnestly the obedient scarecrow applied his lips to the enchanted pipe, the more distinctly was Feathertop's human likeness focused-upon *his* visible realities, and more importantly, the more sagacious his erudite expression grew; and the more life-like his gestures and movements became, and finally, the more intelligibly audible his high-pitched voice resounded.

The figure's now royal-in-appearance garments too, glistened so much the brighter, emanating an illusory magnificence. The very pipe, in which burned the spell of all *that* evolving fantastic wonderwork, ceased to appear as a smoke-blackened, earthen stump.

"Hold thou pipe firmly and securely, my precious one," advised she, "while I fill it for thee again. The device is your lifeline for breathing, and it's your wonderful guarantee of achieving success in the outside mortal world. Everyone's waiting for your straw ass to appear on stage out there."

It was sorrowful to behold how the fine noble gentleman began to quickly fade back into a scarecrow, while Mother Rigby quickly shook the ashes out of the pipe and proceeded to replenish it from her tobacco-box. The evolving crisis demanded immediate resolution.

"Dickon," cried the demanding bitch in her high, sharp tone. "Another coal must be delivered for this blasted pipe! I can't wait until alternative fuels like wind power and solar energy are finally perfected and available on the black market!"

No sooner were those imperative words uttered than the intensely red speck of fire was again glowing and flourishing within the occult pipe-bowl. And the scarecrow, without waiting for the witch's bidding, applied the tube to his lips and drew in a few short, convulsive whiffs, which soon, however, became regular and equally repetitious inhalations.

"What a drag my new life is!" complained Feathertop as he puffed and inhaled upon his pipe. "What a fucked-up but delicious drag!"

"Now, mine own heart's darling," a relieved Mother Rigby spoke, "whatever may happen to thee, thou must stick to thy magical pipe. Thy life is in it; and that, at least, you now know quite well, if you know any relevant bull-shit at all. Stick to thy pipe, I say! Smoke, puff, and blow thy clouds into all *their* grateful faces; and tell the knuckle-brained, hollow-headed people, if any question be made about your indulgent habit, that it is expressly being performed for thy own health purposes, and for thy own personal satisfaction, and that your neurosurgeon physician, and also your very knowledgeable foreign apothecary, ordered thee to smoke incessantly."

"But how do I keep the damned thing going if you're not around to kindle it?" scrupulously asked the scarecrow. 'If this thing goes out, or is ever extinguished, then I'm really fucked and extinguished, too!"

"Ah, my sweet one; when thou shall find thy pipe getting low, go apart from the mortals, and station your cute ass into some remote corner, and (first filling thyself with smoke) cry sharply, 'Dickon, a fresh pipe of new tobacco!' And then bellow, 'Dickon, bring another burning coal for my fatigued pipe!' And soon, you'll have enough fuel into thy pretty mouth as speedily as may be."

"And if I am dilatory and summon this genie Dickon too late?"

"Then, instead of you existing as a gallant gentleman dressed in a gold-laced coat, thou will be converted into but a jumble of sticks and tattered clothes, and a bag of straw, and a withered pumpkin unworthy of making any pie! Now depart, my treasure," commanded the crazed sorceress, "and may good luck go with thee! But if your dick falls off, don't call Dickon! Just summon him if you need another required hot coal or new tobacco inserted into your pipe."

"Never fear, Mother-fucker, er, I meant to say, Mother!" the now-confident configured figure answered, speaking in a stout egotistical voice, and sending forth a courageous whiff of dense smoke, Feathertop then sagaciously pledged, "I will thrive in human society, as an honest impostor and a phony gentleman may not!"

"Oh, your M. F. comical frivolity will be the death of me yet!" cried the old witch, satisfactorily convulsed with laughter. "And that last expletive of yours was well said. 'If an honest impostor and a phony gentleman may not!' Ha, ha, ha! Thou will play thy part to perfection without any Shakespeare or Cervantes needed to give you the correct lexicon. Get along with thee for being a pretentious smart fellow," insisted the impulsive hag. "And I'll wager on thy head, as a man of pith and substance, with a brain and with what they in cultured society call a heart, a head, a dick, a potent set of balls, along with a nice ass, too, and all else that a man should have as usable social weapons, against any other thing ambling around the indigenous countryside on two legs. I hold myself a better witch than I had been yesterday, for thy own sake and safety. Did not I make thee almost entirely from discarded rubbish?" Mother Rigby rhetorically asked. "And I defy any arrogant copycat witch operating a black magic business anywhere in New England to duplicitously make a duplicate splendid masterpiece such as you! Here now; take my staff along with thee to the local town!"

The staff, though it was but a plain oaken stick, immediately took the aspect of a gold-headed cane.

"I thought that Dickon was your only staff!" Feathertop jested and gestured like an accomplished jester.

"Ha, ha, ha! You belong on Puritan Comedy Central now performing at the Salem Stocks and Bonds Torture and Lynching Club," guffawed Mother Rigby. "Remember *this* basic truth, my Lad. That gold head atop your cane has as much sense in it as thine own miracle pumpkin head possesses, and it will deftly guide your ass straight to Worshipful Master Jeremiah Gookin's palatial door. Get thee gone, my pretty pet," boomed the decrepit sorceress. "Yes, my darling; my precious one, my opulent treasure; and if any itinerant asshole meandering-around out there stupidly asks thy name, tell the freaky shit-head that your code-name identity is 'Feathertop', and nothing more. For thou hast a lengthy rooster feather implanted into thy three-sided hat, and I've shrewdly thrust a handful of duck feathers into thy empty head, so that you can quickly duck-down if ever attacked. And oh yes," the witch stipulated and cackled. "Thy wig, too, is of the fashion of which the more-sophisticated aristocrats of this age call 'Feathertop', so my pretty, Feathertop be thy official name! You'll impress the wealthy old simpleton Judge Gookin that you're the finest ambassador traveling about the New World; the Old World; the Syndicate Underworld, and the dreaded Afterworld all put together, ha, ha, ha!"

* * * * * * * * * * * * *

And, issuing-out on a narrow weedy path from the shoddy cottage, Feathertop strode manfully towards the nearby town. Mother Rigby stood at the threshold, well-pleased to see how the majestic sunbeams glistened upon her mobile "special invention", as if all his artificial magnificence constituted real attributes, and now how diligently and lovingly the "newly-arrived mortal" smoked his illustrious pipe, and how handsomely the dignified fellow sauntered and farted, in spite of a little stiffness of his legs, and minor arthritis hurting inside his semi-erect stick dick.

Later that morning, when the principal street of the neighboring town was just at its acme of hustle and bustle, the form of a very distinguished figure was seen ambling and gallivanting on the crowded sidewalk. The gentleman's discernible attitude, as well as his flamboyant garments betokened nothing short of European nobility. The zesty zany pedestrian wore a richly-embroidered plum-colored coat; a waistcoat of costly velvet that was magnificently adorned with golden foliage; a pair of splendid scarlet breeches; pink linen underwear, and the finest and glossiest of white silk stockings.

On the breast of his imperial coat, a shiny platinum star glistened, the stellar object symbolizing a badge of royal French political influence. The merry visitor managed and manipulated his gold-headed cane with an airy grace, a style of conduct emblematic of the fine gentlemen of the pre-war period in American history. And to give the highest possible finish to his visual equipment, Feathertop sported lace ruffles at his wrists' sleeves, a pattern of a most ethereal delicacy, sufficiently avouching how idle and aristocratic must be *his* hands, which the rare material had half conspicuously concealed.

It was a remarkable point in the accoutrement of this brilliant personage that the uncoordinated guest held in his left hand a fantastic kind of pipe, with an exquisitely painted bowl, and an accompanying elegant amber mouthpiece. This smoking instrument the fellow deftly applied to his lips as often as every five or six paces, and the sartorial-attired visitor intermittently inhaled a deep whiff of smoke, which after being retained a moment in his lungs, might be seen to casually eddy gracefully from his mouth and nostrils, just as an opera soprano diva might do while smoking marijuana joints inside her backstage dressing room.

As may well be supposed, the street pedestrians were all astir with gossip and chatter to find-out and discover the stranger's rather unique name and general purpose.

"It is some great nobleman to be sure, beyond question," remarked one of the more perceptive townspeople. "Do you see the impressive star at his breast? This most splendid man must've originated from another country, or continent, or perhaps from another planet."

"Nay; it is too bright to be seen," said another gentleman bystander with his mouth agape and his right arm akimbo. "Yes, he must indeed be an important nobleman, as you say and suggest. But by what conveyance, think you, can his masterful lordship has voyaged or travelled hither? There has been no vessel from the old country for a month past; and if our tourist has arrived overland from the south, let's say by Providence from Providence, pray where the hell are his attendants, his luggage, and his equipment?"

"Obviously, the regal personage needs no equipage to further define his high rank," commented a third male resident. "If he came among us in rags, nobility would shine through a hole in his elbow. I never saw such integrity evident in a queer, unorthodox gait. The gentleman, I believe, has the old Norman blood liberally flowing in his veins; I warrant him that accolade. He isn't of lowly Saxon legacy, that's for damned sure! Perhaps he's French! I can theorize and determine that fact from the gray poop on his left hand."

"I rather take him to be a stern Dutchman, or one of your high-ranking Germans," interpreted and insisted another curious city citizen. "The men of those countries have always the pipe at their mouths. That intelligent social habit allows the clever savants to deftly avoid taking the gas pipe!"

"And so has a Turk those pertinent characteristics," answered his equally-befuddled same-sex companion. "But in my keen judgment, this gay-looking, effeminate stranger hath been bred at the French court, and hath at Versailles learned politeness and grace of manner, which none understand so well as the nobility of France. Just check-out that gait, now! A vulgar spectator might deem it stiff; he or she might call it a hitch and jerk; but to my hawk eye, it hath an unspeakable majesty, and must've been acquired by constant observation of the deportment of the Grand King Louis XIII. The stranger's character and office are evident enough in his public deportment. Our noble visitor is no doubt an eminent French ambassador, dispatched to America to treaty with our rulers about the cession of Canada. Perhaps we can introduce ourselves to him, and arrange to have a tremendous threesome at the local Pussy Cat House and Pecker Pumping Café over on the corner of Prostitute and Gay."

"More probably our impeccable guest is a debonair Spaniard," said another imperceptive gossiper, "and hence his yellow banana complexion; or, most likely, he is from Havana, or from some malaria port on the Spanish Main, and he's come here to make investigation about the Jolly Roger piracies which our government is thought to be furtively conniving. Remember, there's a skull and crossbones fraternity thriving over at Harvard. And may I add," further contributed the partially-blind observer having a black patch over his right eye, "those settlers in Peru and Mexico have skins as yellow as the gold which they dig out of their lucrative mines."

"Yellow or not," an enamored lady about to orgasm yelled. "He's a sensationally beautiful man, so tall, so slender! Such a fine, noble face, with so well-shaped a nose, and all *that* exquisite delicacy of expression about the mouth and crotch! And, bless me, how bright his breast star is! It positively shoots out flames, just like heated semen entering my....!"

128

"So do your eyes perceive truth, my fair lady," said the approaching stranger, with a diplomatic bow, and then his artificial mouth yielding a puff from his hypnotic pipe, for Feathertop was just passing at that instant.

"Upon my honor, his fabulous pipe makes mine look like a piece of shit," commended the lady's horny husband.

The enamored woman ignored her spouse's nonsensical articulation. "Was ever so original and marvelous a compliment ever uttered?" murmured the infatuated lady, in an ecstasy of total delight, as the aroused wife experienced a massive orgasm for the fifth time in thirty-seconds. "I'm so happy I have come, er, I mean *he* has come!"

Amid the general admiration that had been excited by the stranger's sudden appearance in the mediocre town, there were only two dissenting voices present among the spectators. One was that of an impertinent cur, which after snuffing at the heels of the glistening figure, the disappointed canine put its tail between its legs and skulked into its master's back-yard, vociferating an execrable howl. The other tough critic was a young child, who squalled at the fullest stretch of his lungs, and babbled some unintelligible jargon about a "silly-looking pumpkin head that looks somewhat like a huge orange's ass."

Feathertop, meanwhile, pursued his way along the crowded street. Except for the few complimentary words, which the sophisticated hiker had spoken to the enraptured woman, whom the enthusiastic scarecrow creatively referred to as "Lady Climax" without ever knowing her real name, and virtually ignoring the presence of the accompanying male bystanders, the new arrival seemed wholly-absorbed in ambitiously smoking his pipe, and apparently interested in nothing else.

With a noisy crowd gathering behind his footsteps, the genial trekker finally reached the mansion-house of the worshipful Justice Gookin. Feathertop unfastened and entered the gate, and in an awkward fashion, tripped while ascending the red-brick steps leading to the front door, where the uninvited guest then gently knocked. In the interim, before his summons had been answered, the "queer stranger" was noticed by dependable witnesses to wildly shake the ashes out of his intriguing pipe.

"What did he say in that sharp voice?" inquired one of the nosy spectators. "Is he the king's new tax collector? Fuck George the Third. I say the ignoble shit-head ought to be sodomized by every Tom Turkey, Richard, and harried asshole in the colonies!"

"Nay, I know not," answered his critical friend. "But the sun reflecting off his expensive clothes dazzles my eyes strangely. How dim and faded his lordship looks all of a sudden, before he again puffs on that incomparable pipe! Bless my wits, what the fuck's the matter with me? Reality seems to be a fucked-up illusion!"

"The wonder is," mentioned his more-than-gay companion, "that his nifty pipe, which was out only an instant ago, should be all glowing again, and it possesses the reddest coal I've ever seen. There is something more-than-mysterious about this strange stranger. What a whiff of smoke was *that* last exhale! Dim and faded did you call him? Why, as he turns about toward us, the star on his breast is all ablaze. Let's go home for some quick sodomy before that star leaps off his coat and penetrates and sears both of our vulnerable assholes."

The door to the singular Gookin mansion being now opened, Feathertop unexpectedly turned toward the fascinated crowd, made a stately bend of his body like a great man acknowledging the reverence of the lackluster proletarian social rank, and then the protagonist vanished into the estate's massive foyer.

Indeed, only the mangy dog and the bratty toddler had recognized the honest-to-goodness fact that Feathertop was, in perfect truth, a total fraud.

* * * * * * * * * * * *

Our legend here loses somewhat of its continuity, and I'll deliberately be bypassing over the preliminary explanation between Feathertop and the wealthy import/export merchant, Honorable Judge Jeremiah Gookin, who (as formerly directed by Mother Rigby) journeyed in quest of punctually courting the pretty and petite Miss Polly Gookin.

The lass was a fair damsel featuring a soft, round figure, having light beige hair and blue eyes, and a decent rosy face, along with a never-molested brown hairy pussy, which in total, all seemed neither very shrewd nor very simple. This well-educated young lady had caught a glimpse of the glistening stranger while Feathertop had been standing upon the porch's threshold, and Polly Gookin had forthwith put on a laced cap, a string of beads, her finest kerchief, and her stiffest damask petticoat in preparation for her sought-after impending interview with the handsome visiting guest.

Hurrying from her bedroom chamber to the downstairs parlor, Maiden Gookin had ever since been viewing herself in the large hall looking-glass, and perfunctorily practicing pretty smiles and curtsies, and now that self-conscious activity was being followed by ceremoniously role-playing, weirdly kissing her hand, likewise in the tall hall mirror, next tossing her head backwards, and then adroitly managing her light fan; and also scratching her half-turned fanny.

No sooner had Polly heard her rich father's irregular gouty footsteps approaching the parlor door, Judge Gookin's unorthodox pace, which was accompanied by the stiff clatter of Feathertop's high-heeled leather

130

boots, prompted the young, non-talented lady to commence warbling an improvised song at the piano, with her screeching voice truly sounding like complete and utter dissonance.

"Polly! Daughter Polly!" the embarrassed cranky merchant screamed. "Come hither, child. I'd like to introduce you to a venerable visiting gentleman. This foremost guest ambassador," continued Judge Gookin, presenting the manufactured stranger to Polly, "is the Chevalier Feathertop; nay, I beg his noble *pardon,* even though he's not a warden, and I'm not a prisoner incarcerated in a jail. My Lord Feathertop has, in good faith and trust, brought me a token of remembrance from an ancient French friend of mine. Pay your duty to his lordship, my child, and cordially honor our eminent guest as his quality and rank rightly deserves."

After those flattering words of stilted introduction, the worshipful magistrate immediately quitted the room to take his scheduled morning dump. But, even in that brief moment, had the fair Polly glanced aside at her father instead of devoting herself wholly to the brilliant skinny guest, the pretty daughter might have taken warning of some unearthly, outlandish mischief at hand.

The old man had become nervous, fidgety, and very pale prior to impetuously leaving the room. Feathertop, because of his stout frankness and innocent testimony, had inadvertently scared the crap out of elderly Gookin, because the old fart comprehended that the glorified guest had perceptively understood the Judge better and more thoroughly that the avaricious, vain Magistrate actually knew about himself.

It so happened that the mansion's parlor door was partly of glass, shaded by a silken curtain, the folds of which hung a little awry. So strong was the frightened merchant's interest in witnessing what was to ensue between the fair Polly and the gallant Feathertop that, after hastily abandoning the parlor room, and then speedily taking his raunchy crap, and next only half-wiping his smelly ass, the craven colonial Solon could by no means refrain from the temptation of peeping through the curtain's crevice.

But there was nothing very miraculous to be seen; nothing except the trifles previously noticed; said trifles to confirm the idea of a supernatural peril descending-upon and evilly-enveloping the pretty Miss Polly Gookin. The stranger, it is true, was evidently a thorough and practiced traveler of worldly grandeur, systematic and self-possessed, and therefore the sort of person to whom a parent ought not to confide a simple, young girl without due watchfulness, because obviously, Ambassador Feathertop was so much a carbon copy of vain, avaricious Judge Gookin in both thought and deed.

But pretty, sex-curious Polly Gookin felt not those aroused suspicions. The newly-acquainted pair was now promenading the expansive room: Feathertop with his dainty stride and no less dainty grimace, and the girl with a native maidenly grace, her tits just touched by the greedy visitor, but her dampening pussy not yet spoiled, of which the former advance had evidently infuriated the petrified, eavesdropping Judge.

The longer the small-talk conversation continued, along with the taboo body touching and pursuant male exploration, the more charmed was pretty Polly, until within the first quarter of an hour (as the old Magistrate noted by his ticking, shit-stained, smelly watch), the little pussy-wet chickadee was certainly beginning to fall in love. Nor need it have been witchcraft that had smoothly subdued the rich girl in such a hurry; the poor child's heart, it may be, was so very fervent that it melted with its own warmth as reflected from the hollow semblance of a lover, and his hot, hypnotic coal-lit pipe. Even Miss Gookin's gooky crotch was sticky and damp from the general body melt, and now Polly strongly desired an erect firecracker to explode warm juice deep inside her eager-beaver, hot pink love tunnel.

No matter what Feathertop divulged, his words found depth and reverberation inside her receptive ears; no matter what the impressive scarecrow did, like grabbing her tits, or rubbing her pubic box through her raised dress, his action was heroic to her fascinated eye. And by this time, it is to be supposed there was a large blush on Polly's cheek; a tender smile about her mouth, and a liquid softness in her amorous glance; while the visitor's breast star kept bouncing in and out upon Feathertop's coat, and while comical little two-dimensional alien demons arcanely careened and danced with more frantic merriment than ever, all about the circumference of *his* enchanted pipe bowl.

By and by, aroused Feathertop paused and hesitated, and throwing himself into an imposing attitude, seemed to summon the fair girl to survey his desirable figure; to admire his throbbing prosthetic crotch stick, and to resist his allurement no longer. "Well Bitch, do you want to screw or don't you!" Feathertop loudly implored. "I'm tired of this stupid-assed foreplay bull-shit! I want the real thing now!"

The maiden raised her eyes and suffered them to linger upon her Casanova companion with a bashful and fearful stare. Then, Polly cast a glance towards the full-length looking-glass in front of which the pair happened to be standing. The object was one of the truest plates in the world, and incapable of fake flattery. The mirror's reflection compelled the high-society young lady to let-out a frightful shriek. The horrified damsel began collapsing from the thin stranger's side, with her eyes gazing at her avaricious date for a moment, in wildest dismay, and then

132

Honorable Judge Gookin's daughter sank-down in an unconscious state upon the white marble floor.

"What's this dumb-ass canard all about?" shouted the fully confused suitor. "I haven't even lifted your dress and successfully pulled your undies down?"

Feathertop, likewise, then looked towards the other revelation mirror located over the mantel, and there beheld, not the glittering mockery of his outside appearance, but instead a lucid picture portraying the sordid patchwork of his real composition, stripped of all witchcraft embellishments. Angry and frustrated, the pathetic scarecrow turned-around, gave the spying Judge Gookin the middle finger, and then briskly hustled out of the magnificent mansion.

* * * * * * * * * * * * *

Mother Rigby was comfortably seated by her kitchen hearth in the twilight of that eventful day, and the wretched wench had just shaken the excess ashes out of a new pipe, when the devious witch heard a hurried tramp of footsteps approaching along the side road. Yet, it did not seem so much the sound of tramping human footsteps as it did the clatter of sticks, or the annoying rattling of dry bones.

'Ha!' thought the old witch, 'What step is that? Whose skeleton is out of its grave now, I wonder? Could it be Lady Cadaver?'

A rather disfigured figure burst headlong through the opened cottage door. Feathertop's pipe was still alight; the breast star still-flamed upon his outer coat; the dazzling embroidery remained glowing upon his regal garments; nor had the deteriorating scarecrow lost, in any degree or manner that could be discerned, the essential aspect that assimilated his identification with *our* mortal human brotherhood. But yet, in some indescribable way (as is the case with all that has deluded us when once found-out after being suspected), the vivid burden of guilt was being painfully felt beneath the scarecrow's cunning external facade.

"What has gone wrong?" the surprised witch demanded. "Did yonder sniffling hypocrite Judge Gookin thrust my darling invention from his elaborate door? The fucked-up villain! I'll send twenty hellish fiends to torment the dumb-fuck until the egocentric dunce eventually offers thee his virgin daughter on his bended knees!"

"No, Mother," Feathertop replied quite despondently. "It was not *that* development which has addled my straw brain. The asshole Judge has little to do with my current melancholy."

"Did the naïve girl scorn my precious one?" Mother Rigby asked, her fierce eyes glowing like two lit anthracite coals. "If she has abused you one iota, I'll gladly cover her immaculate face with pimples and blackheads! Polly Gookin's nose shall be as red as the coal burning inside thy pipe! Her front teeth shall drop-out, and then her infected gums will be ejected, too! In a week hence, the little bitch shall not be worth thy having! Now go and try our little experiment again. Here are two lousy coppers, and I don't mean a pair of drunken town constables, either!"

"I can't be bribed, Mother! I just can't! I feel I must exit the mortal's world in total tranquility!"

"Well then, handsome scarecrow; keep your 'chin high'!"

"Speak plain English, Mother! I can't fuckin' talk or understand Chinese or Swahili! And please don't be envious! Let rich Miss Polly alone, Mother," poor Feathertop answered. "The girl was half-won by my seductive advances; and methinks a kiss from her sweet lips might've made me altogether human. But," the lugubrious wretch added after a brief pause and then a candid howl of self-contempt, "I've seen myself accurately, Mother! I've seen myself for the wretched, miserable, greedy, empty thing that I really am! This is my humble intent, and I wish I shall no longer exist as a living being!"

Snatching the magical pipe from his own mouth, the disconsolate scarecrow violently flung the object with all his might against the cottage chimney, and at the next instant, sank upon the floor, immediately disintegrating into a medley of straw and tattered garments, with some sharp sticks protruding from the whole heap, and a shriveled, partially-shattered pumpkin situated in the midst. The eyeholes were now eerily lusterless; but the rudely-carved gap, that just before had been a mouth, still seemed to twist itself into a despairing grin, and had so far remained human in appearance.

"Poor Fellow!" Mother Rigby lamented, with a rueful glance at the macabre relics of her ill-fated experiment. "My poor, dear, pretty invention; yes, it is my poor Master Feathertop! Thousands upon thousands of coxcombs and charlatans inhabit this lackluster world, made-up of just such a jumble of worn-out, forgotten, and good-for-nothing trash as poor Feathertop had been in the beginning, and is now! Yet those various inanimate objects live and now exist separately in fair repute, and never see themselves for precisely what the hell they are. And why should my all-too-honest puppet be the only one in this fucked-up world to actually fully-know himself, and then wickedly perish for it?"

While thus muttering, the sorrowed witch had filled a fresh pipe of pungent tobacco, and neurotically, the hideous hag held the stem between her rheumatic fingers, being doubtful whether to thrust the object into her own mouth or into smiling, dying Feathertop's.

"Poor Feathertop!" Mother Rigby sadly continued her mourning. "I could easily give him another chance, and send the lad forth again into formal society tomorrow. But no; his feelings are too tender, and his sensibilities are rather too deep to risk another complicated misadventure. My poor darling seems to have too much heart to bustle for his own advantage, especially in such an empty and heartless human world. Well! Well!" Mother Rigby realized a fitting conclusion to her overwhelming anguish. "I'll make a legitimate scarecrow of him after all. Tis an innocent and useful vocation, that being a useful scarecrow; and it'll suit my darling well; and if each of his human brethren had as fit a vocation or avocation as his, it would be much the better for all of mankind. And as for this precious pipe of tobacco, I fuckin' need it more than he does."

The pensive witch then paused for a moment to formulate in her mind several final thoughts. "The Judge, I understand, is planning on building a new museum in town, the Gookinheim, I believe. Perhaps the remnants of poor, defeated, valiant Feathertop can eventually be put on exhibit there!"

So, after muttering *that* mirthless summary, aggrieved Mother Rigby placed the familiar stem between her dry lips. "Dickon!" cried the contemporary sorceress in her high-pitched, sharp staccato. "Bring another sizzling coal for my pipe, and deliver it on the double!"

"The Golden Fleece"

When Jason, the son of the dethroned King of Ioclus, was a little boy, he was really little. Aeson was the aforementioned dethroned King, whose infant son had been rescued and escorted out of the city to safety by a loyal royal adviser to the deposed ruler, during the swift and violent insurrection. The soon-to-be toddler was taken to Chiron, a stern, well-disciplined Centaur who operated the queerest of academic schools in a remote cave for prospective effeminate boys, who probably would all eventually grow-up into full-fledged, gay faggots and transvestites.

Chiron the Centaur was both a quadruped and a bi-penal, meaning that the odd tutor had the legs and body of a white horse, the head and shoulders of a man, and the famous beast possessed two very long independent dicks. Despite his weird physical appearance, Chiron was a superb teacher and scholar who, on occasion, demonstrated a nasty disposition. Some of the Centaur's more renowned students had been Philoctetes, who later killed Paris, and a few other important cities; Asclepius, who became a notorious doctor; Hercules, a legendary hero strongman, and also "that heel Achilles", who gradually matured into a prominent Greek hero during the *Trojan War*, also known to more serious historians as "the prophylactic conflict".

The erudite Centaur Chiron taught his distinguished pupils how to play the harp, and how to kill harpies; how to cure diseases, along with curing smoked ham and smoked tobacco all at the same time; how to use the sword and the shield in order to kick ass; how to read and write; and finally, how to jerk-off using only horse's hooves.

When Jason was-six-years-old, the child prodigy asked Chiron a very intelligent question. "I'd rather see women take-off their clothes at the local strip mall than engage in all of this homosexual behavior you've been teaching me," the lad tersely stated. "Why can't we learn some basic moral heterosexuality at this damned cave school? Do you want us to evolve into culturally retarded cave men or what?"

"Shut the hell up and keep sucking my two long flaccid dicks until they get hard!" Chiron answered in a very perturbed tone of voice. "When you become my age, Jason, you can teach your own kids anything you fuckin' want, you little snot-nosed cock-sucker! But until then, you're under *my* fuckin' jurisdiction!"

And so, Jason had to suck-up to Chiron from when the rebel was a little tyke, up to the time the son of Aeson was a fully-grown teeny-bopper. Upon reaching his eighteenth birthday, Jason was ready to go out into the fucked-up world and seek his already-prescribed and fame and fortune.

"Is it true, Chiron, that I'm a prince, and that my shameful Uncle Pelias had stolen my father's throne away from him?" Jason asked Chiron right before receiving his graduation sheepskin, which the recipient proudly wore over his athletic body, along with his leopard skin, which made the inquisitive Prince easy to spot from a distance.

"No, Pelias sits on the same throne your father Aeson had," the Centaur humorously replied. "So, your father's throne was not taken in any grand larceny felony. But your criminal Uncle Pelias is a real mother-fucker because he's been porking your mother all these past eighteen-years. Now, if demented Pelias and your mother were totally gay like I am, that sort of adulterous bull-shit would've never happened between your promiscuous mommy, and your uncle, over in the *hamlet* of Iolcus."

"I'll punish my immoral Uncle Pelias for being such a cad like legendary Cadmus was," Jason promised his mentor Chiron. "I'm not gonna' fuckin' *horse-around* in a dank and dreary cave the rest of my life like you've stupidly elected to do!"

Chiron had given Jason two spears (that incidentally were not from Brittany), and a new pair of sandals as graduation presents, and soon the proud young man left "the Cave Academy" and proceeded on his merry way towards Iolcus. A half-hour later, the adventurous fellow came to a river-rapids, and instead of walking downstream and crossing where the water was less turbulent and shallow, the stubborn idiot began fording the fast-flowing current right at its most difficult crossing. The eddying, roaring stream soon caught Jason off-guard in his haste, for it was springtime, and the river was much broader than it was during the non-rainy season, and the melting snow complicated matters by cascading-down from distant *Mt. Olympus*.

The young man paused in the middle of the swift current to consider his options and other future stock investment strategies. 'I must be careful. There are many jagged rocks here in the middle,' Jason analyzed and evaluated. And when the carcasses of several drowned sheep, cows, horses, elephants, and hippos floated by the stationary youth, the haughty teenager finally realized and interpreted correctly that his ass had been in the midst of a dangerous situation in progress.

'I can't swim against such a damned strong current,' the callow fellow considered. 'And worst of all, I can't even fuckin' swim.' Then, Jason reflected some more. 'My mentor and tormentor Chiron had no wild river flowing through his smelly cave to teach me *that* particular skill. Oh shit! I've lodged my right foot between two goddamned jagged rocks! What a fuckin' bummer this predicament is! It's a good thing that my fuckin' dick and balls are still safely attached!'

"Are you experiencing a degree of difficulty?" a curious female voice asked the troubled neophyte. "You must not have had a decent education, since apparently, you have not been prepared to cross such a rushing stream as this sucker happens to be."

Jason was more embarrassed than offended, even though the lad was quite aware that his life was at least temporarily in jeopardy. And being directly chided by an old wrinkle-faced woman was perhaps the ultimate of insults for a conceited and vindictive young man to have to suffer and endure.

"Perhaps you ought to yell for Chiron the Centaur to arrive and rescue you from your uncomfortable dilemma," the old hag further admonished her humiliated listener. "But that egotistical dumb bastard doesn't know how to swim worth a damned rat's ass, either!"

The encumbered river-crosser studied the old lady's appearance and noticed that she wore a grimy old drab shawl over her unkempt, mediocre tunic; held a crooked, old staff in her left hand with a wooden cuckoo carved on top, and furthermore, carried a half rotten pomegranate (an out of season fruit) in her left palm. And Jason also noticed that a tame, dependent peacock stood by the old bitch's side.

"If I didn't have bad cases of arthritis and rheumatism right now," the old hag complained and commented, "and if I were a mere hundred-years younger, then I would salvage you from your *current* problem. Where are you heading, Jason?"

The son of Aeson was startled that the hoary, gray-haired woman knew his name, his former teacher's identity, *his* general background, and his present uncomfortable problem in the river. "Oh, psychic hideous-looking bag lady," Jason pleaded. "I'm heading to Iolcus to challenge King Pelias to abdicate his confiscated throne and relinquish it to me, the rightful heir, which originally and legitimately belonged to my father Aeson," the naïve, idealistic lad thoroughly explained. "But right now, I'm experiencing a rather upsetting obstacle that's severely hindering my necessary progress."

"Well then, Jason, I happen to know exactly what you're up to. You're *up to* your waist in the roaring river, ha, ha, ha," the old woman humorously giggled. "And when you're through giving me a lot of irrelevant bull-shit, I request that you take me upon your back, so that I may cross the river with minimum danger. Since there aren't any goddamned *Boy Scouts* around yet, please forgive the inane anachronism, your awkward services will just have to suffice. My peacock and I have some important business to conduct on the other side. But first Jason, you must empty the urine from your *peacock* into the swirling stream. Ha, ha, ha, ha! And please don't fuckin' *double-cross* me, ya' hear, ha, ha, ha! I only wanna' go one damned way, and I don't request round-trip service from you, ha, ha, ha!"

"Good old hag bag woman," Jason sincerely answered. "Your business cannot possibly rival my pursuit of removing a most-evil, illegitimate King from my father's throne. And if I should stumble transporting you to the other side, we'll both surely drown, and soon be really going to the other side on Charon's barge across the *River Styx* into subterranean Hades. In the final analysis, I doubt whether I'm strong enough to convey you across this turbulent stream against such a wild and forceful, rapid-flowing rapids. For you see, old hag," the youth eloquently clarified, "I'm blue-blooded, and was not born into damned mainstream society."

"Look, Asshole, if you aren't strong enough to carry my butt to the left bank that's here in Greece and not in Paris, France," the elderly wench rankled, "then you certainly aren't strong enough to remove King Pelias from his goddamned throne. You don't seem to have the testicles or the required sperm count to lead a successful coup d' etat, whatever the fuck that is! Now either carry me across the stream, or else live in humility and defeat for the remainder of your already fucked-up life!"

"Okay, you old dirt-bag, you win," the brawny youth conceded. "If you can leap upon my back, I'll gladly conduct you to the other side without even desiring a toll, a fee, or a raunchy lousy rotten piece of geriatric ass. I'd rather have us drown together than to see you drown in these rapids while my damned foot is helplessly caught between two rocks. We might as well fuckin' drown together, old woman. That way your certain demise will not be on my conscience, for it will have happened at *your* own suspect volition."

Much to Jason's astonishment, the old bitch carefully placed her peacock upon her right shoulder; took twenty-paces backwards, and then possibly believing that she was Archimedes, the old dame let out a shout of "Eureka!" as she fiercely sprinted to the river's edge. The hoary lady then used her staff with the cuckoo on its end, and acting very cuckoo herself', the aged bitch planted the long stick into the ground as she hustled forward, and then athletically pole-vaulted onto Jason's back. The jolt from the impact momentarily sent Jason underwater, and when the kingdom-less prince violently arose with the old woman still desperately clinging to his back, the exiled heir had accidentally turned his right foot, and incidentally freed his aching ankle from its snare.

Jason courageously staggered through the surging currents to the opposite bank, using both his spear and his sword as improvised wading sticks. "Oh shit!" Jason exclaimed. "I have lost my right sandal in a river crevice. Now, I'll be the fuckin' laughing stock of King Pelias's court, appearing in front of him with only one golden-stringed sandal. What a sandal scandal that shit-eatin' event will be!"

Upon reaching and climbing the other bank of the raging river, the depressed-but-aspiring Prince stooped-down to allow his passenger to drop from his posterior onto the pebble-laden sand. And after then standing erect, the old hag had some truly consoling words to deliver.

"Don't take your sandal loss to heart," the hideous-looking lady imperatively lectured. "Now, I'm quite certain that you're the lad that the garrulous Speaking Oak had been describing to me. That tree could out-predict the much-praised *Oracle of Delphi,* and also the equally gifted *Augur of Philadelphia.*"

"But what of my missing sandal?" Jason muttered and complained. "Malicious Uncle King Pelias is liable to think that I'm Shoeless Joe Jacksonocles, and not his feared nephew Jason, the rightful heir to *his* father's throne. I guess I won't be vacationing at any Greek *Sandals* resort any time in the fuckin' near future."

"I assure you that a new pair of sandals will be forthcoming in due time," the old bag stated with certainty and conviction. "And when Pelias takes a gander at your bare right foot, his face will turn as pallid as my smelly albino ass. Now, follow your path to Iolcus with my humble blessing, kind Jason. And after you're triumphant in your aspirations, and finally ascend to your high throne, please remember this wretched, decrepit, old bitch that you had carried across this fucked-up river."

The ancient-looking dame with the curved back and hunched shoulders then hobbled-off giving the youth a broad smile, and winking her large brown eyes, as if she was flirting with or favoring him. And Jason received the fanciful impression that there was something wonderfully majestic about the mysterious woman's general demeanor, despite her apparent aging handicaps, arthritis, and unsteady gait. And the old hag's peacock then fluttered-down off the woman's shoulder, spread its feathers, and exposed its tiny attractive ass specifically for Jason's attention, admiration, and approval.

When the old woman and her handsome bird were out of sight (neither of them were actually blind), Jason proceeded onward with his vital trek to Iolcus. 'My father would be generous and considerate enough to have a bridge built over that wild river,' the boy contemplated. 'But cheap parsimonious old Uncle Pelias doesn't even own a goddamned unabridged dictionary. What a waste of protoplasm that miserable son-of-a-bitch is! Wait a minute! I don't want to dishonor my damned anonymous, paternal grandmother!"

In another hour, the obstinate wanderer arrived at the outskirts of a seashore city situated at the base of a high mountain. In the distance, a huge puff of smoke was wafting skyward, and so Jason felt compelled to inquire of a stranger what large object was being burned in the distance.

"That over yonder is the city of Iolcus," a blind man answered, "and we people are the subjects and predicates of our ruler King Pelias, who is presently in the process of sacrificing a sacred bull to Poseidon, Lord of the Oceans, along with being the official area presider of all roosters, and of all the local chickens of the sea. That dark smoke your eyes perceive is rising from the city's centrally-situated public worshiping altar. Everything in the bull's body is being incinerated, even all the bulls-eyes, and all the bull-shit, too."

Another more curious stranger in the crowd eavesdropping on the hollow bull-shit conversation observed that Jason had a missing sandal, and also noticed that the lad's general apparel, featuring a leopard's skin, was quite unlike the more modest fashion trends prevalent in Iolcus. Soon, the new arrival became quite embarrassed at all the natural crowd scrutiny.

"Look at him! Stare your eyeballs upon him will ya'!" everyone began jabbering. "Do you see that he wears only one sandal? He's the dreaded man with one sandal. What does he plan to do? What pithy remarks will Pelias say to this pathetic, alien upstart?"

'These assholes must be very ill-bred to act like complete obnoxious jerk-offs, behaving so indiscreetly in public,' Jason thought as the vernal visitor hurried through the gathered throng, and soon wound-up standing near the sacrificial bull and bull-shit altar. 'Shit! The smell of that smoking bull is making me damned hungry for delicious barbecued beef.'

The crowd's noise suddenly distracted King Pelias from his official ceremonial capacity, and the tyrant turned-around with a frown upon his countenance, and the despot focused his beady pupils in the direction of Jason. But the multitude was so densely crammed around the foreign visitor that the perturbed King was presently unaware of the young man's missing sandal.

"How dare you interrupt my sacred bull being solemnly sacrificed to Lord Poseidon!" the King blatantly chastised. "Who the fuck are you that violates my time-honored ritual? What written right do you have to disturb my unwritten rite? Speak now, or forever hold your peace, and also your endangered testicles."

"Your Majesty, you must blame your rude and detestable subjects for making such a disruptive ruckus," Jason ineffectively argued. "The idiots are bickering and gossiping very loudly, just because my damned right foot happens to be bare. Is such a trivial, accidental, non-intentional matter such as a lost sandal a fuckin' egregious crime, or an unforgivable

142

indecent immorality around here? Are your subjects and predicates a bunch of mini-minded pinheads, or what?"

The despotic monarch instinctively glanced-down at Jason's walking appendages, and then predictably gasped in alarm. "Ha! You are indeed a one sandaled insolent asshole! What the fuck should I do with you?" the crimson-faced Pelias stammered as the dastardly scoundrel angrily and tightly held the bloodstained sacrificial knife in his right hand.

A murmur arose from the restless witnesses to the peculiar confrontation, and then the aforementioned wise, blind, old geezer in the crowd gleefully screamed-out, "The one-sandaled man has finally come. The remainder of the fuckin' prophecy must be fulfilled. The son of King Aeson has...." And then, quite unfortunately, the old blind prophet clutched his chest, and instantly fell dead to the ground.

Seventeen-years prior, the very revered Speaking Oak of Dodona had informed King Pelias that a man wearing only one sandal would show-up in Iolcus to remove the illegitimate monarch from dominion over the exploited citizens, subjects and predicates. And Pelias had created a royal edict that no one with only one sandal should ever appear in his midst. The regal treasury had financed thousands of pairs of sandals so that Pelias would be free to wander about his capital without dread of being assassinated by some athlete with athlete's feet, brazenly wearing insufficient footgear. And now, because of the controversial sandal incident, along with Jason's defiant attitude, wicked King Pelias had been publicly agitated and exceedingly insulted to the point of insane madness.

"My good young fellow," the pernicious, illegitimate King feigned in a much calmer voice. "You are indeed welcome to tarry in Iolcus. However, we are civilized people and not savage hunters, and we do not wear primitive garb such as leopard skins in this tranquil, peace-loving, homosexual city. Just because my' chatty subjects live in an urban area, doesn't fuckin' necessarily have to mean that the residents must act urbane. Pray tell, young pecker-head," the King chastised. "Who in their right mind educated you? Where did you receive your stinking, controlled arrogance, which is quite demonstrative and observable?"

"The profound saying is true that a leopard skin and its wearer doesn't change its or *his* spots," the proud new arrival stoutly stated. "I am Jason, and I've been faithfully instructed by the noble Chiron the Centaur, who has taught me medicine, music, horsemanship, battle combat, and how to immediately recognize dangerous jerk-offs when I encounter them!"

"I've heard of this peculiar individual Chiron, although he is definitely no pal-o-mino," Pelias answered with a lame pun. "And you, young man, had to put up with *his* fundamentalist horse-shit for a number of years, I suppose," the King further chided. "Anyway, young Jason, since you're obviously very scholarly, I have a specific philosophical question to advance. Are you willing to respond to my interrogatory?"

"I don't pretend to have mastered wisdom," Jason modestly replied. "In fact, I have yet to possess adequate knowledge in the more-simple mundane school subjects like gym and cafeteria."

The diabolical King's true intentions were to trick and then trap the gullible youth into an uncompromising situation that would ultimately cause extensive suffering and eventual destruction to Pelias's inexperienced "wet-behind-the-ears" novice rival. The monarch formed a smile upon his now florid ruddy face, and then asked his tormentor a rather poignant question.

"Intrepid Jason, what would you do if a man were out to ruin your admirable reputation, and had a mind bent on slaying you? If you were a king, Jason, what would you do within the jurisdiction of your power to fuckin' counteract and stifle the no-good bastard?"

Jason studied the evil and the malice that were being expressed upon King Pelias's broad grimace. 'I cannot tell a lie and I must exhibit good public decorum, even though I despise my mother-fuckin' uncle with an angry passion that defies description or explanation!' Jason considered. 'The son-of-a-bitch knows who the fuck I am, and is now contemplating having me publicly mortified, and then officially slain in cold blood. But I must keep my word and earnestly answer the no-good, gutless piss-head!'

"If such a persistent man bothered the hell out of me," Jason boldly-but-imprudently declared, "I would most-certainly send that annoying tormentor in quest of the legendary Golden Fleece. That almost impossible enterprise should keep my wick-dicked adversary occupied, and more-than-likely, would eventually terminate in getting the dirty, conniving prick either maimed or killed!"

King Pelias's eyes sparkled with greed and great satisfaction. "Well then, brash Asshole with the singular sandal; go and bring me back the magical Golden Fleece, since you've been so damned impetuous and outrageously *ram*bunctious."

"I shall go on this dangerous exploit," Jason answered with evident dignity. "And if I fail, that means that you, cruel Pelias, will retain your crown. But if I succeed and come back to Iolcus with the grand prize, then craven false King Pelias, you must surrender your unearned throne; your unearned wealth; your unearned scepter, and all of your 'unearned runs' to the crap-house."

"That I will gladly and voluntarily do," the prevaricating ruler sneered and vowed before his appalled and resentful subjects. "I shall meanwhile keep my extensive properties and gold coins safely in my custody, until you've satisfactorily completed your self-defined, silly, impossible escapade."

Jason left the center of the jeering throng, and sought-out the services of the world's greatest boat builder, a craftsman named Argus, who was very happy to accommodate the youth for promise of a cut of the profits in obtaining the remarkable Golden Fleece, and for one percent of Iolcus's annual taxation revenues upon Pelias's abdication from power.

"No ship of such colossal dimensions has ever been constructed," Jason marveled and confirmed to Argus. "Many timbers must he hewed, and at least six-months of time devoted to completing the massive project. But we can't sail all the way to Colchis in a chariot."

"If the crew you fuckin' assemble is as fine as this ship will be," Argus honestly remarked, "then thanks to you Jason, *my boat* will have finally come in."

Messengers were soon dispatched to every Greek city to recruit the best warriors to journey on the fabulous expedition. Only forty-nine of the bravest soldiers would be chosen for the quasi-military campaign, voyaging to the other side of the Black Sea in "the *Argo*," and the crew would be logically called "the Argonauts", named after the ship, which was named after the famous fucked-up shipbuilder, who regrettably had been named after the extremely fucked-up city of Argos.

"I'll be the fiftieth asshole Argonaut aboard the *Argo*," Jason told Argus from Argos. "I say we have a fifty-fifty chance of succeeding," the expedition leader joked. "That is, if the son-of-a-bitchin' Golden Fleece really exists, and isn't just a wild myth circulating all over the goddamned known ancient world."

"That's what makes mythology interesting," Argus blithely agreed with a wink of his right eye. "And anyway, Jason. It's really great being a character in this new myth that's being developed. I mean, who the fuck needs history when we could all fuckin' argue and debate all day long about bull-shit mythology?"

Daring and adventurous young champions from all over Greece were immediately attracted and then drawn to Iolcus, bearing bronze helmets, swords, and shields. The forty-nine best candidates were selected after competing in numerous athletic contests, and among them were the best boxers, wrestlers, mud wrestlers, javelin throwers, swimmers, pussy-lappers, and masturbators in all of *that* totally-bizarre part of the ancient world. The qualifiers eagerly climbed-up the *Argo's* gang-bang-plank, many of whom had been educated by the faggot quadruped Chiron the Centaur, who always desired being the undisputed 'Centaur' of attention while lecturing inside his dirty, stenchy, unkempt cave classroom.

Some of the Centaur's former students that were also mariners to be sailing on the *Argo* were the mighty Hercules; twin brothers Castor and

Pollux, and the legendary Theseus, who had just recently slaughtered the savage Minotaur. Other famous heroes participating on the daring mission were keen-eyed Lynceus; the noble musician Orpheus, and to appease the influential woman's rights' liberals, Jason had selected Atalanta, who had been weaned by a mountain bear, but who screwed like a mink. And so, the Argonauts would have a wonderful available piece of ass, along with great blowjobs daily to keep themselves happy and motivated on their extended, perfidious, all-encompassing quest of the renowned Golden Fleece.

The young captain appointed Tiphys to be the *Argo's* helmsman and navigator, because *he* was an amateur astronomer (well, actually a dumb-ass astrologer), who understood how zodiac constellations and certain prominent stars (except any from a distant place called *Hollywood)*, could guide the ship through even the most perilous of waters. And Lynceus had been delegated chief lookout, and was stationed at the *Argo's* prow, where the alert fellow could spot various prowlers and potential enemies a full day ahead. "I have twenty-twenty vision," Lynceus amiably informed Commander Jason. "But I have difficulty seeing more than forty fuckin' objects at a time."

The *Argo* finally embarked out to sea, amidst total apathy from the population of Iolcus, but apparent extreme joy on the part of the avaricious King Pelias. The mariner/warriors assiduously stirred their oars in unison into the harbor's deep water, and the *Argo* gently glided in the direction of the northern horizon. Pelias keenly watched the colorful spectacle occurring from a high promontory overlooking his dumpy metropolis.

'Thank Zeus that those stupid fools will never return,' the mendacious monarch reckoned. 'The *Argo's* destiny is nothing but doom and gloom. And with the vivacious broad Atalanta aboard, throw in a little womb and tomb, too! Ha, ha, ha!'

After passing through the Hellespont, the enthusiastic sailors began discussing the origin of the Golden Fleece, which had been a Boeotian ram that had transported two endangered children (way before there were any endangered animal species) over land and sea to the Kingdom of Colchis. The female rider Helle fell-off of the flying ram's back, plummeted into the sea, and as a result, the point where Helle landed became known on all ancient maps as the Hellespont. The young boy, Phrixus, was then transported safely ashore, but the incomparable flying ram became so fatigued that it died as soon as it landed.

Phrixus attempted giving the ram artificial respiration, but by accident, vomited down the benign animal's throat, thus making the poor gasping creature choke to death. The ram's fleece immediately and miraculously turned to gold, and was hung over the branch of a huge oak tree in a secret meadow. Many valiant explorers attempted forays to confiscate the resplendent fleece, but all of the sieges were in vain. No pirates or plunderers were ever capable of fleecing the Golden Fleece from Colchis.

One evening, the Argonauts were resting in their vessel near a certain unnamed island when the crew spotted another much smaller boat heading in their direction. The two sailors aboard turned-out to be exuberant princes that were then returning from Colchis back to their native land.

"The tree on which the Golden Fleece is hung is guarded by a terrible dragon that especially feasts on hunters, sailors, soldiers, and bodyguards," the first out-of-breath prince related to Jason. "And the dragon eats men raw, and especially savors the taste of blood and uncooked flesh."

"You cannot intimidate us with such fanciful bull-shit!" Jason arrogantly answered his nautical guests. "My 'comrades' and I will not turn back, even though none of us are card-carrying communists. And anyway, dear suave princes, voluptuous Atalanta eats me raw and she swallows, too, down in the *Argo's* exclusive galley lounge. The heroine must think my friggin' dick is a goddamned sperm bank!" Jason ejaculated to his thoroughly-amused and extremely effervescent listeners.

"If there's a blow-job or two waiting for me on this magnificent ship," the second foreign prince attested, "then I say fuck the fierce dragon, and put the son-of-a-bitch on hold! Who the hell wants to live a long dull boring life, and then die in a fuckin' rocking chair devoid of gratifying erections? On second thought, now exactly where's this horny, slutty, bitch Atalanta you've been fuckin' bragging so much about? Down in the galley you say?"

Two days later, King Aeetes of Colchis learned of the Argonauts arrival and anchoring in the harbor of his mostly gay and lesbian community, where many promiscuous gays had wild sex on tree limbs, and when the boughs broke, the whimsical faggots would fall. Aeetes sent for Jason, and the youthful Commander, upon initial examination, did not savor the King's stern face, which immediately reminded *him* of his cruel and brutal uncle, the deranged King Pelias of Iolcus.

"Welcome to Colchis, brave Jason," the sly King falsely flattered. "Are you on a random pleasure cruise, looking for loose women? Are you working for a map company and casually exploring the local geography? What personal pursuit has brought your ass to my peaceful court?"

"Your Benign Excellency," Jason began with an exaggerated bow. "I beg you to endorse my noble purpose in coming to Colchis. And do not worry, King Aeetes. The Argonauts are *not* here to round-up faggot homos' and lesbians that abound in your insane land in order to take the lunatics back to Greece to be our fuckin' slaves."

"Then, what exactly brings your fantastic, well-equipped fighting ship here besides the fuckin' wind and currents?" Aeetes suspiciously demanded knowing.

"Kind King," Jason politely replied after clearing his slightly-hoarse throat. "My uncle King Pelias of Iolcus has promised to relinquish his throne to me, if I'm successful in retrieving the illustrious Golden Fleece, and then taking the prize back to Greece and presenting the trophy to him. I humbly solicit your permission in repossessing the world-famous fleece, which as you know, had originated from my native land."

Now the avaricious King Aeetes valued the Golden Fleece even more than he liked kinky gay sex, and even more than the narcissistic moron appreciated four-hour-long erections. The egocentric ruler had trouble disguising the intense scowl seemingly welded upon his already ugly visage. "Jason, you conspiring, distrustful fleecer; are you aware of the dreadful conditions you must complete before ever successfully acquiring the Golden Fleece?"

"I'm fully cognizant of the legend that a carnivorous dragon guards the Golden Fleece in a remote garden or dell," the callow youth communicated. "And I most certainly am aware that I run the risk of being viciously mauled and devoured."

"I see that you've more than adequately studied our culture and customs," Aeetes falsely praised. "But before you can earn the privilege of being greedily consumed by my pet dragon, you must first tame my ferocious fire-breathing bulls that Hephaestus, lame god of *Olympus,* had personally manufactured for me in his laboratory workshop. The blacksmith god has placed a furnace inside each of their stomachs," Aeetes comprehensively explained. "And anyone who approaches either of the formidable beasts will automatically be incinerated by the fuckin' flames that spout-out from their mouths when the bulls belch and snort, and then also shoot fire out of their enormous fat asses when the animals continuously fart. Do you consider my most compelling genuine, true-story bull-shit?" Aeetes requested knowing.

"The danger of your fire-breathing bulls does indeed sound like a lot of phony bull-shit, but I comprehend that their challenge stands in the way of my next objective, which is to kill the savage dragon that guards the magnificent fleece," Jason valiantly and eloquently declared. "Therefore, I must soon satisfactorily complete my significant purpose in coming to Colchis."

"Well, Jason," the King nonchalantly continued in an effort to scare the living and dead shit out of his persistent tormentor. "After you've tamed my erratic bulls, you next are required to yoke them to a plow, and make thirteen deep furrows inside the sacred grove of Ares, *our* mutual god of war. You next must sow the teeth from the already-slain dragon in the field, and fight the armed warriors of the ancient cad Cadmus. Those immortal soldiers that shall spring-up from the sacred soil are invincible, and will ultimately defeat you and your determined Argonauts," the King stressed and snidely snickered. "Have you ever had your ass kicked before by a fuckin' crew of immortal, armed red skeletons?"

"The acclaimed pedagogue Chiron the Centaur had taught me how to fight and defend myself against even the most monstrous and aggressive enemies," Jason boasted. "And inside his cave, we weren't exactly engaged in fuckin' horseplay, either. These immortal non-comical red skeletons with limitless energy absolutely sound like worthy opponents to my well-trained and well-prepared rowdy, doughty crew of ass-kickers."

"Well, sanctimonious Prince Jason, I hope that you aren't too complaisant in rushing to judgment," King Aeetes sternly warned. "Now you and your crew of misfits make yourself comfortable and merry in my palace banquet room, for tomorrow will probably be your last stinking day on this stinkin' fucked-up planet!"

While King Aeetes was bullshitting with Jason and accurately sizing him up, a gorgeous young female was silently standing in a corner of the throne room, and sizing-up the cute bulge between the handsome Greek representative's hairy legs. The knockout girl (the only heterosexual in all of Colchis) was assessing the hero's personal equipment, and a warm, wonderful, scintillating tingle began quivering-away inside her vulnerable crotch area. And when Jason finally departed from the hard-spirited King's presence, the lonely neglected young maiden, who absolutely despised her cold-fish father, discreetly followed the ambitious hero out of the chamber, and immediately initiated a conversation.

"I am the King's only daughter, Medea," the Princess introduced herself. "But you don't have to worry because I don't belong to the Colchis mass media," Medea pathetically jested. "I'm omniscient in some respects, and as long as I remain a virgin, I'll know plenty more than the average deflowered girl does, that's for damned sure. I don't write the damned mythological laws; I only heed and obey the stupid nonsensical traditions that the mandates portend."

"Indeed Medea, if you can deftly assist me in obtaining the Golden Fleece, then you can be independent of your cold-hearted, fucked-up father, and come and live with me in beautiful downtown metropolitan Iolcus," Jason inanely maintained. "And I have a fantastic female friend named Atalanta who will teach you how to properly screw, and how to administer good head in the most correct manner. It'll be worth losing your special virgin powers that you've just alluded to."

"I know how you can tame the fire-breathing bulls, and then plant the dead dragon's teeth in order to obtain possession of the Golden Fleece," Medea intimated to her first genuine heterosexual boyfriend. "And I can't wait to have my hot honey-well explored by your eager fingers. I'm already tingling all over, and can feel my squiggly clit' button throbbing, and hungrily begging to be fondled and massaged."

'This rather strange woman, if not handled properly and delicately, could amount to a very grave threat, even more formidable than the awesome fire-breathing bulls and the sowed dragon's molars and incisors,' the Greek military expedition captain realized and concluded. 'Perhaps this attractive and vivacious bitch is also a damned dangerous witch.'

A moment's pause was broken with Jason advancing the relevant question that had been playing havoc with his unsettled mind. "Medea, are you an enchantress? You appear to have an unusual other-dimension quality about you."

"Indeed, my dear Prince Jason," Aeetes's daughter hesitantly confessed. "And the famous sorceress Circe happens to be my deranged father's sister. I can foretell the future, and I don't know exactly what it looks like, or specify what to say to it. But I can easily identify the old bitch with the obnoxious peacock, the cuckoo staff, and the pomegranate than you had conducted across the raging river that was devoid of white water rafters. And my dear Jason," Medea added, "I also know all about the damned sex games you used to play with that faggot pedophile Centaur Chiron, who had more than sufficiently corrupted your already emotionally scarred childhood through many perverted and unwarranted sexual molestations," the beautiful, virgin witch disclosed. "So, in essence jerk-weed, be careful, because I know what the hell you're thinking before you say it, and I also know what you may attempt speaking otherwise to conceal your secret thoughts and deepest motives."

"The dragon's imminent threat presently doesn't perplex me," Jason honestly admitted. "I'm now more concerned about the fire-breathing bulls that might singe my myriad pubic hairs, and start a roaring inferno in my lower pelvis, which might even then ignite the vital hair follicles in and around my tender asshole."

"When you encounter the brazen bulls, your heart will hold the appropriate solution to their savagery," Medea predicted. "But first and foremost, Jason, you must be insulated from *their* terrible fire-breathing bad breath. Both bull specimens have severely bad cases of halitosis. In *this* metal case I'm holding is a most advantageous ointment that will prevent you from being charred and scorched to embers. But be sure to rub extra amounts of the formula over your dick, balls, and ass, because if those precious organs become burned off your cute, firm, taut body, I might then lose interest in your marriage proposal. Do you read me?"

"Like a book of *Aesop's Fables*," Jason intelligently and creatively answered. "Now please hand me the metal box, and I'll generously apply the lotion in private to my privates. If I allow you to do it Medea," the abashed hero said while abundantly blushing, "then I might squirt several pounds of sperm juice all over the damned place, and immediately lose my strength because I won't have the necessary balls to tame the lousy-breathed, fire-shooting bulls."

"Here you are, my special hero," Medea declared as the princess handed her box to Jason. "I only wish that my sinister father was half as kind-hearted, courteous, considerate, sentimental, romantic, affectionate, sincere, truthful, innocent and well-endowed as you are."

"My heart shall not fail me in this monumental endeavor, except if I suddenly have a massive coronary attack," Jason cleverly conveyed to his lady admirer. "And so, Medea, just give me the time and the place where I might domesticate those ferocious bulls. In the meantime, I'll practice some shadowboxing, and pretend I'm hitting the two snorters right in the center of their bulls-eyes. Maybe it would be safer if I actually hit the nasty shits in the bulls-eyes with fuckin' arrows from my bow, rather than with my mortal clenched fists."

At midnight, steadfast Jason met and embraced Medea outside the impeccable palace garden. Then, the horny, love-blinded Princess betrayed her father and presented her new-found Greek companion with a small wicker basket.

"Here Jason, the dragon's teeth that were pulled and removed by that cad Cadmus a hundred-years-ago are in this wicker," Medea confidentially communicated. "And don't worry one iota about the damned fire-snorting bulls. Their taming will be no more difficult than pulling teeth."

Medea then led her inspired champion to the particular pasture where the fire-breathing bulls were kept, and where the beasts did all of their foul, enormous bull-shitting. The constellations were glistening in the warm summer night sky, and the moon was showing ample reflected sunlight for the two rare heterosexual conspirators to accurately survey their immediate environment.

"The deadly creatures are preoccupied crapping their hot intestines out over there," Medea indicated while pointing to her right. "Allow them to see you Jason, in order to make your impending contest a fair competition. The damned element of surprise is only for weak and wimpy cowards to employ."

"Are you crazy?" Jason shrieked while accidentally disturbing the yonder bull-shitting bulls. "Those monsters have a tremendous size advantage over me and are very experienced at instantaneously turning young men into mini-infernos! According to Lord Hephaestus, I think the scientific process is called spontaneous combustion. Exactly how many unfortunate men have perished attempting to tame those wild beasts?"

"Only several thousand or so," Medea nonchalantly replied. "But none of the idiots had the special magic ointment smeared all over their bodies like you do now. I mean, Prince Jason, I'm getting hot and tingly flashes all over, just thinking about it!"

"Your father probably declares it a holiday whenever someone gets killed trying to settle the brutes' unruly temperaments," the captain of the Argonauts discussed and conveyed to Medea a certain behavioral propensity of her father' Aeetes *he* had heard about. "I think I once read it in a *bull*etin pinned on the public *bull*etin board in the downtown marketplace back in Iolcus."

"Whatever you do, Jason, don't allow doubt to engender fear in your heart," Medea wisely advised her new champion. "Now, exhibit courage and audacity, or else you'll ultimately experience defeat and certain death."

'Maybe I should've stayed in Chiron's secluded cave and enjoyed a safe, happy lifestyle molesting the new crop of kindergarten students,' the somewhat-worried hero meditated. 'It's now time to either show fortitude and dedication, or be converted into a human-sized cinder-fella'.'

Jason kissed Medea on her rosy cheek, and then boldly approached the fire-breathing animals. Four foul streams of hot vapor were simultaneously being released into the atmosphere as if the jets had been expelled from blast furnaces, indicating that the bulls cared nothing about air pollution, or about bull-shit environmental propaganda advanced by radical left-wing liberals. Then, the hot spurts diminished and vanished, but several seconds later, the flames reappeared with even more intensity. The moments' of truth and of survival were now at hand.

"Wow, Medea! Something just occurred to me!" Jason exclaimed while turning-around and speaking to his stationary love. "If those two monsters were sleeping, I'd be slaying a couple of dozing bulls! And whoever heard of anyone, hero or otherwise, killing two bulldozers?"

As Jason approached the temporarily, apathetic, unwary bulls, the beasts were grazing-away knee deep in bull-shit. Momentarily, each began sniffing the air as a distant foreign scent became perceptible to *their* olfactory senses. And when the intrepid interloper came to within a hundred-feet of *their* presence, red hot vapors again shot out of the creatures' nostrils, and lit-up the whole damned vicinity. And when the brave hero came to within twenty-feet of the horned behemoths, sparks were flying everywhere, and four white hot jets went zipping across the pasture and set fire to trees, fences, grass, weeds, and fleeing rodents.

'Thank goodness I'm smeared like a buttered pig with Medea's secret-formula enchanted ointment,' Jason evaluated, 'or otherwise, the white-hot flames would've already made my highly cherished dick into a barbecued wiener, and my ass and asshole into smoked baked ham. I must now cautiously wait for the bulls' expected attack, and be exceptionally patient until their abominable nostrils and assholes finally run out of flames and fuel.'

Just as the snorting animals were about to gore Jason's buttocks all over the now-illuminated pasture, the dauntless hero grabbed one of the creatures by the horns with his vice-like grip, lifted the surprised animal into the air, and then flung the heavy beast directly into its now-delirious mate, with the two astonished predators incidentally goring each other with their ultra-sharp horns.

'That's how to really shoot the bull!' Jason mused. And ever since that memorable day in Colchis, and as a matter of fact, everywhere else in the whole-wide-world, the catchy phrase "taking the bull by the horns" means to abandon fear, and to overcome peril, despite the accompanying adversities and dangers that are presented by the prospective struggle.

It was no elementary task (but a real *harrowing* experience) harnessing the dazed, wounded bulls, and then yoking them to the rusty plow, but like a determined entrepreneur, Jason plowed right into the immense project. And a half hour later, the entire fallow field had been converted to furrowed black earth. Jason then effectively used the dragon's teeth from the wicker basket Medea had so helpfully provided, and quickly and randomly scattered the objects all around the plowed pasture.

'I wonder what the fuck's gonna' happen now?' Jason imagined. 'Certainly, Medea's protective ointment cannot help me against my next obstacle.' Then, the apprehensive prince decided to again consult with his new-found love. "Medea, how long will it take until harvest time for these amazing teeth-seeds? Is there sufficient time to have some kinky safe sex before the nasty warriors from the past appear?"

"A crop of tenacious soldiers will spring-up from the tilled soil very shortly before you can ever have time to achieve a full erection," Medea related in a rather disappointed and depressed tone of voice. "And the red skeleton warriors once killed by that cad Cadmus are violently relentless. Perhaps if you wear my heavy chastity belt, your personals will be spared from brutally being maligned and castrated."

After Jason planted the dreaded teeth seeds, soon, shiny bronze spear tips wormed their way above the ground under the full moon, and a moment later, brass helmets, swords, and shields sporadically penetrated up through the soil. And then, thirteen gruesome red skeletons shot-out above the surface with defiant grim expressions on their very contoured and prominent facial bones. The incredible warriors moved in exact precision and formed a military phalanx, first raising' up their shields to chest level; next lifting their swords above their heads, and then all shouting in unison "Die Asshole!" in a frightening attempt at intimidating their Greek opponent.

A moment later, the unearthly militia slowly advanced forward in very deliberate, rhythmic steps, with their grotesque bones clattering in what amounted to sensational shocking unison. "Come on Jason! Conquer us or die!" the uncanny red skeletons eerily chanted. "You can't keep your privates private from our persistent thrashing swords much longer!"

Jason held his ground with his trembling right hand brandishing his sword, such as the thespian Shake-*speare* must have dramatized on the *Globe Theater's* stage. The stressed-out lad stood there in overwhelming terror, with streams of piss and diarrhea trickling down his sweating legs.

"Guard the Golden Fleece! Don't let this ambitious prick fleece the Golden Fleece from Colchis!" the advancing vanguard all chorused together, while still moving forward in their weird, morbid, highly-animated, choreographed advance.

The trespassing Greek Prince was horrified at the satanic spectacle his eyes perceived. 'I cannot fight this vindictive superior platoon all by myself,' the young intruder logically assessed. 'I must reunite with the valiant stout-hearty Argonauts to make this a more even battle!'

"Quick Jason!" Medea implored. "Pick up a rock, and waste no time hurling it into the center of the advancing vanguard. It is your only available chance of salvation from this fucked-up, supernatural dilemma!"

Jason heeded Medea's intelligent recommendation with little time to spare. The intrepid warrior heaved a rock into the unified aggregation, and it collided with a tall red skeleton's bronze helmet. The projectile bounced-off of the helmet; hit another shorter red skeleton in the face, and then ricocheted off and impacted with a third ancient, red-boned combatant's elbow. The unexpected attack' made the red skeletons lose focus of their prime enemy, and instantaneously, the thirteen idiots began frantically quarrelling, whacking, hacking, punching, stabbing, and decapitating one another. Skeletal arms, legs, heads, torsos, pelvises, and boners were scattered all over the damned oddball combat zone.

'I suppose the best way to get ahead in this world is to become a goddamned headhunter!' Jason mused as the protagonist stooped-down and generally examined a decapitated skull. 'Oh well; savage see, savage do! Just look at those hilarious assholes feverishly punishing and re-killing each other as a result of a simple rock incident that, thanks to Medea, I had instigated!'

"Is that all you can think about after employing such a brilliant stratagem?" Medea lambasted. "I mean, give me my due credit. If it weren't for me, Jason, you'd definitely be Hades-bound right now!"

"Look Medea!" the Greek Prince appreciatively exclaimed. "I gratefully acknowledge your very helpful alliance. Thanks to your remarkable unparalleled genius, all of the antagonistic skeletons have frenetically self-destructed, and have efficiently eliminated each other from being my avowed adversaries."

"Brains,, when used cleverly, always triumph over silly brawn!" Medea philosophically answered her stunned companion. "My father's bodyguards will loyally re-bury their ancestors' remains with honors tomorrow morning. Such is the fate of simple-minded, non-thinking, compliant soldiers, who without question, obey orders that defy both reason and logic. There's more to life Jason than being, and enjoying being, a stupid pathetic fuck-head! Now, go to my father early in the morning," the pretty Princess directed, "and inform him of your success with the fire-breathing bulls and with the red skeleton fanatics. Then, King Aeetes will more-than-likely provide you with additional fucked-up instructions to follow."

At dawn, it finally dawned on Jason that the pure-hearted Commander should leave the drunken Argonauts inside the *Argo's* galley and again visit paranoid King Aeetes in his opulent palace. After entering the official greeting room, the youthful captain from afar was led to the "presence room" to present himself to the King Pelias facsimile.

"Your eyes look weary, Jason," the alarmed King Aeetes somberly began. "And you must've spent a sleepless night jerking-off and fondly dreaming of my nightmare bewitched daughter. You're probably very concerned about my fire-breathing bulls, not to mention the fearless red skeleton soldiers from antiquity. And I warn you, young brazen fool, that if you dare screw Medea, and she loses her singular virgin powers of sorcery and prophecy, then I guarantee you that the least of your hardships will be when I have the Argonauts and *your* wangolas and scrotums sliced-off and fed to my hungry, fire-snorting bulls. If you and your forty-nine assholes came here to sack Colchis," Aeetes vehemently maintained, "then I'll see to it that *your* sacs will be severed from your abdomens as my just and rightful retribution."

"I hate to inform you, Your Vile Majesty, but the tasks you've just described have already been fuckin' performed," Jason indicated with a firm voice to match his firm resolve. "The infernal inferno' bulls have been easily tamed and yoked, and your bull-shit pasture has been painstakingly plowed. Also, the dragon's teeth have been sowed, and I've seen to it that the red skeleton warriors have been soundly trounced, vanquished, and destroyed. And now, King Aeetes," Jason confidently continued, "I hereby request your imperial permission to terminate the ferocious dragon guarding under the oak tree; acquire the Golden Fleece, and abscond from Colchis with both it and your beautiful daughter."

"And you expect me to accede to *those* very unacceptable, intolerable conditions!" Aeetes hollered with visible disdain. "I only make grandiose promises so that pledged words can be broken. That spectacular Golden Fleece possesses the extraordinary ability to cure every malady, sickness, and infirmity. And Jason," the King intimated. "I desperately need the fuckin' thing so that I never ever die from venereal diseases, which for your information, I acquire quite frequently from sodomizing every male or female asshole in sight. And so, I advise you, ambitious fool, to abandon your clownish pursuit of the fleece, or risk surrendering your life to my whim."

"But you've vowed that you would surrender the Golden Fleece if and when I completed the arduous labors you had assigned!" Jason vociferously protested. "Don't you keep your word? Isn't your word your bond and seal?"

"Look, you dumb-ass idealistic imbecile!" Aeetes loudly argued and reprimanded. "Only quixotic suckers, dreamers, and losers keep their' fuckin' promises. And I am knowledgeable that Medea has meticulously assisted you in accomplishing your prodigious enterprises while employing her counsel, enchantments, and her exceptional soothsaying ability. Without her consultation and advice to you, I would now be addressing an inanimate cinder right before my eyes, and not an arrogant, callow, shallow, egotistic gullible fool."

Jason became livid at being denied his most-desired claim. The Greek hero indignantly left the deceitful King's presence, and decided to trek to the *Argo* and awaken the forty-nine drunken Argonauts, who always for some inexplicable reason, fought better when having hangovers, and consequently, hanging over the ship's gunwales and vomiting their healthy guts out. 'We'll raid the Grove of Ares en- masse; slay the maniacal dragon; pilfer the glorious Golden Fleece; kidnap Medea, and sail the fuck out of here heading for Ioclus as soon as possible,' the gallant Greek Prince methodically plotted on the way to his incomparable battleship.

As Jason was sprinting in full battle array towards the *Argo,* he by chance encountered Medea, who also had had a sleepless night thinking about betraying her rich father, and jeopardizing a lucrative inheritance for the ludicrous sake of eloping with a silly, fanciful fellow possessing an impressive firm body, and a throbbing uncircumcised manhood.

"What has my father told you?" Medea anxiously inquired. "I already know from my gift of prophecy, but I desire to hear the truth from your soft, innocent lips."

"Your superficial, selfish, contrarian father will not under any circumstances surrender the Golden Fleece, even after I've fully satisfied all of his demanding requirements," the visiting p,rince confirmed with regret. "Aeetes absolutely refuses to allow me to exterminate the gruesome dragon that guards the tree in the Grove of Ares. This Golden Fleece operation is proving to be a really *tree*-mendous challenge."

"And that's the least of your worries," Medea cried-out while embracing her hero, and feeling his semi-erect pecker rubbing against her crotch's slit', leading to the entrance of her hungry, wet, pink love tunnel. "Be sure to set sail on the *Argo* by sunrise tomorrow morning, or else my repugnant Daddy intends to burn your splendid ship to a crisp, and castrate and then decapitate you and your inebriated crew of rowdies. Now, show patience and fortitude dear Jason, and wait for me right here at midnight. I shall again utilize my enchantments to help you in your honorable and deserving quest. And furthermore," the pretty Princess austerely stipulated, "let's for now forget all about fuckin' sexual intercourse, or else you won't have any genitals to perform sex on me, or on anyone else."

After hiding out in a gay and lesbian community brothel for the next seventeen hours, Jason sauntered-out to the *Argo* to inform his mariners that the foray into the consecrated Grove of Ares was imminent. And after the benevolent and rebellious Medea joined the merry party of revelers outside the sacred Grove, the bevy (upon Jason's insistence) quietly proceeded toward the aforementioned garden where the Golden Fleece sparkled and gleamed as it remained suspended in the distance from a sturdy oak tree. The excited, half-intoxicated Argonauts surreptitiously passed the pasture of the now-dead fire-snorting bulls, where two young offspring were busy licking each other's balls and peckers, while trying to establish a new pecking order, or in this case, a new *peckering* order as the neophyte animals singed and scorched each other's reproductive organs, wildly attempting to determine territorial dominance.

The Greek pirates and Medea stealthily entered the foreboding Holy Grove of Ares, and Medea guided and escorted the entourage to the great oak tree, that for centuries, represented the home base for the miraculous Golden Fleece.

"Look over on that second very strong limb," Medea directed Jason's attention. "See that unique object glistening in the pale moonlight. That resplendent glittering article constitutes your noble quest. That priceless gift is the inimitable, timeless, Golden Fleece. Now all *you* must do to possess it is to soundly vanquish the vile, diabolical dragon."

Jason gingerly stepped closer to the pulsating phenomenon, and his amazed eyes gazed at and admired its golden grandeur. 'So many have perished and lost their lives, dicks, and balls in quest of this very magnificent *sheepskin* that should actually be conferred to me by the reluctant faculty at the prestigious *University of Colchis*,' Jason creatively imagined. 'Now it is time to purloin this treasure to finally complete my most essential mission.'

"Stay still and staunchly guard your family jewels," Medea warned her all-too-impetuous love. "Over yonder is the venomous dragon with its devastating, scaly tail coiled around the legendary oak tree. Watch that innocent antelope aimlessly that's bounding through the Grove of Ares so that you, Jason, could completely fathom the palpable danger that presently imperils you."

The unaware antelope hastened and hopped towards the alluring Golden Fleece, but then the head of the viperous protector lashed-out like a whip, and its fangs seized the unsuspecting creature, and in another minute, the formerly spry, brimming-with-life antelope was crunched in the predator's jaws, and soon mercilessly devoured in one devastating swallow.

The alert dragon perceived that other' encroaching intruders had furtively invaded its off-limits territory. The monster stretched-out its long muscular neck, with its evil mouth wide-open and featuring sharp and lethal carnivorous fangs. Soon, the dragon's main head came to within ten-feet to where Jason, Medea, and the accompanying band of drunken, petrified Argonauts were stationed, frozen, still as statues. The viper's undulating head then came wriggling and waving, and soon managed to reach within a yard of the wary trespassers, and everyone, including Jason, retreated back several feet to avoid being selected and snatched into the loathsome beast's maw.

"Well Jason," Medea remarked. "Before you shit yourself and stink up the whole Holy Grove of Ares, I want to know exactly what you think your chances are of successfully escaping with the Golden Fleece right this very second."

Jason instinctively drew his sword and raised his shield, feigning the external courage to audaciously engage in mortal combat with the formidable viper. The vernal captain's predictable impulsiveness was immediately criticized.

"Don't be absurd!" Medea sarcastically reproached her chosen hero. "Without my vital intercession and scholarly advice, you'll soon be dead meat, and your wonderful penis will cease pulsating and throbbing forever. In this tiny magic metal box is a secret potion that'll prove to be just as potent and wonderful as the hairy pink magic box between my feminine legs."

As the dragon's curious head came to within a foot of Jason and Medea, the Princess neurotically and accidentally dropped the small container onto the ground, and just as Jason was about to be plucked-up and voraciously chewed to tiny bits and morsels, Castor (Pollux's twin brother and certainly one of the more fucked-up Argonauts) came rushing forward and risked his life, tossing a gallon of his home-made Castor Oil into the throat of the repulsive, hissing monster. The foul-tasting, sticky substance initially tranquilized, and then moments later, incapacitated the villainous dragon, which in a matter of thirty additional seconds, collapsed to the ground with a loud thud. But luckily for Castor, the clever chemist had not strained-out the poisonous seeds from the castor plant while producing the Castor Oil, and so, the dragon soon died from an overdose of lethal food.

"That was great quick thinking!" Jason complimented Castor in the midst of boisterous jeering from the still-drunken but very impressed Argonauts. "And it's a good thing neither I nor my crew ever sampled any of your fucked-up liquid experiment. I'd rather drink twenty-gallons of smelly cat piss than a single ounce of that fucked-up Castor Oil."

"My next project, Jason, will entail designing four sets of very sturdy Castor Wheels to serve as rollers to drag or pull a gigantic wooden horse I've been often dreaming nightly about," the imaginative Argonaut revealed. "You never know when an enormous wooden horse needs to be moved to a city's gates in a fuckin' hurry!"

Now, as to why Jason is credited for the heroic deed of killing the terrible dragon is to this day incomprehensible to this writer, and the story directly contradicts *his* tedious impeccable research, for certainly the great achievement ought to be rightfully attributed to the drunken imbecile Castor, who is incidentally discriminated against and despised by every biased chronicler, and by every prejudiced historian who absolutely and positively abhors the lousy, sticky, pungent taste of Castor Oil.

Everyone in the Greek marauding contingent indulgently laughed at Castor's zany description of his next impractical objective. Then, Jason attempted bringing all his crew back to reality by stating something quite rational and plausible.

"Men, let us now possess the Golden Fleece and hightail it the fuck outa' here while we can still piss and shit. King Aeetes plans to burn the *Argo,* with or without us in it," the ship's captain instructed his half-intoxicated crewmen. "And confidentially, my fellow mariners. I've learned from a perfectly reliable source that the dirty bastard has malicious designs of severing our balls and our peckers, too, without even giving us any fuckin' severance pay. So, without articulating any further 'adieu', my sailing companions, let's exhibit alert dispatch, and swiftly sprint our sweaty asses back to the *Argo*."

Jason stood on Castor's broad shoulders, and gently removed the Golden Fleece from its traditional perch. And when the outstanding hero jumped-down to ground level clutching his exceptional prize, some sensation compelled the doughty prince to turn his head to the right, where Jason beheld an old wretched hag holding a cuckoo-headed brown staff, and sporting a peacock sitting motionless upon her right shoulder. Then, the old bag yelled for Jason to immediately return to Iolcus, clapped her hands, and impressively transformed into the beautiful goddess Hera. And in an instant, Zeus's fickle wife gleefully vanished into the atmosphere that surrounded her temporary, majestic presence.

The fifty-one jubilant participants dashed the full mile back to the *Argo,* and without wasting any additional valuable time, the ship's anchor was swiftly hoisted, and soon the sleek state-of-the-art vessel was sailing out of Colchis's narrow harbor and into the deep blue sea. In another five-minutes, the *Argo* was out of harm's way, and was safely being maneuvered by the inebriated mariners back and forth across the Black Sea, until the cheerful crew all finally sobered-up twenty-four hours later, and then finally navigated a straight course to fucked-up Iolcus.

"Pelias will shit himself when he sees me returning with the coveted Golden Fleece," Jason told Medea. "I have, with your illustrious aid, performed the impossible! Now let's get laid while I still have energy enough to grow a decent erection!"

"Just like my ruthless father King Aeetes has already done," the astute prophetess Medea obtusely verified. "As everyone presently knows, 'Birds of a feather often shit together', or more specifically, the flying creatures simply often bombard their droppings at the same time in different places, as is the remarkable case of sullen King Pelias of Iolcus and the dastardly King Aeetes of Colchis."

160

"The Great Carbuncle"

At nightfall, once in the olden time, no one else but me remembers or even cares about, on the rugged side of one of the Crystal Hills, a party of "seeing red adventurers" was gulping-down hard whiskey after a toilsome and fruitless one-week quest in search of the Great Carbuncle, a famous, ruby-red, prodigious gemstone reportedly shaped exactly like a giant foot bunion. The greedy individuals in quest of the legendary giant mineral had trekked to that remote hinterland, arriving in that desolate place not as friends, nor as partners in the wild enterprise, but solely for one purpose. The wannabe' tycoons were obsessed, and greatly compelled, by a selfish and solitary longing to obtain possession of that rather fabled, wondrous red gem.

Their feeling of brotherhood, however, even though one of the scouting party was a scrawny female, was strong enough to induce each rival to contribute a mutual aid in building a rude hut of flimsy branches, and next participate in kindling a great fire composed of shattered dried pines, that had in the recent past, drifted-down the headlong current of the Amonoosuck, on the lower bank of which the melancholy prospectors were scheduled to pass the night, while also passing an abundance of intestinal gas.

One of their number happened to be a veritable shit-head, who had become so estranged from natural sympathies that the emaciated varmint didn't give a crap about anyone, or anything, except the highly-sought-after Great Carbuncle. A vast extent of wilderness lay between the campers and the nearest settlement, which of course was occupied by parasitic lawyers, pimps, politicians and judges.

The roar of the Amonoosuck (which really sucked) would have been too awful for human endurance, while the cascading mountain stream seemed to speak with the wind in fucked-up sinister sounds that made everyone around the blazing campfire constantly and egregiously fart without hardly ever eating or drinking anything.

The competing adventurers, therefore, exchanged somewhat hospitable, civilized greetings, and welcomed one another to the hastily constructed primitive hut, where each prospector was the host (for vicious mosquito and green-headed fly attacks), and all present around the raging fire were the mutual guests of the whole cordially-fake company of selfish competitors.

The new arrivals spread their separate supplies of food upon the flat surface of an enormous rock, and together the fools partook of a general repast. A sentiment of good fellowship was perceptible among the fatigued party, though repressed by the idea that the renewed search for the Great Carbuncle must make the contesting campers separate strangers again in the morning.

Seven resolute men and one young, gaunt-faced, long-haired female warmed themselves together around the roaring fire, which extended its bright wall along the whole front of their improvised wigwam. That night, the six men had forgotten all about their pursuit of the Great Carbuncle, and desired some sexual action with the only woman on the quest, but since she was so skinny and naive, the horny critters soon focused their minds' attention on gaining some much-needed sleep.

The eldest of the group, a tall, lean, weather-beaten, veteran hunter, some sixty-years of age, was clad in the skins of wild animals, whose fashion of dress he excelled in imitating. The forest deer, the timber wolf, and the black bear had long been this moron's most intimate companions. This same old codger from Cleveland was one of those ill-fated mortals, such as the local Indians told of, and often epitomized. All who visited that region knew this particular asshole as "the Seeker", and by no other name except perhaps "the Searcher".

As no one sitting around the campfire could remember when the whiskerando first took-up the gemstone search, there then developed a fable in that section of the valley of the Saco, that for *his* inordinate lust in pursuit of the Great Carbuncle, the dumb-fuck itinerant Seeker had been condemned to wander among the perilous mountains until the end of time, still with the same feverish hopes at sunrise matching the same depressing despair at evening's dusk, all naked ambitions dominating the greedy Searcher's obsessed soul.

Next to the miserable Seeker sat a short-legged, elderly personage, who was wearing a high-crowned hat, and just like his oddly-formed head, the headdress was shaped somewhat like a crucible. This loner was from beyond the sea, a certain Doctor Cacaphodel, who had delusionally believed and insisted that he truly was imperial King Tut reincarnated.

Dr. C. had somehow wilted and dried himself into a facsimile mummy by continually stooping-over charcoal furnaces for four consecutive decades. The dumb-fuck nutcase spent years inhaling unwholesome fumes during his non-productive researches into chemistry and alchemy.

Many wild stories had been told of this oddball fellow Dr. Cacaphodel. One interesting anecdote claimed that the strange jerk-off had graduated from Dartmouth with darts in his mouth, whether true or not, and immediately after that prestigious college commencement, Dr. C. began the commencement of his totally bizarre experimental studies. Later that year, the stupid fool had drained his body of all its richest blood, and wasted it, with other inestimable ingredients, in futilely performing an unsuccessful science investigation. And the freakish shit-head had never been a mentally or physically healthy human, ever since attempting his vain (vein) demonstration.

Another of the intrepid adventurers was Master Ichabod Pigsnort, a weighty, corpulent merchant and selectman of Boston who indeed, as his name suggested, possessed an icky bod. At a young age, Pigsnort had become an elder of the famous Mr. Norton's church, located downtown on Synagogue Street. The dishonorable asshole's numerous enemies had fabricated a ridiculous story describing that Master Pigsnort was accustomed to spending a whole hour after prayer time, every morning and evening, in wallowing-around naked among an immense quantity of sticky pine-tree cones, which Pigsnort eventually sold in order to purchase his wife's sow-looking girlfriend an inexpensive Douglas fir.

. The fourth adventurer to that section of the New England White Mountains had no name or birth certificate that his companions knew of, and was chiefly distinguished by a sneer that always contorted his rather thin visage. The anonymous dumb-shit designated as Mr. No Name #1, or more specifically, 'the Cynic', was distinguishable by a massive pair of square-framed spectacles, which were supposed to deform and discolor the whole face of nature; that is, corresponding to this ridiculous gentleman's fantastically faulty perception.

The fifth mountain explorer likewise at first lacked a name and was appropriately labeled by the others as Mr. No Name #2. This *appellation* was the greater pity, since Mr. No Name #2 appeared to be a pathetic poet coming from a certain *Appalachian* district of New England. "The Poet" was a bright-eyed, middle-aged weirdo whom his colleagues participating in the zany expedition believed maintained an ordinary diet of "fog, morning mist, and a slice of the densest cloud". Every morning "the Preposterous Poet" would awaken with a clear mind and tell the remainder of his company, "Okay fellow assholes; let's get the fog outa' here!"

The sixth psycho of the heterogeneous party was a youthful, effeminate man of haughty mien, and this impostor sat somewhat apart from the rest. The pretender was wearing his plumed hat loftily among his elders, while the fire glittered upon the rich, gaudy embroidery of his feminine apparel. This perverted cross-dresser was none-other-than the fucked-up Lord de Vere, a Frenchman who when at home, was said to spend much of his time inside the burial vault of his dead progenitors, rummaging like an obsessed maniac through their moldy coffins to bone-up on his bizarre fantasies. The disheveled dip-shit was always in search of all the earthly pride and vanity that had been hidden among the decaying bones and dust.

Lastly among the assembled degenerates was a handsome youth clad in rustic garb, and by his side a blooming little female from

Bloomingdale, New Jersey. Her name was Hannah, and her husband's formal designation Matthew. The married idealistic misfits seemed strangely out of place among the whimsical, avaricious fraternity whose total wits had been set agog by the prospect of unilaterally discovering and possessing the Great Carbuncle.

Beneath the shelter of the one and only makeshift hut, sitting near the bright blaze of the same fire, and looking like Indian campfire girls mostly dressed as men, sat this varied group of fucked-up adventurers, with all their energies so intent upon finding a single object, namely the Great Carbuncle. Quite naturally however, several related eccentric circumstances had brought the explorers all mutually traveling to the same desolate New England region.

Dr. Cacaphodel had attentively listened to a traveler's tale of this marvelous red stone in his own distant country. Cacaphodelphia, the chicken and rooster veterinarian turned red gem prospector, had immediately been seized with such a thirst for beholding the fabled red ruby stone as could only be quenched by his capturing its most intense, priceless luster and profitability.

Mr. Ichabod Pigsnort had imagined that he had seen the Great Carbuncle while once being lost with his Uncle Hogshead Pigsnort, a senile, unreliable asylum patient who immediately verified the boar-faced gentleman's fanciful account. After imbibing a gallon of scotch whiskey, and then witnessing the blazing gemstone glaring far out at sea, Pigsnort had felt no rest in all the intervening years, up until now, to frantically initiate his desperate search for fame and fortune.

Our next foolhardy subject, Mr. No Name #1, also referred to as "The Cynic", once being encamped on a hunting expedition a full forty-miles south of the White Mountains, awoke at midnight and beheld the Great Carbuncle gleaming like a blazing meteor in the westward direction of the Green Mountains, so that the shadows of the distant green trees rendered the appearance of being white.

The aforementioned covetous nut-jobs sat in an irregular circle around the campfire, and spoke of the innumerable unsuccessful attempts which had been made to reach the "precise magical spot", its source a brilliant majestic light that overpowered the moon, and almost matched the sun's noon radiance.

Each imbecile smiled scornfully at the madness of every other singular campfire anecdote being revealed, with each dumb-ass sitting in the cold wet mud anticipating better fortune than that experienced in the past by other past frustrated dreamers, yet every ignoramus sitting and listening to another's exaggerated bull-shit automatically nourished a scarcely-hidden conviction that he would himself (masculine by preference here) be the Devil's favored one to ultimately discover the illustrious Great Carbuncle.

As if to allay their too sanguine hopes, the garrulous prevaricators orally reviewed the absurd Indian superstitions which claimed that a "Great Spirit" kept watch over the elusive gem, and the "Wandering Ghost" cunningly bewildered and distracted those who sought the magnificent gemstone. The phantom Indian Spirit would coyly move the precious jewel from peak to peak of the higher hills, or in another scenario, the "supernatural trickster spirit" would deceptively summon a dense mist from the legendary local Enchanted Lake over which the Great Carbuncle presumably hung. But those fucked-up explanatory tales were deemed unworthy of credit by each Doubting Thomas uncomfortably seated in the wet mud around the blazing White Mountain campfire.

In a pause during the preposterous conversation, the wearer of the large spectacles, Mr. No Name #1, amused himself by looking-around upon the gathered party, making each individual, in turn, the object of the sneer which invariably dwelt upon his countenance. Then, the envious Cynic felt compelled to speak.

"So, fellow pilgrims," prefaced the condescending asshole. "Here we are, seven wise men, and one fairly common damsel with tiny tits, who doubtless, is as wise as any farting graybeard in our entire fucked-up company. Yes, fellow greedy bastards, here we are, I say, all bound looking for glory on the same goodly enterprise."

"Look here, just a minute Pilgrim," one of the searchers, Dr. Cacaphodel, instinctively challenged. "What the hell are ya' tryin' to say? I mean, you don't even know your fuckin' name!"

"Methinks, now," resumed Mr. No Name #1, "it would not be amiss that each of us declares what he proposes to do with the Great Carbuncle, provided he has the good fortune to discover and selfishly clutch the renowned jewel. What says our grizzly friend sporting the bear skin? Good Sir Seeker, how do you intend to enjoy the prize which you've been relentlessly pursuing, only you and the Lord knows for how long, trekking your grimy ass all over among the historic Crystal Hills?"

"How should I enjoy it?" bitterly exclaimed the aged Seeker. "I can't have sex with the gem because my limp dick no longer gets even semi-hard! And I hope for no affectionate enjoyment from it, so I won't be romancing the stone; *that* illogical folly has passed long ago! I just want to marvel at its magnificent appearance, and on my deathbed, sell the red stone for a huge sum of money!"

"Ruby, Ruby, Ruby will you be mine, all the time!" satirically sang Dr. Cacaphodel. "Now, I'm the type of guy, who likes to fool around!

Ha, ha, ha! Continue with your lackluster litany, will you Senor Searcher! Ha, ha, ha!"

"Truthfully," the disingenuous Seeker resumed his devious narrative, "I persist in keeping-up the search for this accursed Great Carbuncle because the self-centered ambition of my youth has become a fate upon me in my advanced old age. The thrill of the pursuit alone is my strength to carry on. The arduous quest represents the pure energy of my soul; the warmth of my blood, and the pith and marrow of my decrepit bones! For Gentlemen and Young Lady, I do believe that if I find and own the stone, a miracle will occur, and my limp dick will remain hard until the day I die, even when I take a piss."

"Well, I must confess that my real name is Mr. Charles Paul," Mr. No Name #1 piped-up and contributed to the unrealistic campfire conversation. "And so," the facetious fool proceeded with his suspect commentary, "when I exclusively locate the sought-after gemstone, the Great Carbuncle will be known throughout the civilized world as Mr. Paul's Bunion, ha, ha, ha!"

The Poet, formerly Mr. No Name #2, was then inspired to make a valid criticism directed toward Mr. Charles Paul, formerly Mr. No Name #1, or also the Cynic. "You indeed have the brain of an onion, Mr. Paul Bunion. Your words are corny and not worth repeating, but not quite as corny as your corny feet. So Mr. Charles Paul, you have plenty of gall, and I'll be a monkey's uncle if you're the first to find the singular Carbuncle!"

"What wretched bull-shit you dare utter, Pathetic Poet!" Doctor Cacaphodel objected and protested with philosophic indignation, in defense of the tongue-tied Cynic. "Thou, unsophisticated Poet; you are not worthy to behold the Gem, even from afar. Your beady eyes are incapable of perceiving the genuine luster of that most precious red stone that ever had been concocted in Nature's experimental laboratory. Mine is the sole purpose for which a wise man may desire the possession of the colossal Great Carbuncle. Ruby, ruby; ruby will you be mine!" Dr. Cacaphodel sang.

"Look, Buster, I'm more entitled to the luster," the disgruntled Poet answered and countered. "You, Dr. Cacaphodel, are the fool, *forever* seeking the elusive jewel! So, the next time you sit on your throne, look-down at your shit and pretend that's the stone! And if perchance your bowels can't pass, it's simply because you always speak out of your ass!"

But Dr. C. was not deterred by the Poet's sharp insults. "Immediately, upon obtaining the gem treasure, I shall promptly return to Europe, and after arriving, I'll employ my remaining years in reducing the acquired treasure to its basic mineral elements," Dr. Cacaphobel predicted.

"But breaking-up is so hard to do!" deliberately sang Mr. Pigsnort in impersonation of Dr. C. "I'll bust your stones before you'll ever have the opportunity to meticulously break and examine the legendary gigantic Carbuncle stone."

"But Dr. Cacaphodel's feathers were not the least bit ruffled by Mr. Ichabod Pigsnort's humiliating remarks. "A portion of the stone I shall grind into impalpable powder, but not into gunpowder nor talc; other parts of the majestic composition shall be dissolved in acids, or whatever solvents will act upon so admirable a precious mineral; and the remainder," the boring bull-shitter paused and emphasized, "I'll utilize the rest to melt inside a crucible, or I'll set the remainder on fire with the blow-pipe I had possessed after defeating a formidable African warrior in a past life-or-death, hand-to-hand combat situation. By these various methods," Dr. C. summarized, "I shall gain an accurate analysis, and finally, I'll proudly bestow the results of my labors upon the world, all documented in a massive folio volume, just to break everybody's balls through my clever taunting of their sheer jealousies."

"Excellent nonsense!" exclaimed the former No Name Man #1 with the square-framed spectacles. "Nor, Mr. Charles Paul emphasized, "need you hesitate one scintilla Dr. Cacaphodel, academically deficient sir, on account of your necessary destruction of the most coveted gemstone; since the perusal of your folio may teach every mother's silly-assed, delusional son to concoct an artificial fake Great Carbuncle of his own dumb-ass mineral backyard treasure quest, ha, ha ha."

"But, verily," Master Ichabod Pigsnort interrupted to change the central subject from Dr. Cacaphodel to himself. "For mine own part, I strongly object to the making of these stupid-shit counterfeit mini-gems, as being calculated to reduce the marketable value of the original true whole Carbuncle. I'll be frank, sirs, although my name is Ichabod. I have an expressed interest in keeping-up the giant ruby's price. I've come here and relinquished my regular business habits, leaving my warehouse in the care of my unscrupulous felonious clerks, and putting my credit to great hazard, and furthermore, having put myself in great peril of death or captivity by the accursed local heathen, testicle-swallowing savages."

"Do you possess a Christian bias against Indian tribes and their diatribes?" an amused Dr. Cacaphodel jested to Mr. Pigsnort. "I believe you to be more of a savage than any Cleveland Indian or Washington Redskin!"

Mr. Ichabod Pigsnort ignored his colleague's obnoxious criticisms, and much to his credit and perseverance, stayed on subject. "And all this frivolous nonsense I've just convincingly mentioned is occurring without me ever daring to ask the ineffective prayers and impotent blessings of my mosque's congregation. Indeed fellow Assholes, the quest for the

Great Carbuncle is deemed little better than encountering a traffic collision with the Evil One. Now think ye now, you cantankerous assembled masturbators, that I would've done this totally grievous wrong to endanger my soul; to my body; to my reputation, and to my expansive estate without a reasonable chance of achieving tremendous profit? I maintain that for me to acquire the Great Carbuncle is indeed, a noble and meritorious goal"

"Not I, pious Master Pigsnort," commented the former No Name Man #1 with the spectacular square-framed spectacles. "I, the inimitable Cynic, also known as Mr. Charles Paul, have never laid and ascribed such a great folly to thy testified motivation. I figured that if you, Mr. Pigsnort, wished to be a donkey dick instead of a horse's ass, then I suggest that you go right the fuck ahead with achieving your fantasy fiasco!"

"Truly, I hope not," the lazy merchant challenged, turning his direction to gay Lord De Vere, who was the owner of a chain of bankrupt Gaylord Hotels all over the African Congo. "Now, as far as me ever touching and pilfering from Nature this fantastic Great Carbuncle, I admit that I've never had a mere glimpse of the gigantic gem; but be it only the hundredth part so bright as you disingenuous liars tell me it is, the Ruby Carbuncle will surely out-value the Great Chinese Mogul's best diamond, including his immense baseball-shaped diamond, which the temperamental tyrant holds at an incalculable sum."

"So, what would you do with the precious gem should you claim it as your property?" the normally reticent Seeker asked Lord De Vere. "Would you stick the Carbuncle up your smelly gay asshole and have your male lover sodomize it up to your esophagus with his huge, lengthy dick-stick?"

"Stop being so goddamned ludicrous and insensitive!" Lord De Vere reprimanded the salacious Seeker. "Cease slandering me in this irrational, asinine campfire séance! Despite the fact that I'm sitting-down in this soggy mud puddle, I'm inclined to put the retrieved Great Carbuncle on shipboard, and voyage with it to England, France, Spain, Italy, or into Arab Heathendom, if Providence should send me thither. Using my business acumen," De Vere pontificated, "I'll dispose of the wondrous gemstone to the best bidder among the envious incontinent potentates of the Earth's continents, and I suspect that the successful auction winner may place the Ruby Carbuncle among his most-guarded crown jewels. If any of ye have a wiser plan than mine, let the fucked-up ingrate expound it right this minute."

"That have I, without an infection in my eyes, Lord De Vere, you sordid faggot. Yes, I have a better gem plan to describe, you' mangy maggot!" the argumentative Poet exclaimed. "Do you desire nothing brighter than gold, from the Earth so cold, that thou wouldst transmute, into thy loot, all this ethereal luster, from your windbag bluster, into such dross, just to show us you're the boss! As for myself, in pursuit of my' wealth, hiding the jewel, not like a fool, under my cloak, will be no fuckin' joke. I shall speed me to my attic chamber, to show the world I am a gamer, yes, well-done bound, somewhere around London Town. There, night and day, will I stay, gazing upon it, with no time to shit; my soul, its radiance shall drink, until my ass is tickled pink. And throughout the day's twenty-four hours, it shall be diffused throughout my powers, and gleam brightly ever rosy, in every line of dumb-ass poesy. Thus, long ages after I am gone, the splendor of the Great Carbuncle will linger on!"

"Well spoken, Master Poet!" bespectacled former No Name Man #1 commended. "Hide it under thy threadbare cloak, sayest thou? Why, it will gleam through the myriad holes, and make thee look like a jerk-off jack-o'-lantern! You're a rather strange Poet indeed," the Cynic, Mr. Charles Paul, added. "Most others of your unorthodox ilk write words in verse, but quite ironically, you speak words in verse! How perverse! How fuckin' diverse, too!"

"To think!" ejaculated (here: verbally) the faggot Lord de Vere, mumbling rather to himself than addressing his self-important companions, the best of whom the Frenchman held utterly unworthy of his gay-minded intercourse. "Yes, to think that a rhyming fellow in a tattered cloak should arrogantly talk of conveying the Great Carbuncle to a garret in London's Grub Street! Have not I resolved within myself that the whole Earth contains no fitter ornament for the great hall of my imaginary ancestral castle?"

"You happen to be full of shit, even more so than the entire London sewer system," Dr. Cacaphodel alleged to Lord De Vere in defense of the forgetful Poet. "Now, Mr. Windbag, kindly finish with your implausible oratory so that I may be bored by someone else."

"Here in these White Mountains shall the Carbuncle flame for ages, making a noonday of midnight," Lord De Vere described his implausible illusion. "The stone glittering on the suits of armor, upon the many banners and invaluable tapestries that hang upon my castle hall's walls, and all keeping bright the superb memory of valiant heroes of the past. Wherefore, have all other previous adventurers sought the elusive prize in vain, but that I might win it, and make it a symbol of the glories of my noble family's lofty and notorious incestual line? And never, on the diadem of the glorious White Mountains, did the Great Carbuncle hold a place half so honored as is reserved for it in the main hall of the gay LBGT De Veres' dynasty! Most definitely, *we* are the champions, of the world!"

"Your boasts, Lord De Vere, are ignoble thoughts worthy of immediate disposal and condemnation," evaluated and claimed the hypocritical Seeker, with an obsequious sneer. "Yet, might I presume to say so, that the gleaming gem would make for yourself Lord De Vere a fine rare sepulchral lamp. Indeed, the stunning jewel would display the glories of your lordship's progenitors more truly when safely buried inside the family's imaginary ancestral vault. The Great Carbuncle will never be exhibited inside your silly, pretentious castle. Dissemble all you want, my gay Lord! Dissemble all you want! You, faggot fruitcake, Lord De Vere, are nothing more than the most accomplished asshole champion of the world!"

"Nay, forsooth," observed and responded normally-tranquil and laconic Matthew, the young rustic who had quietly sat hand in hand with his bony, flat-chested, twelve-year-old bride. "The Lordly gentleman has bethought himself of a profitable use for this much sought-after bright red stone. Hannah here, and I, are seeking the fabulous Great Carbuncle for a major purpose of which I cannot presently seem to recollect."

"How, craven Fellow?" his French Lordship exclaimed, in heightened surprise. "Matthew, are you briefly suffering from deep amnesia? Do you remember where your asshole is? Can you recollect where your toddler wife's asshole is? Do either of you' two numbskull juveniles use toilet paper? Tell me Matthew," Lord De Vere persisted in his derision. "What castle or resplendent palace hall hast thou in which to hang the fascinating ruby?"

"No castle or palace," Matthew lowly and humbly replied. "But instead, it'll be exhibited inside as neat a cottage as any within sight of the Crystal Hills. Ye must know, Friends, that Hannah and I, being wedded just the last week by a charlatan Salem witch, have taken-up the search of the Great Carbuncle, simply because we shall need its intense light in the long winter evenings to find comfort with each other. And it'll be such a pretty thing to show the horny, kinky neighbors when the buffoons visit us for foursomes and for six-somes. The Great Carbuncle will shine through our New England cottage so that we may pick-up a pin in any corner to have pin-demonium happen in every room. And the famous gem will set all the windows aglow, as if there were a great fire of corpulent corpses burning inside the dainty cottage's stone chimney crematorium. And then, how pleasant it will be, when we awake in the night to be able to see each other's faces and reproductive organs too, all six of us assholes marveling simultaneously! I can't wait to obtain that most essential gemstone!"

There was a general mass smiling evident among the humored listening adventurers, the collective grins directed at the simplicity of the young couple's simple desired usage in regard to the wondrous and invaluable stone, with which the greatest monarch on Earth might have been proud to adorn his dank palace's stone dungeon wall. Especially former No Name Man #1 with the square-framed spectacles, who had deliberately sneered at the whole company during the entire absurd and lackluster discussion. Now, Mr. Charles Paul twisted his cynical visage into such an expression of ill-natured mirth that Matthew then rather peevishly asked the sardonic agnostic exactly what the sarcastic jerk-off meant to do should *he* possess the Great Carbuncle.

"The Great Carbuncle!" the Chronic Cynic exclaimed, expressing ineffable scorn. "Why, you stupid-shit blockhead; there is no such thing in rerum natura. I've traveled three-thousand-miles to arrive here at this forsaken White Mountain destination, and I'm resolved to set my foot on every slippery peak of these steep hills, and then poke my head into every chasm; into each and every Indian female crack included, for the sole purpose of demonstrating to my satisfaction that the Great Carbuncle is all a totally major fraudulent humbug."

Vain and foolish were the motives that had brought most of the fucked-up adventurers to the remote Crystal Hills; but none so vain, so foolish, and so impious too, as that of the belligerent scoffer wearing the prodigious square-framed spectacles. The Cynic was one of those wretched and evil men whose dark yearnings are totally veiled in secrecy. As the petulant Mr. Charles Paul spoke, several members of the party were startled and distracted by a gleam of red splendor that showed and accentuated the huge shapes of the surrounding mountains, and also the rocky bed of the raging river, the roaring stream reflecting an illumination unlike that of their own raging campfire, bouncing-off the trunks and off the black boughs of the nearby forest trees.

The other daydreaming sitters and squatters of the disorganized expedition listened for the roll of thunder, but their vigilant ears heard nothing, and all were glad when each one recognized that the turbulent atmospheric tempest came not near the general vicinity. The stars, those conspicuous astrological dial points of Heaven, now warned the prospective prospectors to close their eyes to the blazing logs and branches, and then open them, in marvelous dreams, visualizing the mental glow of their transfixed brains, wondrously contemplating yonder Great Carbuncle coming to life.

Later that night, the young married couple had taken their lodging in the farthest corner of the group's rudely-constructed wigwam, and the pair was separated from the rest of the party by a curtain of curiously-woven twigs, such as might have hung, in deep festoons, around the bridal-bower of the late Sam and Janet Evening.

The modest little wife had wrought this odd piece of forest tapestry, while the other guests had been preoccupied bullshitting a lot of bunk about the Great Carbuncle legend. Hannah and her husband Matthew soon fell asleep upon the cold ground with their hands tenderly clasped. The infatuated dreamers awoke at the same instant, and with two happy smiles beaming upon their dual faces, the bride and groom remarkably experienced separate orgasms without ever having rudimentary sex. But no sooner did Hannah recollect where she and Matthew were, that the bride peeped through the narrow slits of the leafy curtain, and noticed that the outer room of the hut was then deserted.

"Up, dear Matthew!" the girl bride cried in haste. "The strange folks, our companions, are all gone! The hut has been abandoned except for us! Up, this very minute, or we shall lose the Great Carbuncle to oddballs even stranger than we are!"

"Holy Hannah! What did you say?" Matthew exclaimed. "I was dreaming about my brothers Mark, Luke and John, and that's the damned gospel truth. Why the hell I had an orgasm with all this sticky stuff over my underwear is indeed a Biblical New Testament mystery! Maybe I'm a faggot like Lord De Vere after all! Better yet, perhaps I'm a born again bisexual!"

"You're a real gem, Matthew," Hannah verified. "But not nearly enough of a gem like the legendary Great Carbuncle is."

In truth, those two poor young souls gazed outside the crudely fabricated wigwam and peered-upon the vague summits of the distant hills, which were presently glittering with that morning's welcoming sun rays. Meanwhile, the other demented adventurers had dreamed of climbing the nearby mineral-rich precipices, and the deserters had intrepidly set-off to realize their mutual fanciful dreams with the earliest appearance of dawn.

But Matthew and Hannah, after arising from their restive slumbers, were as light as two young deer, and the twosome merely stopped to say their morning prayers and wash their faces in a cold pool of the Amonoosuck, and then eagerly taste a morsel of food, ere they turned their faces to the yonder mountain-side.

The folly-oriented sweethearts next toiled up the difficult ascent, gathering strength from their mutual aid and encouragement, which the pair afforded each other. After several slipping and falling accidents, such as a torn robe, a lost shoe, and the entanglement of Hannah's eight-foot-length of hair in a coniferous tree bough, the whimsical lovebirds reached the upper verge of the forest, and were soon faced with pursuing a much more arduous course.

The newlyweds glanced-back at the obscure taiga wilderness which the pair had recently traversed, and now longed to be buried again in its depths, rather than trust undependable fate in their being active participants in so vast and visible a solitude that characterized their planned ascent. Each was independently thinking, 'What the fuck am I doing here?'

"Shall we go on?" Matthew asked, looking upward and throwing his right arm around Hannah's slim waist, both to protect her and to comfort his heart by drawing her closer to it. "I'm used to hairy situations!" the young husband insisted as he latched onto his wife's eight-foot-long shaggy mane.

But the little greedy bride was more than a little greedy, as simple as she was in *that* demanding, uphill situation. Hannah had a woman's love of sparkling jewels, and the girl could not forego the hope of possessing the very brightest gemstone prize in the world, in obvious spite of the serious perils with which the trophy might be won.

"Let us climb a little higher," Hannah suggested, yet tremulously, as she turned her face upward toward the lonely sky while clutching her long mane, which the girl/bride then wrapped-around her waist as an improvised belt. "I feel like I'm your special pony, because I'm a little hoarse now!"

"Come, then my Sweetness," Matthew sternly ordered, mustering his manly courage and drawing Hannah alongside, for his runaway child/bride became timid again at the precise moment that he had grown bolder and fresher.

And upward accordingly clambered the two naïve, obdurate pilgrims in quest of the fabled Great Carbuncle. Their boots were now treading-upon the tops of slick rocks, along with thickly-interwoven branches of snow-white dwarf pines, which, by the growth of centuries, though mossy with age, had barely reached three-feet in height.

Next, the fantasy-minded duo's path arrived at masses and fragments of naked rock heaped confusedly together, suggesting to the husband's fertile mind that this was an omen that Hannah and he were entering into 'a heap of trouble". In this bleak realm of upper-level air, nothing breathed; nothing grew; indeed, nothing mattered except the perilous quest for the Great Carbuncle.

Dense and dark, the swirling mists began gathering in the inviting valley below, casting black spots upon the vast hostile landscape. And soon, the shadows were mystically sailing heavily into one center, as if the loftiest mountain peak had magnetically summoned a council of its kindred clouds. Finally, the random vapors seemingly welded themselves together, as it were, into a thick dismal mass, presenting the appearance of a pavement over which the dual wanderers might have recently trodden to the mountain's base.

And at that juncture, the gullible lovers yearned to behold that vibrant green Earth once again, but this time more intensely. It was then that Matthew and Hannah drew their shivering bodies closer together, with fond and sorrowful mutual gazes, dreading lest the universal cloud should snatch them from each other's sight and grasp, sending the two foolish assholes plummeting and tumbling down the jagged mountainside into the dark valley below.

Hannah's strength had begun to fail, and with that awareness, her courage diminished likewise. The girl's breath grew short as if the dizzy, light-headed bride were suddenly oxygen deprived. The skinny female refused to burden her husband with her hair's difficult weight, which was almost greater than the rest of her. But now, Hannah often tottered against Mathew's side, and then the wretch wearily recovered herself each time from falling by a feeble effort to remain erect. At last, the defeated trekker sank-down upon one of the rocky steps, entirely frustrated, and in a state of mental despair. Hannah's spirit had been decisively vanquished by Nature's apathetic harshness.

"We are lost, dear Matthew," she announced, quite mournfully. "We shall never find our way back to civilization. And oh, dear Husband; how happy we might've been sitting at our kitchen table in our imaginary cottage eating our delectable cheese!"

"Dear Heart! We will yet be happy there, once we can afford to buy a cottage and some delicious cheese to devour," Matthew accurately assessed and answered. "Look in the northern direction. The sunshine penetrates and filters-through the dismal mist. By its aid, I can direct our course to the passage of the nearby Notch. Now, here's my personal advice. Let us go back, my love, and dream no more of the top-notch Great Carbuncle. We can save our pennies and start a profitable cottage cheese cottage industry!"

"The sun cannot be yonder," Hannah noticed and expressed, with a degree of despondency inhabiting her weak, raspy voice. "Judging by the sun's rays, by this time, it must be afternoon. If there could ever be any sunshine here," the apprehensive child-bride hypothesized and nervously contributed, "then the light would come from above our heads, and not from sunbeams (or moonbeams) being shot-out of angels' quivering assholes!"

"But look!" Matthew exclaimed, in a somewhat-altered tone of voice. "Hannah, I do believe I'm beginning to see the light! It is brightening every moment. If not radiant sunshine, what the hell can it be? Is it the Great Carbuncle?"

Nor could the young bride any longer deny that a splendid glistening was slowly breaking through the accumulated dark mist, and the atmospheric phenomenon was gradually changing its dim hue to a dusky red, which in truth, continually grew more vivid, as if brilliant particles were being magically interfused through the gloom without any accompanying doom.

Now also, the thick opaque clouds began rolling-away from the steep mountainside. As the impressive meteorological process continued, the almost-hypnotized couple observed the gleaming of clear-blue water suddenly springing-up, and appearing close at their feet. And almost magically, Matthew and Hannah found themselves standing on the very border of a rather peculiar-but-enticing mountain lake, the water being deep, bright, and calmly beautiful, spreading from brim to brim of a basin that had apparently been supernaturally scooped-out of the solid rock.

A ray of glory seemed to flash across the lake's smooth-as-ice surface. The enthralled climbers closed their eyes with a thrill of awful admiration, a sensation that glowed from the brow of a cliff, the brilliance exhibiting its exotic magnificence over the entire Enchanted Lake. For the simple, impractical, quixotic pair had luckily reached that wondrous Mirage Lake of Mystery, and at last, the dynamic rejuvenated duo had inadvertently discovered the long-sought fabled shrine of the legendary Great Carbuncle!

Matthew and Hannah seemed changed in one another's eyes, in the red brilliancy that flamed-upon their now-florid cheeks, while the illumination's intensity lent the same flaming fire to the lake; to the rocks; to the sky, and to the various mists, which had rolled-back before the light's supreme power. But with their next brief glance, the intrigued pair beheld an object that drew their attention even more than the mighty stone's tremendous splendor.

At the base of the cliff, directly beneath the brilliant Great Carbuncle's reflection, appeared the inanimate figure of a very determined man, with his arms extended in the act of climbing, and his gritty bearded face turned upward, as if to drink the full gush of grandeur that his perceptive greedy eyes were inspecting. But the frightening-in-appearance trespasser suddenly stirred not, no more than if the adamant climber had been changed to marble.

"It's the Seeker," Hannah whispered, convulsively grasping her husband's arm. "Matthew, I think he is as dead, as sure as the mineral Great Carbuncle is not breathing."

"The joy of imminent success has killed him," Matthew replied, trembling violently. "Or, perhaps, the very light of the Great Carbuncle was actually death in disguise! I truly believe that only an accomplished undertaker should expeditiously undertake this sort of fucked-up expedition!"

"The Great Carbuncle!" cried a peevish voice originating from behind them. "The Great Humbug! If you've indeed found it, please, you two juvenile fuck-heads, point it out to me."

Matthew and Hannah turned their frightened heads, and there stood the Cynic, with his prodigious square-framed spectacles set carefully upon his nose, staring intently now at the Enchanted Lake; then at the rocks; then at the distant masses of vapor; now right at the Great Carbuncle itself, yet seemingly as unconscious of its light as if all the scattered clouds had been instantly condensed about his fucked-up body. Though the glowing radiance threw the shadow of the unbeliever at his own feet, as Charles "Diogenes" Paul turned his back upon the glorious glimmering jewel, the doubter would not be convinced that there was the least flickering glimmer present and being generated there.

"Where is your Great Humbug?" the apostate Cynic repeated. "I challenge you to make me see it! If you two imbeciles were taking a crap, I still wouldn't see shit!"

"Over there," Matthew declared, incensed at such perverse blindness, and then roughly grabbing Mr. Charles Paul's two shoulders and swiftly turning the Cynic around towards the illuminated cliff. "Stop being such a blind Asshole! Take off those abominable spectacles, and you cannot help witnessing the Great Carbuncle's stupendous, sublime quality in stark truth!"

The colored spectacles probably darkened the Cynic's eyesight, in at least as great a degree as the smoked glasses through which people gaze at a solar or lunar eclipse. With resolute bravado, however, the contemporary Diogenes snatched the glasses from his nose, and fixed a bold stare, directed full-upon the ruddy blaze of the incomparable Great Carbuncle.

But scarcely had Mr. Charles Paul encountered *its* superb existence, when, with a deep shuddering groan, the faithless fellow dropped his head, and next pressed both hands across his miserable eyes. Thenceforth, there was, in honest veracity, no visible light of the Great Carbuncle; nor any other sign of light on Earth; nor light of Heaven itself, for the poor, self-victimized Cynic was now blinded forever without ever once visiting Venice.

"Matthew," Hannah summoned, shaking and clinging to her neurotic husband for emotional support. "Let us go hence! Unholy shit! I've already crapped my undies three times during this scary mountain episode!"

Matthew quickly recognized that Hannah was feeling faint, and that three quick sessions of devastating diarrhea had completely dehydrated his loyal lady companion. And then kneeling-down, the loving husband supported her in his arms, while he threw some of the thrillingly cold water from the Enchanted Lake upon her face and bosom. The fresh, cold liquid had miraculously revived her.

176

"Yes, Dearest!" Matthew exclaimed, pressing her tremulous form to his breast. "We will go hence, and return to our imaginary humble cottage and eat our imaginary cottage cheese. The blessed sunshine and the quiet moonlight shall soon come through our imaginary bedroom window. We will kindle the cheerful glow of our pretend hearth, at evening tide," the wacky fellow driveled. "And we'll be happy in its light, because it'll soon be nighttime, and we won't be able to sing in the sunshine. But never again, dearest Hannah, will we desire more light from a fucked-up imaginary Great Carbuncle than we should expect the whole wide dumb-fuck world to share with us."

"No," his bride disagreed in regard to satisfying their incessant greed. "For how could we live by day, or sleep by night, in this awful blaze of the Great Carbuncle, which obviously is not imaginary! Stick your rectum near it, and we'll watch the heat burn your tight asshole right off your frail body!"

Out of the hollow of their cupped palms, the confused pair drank each a draught from the Enchanted Lake, which gladly presented the two idealists its uncontaminated, pristine water. Then, lending their guidance to the disillusioned, blinded Cynic, who now uttered not a word, and the Red Glow even stifled *his* groans originating from inside his own most-wretched heart, the disquieted pair began descending the arcane mountain. Yet, as the disappointed duo left the Enchanted Lake's mystic shore, the couple threw farewell glances towards the seemingly bluffing cliff, and their eyes beheld the vapors gathering in dense volumes, through which the legendary gem still burned steadily.

As touching the conditions of the other Great Carbuncle pilgrims, the legend goes on to tell, that the worshipful Master Ichabod Pigsnort soon gave-up the quest and dispensed of it as "a mere desperate speculation", and Ichabod wisely resolved to betake himself again to his familiar warehouse, near the town dock in Boston Harbor, where the insane merchant would conduct wild and raucous tea parties for the local citizens. But, as crestfallen Ichabod Pigsnort passed through the Notch of the mountains, a war party of belligerent Indians captured the unlucky merchant, and the savages hostilely carried their hostage to Montreal, there holding him in bondage, until, by the payment of a heavy ransom, old Ichabod Pigsnort had woefully subtracted from his hoard of accumulated shillings.

By the conniving merchant's long absence, moreover, Mr. Pigsnort's complicated business affairs had become so disordered that, for the rest of his accursed life, instead of him wallowing in silver and gold, the avaricious fool had seldom a sixpence worth of copper. In the end, Ichabod Pigsnort made all of his deposits upon a hollowed-out, oval, wooden plank, where the impoverished fool sat his ass inside his ramshackle, shanty outhouse.

Doctor Cacaphodel, the self-proclaimed alchemist, returned to his laboratory with an enormous fragment of granite, which the asshole assiduously ground into powder; then dissolved in acids; next the maniac melted the particles inside his huge experimental crucible, and ultimately burned the liquid with his reliable blow-pipe. The frenetic nutcase published the results of his questionable experiments in one of the more reputable scientific journals of the day. And, for all those noteworthy purposes, the coveted White Mountain gem itself could not have answered better than the worthless granite that Dr. Cacaphodel had ignorantly taken for granted.

The abstract-minded Poet, also known as Mr. No Name #2, by a somewhat similar mistake to that of his searching associates, made prize of a great piece of ice, which the eternal dreamer had found in a sunless chasm of the mountains, and later, the ignoramus swore that the ordinary ice corresponded, in all points, with *his* general idea of the Great Carbuncle's elemental properties. The critics of this widespread popular saga say that, if the rhymer's stupid-assed poetry lacked the splendor of the fabled gemstone, his insanity retained all the coldness of the ice follies residing and flourishing inside the pathetic Poet's unwitty cranium.

The French Lord de Vere journeyed back to his ancestral hall, where the dimwit contented himself with a wax-lighted chandelier, and filled, in due course of time, another macabre coffin inside the ancestral vault. As the funeral torches gleamed within *that* dark receptacle, there was no need for the divine Great Carbuncle to show or emphasize the vanity of temporal earthly pomp.

The Cynic, also referred to as Mr. Diogenes, and also Mr. No Name #1, miraculously had resurrected himself, and had incredibly survived the treacherous mountain cliff near the Enchanted Lake. Having cast aside his square-framed spectacles, Mr. Charles Paul wandered-about the entire world, exhibiting himself as a miserable trekker, and the insane humanoid was constantly punished with an agonizing desire of again viewing light, atonement for the willful blindness of his former life, thus making 'a spectacle' of himself. The whole night long, the bizarre idiot would lift his splendor-blasted orbs to the overhead moon and stars; Mr. Charles Paul would next turn his face eastward, at sunrise, as duly as a Persian idolater; the Cynic's addled mind symbolically making each afternoon a pilgrimage to Rome, his distrustful imagination witnessing the magnificent illumination of St. Pete's Basilica. And finally, the blind asshole fatefully perished in the Great Fire of London, incinerating himself' into the midst of which the distrustful Cynic had enthusiastically

178

thrust his corporal body, with the desperate idea of catching one feeble ray from the Great Carbuncle's blaze. that in his disturbed mind, was still continuously kindling Earth and Heaven.

Matthew and Hannah spent many peaceful years fondly re-telling the spectacular legend of the Great Carbuncle. The tale, however, towards the close of their lengthy lives, did not meet with the full credence that had been accorded to the legend by those other prospecting imbeciles who had remembered the ancient luster of the famous gem. For it is affirmed that, from the hour when two mortals had shown themselves so simply wise as to reject a jewel which would have dimmed all earthly things, its excellent splendor soon waned.

When the other more greedy pilgrims had eventually reached the craggy cliff at journey's end, the frivolous birdbrains had found only an ordinary opaque stone, with particles of mica glittering upon its otherwise dull surface.

However, in retrospect, an obscure fable states that, as the youthful pair Matthew and Hannah departed the Enchanted Lake, the gigantic glowing gem had suddenly become loosened from the top crag of the overhead precipice, and soon the Great Ruby Carbuncle fell and splashed into the Enchanted Water, and that at noontide, each day hence, the Seeker's lifeless form may still be seen bending over the gargantuan gemstone's tremendous gleam.

A few other bullshitting idle dreamers still believe to this very day that the inestimable colossal red ruby stone is presently blazing on the northern horizon as of old, and the silly-assed faithful still say that the dumb-asses have caught the power of its radiance, like a flash of summer lightning, after getting laid a dozen times in sixty-minutes far down the valley of the White Mountain Notch.

And be it owned and understood that, many a mile from the remote Crystal Hills, I myself' had once seen a wondrous light whirling and rotating-around the very superior mountain summits, and my spirit was both captivated and lured, in devout recollection of the Poet's uncanny verses. And I am both honored and delighted to be the latest and last fucked-up pilgrim alive, still lusting for a brief glimpse of THE GREAT CARBUNCLE.

"Perseus and Medusa"

Acrisius was king of Argos, and the tyrant was so full of shit that the mental case daily sat on a golden toilet instead of upon a golden throne. Besides always taking lengthy craps, slapping his monkey, and scratching his royal ass most of each day, the king (just like all other ancient rulers of Argo) was notorious for telling anyone and everyone who asked about his city-kingdom, "Ar-go fuck yourself'!" The worst part about the entire fiasco was that chronically constipated King Acrisius thought that *his* single redundant hundred-year-old joke was actually funny.

The King of Argos had a beautiful daughter named Danae, who had a bad habit of walking in the woods and then dreaming about getting laid by some horny forest god having multiple sex organs. One day Danae was picking daffodils near a grotto when Zeus, king of the gods, happened to be sauntering by on his way to Ethiopia to visit his fellow Olympian Apollo, who had recently had a new magnificent temple erected in *his* honor in that distant African land below Egypt.

Upon seeing Danae's many charms, Zeus immediately got a gargantuan hard-on, and felt that he had to plant his rod inside the nearest mortal vagina. Danae was mesmerized by the King-god's magic wand, which of course was erect, huge, long, thick, and throbbing. The pretty nymphomaniac then made a major mistake in judgment. Instead of giving Zeus a super-duper excellent blow-job, she got on her back, opened her hairy eager beaver, and had the royal poop pumped out of her until her face nearly turned as purple as Zeus's pulsating bazooka.

A month later, Danae missed her period and discovered that she was indeed pregnant. Her child would be half-*divine* and half-human; whereas, grapes are totally "the vine" fruit, and her child might also be *divine fruit of the womb* if he or she (the potential fruit) turned-out to be gay, either homo' or lesbian.

Danae rushed to her constipated father, Acrisius, seated upon his golden hopper, and told the monarch the bad news. The thoroughly upset full-of-shit king instantly got severe diarrhea, and almost died from a bad case of dehydration.

"Danae, first Lord Zeus screwed the crap out of you in *the forbidden mating woods,* but now he's going to screw me really good, too!" the king lamented while awkwardly wiping his smelly ass with rough cabbage leaves.

"I don't understand exactly what you mean, father?" Danae replied. "I didn't know you had a vagina!"

"Danae, I don't have a goddamned vagina, and if I did, I'd pour cement in the hole, and seal the fucker up! Anyway, my dear daughter,"

Acrisius continued. "A few years back, I had journeyed to *Delphi* to visit Apollo's *Oracle* there, and find out my future!"

"That was more stupid than being screwed by Zeus!" the daughter abruptly answered. "The Oracle always predicts gloom and doom, and never augurs happy tidings. You would've been better off, father, seeing Medusa's face and being turned into stone. Then, you wouldn't have to shit into your golden hopper and suffer dehydration all of the damned time!"

"Anyway, dear daughter," the king went on as the imbecile wiped his fat ass with red onion peels, since he had used-up all the coarse cabbage leaves, "I asked the Oracle if I would ever have a son, but the prophetess predicted that I would only have a daughter, who would eventually bear a son who would eventually grow-up to kill me! And now it's fuckin' happening in real time!" the king insanely screamed. "That blooming seed planted inside your womb is half divine, and when the boy grows-up, he's gonna' eliminate your old man's shittin' ass right off the fuckin' planet!"

"How do you know the sex of the baby that has not yet been born?" Danae challenged. "How do you know I'll definitely have a boy?"

"Because I trust the Oracle a lot more than I trust you and your promiscuous snatcheroo!" the king countered. "And besides Danae, the Oracle has cement up *her* crotch, and wouldn't bull-shit me for sex, or anything else cheap and vulgar, just to get her freakin' rocks off like you've always desire doing!"

Nine months quickly passed. Acrisius became extremely distraught and disconsolate, and not wanting to have Danae executed by the royal hangman, the cruel king placed his daughter and her child in a large chest, and had the pair cast out to sea. The indiscriminate waves carried the floating, waterproof box to the island of Seriphos, where a handsome fisherman named Dictys retrieved Danae and her crying baby from the pounding surf that was violently smashing into treacherous rocks.

Dictys shared his home and possessions with the lovely disowned princess, and with her strong-lunged crybaby son. The fisherman never had sex with the attractive woman because once Dictys learned the boy's father was the chief *Olympian*, the discreet fellow didn't want to be shafted up the ass by one of Zeus's dazzling, electrified billion-volt lightning bolts.

Seventeen-years elapsed, and the boy had matured into a young strong sailor, who journeyed to many islands in the vicinity to engage in trading whores for harlots, and bartering prostitutes for hookers. Danae had named her son Perseus, but all of the natives of Seriphos believed the lad to be "son of Zeus" because of his terrific biceps, his firm chest, and his cute compact butt.

Perseus was adept at boxing, wrestling, bullshitting, and javelin throwing, but the accomplished athlete also possessed admirable social qualities that engendered courtesy, virtue, humility, and justice. But trauma was certain to accompany drama in Perseus's life on the small island of myriad idle gossipers, along with mentally-sick, perpetual masturbators.

Dictys' brother was Polydickdees, ruthless king of Seriphos, who incidentally had three uncircumcised penises. The ruler was extraordinarily evil, cruel, villainous, conniving, greedy, and arrogant. And when Polydickdees saw Danae, his *privates* began *publicly* throbbing and pulsating, like a divining rod, or like Zeus's divine rod. While Perseus was at sea and unable to defend his mother's welfare at home on Seriphos, Polydickdees took Danae away from Dictys' jurisdiction and said to her, "If you will not be my wife, then you'll most-certainly be my servant. What is your response, woman?"

"I wouldn't marry you if you had the only dick and the only set of balls in the whole wide world!" Danae snottily retorted, not knowing that the freak-of-nature king had three uncircumcised peckers and seven uncircumcised testicles. "I'd rather fool around with bananas, squash, and cucumbers than have any kind of sex with you, oral or otherwise, you big, selfish, dumb, braggart asshole!" Danae lambasted Polydickdees.

Meanwhile, on the island of Samos where Perseus's ship was taking on a cargo of harlots, hookers and slaves, the handsome sailor stepped into a nearby woods to take a long leak. A twelve-foot-tall woman approached with a bronze helmet on her head, and the female figure was carrying winged sandals, a bronze shield over her shoulder, and a bronze spear in her right hand.

'When the hell are we Greeks ever going to get out of the damned *Bronze Age?*' Perseus thought. 'There must be more to this stupid age than ridiculous copper and tin alloy!'

The tall luscious babe then spoke to the young sailor, who blushed as the young man tucked his pecker, still dripping urine, back under his tunic. "Perseus, you must perform a special errand for me," the tall deity requested.

"Who are you, giant lady, and how do you know my name is Perseus? Are you a glamorous spy, or are you a gorgeous woodland prostitute? If you want my opinion about woman that put out," the young sailor mentioned, "I'd prefer if you were a gorgeous woodland harlot, for I have no money to pay for a vivacious woodland prostitute!"

"I am neither," the voluptuous goddess disclosed. "I am Pallas Athene, daughter of Lord Zeus, and goddess of *Olympus*. And I can read goodness in a man's heart, and I've readily detected *that* abstract quality in yours. Tell me, dear Perseus," Pallas Athene continued. "Would you rather have a soul of fire, or would you truly prefer a soul of clay?"

Perseus considered the enchanting goddess's proposition, even though Pallas Athene was not trying to proposition him. "Definitely a soul of fire," the lad wisely answered. "For it's a lot better to know adventure and die in the flower of youth than to be like a cow chewing its cud in the field for an entire boring lifetime. For fame and honor go to those possessing souls of fire," the youth eloquently elaborated, "even though those with souls of clay often become rich kings; live in colossal palaces; get laid every night, and can afford all of the best hookers and prostitutes available in the whole damned ancient world!"

"You've chosen wisely," Pallas Athene commended while holding up her bronze shield so that Perseus could view an image that was being reflected from it. "See here, Perseus; do you have the courage to slay *this* terrible monster, Medusa the Gorgon? She has vipers for hair; formidable talons and claws for hands and feet, and the creature bites men's dicks off when giving very bad unprofessional blow-jobs. What do you think of the ugly bitch?"

"She's the most hideous creature my eyes have ever beheld, and I'll certainly cross my legs and eat a pound of saltpeter before I ever confront her," Perseus promised the heavenly goddess. "Where can I find the ugly thing?"

"You're too young at present, and not yet ready to assassinate her," Athene politely chastised. "So, kindly return to Seriphos, and when the time is right, you shall answer the challenge, and be equal to the task," the beautiful goddess promised.

"Okay, I'll be glad to kill Medusa as long as I don't have to lose my virginity, along with my sensitive dick, screwing the venom out of her," Perseus agreed. "For all I know, the Gorgon might have metal jaws planted up her snatch, and that fate might even be worse than receiving a damned fatal blow-job from her ravenous lips, and from her poisonous, dagger-like fangs!"

The goddess then instantaneously vanished *into thin air,* because goddesses, like magicians, wizards and sorcerers, hadn't yet mastered the technique of vanishing into thick air, since factories with smokestacks didn't exist back then to lethally pollute the atmosphere. So, ambitious Perseus obediently returned to Seriphos, where his ears heard gossip that his mother had become a lowly slave in ostentatious King Polydickdees's opulent palace.

The livid young sailor dashed the full mile to the pretentious king's residence, and darted from room to room, desperately searching for his mother. The muscular sailor came across Danae turning a hand millstone and crying her tits off. Evil Polydickdees then entered the chamber, followed by his brother, the benign-but-poor Dictys.

"Craven tyrant!" Perseus recklessly and imprudently shouted at the always-scheming king. The enraged *Adonis* quickly lifted up the simple hand-operated machine that Danae had been rotating. "Mom!" the incensed sailor yelled. "Has *this* mother-fucker been screwing you against your will?" Perseus bellowed as *he* raised-up the run-of-the-mill basic everyday grindstone to use to split-open the suddenly fearful king's cranium.

"Please, my son. Show tolerance and restraint!" Danae begged. "We are but lowly strangers in this hostile land, and must act humbly and not haughtily, although I wish you could break Polydickdees' head, ass, and balls open before I have to again diligently *put my nose to the damned grindstone!*"

"Your mother is right!" counseled passive and wise Dictys. "If you do to my wicked brother what we'd all like to do to my wicked brother," the honorable fisherman noted, "then all of the ignorant people of Seriphos will fall upon us, and then viciously kill us. That's because all of the fucked-up people of Seriphos love being governed by my fucked-up, evil, reprehensible brother. How could I ever explain it to you more logically?"

Polydickdees had been trembling as if the repugnant despot had been experiencing a one-man earthquake. Perseus lowered the heavy hand mill that had been elevated above his head, set it upon the stone floor, and then quickly ceased being so *mill*itant. The son of Zeus grabbed his mother's hand and conducted her to the island's temple of Pallas Athene, where Danae was accepted by the resident priestess as a floor and altar sweeper, along with being a temple marquee scrubber, and a dust and ass wiper, because vacuum cleaners, feather-dusters, and utilitarian toilet paper hadn't yet been invented.

Now, pernicious Polydickdees was a cunning old bastard, and the son-of-a-bitch plotted to somehow get Danae back in *his* custody, and permanently removed from the temple's safe sanctuary. Of course, the king could have sent his soldiers to kidnap Danae at the temple, or to kill the impudent Perseus and the benevolent Dictys at their home, but the sinister distator had never endorsed simple solutions to complex problems, and preferred living and anguishing with difficult decisions.

So, the nefarious king schemed-up a rather complicated trap to send his chief nemesis on "an impossible mission of no return". Polydickdees organized a massive feast, and invited all of the island's nobility and dignitaries, including Perseus, to the grand banquet, designed to pay homage to the king and to *his* very prosperous land.

Every guest brought an expensive gift, and presented his or her item to the ignoble monarch. Then, the villainous royal asshole summoned Perseus to *his* throne for everyone to witness a contrived confrontation, and the shrewd ruler cunningly asked the embarrassed lad, "Perseus, I have invited you to my splendid celebration, but where is your' gift to present to your honorable king?"

Perseus was unaware of such a custom, and stood humiliated before the curious assemblage of pompous aristocrats. The very embarrassed mariner blushed, and then was so nervous when the youthful sailor stuttered, "I have not brought anything because I'm an impoverished mariner, who can barely provide for my own basic needs, which incidentally don't include expensive hookers, risqué couch dancers, and kinky prostitutes."

"This insolent young man," the king preached to the pride and flower of *his* corrupt realm, "had been washed ashore onto our peaceful island. We've dutifully given him asylum and residency, and now the ungrateful fool demonstrates his thanks by not bringing his king a worthy gift. You even claim to be the son of Zeus! I say, Perseus; you're simply an illegitimate vagabond pretending to be of divine descent! How do you' account for yourself, you ludicrous, ridiculous, fabricating fucked-up simpleton?"

The insulted young sailor grew angry with abundant shame and pride, and cried-out for all of the shocked audience of prominent guests to hear, "I shall bring your majesty a present nobler than any you have thus received at your feast!" Danae's son pledged without having any specific idea of what such a gift might be, or even what the hell he was talking about.

"Well then," Polydickdees pressed on. "Exactly what might this superior gift be? Pray tell, Perseus. Let the people of Seriphos know its description and its true value!"

Everyone in the crowded throne chamber boisterously laughed at the king's derision of the almost-destitute young sailor, who boasted that he was indeed the son of the chief-god of the universe. The young attendee then vaguely remembered the beautiful tall woman he had encountered on Samos, and reckoned that now was the time to exhibit the courage her powerful words had instilled in him.

"King Polydickdees," Perseus uttered in a stronger voice than he had exhibited before. "I shall bring you the head of Medusa the Gorgon. That awesome prize will be my special gift to you!"

All the guests in attendance gasped at the young man's bravado. The naïve sailor had played right into the king's plan to get the boy off the island, so that Polydickdees could then permanently capture Danae from the temple, take her to his palace, and then screw the shit out of her ten times each night with his incredible three dicks and seven swollen testicles. "You have foolishly promised to bring me Medusa's head?" the king wildly chuckled and sneered. "Well then, junior jerk-off; leave Seriphos immediately to engage in your dumb-ass, frivolous quest. And don't come back to this island until Medusa has given you some head! Ha, ha, ha, ha!"

The son of Zeus and Danae finally realized that the sly king had cleverly tricked his ass, and the insulted young man left the great feast being jeered and mocked by the five-hundred jovial guests, who all loved being governed by the cruelest and most deplorable king east of the *Pillars of Hercules*.

Perseus was disgusted with his own gullibility. The troubled youth ambled out to the island's high cliffs overlooking the sea, and prayed that Pallas Athene would come to assist him in undertaking *his* extremely dangerous exploit. Three times the youth wept and begged for the goddess to appear, and when despair had virtually saturated his soul, a wonderful mist was discernible upon the eastern horizon, and soon drifted-over to the cliff where the hoodwinked adolescent had been standing. A sparkling, celestial figure slowly-emerged from the illuminated haze.

"Perseus," Pallas Athene greeted. "Raise your head up high and be proud of the noble virtues that inhabit your heart. Take this bronze sword, shield, helmet, along with these winged sandals, and wear them proudly on your daring quest. Now, it is time for you to achieve honor, and convincingly slay Medusa the Gorgon," the goddess announced. "Then, you'll promptly take her head back to Polydickdees as you have so valiantly promised. Your will shall be vindicated by beating the shit out of Medusa, and then turning Polydickdees to stone at his palace!"

"Gee, Pallas Athene. I really made a complete asshole out of myself at my opening act at the palace!" Perseus admitted with an innocent smile. "Please show me how I can redeem my lost credibility."

Athene further explained that her hero had to venture-out on a perilous seven-year-journey to the end of the known world, and that if Perseus was ever overcome by cowardice, then the youth would surely perish with a *soul of clay* in the shadowy "Unshapen Land".

"But how can I slay Medusa if her despicable face will turn me into stone?" Perseus insisted on knowing. "It's bad enough that I now have rocks in my head, let alone a petrified matching stone face to boot!"

"All of that crazy information you'll learn in due time," the goddess sincerely pledged. "This unique expedition of yours must be accomplished in many small steps. First, you must go north and visit the three Gray Sisters, who'll give you specific directions to the Three Daughters of the Evening Star, who dance around the *Golden Apple Tree* like sex-starved, horny lesbians. The daughters will provide you with the correct directions on how to find Medusa's diabolical lair!"

"But how the fuck can I ever kill Medusa if one brief glance at her despicable face will simultaneously freeze my ass, dick, balls, and sperm into solid stone!" Perseus demanded.

"You shall see her reflection in your invincible bronze shield, and then smite the detestable monster with this magic bronze sword," Pallas Athene divulged to her fascinated listener. "Then, you'll stuff her shit-ugly head inside this shit-ugly goatskin sack, and transport it to King Polydickdees for *his* personal inspection."

"But how can I fuckin' cross the seas without a sturdy ship?" Perseus inquired. "I can't even swim a stroke, even though I'm a goddamned experienced sailor!"

"Put these divine winged sandals upon your feet. They'll guide you across the winds to your particular destinations," the goddess patiently explained. "Wear the sandals proudly, along with the bronze shield, bronze sword, and the bronze helmet. Now venture-out into mythology, and start kicking some enemy ass!"

"Can't I at least say goodbye to my mother and to kind Dictys?" the soon-to-be hero asked. "The two have done much to develop my character!"

"No, you may not!" Pallas Athene imperatively stated. "It's now time for *you* to trust the will of the gods, and to discard aside mortal emotions and human associations. Cast your fate to the winds, Perseus. Aspire to a higher power, and then glory and fame will be your legacy forever!"

The glittering cloud descended from the stratosphere, and again enveloped the celestial goddess, and it soon glided out over the sea, and disappeared over the eastern horizon from where it had come. Perseus adorned his feet with the splendid winged sandals; placed the bronze helmet upon his head; lifted-up his new sword and shield, and then gently floated-up into the air. Soon, the airborne hero became adept at regulating both his flying speed and his altitude, and after an hour of assiduous practice, the prospective champion set-out on his great quest, possessing a joyful stout heart.

The lad was thoroughly enjoying the thrill of flight, and after beating several falcons in several impromptu sky races, Perseus buzzed the cities of Athens and Thebes, scaring the shit and the piss out of the daily pedestrians, who were distracted from shopping in the busy marketplaces. And after several months of showing off his aerial skills all over Greece, brave Perseus came to an ominous moor, which after a hundred-miles, gradually converted into a vast sheet of ice.

The courageous fellow then followed an obscure mountain trail through an intense blizzard until the excited adventurer finally reached the isolated cave of the notorious Three Gray Sisters, who were too ugly and wicked to ever be ancient nuns, or to even be over-the-hill hookers.

The three old, blind bitches were grotesque-looking, warty-faced witches that were preoccupied passing their single eye amongst themselves, and arguing incessantly about *its* possession. The illustrious young hero pitied the Three Gray Sisters, who actually didn't give a shit or a damn about pity for each other, or for that matter pity toward anyone else on the whole goddamned planet.

"Oh, noble Three Gray Sisters. I am Perseus," the young stud formally introduced himself to the hideous hags. "And I need some vital information. Please tell me the directions to find Medusa the Gorgon, for I don't have a map, or even a compass!"

"You have the voice of a child of man," the first perceptive ugly sister answered. "Who are you really, oh intrepid mortal?" the witch asked, for in her heart, the old bitch really wanted to get laid because she hadn't had any decent sex from a stiff cock in over five-thousand-years. "Holy Hera! I haven't been pumped since I had 'menopause' over five-millennia ago," the hoary whore remarked. "And the *men* have *paused* porking me, ever since my once juicy love canal dried-up!"

"The rulers of *Olympus* have dispatched me to find the repulsive Gorgon, and to gain knowledge of her whereabouts from you Three Gray Sisters," Perseus claimed. "Don't you three 'sisters' have a *Mother Superior* I can speak with?"

"Look, jerk-weed!" the second cantankerous sister's voice boomed. "You might have to eat all three of our ancient dried-up, smelly, lice-infected cunts if you don't cooperate with our easy demands. We are kin to the Titans, and also to the Gorgons, and to the Monsters of Antiquity, too," the second cauldron guardian laboriously explained. "And we want *you* to know that we despise the new rulers of *Olympus,* and also their fucked-up human worshipers!"

"Listen, twisted Sister," the bold young adventurer answered the most horrible-looking hag of the three. "I would rather jerk-off naked in *that* wicked blizzard out there than eat or screw any of your raunchy, smelly, dried-up, arid, useless pussies. Now then," Perseus adamantly continued. "Tell me the way to Medusa!"

"Who is this insolent pecker-head who dares invade our privacy?" the third withered, pallid-faced Gray Sister insisted on knowing. "Give me the eye so that I may evaluate *his* appearance, and admire his muscular physique, and imagine and fanta*size* the 'size' and length of his hairy pussy plunger!"

As the three ugly, warty, ashen-faced sisters grappled and groped for the singular magical eye, which the gruesome trio had been passing and sharing amongst themselves, Perseus reached-out his free hand, and grabbed *their* only window to the world. "Now then, you ugly, ingrate bitches. I now have your sacred eye in my possession. I insist that you please tell me where the Gorgon resides, or I shall confiscate your most-essential eye; I will fly to the moon, and deposit your' seeing device inside an active volcanic crater," the angry traveler threatened. "And try pissing me off some more with your stupid rhetoric, and I'll cut off your distorted heads, along with your flaccid tits, with my magic bronze sword, and I'll gladly donate the amputated relics to the *Athenian Mythological Museum of Unnatural History.*"

"You wouldn't dare!" the first wretched-looking old hag exclaimed. "You haven't the testicles or the sperm to attempt that!"

"If you don't cooperate and give me accurate directions," Perseus emphatically predicted, "then I'll make all three of you pathetic, stubborn, miserable blind bitches' lick and suck on my stenchy hemorrhoids, until the suckers disappear right out of my hairy, infected asshole!"

"Okay, you win this time, you conniving young bastard!" the first disgusting witch acknowledged and compromised. "Go south toward the sun, and you'll arrive at the *Golden Apple Tree* with three young maidens merrily dancing around it. The beauties are the *Hesperides,* daughters of the Titan Atlas's brother, and they'll give you the necessary directions to Medusa's secret island," the old bag disclosed. "Now, give us back our vital eye, so that at least one of us can view your form, and fantasize about having hot sex with a young stud-meister such as yourself!"

The hero returned the portable eye to its rightful owners, left the dismal, isolated ice cave, and continued southward, flying over desolate mountains and weedy meadows until the skilled aviator observed a tremendous form in the distance, holding-up the sky, and separating it from the earth. 'That is Atlas,' Perseus reckoned. 'And some day he'll be relieved of this important duty, and then finally go into the lucrative business of manufacturing reference books for libraries and for school classrooms.'

Then, the young champion heard sweet angelic female voices harmoniously singing, so he descended from the clouds and viewed the *Daughters of the Evening Star* prancing and dancing around a magnificent apple tree, featuring large golden fruit suspended upon its wonderful limbs.

The beautiful, cheerful *Daughters of the Hesperides* held hands and enthusiastically danced-around the fabulous *Golden Apple Tree,* which had a listless, lazy dragon coiled around its base. The blithe nymphs ceased their merriment upon detecting the arrival of the valiant crusader against evil injustices.

"Who the hell are you?" the first blonde-haired beauty asked with half of her golden bush, and all of her firm tits hanging out of her loose-fitting tunic. "Are you *Hercules* come to steal golden apples from our incomparable tree?"

"No, fair maidens," the young champion candidly replied. "My name is Perseus, but you're positively right about one thing. The goddess Pallas Athene has sent me on a *Herculean* labor. You must show me the way to Medusa the Gorgon's secret lair!"

"Not just yet!" the second blonde-haired and blonde-bushed maiden imperatively answered. "Come dance with us. Then, we'll let you play with us, too!"

"Well, I must admit, that's a mighty big temptation you've offered me!" Perseus exclaimed as he licked his lips while thinking about *those* other lips between the comely girls' perfectly-structured legs. "You just aren't paying *lip service* to what we'll be doing, are you?" Perseus begged for positive verification.

"No, but you can masturbate any and all of us," the third horny nymph informed. "But you cannot penetrate our maidenheads, because we must remain virgins in order to perform our monotonous function. But we do give good blow-jobs that are guaranteed to make you come again!" the *comely* nymph confidently stated.

"Well, that's all very nice and proper," the hero aptly agreed. "But I'll have to take a rain-check on your generous offer. I'm obligated by promise to perform a vital errand for the Immortals, but after I'm finished the *Promethean* chore," Perseus elaborated, "even though I am not Prometheus, I can then also lose *my* virginity, and even my maidenhead too, if I have one near my prostate!"

Then, the fair damsels cried and slobbered all over the place, and also all over each other, whimpering, "Medusa will surely turn you into stone. Then, you'll never have the pleasure of massaging our hot, wet, pink, blonde fluffy beavers, or sucking on our firm erect succulent nipples," the first nymph regretted. "Won't you please reconsider? That scumbag Medusa lives in an alien *cunt*ry."

"I assure you, fair maidens. I'll not be converted into stone by some ugly hussy!" Perseus warranted. "Now, if you presently tell me the precise directions to her remote lair, I can then be on my way. The sooner I can leave, the sooner I can return here and learn some fine hands-on hedonism."

"Very well, then!" the second blonde damsel agreed as she scrutinized the impressive bulge protruding below the center of Perseus's sexy, orange tunic. "The knowledge you seek is not within our scope of experience, but if you request that same information from the Titan Atlas, who can see far into the distant Unshapen Land from his position of holding up the sky, he'll probably gladly help you."

The favorite of Pallas Athene accompanied the luscious blonde knockouts up the side of a steep mountain where their uncle was busy keeping the sky separated from the Earth.

"Uncle, please assist this young man," the first maiden yelled-up and requested. "He requires knowing the location of Medusa the Gorgon's den. Is it somewhere in Denmark?"

"I can see in the distance the Gorgon resting in the shade of a primitive island, but kind stranger," Atlas cautioned, "you cannot approach the island unless your identity is cloaked by the *Hat of Darkness*. Then, Medusa might be able to smell your presence, but won't be able to see you, even with *her* keen eyesight."

"Well then, kind Atlas," Perseus wondered and asked. "Where is this unique *Hat of Darkness?* Where could I locate it?"

"*The Hat* is hidden in the depths of *Hades*, but my immortal nieces could easily retrieve the cap for you. But in payment for rendering that favor," Atlas continued, "I must receive one in return."

"What would you like me to do for you?" the bronze-helmeted champion curiously asked. "Would you like me to scratch your balls, or massage your ass?"

"No, Perseus. This fuckin' task of holding up the sky is far too tedious and boring for even a Titan to perform," Atlas persuasively complained. "So, if you are successful in butchering Medusa's head off, show it to my face, so that I may be turned to stone. Then, my horrible gruesome assignment will be that much less difficult for the remainder of eternity!"

"That's a deal!" Perseus euphorically acceded. "You can be the envy of every drunk's most passionate desire. Atlas my friend. I want you to just think about your future status for a second. You will be *stoned* for all eternity!"

The *Daughters of the Evening Star* took a secret passage leading into the side of the mountain; which led to a macabre tunnel; which gradually descended fifteen-miles into the Earth's core. A full week transpired, until the three blonde dolls finally completed their perilous mission, and ascended to the Earth's surface, carrying the inimitable *Hat of Darkness* as their prized trophy.

"Thank you, kind sisters of mercy, for obtaining this terrific gift," the young adventurer from Seriphos declared. "And I'll be thinking all about your hot, wet, pink, blonde pussies, and your firm, erect, succulent nipples all the way to Medusa's lair, I assure you."

And then the young stud placed the extraordinary *Hat of Darkness* on top of his bronze helmet. In seconds, the sailor-turned-hero vanished from sight, laughing like a maniac as the jolly crusader cavorted-around in his invisible state, tickling the fair maidens under their arms, and then feeling and squeezing their firm tits, featuring very erect, succulent nipples.

Perseus flew onward toward the Unshapen Land that had been alluded to and indicated by Atlas. Ahead, the hero could see the three sleeping Gorgons' talons glistening in the morning sunlight, and the on-a-mission champion instantly forgot about contemplating the fair damsels' blonde pussies and firm tits, while concentrating all of his mental dynamics on the immediate task at hand. 'Pallas Athene suggested that I fly aloft and glance at Medusa's image in my bronze shield,' the daring fellow remembered. 'If my back is to the sun, then I could more easily accomplish *her* expectation.'

The hero's invisible form furtively flew above the three lethargic, inattentive Gorgons, all sleeping and basking in the sunlight as if the monsters were lazy dinosaurs grazing in grassy lands, unaware of a meteor hurtling through the atmosphere, ready to destroy their existence. Perseus's hand trembled as the encroacher held his bronze sword aloft, for the ferocious Gorgons looked rather invincible, even while resting in their non-aggressive state. Medusa was rolling and tossing back and forth in her sleep, perhaps having a premonition of impending disaster.

Pallas Athene's champion gazed into *his* bronze shield, which served as a reliable mirror, and the trespasser viewed the beast's horrendous locks that were now identifiable as moving, living serpents. The monster's sharp fangs protruded out of the sides of her evil mouth, and even as she slept, the creature hissed intermittently. Medusa was so foul and so wicked-looking that Perseus felt inspired to immediately initiate his "supernatural errand". Looking into the immortal bronze shield, the determined assassin savagely swung his sword, and his aim and effort had been true to the mark. In one mighty twist of the arm and wrist, the repulsive creature had been decapitated.

The victor reached-down, and without directly looking, grabbed the bloody head, and adroitly inserted it into the goatskin sack. 'Now, I gotta' get the fuck outa' here in a hurry!' the triumphant hero anxiously thought.

Medusa's body flipped, flapped, and flopped all over the rugged terrain, instantly waking-up her savage sisters from *their* slumbers. In a second, Perseus was again airborne, and as the perplexed sisters searched in vain for the invisible assassin, the murderer was entirely hidden from their scrutiny by the very effective *Hat of Darkness*. The enraged Gorgon sisters flew-off, and four times circled the rocky ledge where the surprise assault had occurred, but no evidence of any culprit was anywhere to be seen or found. Only a flying goatskin bag could be detected in the far distance, speeding-away toward the western horizon.

"Serve me well, my swift winged sandals," Perseus implored. "Give me the lightning speed of Hermes to escape the vindictive beasts on my trail, lusting for sour revenge."

The intrepid assassin flew south across the Mediterranean Sea, and soon Perseus arrived at northern Africa, the land of the *Golden Apple Tree,* and also the *Daughters of the Evening Star.* The two determined Gorgons finally abandoned their futile pursuit, with the approach of evening and the nearby Mediterranean Sea marking both time and geographic boundaries for *their* exhausted bodies to honor.

After landing on the African peninsula bordering the spectacular *Golden Apple Tree*, Perseus gallantly trekked over to the vicinity of beleaguered Atlas to finally fulfill his grateful promise made to the grieving Titan.

"Satisfy your pledge to me!" Atlas urged the successful youth. "Show me the bitch's fuckin' ugly puss, so that I can escape my *Olympian* punishment, and be transformed into stone for all eternity. I demand you turn me into an inanimate mountain crag right now!"

And Perseus honored his responsibility to the melancholy, woeful giant by removing the bloody Gorgon's head from the goatskin bag, and then showing its' cursed horrible face to the colossal figure. Instantaneously, the Titan changed into a jagged mountain peak, and the surrounding northern African ridges still, to this day, bear the giant's familiar name, the *Atlas Mountains.*

Then, Perseus enclosed the Gorgon's head inside the thick goatskin sack, so that no further damage or transformation could accidentally result from its accidental exposure. The three blonde maidens came sprinting-up the mountain trail to inspect their uncle's new radical, rock-hard appearance and sang several verses of: "Turn to stone; turn to stone; Uncle Atlas has turned to stone!"

"He's now as solid as *Gibraltar,*" the first nymph attested.

"Uncle Atlas can now be one of the *Pillars of Hercules*," the second golden-hair vixen marveled.

"Uncle is finally out of his misery!" the third *Hesperides'* daughter gleefully shouted. "Now Perseus, just point Medusa's head at your' pecker so that it might turn hard, too!"

"Sorry, ladies," the chaste-hearted champion idealist answered. "I promise to come back some day with a huge erection to satisfy all three of you young horny bitches. But right now, I must consummate my important journey."

"Perseus, take with you *this* wonderful fruit," the second nymph insisted as the blonde maiden held out one of the lustrous golden apples. "It has sufficient energy to sustain you for a full week!"

"And don't forget to come back to northern Africa so that you can fondle our tits and do anything you'd like to our eager-beaver pussies!" the third young maiden reminded.

"Now, fly eastward over the drab Libyan shore, and from there, zoom north to the land of Greece," the first lovely damsel instructed. "And please, Perseus; retain your sacred virginity and save it for *us* horny young broads to claim!"

The three blonde maidens then all kissed Perseus upon his lips and face, and the enthralled favorite of Pallas Athene ascended into the air, and followed the three daughters' explicit directions, heading straight to the Libyan coast. From there, the son of Danae would continue his flight odyssey to Seriphos, where the returning hero would discard the goatskin sack outside the palace and then nonchalantly present vile Polydickdees with Medusa's grotesque face and head.

"Dr. Heidegger's Experiment"

That very erudite and eccentric chemical-mixing scientist, Dr. Ludwig Heidegger, who had migrated to the United States from Heidelberg, Germany in his youth, invited four old friends to his dark, secluded New Hampshire mansion. The purpose for the hastily arranged assemblage was to formally conduct a secret seminar inside the Professor's spacious study. Although the good doctor strongly wished to reminisce past events with his venerable acquaintances, and also nostalgically review old times, his principal motivation was to gradually expose his aged comrades to the radical idea of becoming central subjects in a "marvelous miraculous experiment".

Three white-bearded, very elderly gentlemen who attended the oddball consultation were Mr. Melvin Melbourne from Australia; Mr. Gaston Gascoigne from Paris, France, and Colonel Kile Killigrew from Western Pennsylvania. One aged wrinkle-faced woman was also in the visiting geriatrics' contingent, Miss Wilma Whyknot, from the New York City Battery District, where the indigent woman now sleeps as a hapless bag-lady in the battery's bus, subway, and train terminals.

Each of the carefully selected guests to Dr. Ludwig Heidegger's secluded laboratory had encountered bad luck in life, and certainly would have been much happier dead-than-alive at age ninety-five.

Especially Miss Wilma Whyknot, who presently looked like Cleopatra does right now. In her younger days, the former spitfire had been a daring, promiscuous bitch, who had had intense love affairs with Mr. Melbourne, with Mr. Gascoigne, with Colonel Killigrew, and last but not least, with the eminent Dr. Heidegger, when the hag had lived in Mass-a-two-shits.

It had been gossiped around all of Puritanical New England that Wilma Whyknot was indeed an ancient slutty hoary whore, who had myriad romantic love affairs with Thomas Jefferson, with Alexander Hamilton, and also with nefarious Aaron Burr, and that the jilted Burr had brutally shot and killed Hamilton in a Weehawken, New Jersey pistol duel that had been waged over vixen Wilma Whyknot's then voluptuous body.

In Australia, Mr. Melvin Melbourne had once been a well-to-do grocery store distributor, but then "the mate" became involved in a crazy business investment, selling kangaroo meat to vegetarian-style supermarket chains. Melbourne soon lost his entire fortune, and officially became bankrupt, unhappily living in a Melbourne, Florida hippie commune, the failed entrepreneur harshly being relegated to the status of a more-than-desperate food stamps and welfare recipient.

Mr. Gaston Gascoigne has chronically suffered from gastritis and colitis, ever since the Frenchman had first plopped his fat ass onto a toilet seat. Wilma Whyknot recalls that the gaseous jerk would fart relentless every time the amorous pair would engage in crazy frenetic sex. Even though "that harpy" Wilma would tell Gaston "Stop farting around," the poor fellow had no control over his spastic intestines, and the unfortunate "French hemorrhage" asshole always had the sorest anus around.

Colonel Kile Killigrew, whose many belligerent ancestors represented the Union during the bloody Civil War, hated any rebel or Confederate descendant born south of the historic Mason-Dixon Line. But in his perverted youth, the Colonel regarded himself as a veritable sex machine, bragging that he carried in his system a dozen sexually transmitted diseases including syphilis, gonorrhea, chancroid, and nymphomania lymphogranuloma. But over the years, the antebellum erection champion had gained immunity to all of the potentially lethal maladies. Occasionally, the now-sperm-less, retired Army officer avoids the traditional V.A. Hospitals, and goes for special treatment directly to the government's highly-acclaimed National V.D. and HIV Medical Center.

"My dear valued, old friends," Dr. Heidegger began his extemporaneous salutation. "Welcome to my humble haunted house, er, I meant to say, 'my modest home'. I urgently need your help in participating in one of my favorite experiments that I often use to amuse myself, frequently performing and perfecting the demonstration right here in my comfortable study. Oh now, I'm so awfully sorry," the absent-minded Alzheimer's candidate apologized. "My study is the adjoining room. This friggn' part of my mansion is the fuckin' foyer!"

"What is your mysterious study like?" Mr. Melvin Melbourne curiously asked. "Is it similar to a university library that's loaded with empty book shelves?"

"My study is actually an old-fashioned room that features tremendous spider webs and cob-webs all over the friggin' walls and ceiling, and I must admit that it is a veritable paradise for voracious insects and mice, and besides *that* dull stupid shit, the entire damned place has plenty of dust, along with scads of accumulated filth in every corner," Heidegger calmly admitted and confessed. "And although I had been born in Hamburg, Germany, and then growing-up in Heidelberg, I only know a little German, and his name is Gunther Fadorkenbender, living way up in Dixville Notch. And regrettably," the garrulous Professor finished, "all of my books are in German and in Austrian, but to my frustration, I only know how to speak and read English and Mandarin Chinese."

Dr. Ludwig Heidegger next led his four very impressed guests from the massive foyer, and then meandered down the long drafty corridor serving as a portal into the aforementioned Grand Study, which also alternated as the scientist's personal laboratory, the exact setting where the fanatic intensively labored day and night on myriad obscure and insignificant projects.

The century-old guide next proudly showed his almost-blind visitors an immense marble statue of the Greek physician Hippocrates, seen peering intently into a naked woman's vagina, with his left hand shoved inside the lady patient's sex tunnel, all the way up to the kinky Greek examiner's elbow.

Then, quirky Dr. Heidegger opened the squeaky panel doors to a seven-foot-high wooden storage closet, and to everyone witnessing the intriguing spectacle, the four visitors were instantly shocked, viewing two skeletons incessantly rattling back and forth against each other in what truly-constituted a rather entertaining-but-weird, anatomical sex orgy.

"When I open the study's windows during a hurricane or blizzard," the unorthodox Professor explained to his now-fascinated audience, "the skeletons really move much better with the wicked wind blowing the dangling sons-a-bitches around in a frenzy. The only problem I have with the cute closet display is that both skeletons are males. I mean, I could have a gigantic gender lawsuit on my hands from the litigious gay and lesbian *community,* wherever the hell *that* fucked-up town is located! I mean, even the fucked-up trans-gender freaks will take me to court over this totally dumb-ass homosexual bull-shit!"

Between two of the more-grimy vertical bookcases was situated an enormous mirror with a faded gold-gilt frame. It had been rumored throughout the whole New England region that all of the Professor's dead former patrons were now spooky goblins and ghouls, all arcanely stashed inside the black magic looking glass, and that the trapped spirits would occasionally stick their ghostly heads outside the frame, whenever stragglers into the dilapidated mansion would be glancing away from the bizarre-looking, ominous mirror.

On the opposite side of the peculiar "museum" was a young lady's portrait, the said female wearing a dull dress, emblematic of a previous century, and the attractive apparel had been woven from imported silk along with an expensive satin fabric.

Melvin Melbourne, Gaston Gascoigne, Colonel Kile Killigrew, and Miss Wilma Whyknot all noticed in sheer amazement that when the sunshine shafts penetrated the dirty windows and then shone directly into the eerie library/study, the young woman's wedding dress would transform from being opaque to being transparent, and the beautiful lady would be exposed stark naked, with all of her pubic hairs and her fine succulent breasts and nipples being fully on display. And then conversely, when the drifting clouds took control of the sky and obscured the sun's radiant rays, the comely woman in the wall painting would be respectably fully clothed once again.

"That's not me up there!" Miss Whyknot observed and exclaimed. "That's the knockout bitch you dumped me for, isn't it Ludwig!"

"Yes Wilma," Dr. Heidegger confirmed. "That lady portrayed in the painting is my' former fiancee, Sylvia Ward. The night before our wedding, my love felt ill, so I gave her a medicinal formula I had been assiduously working on, but delicate Sylvia reacted negatively to the medication and died within an hour," the Professor lamented. "I've since sold the toxic formula to several state penitentiaries, who now use the special chemical solution to execute Death Row prisoners, instead of utilizing costly electric chairs that incidentally are not environmentally-friendly, wasting too much voltage energy and thus, egregiously polluting the pristine atmosphere."

"Doctor, what's that huge volume over there?" Gaston Gascoigne wanted to know. "I've never seen a book quite that enormous anywhere!"

Just then the sunshine shone through the south-side windows, and Sylvia Ward instantly again became naked. Also, the two male closet skeletons were now facing in the same direction, and engaging in humpty-rumpty sodomy, and in addition, noble Hippocrates was now sniffing his stinky middle finger with a broad, snarky smile evident upon his ancient Greek countenance.

Soon, the seemingly enchanted study became rather shadowy again, when the sun retreated behind a dark cloud, and everything in the creepy room returned to its original appearance, including the homosexual skeletons, the weird marble "Hippocrates Statue", along with the oddball "Sylvia Ward Portrait".

"Is that gargantuan book sitting there on the table titled *Mountain of Truth?*" Colonel Killigrew nervously asked. "It's so dust-laden that I can't discern the precise cover language."

"No Sir," Dr. Heidegger promptly answered in a deep mellow voice. "The goddamned title is *The Fountain of Youth!* I found that almost indecipherable volume while exploring for El Dorado up in the Amos Mountains, which as you might know, parallel the Andes. That little vignette I've just mentioned appropriately explains *that* exotic book cover, that is proudly featuring a forgotten range of high mountain peaks."

* * * * * * * * * * * *

While the five senile assholes were gathered around Dr. Ludwig Heidegger's oval study table discussing old mutual friends that had died, specifically Sarah Yeahvo, Kenny Bunkport, and "Shy Ann" Wyoming, the sunlight again reflected through the south-side window panes, which made the four visiting, senior-senior-senior citizens *reflect* on what the hell their notoriously demented host was attempting to communicate.

Professor Heidegger, former head of the science department at the famed Driftwood Naval Academy, located somewhere on the north bank of the Susquehanna River in Pennsylvania, commenced with his mind-boggling narrative. "My dear old friends, and I do mean old," the whacky Professor sarcastically emphasized. "First of all, you four withered-up itinerants should be wearing name tags so that I could fuckin' remember who the hell I had sent invitations to."

Melvin Melbourne cleared his throat, and the bankrupt charlatan rudely interrupted the forgetful host, who was presently suffering from a bad case of exaggerated dementia. "Dr. H., how come there are four empty champagne glasses upon the oval table? Are your four undistinguished guests sitting here going to drink air? On second thought, I think we all badly need oxygen, ha, ha, ha!"

"The four stemmed glasses are on the table so that you dumb-ass wretches could assist me in conducting a very odd-but-phenomenal experiment," Professor H. (who actually felt and looked like H) revealed. "Within the confines of this study/laboratory, I wish to learn the outcome of my life's work; that is, before I fuckin' die and go to Heaven, Hell, Purgatory, Limbo, or maybe to Nowhere, except into the goddamned ground!"

"Who gives a royal flying shit!" Melvin Melbourne gruffly butted-in, trying to steal the now-annoyed Professor's verbal thunder. "When you're dead, you don't fuckin' know anything!"

"You might be nimble enough to vault into your vault!" cryptically joked Colonel Kile Killigrew to flabbergasted Melvin Melbourne. "That type of amusing endeavor would be quite an undertaking, even without the aid of an undertaker dying from HIV/AIDS, ha, ha, ha!"

"We're all obviously suffering from advanced Iron Deficiency Anemia," objectively jested Miss Wilma Whyknot. "So *why not* serve us four old farts some delicious Geriatric Punch, ha, ha, ha! Especially for my old gaseous lover, Mr. Gascoigne here, who I think eats too much goddamned broccoli!"

"Didn't you use to be a bank teller before you were a teller of tall tales?" Gaston Gascoigne merrily expressed to demoralized Dr. Heidegger, before egregiously farting a loud gas bomb blast lasting for forty-seven and a half seconds. "Dr., are you going to show us how you can annihilate a defenseless white mouse in an air pump, or are we going to examine one of Methuselah's five-thousand-year-old sperm cells under a microscope?"

The three other jollied guests all laughed, burped, belched, and farted in response to Gaston Gascoigne's fairly-whimsical remarks. But their all-too-serious host evidently was not in a similar jocular frame of mind.

"You're not too far away from the very essence of my innovative theory," Dr. Heidegger replied, before rising-up from the musty oval table, and then slowly limping across the large neglected room, returning just as deliberately while gingerly carrying the giant black heavy book, showing the obscure Amos Mountain peaks on its begrimed cover.

The rather clandestine Professor carefully opened the silver clasp bindings, and reaching between the first and second pages, the possessed demonstrator cautiously removed what appeared to be the remnants of a withered rose, or what appeared to be *that* particular flower variety.

After everyone quieted-down from enjoying the previous ongoing ludicrous conversation, the good Dr. solemnly addressed his cynical doubters. "This half-crumbled rose that I'm now holding in my quivering hand had blossomed fifty some years ago. My lovely fiancee Sylvia Ward had given this flower memento to me to wear in the lapel of my 'tuxedo' on *our* wedding day."

"Yes Professor, but I suppose the only tucks any of us now know are the stenchy suppositories we use to purify our smelly assholes, ha, ha, ha!" Melvin Melbourne articulated as his three equally-asinine associates also simultaneously guffawed.

Ignoring the totally preposterous goof-ball remark, along with the resulting laughter, undaunted Dr. Ludwig Heidegger continued with his esoteric exposition. The four dubious attendees finally fathomed that the profound Professor was deadly serious about further delivering his strange lecture.

"For over half a century, this treasured flower I've kept between the pages of the classic old volume, but now tell me. Do any of you' Neanderthal knuckle-dragging skeptics believe one iota that this withered flower can be revived back to its glory days' fresh blossom?"

"Your former Scottish servant, Wilt "the Kilt Chamberlain, decaying horizontally inside his extra-long grave, looks better than *that* lifeless rose does!" Wilma Whyknot evaluated and commented. "You must be a blooming idiot Professor, ha, ha, ha! My dried-up pussy will grow thick, brown, curly hair again, before that wilted rose is ever rejuvenated! Ha, ha, ha!"

"Just watch this unique bull-shit!" demanded the now-insulted Professor. "That asshole Shakespeare had it all wrong. This rose is more than a mere rose! Your full-of-shit doubting minds are analogous to your shrunken brains being 'skeptic' tanks, that are full of diarrhea! You four facetious assholes will soon learn and appreciate the explicit veracity of my sublime words!"

On-a-mission Professor Heidegger then removed a mint-colored vase that had been obscurely covered by a green cloth shroud, the commonplace object being taken from a previously unnoticed bookcase that had been occupying a space upon a dusty side wall. The determined demonstrator next meticulously dropped the lifeless rose into the murky water contained inside the "magical vase". At first, the lifeless flower was simply floating on top of the cloudy-but-mysterious liquid solution.

"Is that water well water or tap water?" gaseous Gaston Gascoigne asked the experimenter. "That water must be tap water, because it doesn't look too well to me! Ha, ha, ha!" the flamboyant asshole remarked before loudly tooting a large quantity of expendable gas (for thirty-seconds) from his erratic asshole.

"Doubting Thomas," Dr. H. caustically criticized gaseous Gaston. "Now, I hereby accuse each of you other three noodle-brained buffoons of also being a doltish Doubting Thomas. None of you hare-brained fools would've believed Jesus at the Biblical Cana Wedding Feast, even if the Lord had changed the wine that He had transformed from water, back into water again!"

Soon, a most incredible alteration in the experimental rose's composition started to occur. The separate petals began assuming a deeper red texture, and the flower itself was emerging from its deathlike state of existence, or non-existence, if you prefer the latter terminology. Then suddenly, without any sign or notice, the slender tender stem and leaves mystically turned green and vibrant.

"This is certainly a deception, a flimsy carnival side-show trick I once saw performed on the Coney Island Boardwalk," Colonel Kile Killigrew remembered and orally shared. "Or perhaps it was on the Atlantic City Boardwalk! I can't seem to accurately recall. But you do recollect, don't you Wilma? We were shacked-up in a fleabag hotel screwing-away like addicted minks, pleasurably enjoying your intense sex drive; you were like an animal in estrus; yes Wilma, we were humping and pumping away, in a fleabag hotel just off of Surf Avenue! Then, we walked all over the damned place, looking for a tree growing in Brooklyn."

"Have you never heard of the exotic Fountain of Youth, Colonel?" Dr. H. asked Kile Killigrew. "The Spanish explorer Ponce de Leon searched for the fabled wonder in vain, all throughout Florida. Yes, the fabulous 'flower state', around three centuries ago. But the lost wanderer never searched for the Fountain in the right place," the Professor professed. "However, a dear friend of mine living near Lake Macaco had remarkably discovered the legendary Fount, and this nondescript mint-green vase contains water from the miraculous underground spring. Even though its wonderful spring water, you can drink it summer, fall, and winter, too! I promise you Folks, this vial is not vile at all!"

"Holy shit!" Melvin Melbourne rather boisterously exclaimed. "I could sprinkle some of that terrific crap on my dick, and it'll get hard for the first time in forty-years! And my tiny shriveled-up balls could be resuscitated, too!"

"I need that magic water applied to my scrawny chest to firm-up my sagging tits!" Wilma Whyknot excitedly yelled. "My flabby nipples will become big suckers once again! And my clit will get hard once more, and be just as big as Gaston's erection used to be!"

"I'll have more erections than any friggin' builder or architect ever did, including that dead guy, Frank Lloyd Wright!" Gaston Gascoigne enthusiastically shouted. "I'll be able to pop semen all over the damned place, even more so than the brawniest seamen out there sailing the oceans! As I used to say before getting laid back in the good old days, 'A little squirt never hurts!' But honestly, too much sex could also fag-out a gay French faggot like me, Gaston Gascoigne!"

Staring curiously at the ordinary-looking vase full of murky Fountain of Youth water, Colonel Kile Killigrew, no longer looking like 'Death Warmed Over', inanely yelled-out an imaginative exclamatory sentence for all present to hear, "Dr. Heidegger, take me to your liter!"

Indeed, the dumb-assed veteran military officer from Western Pennsylvania now sounded very much like a common, stereo-typical, fucked-up space alien.

* * * * * * * * * * * *

Seeing that his old flame Wilma Whyknot was looking forward to the prospect of having her clitoris perk-up to its former teenage hardness, Dr. Heidegger became inspired to pour the muddy water taken from the purported Fountain of Youth into the four filthy champagne glasses. Tiny bubbles percolated at the glass bottom and then, the little air pockets gradually rose-up to the surface, magnificently exploding in each example, forming into a lustrous, silver liquid surface.

"Before you partake of your drink," the absent-minded Professor stressed to his over-anxious guests, "remember all of the monumental mistakes you've experienced in your lackluster past lives, and then think of constructive ways you can deal with those perils the second time around on life's wondrous carousel."

"Fuck your philosophical bull-shit!" irate Melvin Melbourne demanded. "Pour us the freakin' magic water before it evaporates into useless hydrogen and oxygen molecules! I don't want to be a goddamned model citizen!" the transplanted Australian vehemently yelled. "I just want to screw a few good-looking bitches, who *are* gorgeous models, and who might incidentally be non-model citizens also! I'll even screw some fat ugly illegal Mexican whores if I get horny enough! Si, mucho gorda feo muchachas! Si Senor Heidegger!"

"But Friends," Dr. Heidegger futilely objected. "Just consider what a marvelous advantage you're being offered right this moment. It would be a shameful sin if you dunces didn't practice more wisdom and more virtue on your second, more-opportune tour of human duty, so to speak."

"Cut the silly-assed, sanctimonious bull-shit, and start pouring the goddamned muddy water," Gaston insisted before expelling a devastating blast of gas, this time propelling his ass right off his chair, and then sending his body two feet into the air. "We're too fuckin' old to joyfully sin without the help of the Fountain's magic water!"

"But what about today's vulnerable youth being tempted by drugs, sex, and alcohol?" the benign retired Driftwood Naval Academy Professor academically challenged his academically-challenged listeners. "What about today's endangered youth?"

"Fuck them!" Melvin Melbourne exclaimed. "Shit on the acne-faced shit-heads' heads!"

"But isn't there more to precious human life than a very limited, self-centered, biological, animal-type existence?" the ball-busting, water-pouring host requested, all the while seeking some semblance of constructive verbal reactions.

"I hope the miraculous water doesn't grow teeth upon Wilma's gums!" Colonel Killigrew contributed to the zany general oral debacle. "She gave tremendous blow-jobs when the promiscuous bitch had a full set of choppers anchored in her mouth, but with only gums to suck with, holy shit America! My balls are beginning to ache! I think I'm goin' to pop a huge premature load into my clean white underwear, even before ever drinking the fine elixir!"

"Drink hardily, then, and be satisfied to your heart's content!" Dr. Heidegger sternly instructed, bowing his head and waving his right arm like a respectful Indian servant. "And drink to your dicks and tits' content, too! The amazing stuff I'm gonna' serve you will work better than testosterone in men, and even better than estrogen in a horny woman like Wilma."

"Stop with all of the lousy pedantic profundity!" sex-starved Wilma Whyknot hollered. "This rather stimulating hormone you're suggesting will once again make *this* veteran *whore moan*, ha, ha, ha!" Then, the all-too-thrilled, cantankerous, alligator-skinned, lunatic bitch indulgently imbibed all but a remaining few ounces of her imported Fountain of Youth water.

"This muddy water tastes like cat piss!" gaseous Gaston loudly complained, before farting a deep hole into his chair's soft upholstery.

"I understand that swallowing-down cat piss could send the dumb-fuck experimental drinker into a suspended catastrophic, catatonic state. Now Gaston, have you ever drunk cat piss to be able to confidently make *that* rather unethical-sounding, totally-distasteful statement?" Melvin Melbourne challenged his former rival for Miss Wilma Whyknot's infamous sexual favors.

"No Melvin, but confidentially, I've only smelled cat piss from a distance at the neighborhood kennel, but I do have box-wood hedges all around my property, and box-wood smells almost-identical to cat piss. In fact," Gaston further elaborated on the wholly boring subject, "every day I would see a large family of cats pissing on my cherished hedge. But unlike the bothersome stray cats roaming around, I've perceptively noticed that the more discriminating canines on my block all piss on dogwood trees, instead of on my fragrant box-wood hedges! However, the other less-sophisticated, imbecile mutts in my neighborhood are always pissing on and barking up the wrong friggin' trees, that is to say, oak, birch, pine, maple and elm!"

"It's a good thing you all have advanced Parkinson's," Dr. Heidegger observed and mentioned. "The shaking of your hands while gripping your glasses mixes-up and stirs the Fountain formula most excellently. Someday, I'll be able to put every fucked-up nursing home and adult diaper company out of business with this wizard-like, Florida water!"

Suddenly, the flaccid faces of all four invited guests began glowing and brightening, and soon a healthy ruddy color appeared on their formerly pallid cheeks; in fact, on all their faces, and also, on the cheeks situated upon their ancient buttocks, too. Mr. Melbourne, Mr. Gascoigne, Colonel Killigrew, and Miss Whyknot no longer looked like morbid funeral parlor corpses about to be cremated.

"Give me more damned water!" Melbourne demanded like a bratty toddler in a high chair. "My limp dick has partially erected while I was looking at Wilma's tits firming-up! Hurry-up Heidegger, before I lose my miniature hard-on! And I really don't give a skunk's shit if I damage my brain with all the blood surging-down from my head to my throbbing pecker. I gotta' keep the damned thing alive and growing! I want more water Heidegger, and I want it now!"

"Patience! Patience my Man!" counseled the very suave Professor. "Just pretend you're a successful medical doctor, and that you have lots of patients, ha ha, ha!"

More supernatural water was being poured from the mint-green vase into the four champagne glasses, and the recipient merry revelers greedily gulped-down the liquid as if it were refreshing cold soda pop on a sultry summer day. The hideous silver hairs on the elderly guests' balding heads were slowly losing their boring grayish hue, and when the study's heavy wooden oval table rose-up six-inches off the floor, all because of Melbourne, Gascoigne and Killigrew's new-found erections, all six avaricious eyes quickly turned-upon elegant-looking and now-sensuous Wilma Whyknot.

"Wilma, you look absolutely charming!" the disreputable conniver Gaston Gascoigne hungrily declared, just as his next powerful anal toot nearly obliterated his expensive trousers.

Instead of masturbating in public, the three horny gentlemen quickly stripped-down nude, and then immediately began wildly pursuing Wilma Whyknot around the study's oval table like dizzy sex-starved maniacs.

"No more vicarious sex for me!" screamed a hot-to-trot Colonel Killigrew. "I want the real thing baby! Yes sir, the real thing!"

"No more casino card playing for me! I'm tired of losing at gambling!" Gaston fanatically bellowed. "Now I want the real deal! Yes, I want the real deal, and nothing else: The Queen of Hearts and not the damned Queen of Diamonds!"

"No more me idiotically looking at merino sheep and hairy wallaby assholes!" Melvin Melbourne yelped. "This fuckin' time it's gonna' be boner-fide penetration! Forget my prized donkey Monica doing my favorite mule Clinton! I want to be fucked and not sucked!"

"I want to be screwed badly, too!" shouted the already-fatigued table-racing harlot, being relentlessly chased by the lustful male trio. "But I want to be porked by only one horny jerk-off at a time!"

'Holy hormones!' Dr. Heidegger disgustingly thought. 'Those three assholes desiring to rape Miss Whyknot don't give a shit whether or not they have ribbed condoms! And I now understand that *that* Fountain of Youth miracle water is a fantastic aphrodisiac, too! Forget me putting the profitable nursing homes and the lucrative adult diaper industry out of business! I'm gonna' be destroying the blue sex pill market, too!'

"We're gonna' get ya' Wilma, and spread those Rockette legs wide open!" Melbourne yelled ahead to the former harlot, sounding a little like futuristic cartoonish Fred Flintstone. "Keep circling the damned table! But we're gonna' get you good! Your wet pink snatcheroo is gonna' be pumped dry!"

Professor Heidegger simply stood in a far corner of his musty study with his jaws agape, peering incredulously at the naked men's dandy hard-ons, flapping violently up and down, during their hot cunt-hunt pursuit.

"Look here you fanatical nutcases!" Dr. Heidegger shrieked above the chaotic din. "Now I know for sure that frivolous self-centered assholes like you four ingrates are rapidly turning the majestic United States of America into a Third World Banana Republic!"

* * * * * * * * * * * *

When Miss Wilma Whyknot's lungs finally ran out of breath, the exhausted-and-retired New York City prostitute was immediately gang tackled by the three more-than-eager nude gigolos, who during the turbulent tumult, hadn't realized that the trio had lost their impressive erections while grappling and fighting with each other for "first dibs", for "sloppy seconds", and for "who gives a shit, messy-thirds".

Miss Wilma Whyknot now also was extremely disappointed at not getting gang-banged into ecstasy upon the immense study's dirty oak-planked floor. And when the four dazed, naked, sex-marathon participants rose-up from their knees to their feet, pissed-off Wilma, feeling ignored and abused, swiftly kicked all three disconsolate and sexually-frustrated paramours very forcefully into their now-dormant and inert testicles.

But when the four struggling lunatics had been frenetically rolling-around upon the study's sordid floor, no one except alert Dr. Ludwig Heidegger had comprehended that the extended scuffle and the ensuing fracas had caused the mint-green vase to fall off of the oak table, and then completely shatter upon gravity's impact.

Finally realizing what damage had occurred, all four miserable morons got-down on their hands and knees, and began aggressively licking the dirty planks, their parched tongues in desperate quest of the remaining minuscule droplets and beads of invaluable and indispensable Fountain of Youth water.

The four elderly, misguided fools all stared at unfazed Dr. Heidegger, who was then sitting in his favorite red velvet wood-carved armchair. The shrewd scientist was passionately holding the again-withered rose given to him by Miss Sylvia Ward, fifty-three years prior, the selfsame flower that Ludwig had recently rescued from the shattered mint-green flower vase.

"My dick is absolutely limp!" moaned extremely distressed Melvin Melbourne.

"My balls are shriveled," cried garrulous Gaston Gascoigne. "I think they're disintegrating as I speak! I'm so fuckin' pooped I can't even poop or fart!"

"My tits are horribly flabby and sagging again, and my lush brown pussy hair has mysteriously disappeared," volatile and obsolete whore Miss Wilma Whyknot vehemently bitched. "Somebody must've put vanishing cream in that fucked-up spiked Fountain of Youth water!"

"Yes, my old Friends, you're all impotent shit-heads again," Dr. Heidegger verified. "And unfortunately, I've just received word yesterday that my old acquaintance down in Florida has passed-away.

Leon de Ponce was really and truly the only person who knew exactly where the singular Fountain of Youth is located!"

And then, the eccentric Professor casually limped-out of the library/study, and methodically progressed through the tall thick doors into the red-carpeted foyer. Several moments later, distinct clanking sounds were discerned, and after the metal window shutters slammed closed, the four pathetically-trapped elders finally fathomed that they had become incarcerated invitees locked inside the bizarre room.

A dim dull light being emitted from the chamber's four tall oval table candles revealed Sylvia Ward alternating inside the fearful wall portrait from being fully-clothed, to being totally nude; and then numerous pale-faced dead medical patients were sticking their eerie heads in and out of the room's dreadful wall mirror; and the two male skeletons were again enacting their perverted sodomy; and finally, Hippocrates began dashing-around the accursed study, wielding two sharp daggers in his massive white marble hands.

Before any of the doomed hostages could scream, shout, or even emit gas, a small square trap opened in the side wall, and Dr. Ludwig Heidegger's scary voice declared, "Well my former Friends from the distant past, I've decided that you've all lived on this planet for far too long. Yes, I am indeed playing God! I've intelligently retained several additional vases of the sensational Fountain of Youth formula down in my dank cellar, so I plan on being around this isolated part of New Hampshire for at least another century or so."

"What's to become of us?" yelled-out a now-hysterical Wilma Whyknot, who had swiftly scurried to a web-infested corner to temporarily evade the formidable stalking of Hippocrates, a now-living, animated lethal statue.

"My dear Wilma," Dr. Heidegger condescendingly answered and then snickered. "I'm getting overwhelmingly bored being a chemist, a pharmacist, a medical doctor, and a college instructor these past seventy-years. And so, I'm finally graduating from Mortuary Science School, but in order to be fully certified, I must first dissect four fresh corpses, and then write a comprehensive thesis on my results to allow me to finally qualify for receiving my diploma."

"You can't do this unthinkable mortal sin to us!" shrieked a fully-delirious Melvin Melbourne, whom lethal Hippocrates was now keenly eyeing. "This travesty you're engaged in is undoubtedly malicious criminal behavior! You'll pay for your dastardly felonies, I'm sure of it! The police will eventually track you down!"

"After the four of you foolish nitwits are stone-cold dead," Professor Heidegger's voice calmly and eerily informed his prospective victims through the square trap hatch in the side wall, "I'll have loyal

Hippocrates carry each of you one at a time down to my cellar morgue, where I'll diligently commence working on my most difficult Mortuary School Thesis!"

"Theseus and the Minotaur"

In the old city of Troezene, at the foot and toes of a lofty mountain, there lived, a very long time ago, a proud little tyke named Theseus. His grandfather, King Pittheus, was the sovereign of that pitiful country, and the ruler was reckoned by dumb-ass scholars to be a very wise man, so that Theseus, being brought-up inside the royal palace, and being naturally a quasi-bright lad, could hardly fail at profiting by listening to, and heeding, King Pittheus's pithy instructions.

The mother of Theseus was Aethra. As for his missing father, the boy had never seen the itinerant, philandering gigolo. But from his earliest remembrance, Aethra used to accompany little Theseus into a dark woods, and the pair would sit-down upon a moss-covered rock, which was deeply sunken into the solid earth. There, Aethra often conversed with her all-too-inquisitive son about his deadbeat father, and the mother monotonously declared that the avowed womanizer was called Aegeus, and that her husband was a great king, and sternly ruled over distant Attica.

Aegeus dwelt at Athens, which was as famous a city as any other fucked-up place in the ancient mythological world. Theseus was very fond of hearing about sperm-laden King Aegeus, and often asked his good mother Aethra why the cheating sex-addict did not come and live with them at Troezene. The curious youngster also wondered how many thousands of biological half-brothers and half-sisters Theseus actually had scattered throughout the entire Aegean Sea, which gets older and older with each passing day.

"Ah, my dear son," Aethra answered, with a heavy sigh. "A monarch has his people to take care of, and not just provide for one of his one-night flings, like poor little old me. The Athenian men and women over whom Aegeus now rules, take the place of his children, and your biological father can seldom spare time to love his own son as other more normal derelict parents do. Your philandering dad will never be able to leave his important kingdom for the sake of seeing his neglected little boy, or me, his once knocked-up mistress."

"Well, but, dear mother," Theseus apprehensively wondered and asked. "Why can't I go to this famous city of Athens, and tell sperm-sharing King Aegeus that I'm his son? Someday, I'll have sperm to shoot all over the region just like pop does, whenever he pops his hyperactive weasel!"

"That may happen by and by," saddened Aethra admitted. "Be patient, Theseus, and we shall see what the hell we shall see. You're not yet big and strong enough to set-out on such a dangerous and historic errand. Perhaps after you grow a crop of hair around your tiny pecker, you'll be ready to finally set sail into the sunset!"

"And how soon shall I be strong enough to seek my fame and fortune?" Theseus persisted in inquiring. "I can already lift a leaking ten pound bag of bird feces over my head!"

"You're but a tiny lad with diminutive-sized testicles," indiscreetly replied his mother. "See if you can lift this moss-laden rock on which we're sitting?"

The little fellow had a greatly distorted opinion of his own strength. So, grasping the rough edges of the colossal, mossy rock, the diminutive braggart tugged and toiled strenuously, and got himself quite out of breath in the interim, without being able to even slightly budge the heavy stone, which seemed to be rooted quite deeply into the ground. No wonder that the ambitious wimp could not move the hefty boulder; for the object would have taken all the force of a very strong hero, like legendary Hercules, to successfully lift it out of its earthy bed.

Aethra stood looking on, with a sad kind of a smile featured upon her rosy lips. "You see how it is, my dear Theseus. You must possess far more strength than now before I can ever trust you to venture-off to Athens, and tell apathetic King Aegeus that you're his lousy bastard son. But when you can lift and move this rock," the mother indicated and emphasized, "you can show me and describe precisely what is hidden beneath it. Then, I promise you'll have my expressed permission to depart to Athens across the vast, perilous sea."

A dozen times after *that* empty discussion, Theseus did ask his mother whether it was yet time for him to travel to Athens to visit his father, and there, lose his virginity. And still, his mother pointed to the enormous rock, and told her son that for years to come, the puny wise-ass could not be strong enough to move the colossal boulder.

And again and again, the rosy-cheeked, curly-headed boy would tug and strain, giving the lad painful double-hernias all over his frail body. Meanwhile, the huge stone seemed to be sinking more and more into the immovable ground. Over the years, the moss covering the immense rock became thicker and thicker, until at last the colorful green boulder looked almost like a soft green seat, with only a few gray knobs of granite, and overhanging sprouting trees, branching-out from its round surface.

But, difficult as the entire matter looked, Theseus was now growing-up to be such a vigorous youth, that in his own inflated opinion, the time would quickly arrive when the frustrated lad might hope to get the upper hand of that ponderous lump of stone. 'Mother says I've got rocks in my head, so in truth, I'm a kinsman to this motherless green boulder!'

Several years afterwards, when the mother and son were again sitting upon the moss-covered stone, Aethra had once more told her obdurate son the often-repeated story of his wayward father, and how gladly Aegeus would receive Theseus at his stately Athenian palace, and how the pussy-crazy king would present the youth to his noble courtiers and the city's noblest citizens, and tell the fuck-heads that Theseus was the prospective heir to *his* myriad dominions. The eyes of the obstinate teenager glowed with enthusiasm and avarice, and the adolescent conniver would hardly sit still to again hear his mother speak the hackneyed prediction. "Yes, Mother," the eager young punk resolutely proclaimed. "The time has come!"

Then, Theseus bent himself in good earnest to endeavor performing the arduous task, and the lad strained every sinew, with admirable manly strength and dexterity. The attempter put his whole brave heart into the gallant effort, violently wrestling with the huge, sluggish stone, as if the inanimate object had been a living enemy.

The adamant asshole heaved, lifted, and resolved to succeed, or else be destined to perish there as a defeated born loser, and allow the rock forever to be *his* monument to failure!

Aethra stood alongside, gazing at Theseus in his great struggle, and the woman clasped her hands, partly with a mother's pride, and partly with a mother's sorrow. Suddenly, the great rock stirred! Yes, it was now raised slowly from the bedded moss and earth, uprooting the shrubs, weeds, trees, and wild flowers along with it, and was then amazingly turned upon its side. Theseus had, at last, handily conquered the incredible task at hand!

While taking much-deserved deep breaths, the triumphant, acne-faced teenager looked joyfully at his astounded mother, and she smiled upon him through her alligator-type crocodile tears.

"Yes, Theseus," Aethra acknowledged and remarked. "The time has come, and thank Zeus that you must stay no longer at my side! See what King Aegeus, your royal father, left for you lying beneath the stone, when the bastard had first lifted the huge rock in his mighty arms, and laid it upon the spot, precisely where you've now majestically removed and placed it."

Theseus looked carefully, and his eyes observed that the immense rock had been placed over another partially-concealed slab of stone, the newly-discovered hollow containing a narrow cavity within it. The newly-discovered shape had wooden walls and resembled a roughly-made chest or coffer, of which the upper mass had served as the protective lid. Within the framed hollow lay a sword, with a golden hilt, and a neat pair of "magical sandals".

"That was your father's favorite sword," Arethea recognized and informed. "And those were his comfortable sandals. When the womanizer left this land to become king of Athens, Aegeus bade me treat you as a child until you should prove yourself a man by lifting and moving *that* enormous stone. With that challenging task being accomplished, you are to put on *his* sandals, in order to follow in your father's footsteps, and to next gird on your waist his invincible sword, so that you may fight giants, and dragons, and harlots, and harpies, and blind old geezers, as King Aegeus had done in his glorious youth."

"I'll set-out for Athens this very day!" Theseus excitedly revealed. "Now, I'm finally ready to meet my negligent, arrogant old man, and finally get my first official coming-of-age piece of ass."

"Thank Zeus!" Aethra euphorically exclaimed. "Theseus, you have no idea what dismal drudgery it has been for me having your smart-ass tethered to my apron strings these past horrible eighteen years! Don't let the front door collide with your ass on the way out! Good bye, and good riddance!"

* * * * * * * * * * * *

As already established, Theseus was an ancient Greek hero from Troezene that led a very Spartan existence while living his childhood in southern Greece, and later visiting Crete, which was an island situated next to shitty Excrete. In fact, many college literature students have written their theses on the legendary Theseus. The popular champion was featured in three of Euripides' plays, and after another playwright named Sophocles tore-up the three Theseus' scripts, a third drama writer named Aeschylus shouted at Sophocles, "*You rippa' these*? Why are you' such a dumb destructive fuck! *You menna' these* now, you stupid shit!"

As already mentioned, Theseus was the son of Aegeus, King of Athens, but his strange, estranged father thought that his bratty, egotistical kid would be a nuisance, so the paranoid ruler had his progeny live with *his* bitchy mother in southern Greece. Aegeus was very superstitious, and religiously honored a silly prophecy that a blind, deaf-and-dumb soothsayer had once predicted to the easily influenced, paranoid Athenian king.

'I'll bury this sword and soldier's sandals in this hollow,' the king thought after dropping his pregnant wife off in southern Greece. 'And then, I'll place this boulder over it. I hope this rolling stone gathers no moss, while I'm pushing it toward the two buried items inside the hollow,' Aegeus reflected without ever using any mirror. 'When my obnoxious son becomes strong enough to roll the giant rock off the hole all by himself,' the king imagined, 'then he'll be mature enough to live with me in Athens, where I can thoroughly corrupt his morals, and make his vulnerable mind totally fucked-up and decadent, just like mine is.'

When Theseus finally became old and strong enough to move the rock, the "Prince" consulted two stone rolling engineer friends, named Mik and Jagged, to render relevant advice, so as already related, after Theseus's mother showed him the boulder for the thousandth time, the prodigious lad easily moved the object and discovered the fighting bronze sword and soldier's sandals underneath.

"Now, I can journey to Athens and sleep with father instead of shacking-up with you," Theseus told his haughty, promiscuous, incestual, whoring mother. "I'm through with rolling boulders. Find another damned little toddler to abuse and molest!"

"The time has come for you to get the *Hades* out of here," the disgusted mother related to her discourteous, narcissistic son. "Your grandfather wants to see you leave the city too, because he believes you're an absolute arrogant, punk hooligan. Now Theseus," Arethea instructed. "Go' directly to the dock, and climb-aboard the next friggin' boat sailin' to Athens."

"I refuse to make the trip by water," Theseus protested. "The voyage would be too safe, and too simple for me to complete. I mean, Mom, if I'm to ever become a great hero, I need challenges and difficult problems. How the fuck am I ever goin' to become a legend by just sailin' around in a dip-shit wooden boat with asshole weak and wimpy, senior-citizen, sightseeing tourists all the way to Athens?"

"Your older cousin, Hercules, rides in boats and ships all the time," the teenager's mother reminded him, "and *he's* already regarded as an accomplished hero. I believe that the younger generation always has to make things more complicated than the assigned chores really have to be!" the mother chided. "Why do you always have to impetuously prove something without thinking it through?"

"May you grow a second asshole, and may it appear between your tiny tits!" Theseus exclaimed as the insulted youth indirectly favored his aberrant father, denouncing his mother and her feckless, aristocratic, cowardly family. "You'll never grow or have balls for as long as you live!" the boy disrespectfully chastised his already-distressed mother.

"I hope you live a dangerous and adventurous life, my son," Theseus's mother prattled. "For I can plainly see that you're just as conceited and just as reprehensible as your pretentious father is. So, it's gotta' be *my way* or the highway, if ya' don't want to shape-up and ship-out!"

"Mother, I only wish that we ancient Greeks had last names, for if we did, I'm certain that *your* contemptible last name would be Fucker!" Theseus maliciously cursed as the stubborn youth set-out on foot north in the direction of Athens.

"You'll lead a hard harsh life, and your ship will never come in!" the mother shouted and predicted.

"Eat my royal salami!" Theseus turned and nastily hollered-back. "Then, you'll have a major reverse *edible* complex! I've had it with your ignorant daily bull-shit!"

* * * * * * * * * * * * *

The overland trip to Athens was long and arduous. Many avaricious, heinous thieves and bandits hid along the popular trail, waiting to pounce upon any itinerant traveler. But magnificent Theseus was not stifled by any lowlife threats jeopardizing his safety.

"Give us your money," the leader of three robbers demanded in one particular ambush near Corinth.

"I have no money and don't give a shit what you say!" Theseus boldly answered. "Now fuck-off, assholes!"

"Then, I recommend that you kneel-down, so that after *we* pilfer your gold and silver coins, we may lift and toss you over the side of the cliff into the raging sea!" the second robber insisted.

"I've already told you dumb-dicks to 'fuck-off!" Theseus angrily demanded. "What you have threatened me, I shall certainly do to you! Fuck-off, and find someone weaker and richer than I am to rob!"

The infuriated hero then grabbed the first surprised trail thief, hoisted the scumbag over *his* head, and flung the screaming bandit off the precipice into what would later become known as the Aegean Sea, which would be officially named after the lad's aging father, Aegeus, ages later. Then, audacious Theseus knocked the other two aggressors unconscious with his bare clenched fists. When the pair of hostile highwaymen finally revived, the now-delirious shit-heads found themselves tethered to two pine trees that had been bent to the ground.

"What the fuck's goin' on?" the first thoroughly paranoid path villain yelled. "Damned *Oracle of Delphi!* Your terrible prediction has come to fruition! This pugnacious punk lunatic is gonna' tear me limb from limb!"

"I hope you two are prepared to go your separate ways!" Theseus laughed. "And splittin' headaches are nothin' compared to the splittin' bodies I'm about to administer!"

"Untie us and we'll promise to do anything you ask!" the first robber pleaded. "I'll wash and lick your grimy feet; wipe your dirty smelly ass clean; massage your raunchy dick every hour, oh well; I suppose I'll do just about anything you command!"

"Fuck you!" Theseus yelled as he released the trees from their tethers with one swift swipe of his trusty bronze sword. The two apprehensive thieves were simultaneously catapulted into the air, and in a second, separated into four pieces, as their dismembered bodies soared-off the precipice, and into the yet unnamed Aegean Sea, situated a hundred-yards below. "That oughta' teach you dunce-headed hoodlums from fuckin' with me!"

Theseus had killed over a hundred diabolical bandits in his conflict-oriented trek from Sparta to Athens, and finally, it was now safe for politicians, priests, pedophiles, and other less dangerous crooks to travel about ancient Greece unmolested.

When Theseus finally reached his destination, the Athenians had heard of his successful campaign against BASTARDS (Bandits Association for the Systematic Thievery of Athenians, Retards, Dumb-asses and Spartans), King Aegeus had also been briefed of a bold young hero that had recently entered his city. The ruler invited the yahoo by messenger (but not by *Yahoo Messenger*) to attend a banquet that was coincidentally being given on that very day, being celebrated to honor no one, or nothing.

'I'll poison the young punk at my exquisite banquet,' the king thought while not realizing or caring that the callow vigilante might indeed be *his* exiled son. A witch named Medea had planted *that* evil thought in King Aegeus's underdeveloped brain. Medea wanted to have full influence over the Athenian ruler, and the gifted enchantress knew by prophecy that Theseus was the monarch's only son, and the clever witch wanted the kid out of the picture, so that the greedy female could continue running the city and its profitable businesses, while using the dummy king as her obedient puppet.

At the raucous banquet, Medea was about to hand Theseus a chalice filled with wine laced with poison, but the young hero inadvertently dropped his bronze sword onto the palace's stone floor. The king instantly recognized the bronze sword as the one that *he* had surreptitiously buried under the boulder in southern Greece, which was even worse than being buried for seventeen-years in ancient greasy grease. The king instinctively knocked the poisoned cup out of Medea's hand onto the stone floor, and the witch imaginatively used her magical powers to disappear to Asia Minor, where minors under the age of eighteen were officially allowed by law to drink wine, beer, liquor, sperm juice, and poison.

"People of Athens," Aegeus announced. "May I introduce to you my son and heir, Prince Theseus!"

"Fuck both you and him!" everyone in attendance sarcastically jeered. "Get some new worthwhile genetics in your accursed, inferior family tree!"

"When's the royal orgy going to begin?" another guest yelled. "I feel like being a *bisexual* tonight!"

"I'd rather be *introduced* to venereal disease than to a slime-ball like immature Theseus!" another celebrator boomed.

"Just what this already fucked-up city needs is another perverted, pompous, royal asshole!" the thousand guests all amazingly shouted *in unison,* even though they all were *in Athens.*

Meanwhile, scheming King Aegeus was contemplating a contemptible plot to eliminate the threat of Theseus ever prematurely stealing the monarch's power, wealth, concubines, sluts, dildos, and glory. The unscrupulous king escorted the pure-hearted Theseus out of the regal banquet chamber and into *his* private ornate lounge to make the chaste lad a special offer.

"My son, Theseus," Aegeus began. "I have a special 'proposal' for you to consider."

"I don't want to marry any damn man who proposes to me," the argumentative hero loudly replied. "Especially a psychologically dysfunctional man, who happens to be my' fucked-up father!"

"No-no, my son," the king heartily laughed. "I want you to go on a specially assigned quest to rid my soul of a certain guilt that persistently haunts me."

"Special quest?" Theseus's eyes lit-up as the want-to-be hero evaluated the prospect of finally experiencing a real adventurous exploit. "Do you want me to break up lesbian love triangles back in Corinth? What about me eliminating all homosexual romantic love-triangles and sex-trapezoids in Attica?" the young handsome prince inquired.

"I assure you, Theseus, that you'll be under aging King Aegeus's aegis!" the father persuasively alliterated.

'I would rather be standing at the base of *Mt. Olympus* when it finally crumbles and tumbles to the ground,' Theseus cynically thought but did not share.

King Aegeus proceeded to tell his mercurial-minded son about the legendary King Minos, ruler of the island of Crete, situated right next to shitty Excrete. Minos had lost his only son Androgeus to a terrible tragedy. The cretin Cretan king had sent Androgeus to Athens to discuss with King Aegeus the exciting plan of trading wives for nymphomaniac whores.

"Theseus," Aegeus said to his pristine and idealistic son. "I foolishly told Androgeus about a very dangerous horny bull that had been terrorizing the outskirts of Athens, and also, the outskirts and undergarments of all women living around or near the city. The lustful, horny beast wanted to screw beautiful women instead of simply obeying nature and being content porking cows."

"What did you do to Androgeus that was so foolish?" Theseus innocently asked, without suspecting how big of a conniving, devious prick his father actually was.

"When Androgeus heard me talking about this special perverted bull," Aegeus continued, "the glory-seeking thug volunteered to go and kill the sex-crazed creature, and I stupidly allowed him to pursue his wild fantasy. Then, the horny bull mercilessly gored and killed Androgeus, and distraught King Minos became excessively pissed-off about *his* son's unnecessary death."

Aegeus next explained that Minos sent his best elite soldiers to invade Athens, and threatened to burn *his* splendid metropolis to cinders if the beleaguered king didn't send seven fair maidens and seven virgin males to Crete every nine years to be offered to the mighty Minotaur to devour.

"The minute tour?" Theseus asked. "How could a *minute tour* of any government building devour fourteen innocent teenagers?"

"My dear fucked-up son," Aegeus interrupted. "The Minotaur is a horrible monster that has the head of a bull and the body of a man, and I tell you, Theseus, that's no goddamned bull-shit. The grotesque creature was the offspring of Minos's wife Queen Pasiphae and a studly bull. Pasiphae preferred having sex with bulls, horses, donkeys and elephants, or just about any animal that had a dick longer and thicker than a man's leg."

"Wow!" Theseus marveled. "Then Minos's wife never had sex with a rooster, so that this tale you're presently relating could never be misconstrued as your typical cock and bull story."

"Exactly," King Aegeus petulantly agreed, "Queen Pasiphae hated roosters with a passion and would often repeatedly scream-out during nightmare orgasms, 'Any animal's cock'll do, besides a cock-a-doodle-do'!"

"How did King Minos get possession of such an extraordinary creature as this Minotaur you've been describing?" Theseus asked his demented, degenerate father.

"A magnificent bull was given to Minos by the sea-god Poseidon," Aegeus explained to his fascinated son. "Poseidon strictly instructed Minos to sacrifice the bull to the gods, but Minos refused to do so. The asshole king was an impotent voyeur, who only got half an erection watching the horny bull fuck the shit out of Queen Pasiphae twenty-four times a day," Aegeus graphically elaborated. "Then, a son was born to Pasiphae, and the offspring was the gruesome-looking, big-dicked, very horny Minotaur."

Theseus learned from his father that Minos had commissioned the services of a great Greek architect named Daedalus, who had designed and supervised the construction of a vast network of underground caves and tunnels that formed a virtually inescapable dark maze beneath the Cretan palace at Knossos. Every nine-years, the fourteen young Athenian virgins were cruelly placed inside the incredible, a-maze-ing labyrinth, and were eventually individually and brutally slaughtered, and then, voraciously consumed by the wholly heinous Minotaur.

"So, what the fuck does all of this damned stupid Minotaur bull-shit have to do with the reason for *my* quest?" the now-perturbed Theseus inquisitively asked his father.

"Within a week, the next fourteen Athenian youths are scheduled to leave Athens and voyage to Crete, only to be thrown to the wretched beast," Aegeus divulged. "And you, my son, must venture to Crete and slay the vile Minotaur before the innocent virgins are sodomized, screwed, and then ultimately devoured."

"I hereby volunteer to be one of the young males to be sacrificed!" Theseus cavalierly announced to his father. "I gotta' get my first big exploit under my belt, and besides, I might actually enjoy being sodomized by the savage monster."

"Are you a virgin?" Aegeus curiously asked.

"Fuckin'A!" Theseus proudly declared. "Before the ship returns to Athens, I shall lower the bad news black sail, and raise the white one, so that *you* will know in advance of my conquest of the Minotaur," the eager prince stated. "Now father; please leave me the fuck alone while I formulate a clever ruse to employ!"

'That is quite good my accursed son,' Aegeus meditated. 'After you're killed by the monster, my debt to Minos will have been erased, and my imperial dominance fully secured, with me being the kingpin here in Athens. My supreme will shall be unchallenged by Crete!'

The fourteen sacrificial victims arrived in Crete by ship from Athens, and were forced to march in a procession that paraded throughout the city of Knossos, which had only two one-way streets. The fourteen prospective victims were showered with bull sperm, cow ovarian eggs, and the prospective victims felt and heard lots of bull-shit being vociferously yelled at them. Ariadne, the daughter of King Minos, was in the crowd throwing hard and soft bull manure at the fourteen unfortunate Athenians, when the knockout maiden noticed Theseus's muscular body, and immediately fell in love.

"Daedalus," Ariadne said to the drunken reveler standing next to her. "Kindly tell me, great architect. How can a person escape the labyrinth that you and your son Icarus had designed and had constructed beneath my father's palace. How does a person, like myself', who doesn't have the wonderful gift of tunnel vision, get out of that freakin' underground maze?"

"Okay, Ariadne, I'll tell you everything if you promise to give me a quality royal blow-job, and then sit on my face with your bare ass, and frenetically maneuver and rivet your wet twat over my nostrils for at least an hour," Daedalus stipulated.

"It's a deal!" Ariadne enthusiastically replied. "But I don't want your long nose bustin' my cherry before my chosen lover has the opportunity to pump the poop out of me!"

Later that afternoon, Ariadne had several soldiers escort the chaste-hearted, courageous Theseus to her royal bedroom. The young hero eagerly listened to the princess's proposal, as his eyes remained fastened upon Ariadne's rock-solid, tits having beautiful, round, protruding nipples, delightfully showing through the well-built young lady's sheer-thin-white tunic.

"I shall help you escape the labyrinth if you promise to take me to Athens and then marry me," Ariadne directly suggested. "I need to escape outa' this fuckin' desert-island dump, and get the *Hades* away from my fucked-up, voyeur father, and my mentally-sick, sex-crazed bull-screwin' mother."

"I promise to take you home to Athens as long as you don't fuck-around, having perverted sex with bulls, horses, donkeys, and elephants!" Theseus sternly returned. "To tell you the truth, Ariadne, their long thick dicks make me feel rather inferior."

"I promise!" the obliging princess agreed. "Now take this ball of thread, and I'll tell ya' exactly how to use it."

That night, Theseus entered the pitch-black labyrinth through a well-concealed secret palace door. The hero tightly tied a loop of string around the wooden door's latch; kissed Ariadne for good luck, and then proceeded into the dark and perilous labyrinth. All the while, the hero unwound the ball of string that was now his sole connection with civilization, along with the outside world.

Theseus ventured forward in the cold, dank blackness, searching and listening for any sound of the dreadful heinous monster. The nervous dark-maze explorer soon heard a loud snoring originating in the far distance. A minute later, the intruder fell over the suddenly-startled Minotaur, and then took the bull by the horns, smashing the beast's skull repeatedly against the dense, underground, rock walls. And then, Theseus beat the living bull-shit out of the snarling, growling beast, by pounding the Minotaur relentlessly with his clenched fists, alternately in the balls, and then in the face. Soon, the defeated creature had been brutally battered to death, and its lungs breathed no more.

Theseus lifted himself up from atop his terrible adversary; luckily found the ball of string upon the ground, and followed its path along three subterranean corridors, back to the concealed palace door from which the hero had entered the amazing maze.

"Oh, my marvelous hero, you have returned alive!" Ariadne shrieked and yelled as the thrilled princess threw her arms around her new-found idol's broad shoulders.

"I don't play *second string* to nobody, not even a fuckin' Minotaur!" Theseus boasted as the victorious youth casually dropped what remained of the ball of string to the re-entered palace's white marble floor.

The thirteen virgins (excluding Theseus and Ariadne, both of whom were definitely not certifiable virgins) speedily fled back to the Athenian ship. In no time, the escaped couple was heading north by northwest, and the following morning, the merchant vessel docked at the island of Naxos, only a few nautical miles from Nachos.

"Oh, my brave Theseus!" Ariadne exclaimed. "I'm extremely seasick, and I've already vomited-up half my lungs, and a third of my stomach. Please leave me on this island until I fully recover from my nausea," the princess wept. "Then, by all means, return here to Naxos and take me to Athens with you!"

"All right, Ariadne!" Theseus consented. "I approve of your wise recommendation. But I insist that if you would simply give me a deep-throated blowjob, then all of that nasty sour stomach fluid would quickly exit your mouth, after I pop my biggest load ever down your gorgeous throat!"

When the Athenian ship left Naxos, and finally neared its ultimate destination, Theseus was thinking about Ariadne giving him the best blow-job ever, and the distracted passenger forgot to take-down the black sail, and hoist-up the white one. King Aegeus was watching the black-sailed ship from the summit of the city's *Acropolis*. 'This is great!' the ruler concluded. 'My son Theseus is dead, and the black sail has been raised, indicating *that* wonderful bad news. I now can rule Athens unimpeded and unchallenged by any other young, asshole, idealistic whippersnapper thinking and acting like myself!'

Theseus's mind broke-off from its idle reverie, long enough for the Minotaur conqueror to realize that he had been morally obligated to his royal father to lower the black sail, and then raise the white one, signifying *his* glorious triumph in Crete over the ghastly and lethal satanic Minotaur.

Seeing the white sail being hoisted up the ship's mast, Aegeus became abundantly depressed, paranoid, livid, crazy, despondent, melancholy, neurotic, and lugubrious, all at the same time. The confused and agitated suicide victim leaped from the *Acropolis,* and swiftly plummeted-down, crashing into the small temple of Athena, where the insane king instantly ruptured both of his *temples,* and immediately died upon impact. Aegeus's body then continued rolling all the way to the roaring sea, and finally, fell off another cliff into the dark blue water. Hence, the geographic area is now known and identified as the Aegean Sea.

And that's precisely how intrepid Theseus had killed the pernicious Minotaur, and then easily became by default (through no fault of his own) the rightful ruler of Athens.

This final scenario involving his aberrant father was indeed melancholy news for Prince Theseus, who, when the impetuous lad had stepped ashore, found himself king of all the peninsula, and such a tremendous turn of fortune was enough to make any young man feel very much exhilaration. However, bold Theseus sent for his estranged mother to voyage to Athens, and by taking her sage advice regarding idiotic bureaucratic matters of state, the intrepid fellow became a very excellent and outstanding monarch, and unlike *his* nefarious father, was greatly beloved by his new-found subjects.

"The Birthmark"

In the latter part of the last century, there lived a rather confused young man of weird science and strange medicine, a failing experimenter proficient in every branch and twig of natural philosophy, who not long before our story opens, had made experience of a spiritual (sexual) affinity more attractive than any chemically-produced orgasm that the weirdo fool/pretender had ever concocted. This bizarre mad neurotic asshole had left his laboratory to the care of an incompetent assistant; escaped from the workplace's dense furnace smoke; washed the dark stain of acids from his exploratory fingers, and somehow managed to persuade a beautiful woman to become his lawful wedded wife.

In those most-peculiar days, with the recent discovery of electricity, along with other kindred mysteries of Nature being explored, novel paths were being opened into the new region of "scientific miracles". It was not unusual, therefore, for the love of science to become a cultural enemy of marital love.

The higher intellect, the imagination, the entrepreneurial spirit, and even the emotions of the heart, might all find their congenial harmony in lofty pursuits, which would ascend from one step of powerful intelligence to another, until a naive philosopher should lay his hand upon the 'Divine Universe's secrets of creative force'.

We know not whether Elmer Hamilton possessed this degree of faith in science's ultimate control over Nature, and *his* chauvinistic control over kinky females, perverted bisexuals, and horny lesbians. Since the Harvard Philosophy School's educated scholar had not been properly breast-fed as an infant, at age twenty-two, Elmer Hamilton had seriously abandoned Socrates, Plato, and Aristotle, and soon devoted his full energy and effort to the pursuit of sophisticated scientific studies. Elmer's love for his young wife's luscious knockers might have at times proven to be a stronger craving than his compulsive fascination with his secret scientific endeavors.

Such a spiritual/scientific union accordingly took place, and was attended with truly remarkable consequences, accompanied by a deeply impressive Puritan code of moral conduct. One day, very soon after the couple's hasty elopement and subsequent marriage, Elmer sat gazing at his wife's nicely formed tits, and then peered at her flawed face, which featured a large black birthmark that violated *his* narrow concept of feminine perfection.

'Shit!' Elmer disgustedly thought. 'I can't have friggin' sex with science. I gotta' have sex with my vivacious wife, but every time I look at the well-stacked broad in broad daylight, I fuckin' lose my erection!" Then, the very frustrated fellow dejectedly addressed his well-built wife.

"Georgiana," the newly-married husband commenced speaking. "Has it ever occurred to you that the grotesque-looking black birthmark upon your right cheek might be either medically or scientifically removed?"

"No, indeed," the wife readily replied, smiling like an attractive virgin. But then, perceiving the seriousness of *his* manner and tone of voice, Georgiana blushed deeply and further answered. "To tell you the truth, Elmer, the ugly blemish has been so often called a charm by my lying parents that I was always childish enough to imagine it might actually be so glamorous. I mean, haven't you ever heard of something called 'a beauty mark'?"

"Ah, upon another face perhaps, that two-inch-in-diameter black mole might be a charm to someone like a blind Dracula," the wife's momentarily distraught husband babbled. "But never upon yours. No, dearest, Georgiana. You came so nearly perfect from the hand of Nature that *this* physical defect, which we hesitate whether to term a defect or define it as an obtrusive beauty mark, well, the sight of it being so large absolutely shocks me. I consider the abnormal-in-size, very visible mark to be quite imperfect. If sin has physical existence, then that gross-looking, so-called beauty mark upon your right cheek makes your goddamned face, in my perceptive eyes, uglier than fuckin' mortal sin!"

"Shocks you, you say, my inconsiderate arrogant, Husband! Your insensitive negative re*mark* truly offends me." The discreet wife's face at first reddened with momentary anger, but then the upset spouse found herself emotionally bursting into tears. "Please explain why you had taken me from my mother's side? I was completely happy being a damned spoiled-brat momma's girl. You must know, as a man of academic studies, that you cannot love what shocks you! Your attitude I find more hideous than my very visible facial defect! I recommend Husband, that you stop behaving and sounding like a chauvinistic champion asshole! Haven't you ever heard the common expression, 'Beauty is only skin deep'!"

To acknowledge this conversation in vivid interpretation, it must be mentioned that in the center of Georgiana's right cheek (the one on her damned face) was a singular huge, raised black growth, deeply interwoven, as it were, with the texture and substance of her otherwise gorgeous visage, which in her spouse's mind, had radically changed the complexion of everything beautiful.

"I resent, Elmer Hamilton, that you are glued to your secret scientific experiments, and not at all stuck on me, all because of my unique beauty mark, which your warped mind considers a grotesque and ugly external characteristic."

"Georgiana, I have the ideal solution. I believe that the large birth mark upon your right cheek can be surgically removed. If it is excised,

I'm sure that our love life will be rekindled once it is gone. As it is right now, a castrated eunuch gets more erections than I do!"

In the usual state of her alluring flesh, a healthy-though-delicate florid bloom, the reprehensible 'beauty mark' wore a tint of deeper crimson, which imperfectly defined its shape amid the surrounding skin's rosiness. Thus, unless screwing his wife in the dark, Elmer Hamilton could not achieve, let alone sustain, a decent erection, even after the crackpot had eaten three pounds of raw clams and oysters.

Every time Georgiana blushed, the foul-looking mark gradually became more indistinct, and finally, virtually-vanished amid the triumphant surge of blood that bathed the whole right cheek with its brilliant glow. But if any shifting motion caused her distinctive features to turn pale, there was the mark, expanding again, like a crimson stain upon the soft snow, a manifestation that Elmer sometimes deemed a dreadful representation that literally scared the remaining shit and piss out of him.

The black growth's shape bore a little similarity to a human hand, though resembling fingers belonging to the smallest African pygmy. Georgiana's former suitors were wont to say that some fairy (gay lesbian pixie), at the wife's birth hour, had laid her tiny hand upon the infant's right cheek, and *that* enactment left the unique impression there, that both detracted and distracted from the young lady's magnificent body and overall terrific physical appearance.

Many desperate suitors would have risked life and limb for the unique privilege of pressing their lips to Georgiana's extended hand, and then gently and gradually moving towards the girl's fabulous tits, and next to the doll's delightful brown, fluffy pubic garden. It must not be concealed, however, that the repulsive impression wrought by *that* major facial blemish had aroused genuine concern and disappointment among all Mrs. Hamilton's former suitors.

Some fastidious persons (but they were exclusively of Georgiana's own sex) affirmed that the "bloody-looking hand", as the critical observers often chose to call the gross-looking facial mark, quite destroyed the effect of the woman's general beauty, and that the black and crimson item rendered her overall countenance even more hideous than a witch's warty face.

But it would be as reasonable to claim that one of those small blue stains which sometimes occur in the purest statuary marble would convert the original 'Eve of Powers' into a horrendous-looking monster. Horny male observers, if the birthmark did not heighten their instinctive admiration, contented themselves with wishing, "The frightening growth should go the fuck away with soap and scrubbing, but *that* fantasy is just wishful thinking!"

After Elmer's elopement and rapid marriage, for the groom had thought little or nothing of the matter before, the harebrained idiot discovered that he had always been dehydrated because the blemish would daily frighten the accumulated fecal matter out of both his colon and his semi-colon.

Had Georgiana been less beautiful, let's say like mythological Medusa the Gorgon, for example, if Envy's self could have found no one else to sneer at, or find fault with, then Elmer Hamilton might have felt his affection heightened by the prettiness of that diabolical black and crimson facial imperfection, now most-evidently portrayed; and now showing itself daily, like an evil lighthouse with every pulse of emotion that throbbed within Georgiana's heart, and also pulsating inside her swollen clit, that also no longer could be satisfied.

But seeing his wife's curvaceous body, otherwise so perfect, greatly disappointed Elmer, being vastly frustrated, now found this one prominent defect grow more and more intolerable with every passing moment of his conflictive life.

It was the fatal flaw of humanity which Nature (in one shape or another) stamps ineffaceably on all her custom-made productions, either to imply that the living creations are temporary and finite, or that their unattainable perfection must be wrought by toil, frustration, rejection, and pain. It's as if Nature is communicating to us mere mortals: "Hey human assholes. Nobody's fuckin' perfect!"

'I was so anxious to get laid with someone that I had overlooked Georgiana's marred face that's now giving me the creepy overlooks,' Elmer reckoned. 'At least, before we were married, I could jerk-off and achieve getting my rocks activated. Now, I'm entirely impotent, not only in bed, but also in the bathroom, and in the goddamned closet, too! Shit! That blighted crimson and black deformity is uglier that the scarlet pimple-nel's hideous pimple ever was!'

In this manner, Elmer had rashly concluded that the despicable mark was a symbol of his wife's liability to sin, sorrow, decay, death, and possibly bisexuality. For indeed, in *his* mind, a cause-effect relationship existed with all of those aforementioned bewildering, bull-shit factors interacting. In truth, our main character's somber imagination soon rendered and determined that the birthmark was certainly a very frightful object that might even turn him to stone, or perhaps lead, or maybe even into a pencil-necked geek with plenty of graphite inside.

Self-conscious Georgiana soon learned to shudder at *his* deliberate, transfixed lengthy gaze. Her right cheek needed but a glance to affect the peculiar expression that his face often wore to change the rosiness of her cheek into a deathlike paleness, amid which the crimson facial hand was brought strongly out into what seemed bold-relief prominence, similar to a smattering of ruby mineral upon the whitest pure marble, scaring the feces and the piss out of Elmer Hamilton's ass and dick.

* * * * * * * * * * * * *

Late one night, when the oil lamp-lights were growing dim, so as hardly to betray the exaggerated stain quite evident upon the poor wife's right cheek, Georgiana herself, for the first time, voluntarily took up the taboo family subject in general conversation.

"Do you remember, my dear Elmer," Georgiana prefaced, with a feeble attempt at achieving a smile, "have you any recollection of a nightmare you had last night about this odious growing black hand growing bigger each day upon my face? Why did you shriek without waking-up? Was my beauty mark strangling you? Was it strangling me? Was it strangling us?"

"None! None of those daft scenarios whatsoever!" Elmer guiltily replied. But then, the unemployed wannabe' dermatologist added, in a dry, cold tone, affected for the sake of concealing the real depth of his appalled suppressed emotion, "I might as well dream of being devoured by the abominable transforming mole, thriving upon your otherwise beautiful face; for before I fell asleep, the increasing-in-size mole had taken a pretty firm hold of my fanny, er, I mean, my fancy."

"And then, you actually did dream of my right cheek terrorizing you?" Georgiana hastily continued, for the sensitive female dreaded lest a gush of tears should interrupt what despair she had to disclose. "A terrible dream that non-Puritans call a female horse in the dark, er, that is to say, the superstitious gossiping majority in the town call your haunting dilemma 'a nightmare'! I wonder if you could forget the toxic community gossip abounding about my enlarged beauty mark," the upset wife communicated. "A twin sister blemish is in my heart now, and I hereby believe that we must have it also taken out! Reflect seriously on what troubles you, my husband; for by all means, I would have you recall *that* devilish dream you had experienced last night. I indeed must get rid of the two hellish moles: the one on my face, and symbolically, the same damned one residing inside and contaminating my vulnerable heart!"

Elmer now fully-remembered the essence of his disturbing dream. The perplexed husband had imagined himself working in his secret laboratory with his moronic, lame servant, Aminadab. In Hamilton's nightmare, the madman was attempting a critical operation for the removal of the contemptible birthmark, but the deeper the knife dug, the deeper sank the facial black and crimson hand, until at length, its tiny grasp appeared to have gone-down through the wife's throat and chest, next catching hold of Georgiana's duplicate malicious mole inhabiting her tender heart; however, the distressed housewife's wannabe' plastic surgeon was inexorably resolved to aggressively and persistently cut-away the unnerving facial growth.

When the horrifying dream had risen from the husband's subconscious, and had shaped itself perfectly into his memory, Elmer Hamilton sat reticent in his wife's presence with a culpable feeling of not being able to successfully surgically remove the fucked-up facial mole from her right cheek. Until now, the quixotic loser had not been aware of the tyrannical influence acquired by one powerful idea prevailing over *his* weak mind, and the determined, obsessed jerk also lacked awareness of the lengths to which the perplexed ignoramus might find (within his lost-in-space heart) an area reserved for giving himself both tranquil peace of mind and a nice piece of ass.

"Elmer Hamilton," Georgiana solemnly resumed her criticism. "I know not what may be the cost to both of us to rid me of this potentially fatal birthmark, that even at times, scares the living shit out of me. Perhaps its removal may cause a cureless deformity, making me suddenly becoming eligible for the Miss Ugly Puritan America Contest; or it may be the mole's stain goes as deep as life itself, saturating right-down to my vagina and ovaries, and thus, evilly contaminating my unfertilized eggs. Again now, for the hundredth monotonous time, do we know that there is a possibility, on any terms, of unclasping the firm grip of this little black facial hand which had been laid upon my face before I ever came into this ass-backward world during a very difficult breech birth? This horrible defect existed months before I was ever hatched from my mother's egg?"

"Dearest Georgiana; I've spent much thought meditating upon the bitchin' subject," Elmer austerely interrupted. "I'm now totally convinced of the perfect practicability of your hideous mole's permanent removal. I'll use the longest, sharpest knife in the kitchen cutlery drawer to excise the nasty son-of-a-bitch from your right cheek. I'll perform the skin operation without ever spending a minute inside a medical school seminar lecture hall."

"If there be the remotest possibility of it ever occurring," Georgiana somberly continued, "then let the attempt be made at whatever risk. Do you realize, my dear Elmer, that I could become a female *Scar*-amouche? I insist that the danger of a rare operation means absolutely nothing to me, for life, while this hateful mark makes me the object of your great horror and utter disgust, my mediocre existence is currently a heavy burden, which I would fling down with joy if you could skillfully excise the black and crimson mole from my right cheek. Either remove this dreadful black hand embedded in my face, or take my wretched life!" the wife emphatically demanded. "In truth, I believe that you possess deep medical knowledge, that's something akin to weird science. I suspect that you've achieved great wonders inside your' failed experiments down in your secret basement laboratory. Cannot you remove this horrendous birthmark, which I often cover with the tips of eight small fingers and two tiny thumbs? Is this complex operation to which you allude beyond your limited flimsy education? So, Husband, for the sake of your own peace, and to save your poor wife from your vulgar madness, let's get it on? For indeed, dear wacky Husband, I sincerely pledge that you're the only one I shall ever allow to disfigure and distort my face!"

"Noblest, dearest, most tender Wife," the psychotic spouse rapturously praised. "Doubt not my skill and power. I've already given this matter the deepest thought, yes, thought which might almost have enlightened me to create a splendid being less perfect than yourself'. For as you know from our bed adventures, rolling-around under the sheets in the dark, when I cannot see your scary blemish, I just love the prospect of love tunnel penetration; and conversely, you love to be penetrated. Now then, my sweet Georgiana," the wholly mortified husband equivocated. "You've led me deeper than ever into the heart of Texas, er, I mean into the heart of medical science. Although I've never attended medical school, I feel myself fully competent to render your dear right cheek as becoming as faultless as its fellow left-side slab of flesh; and then, most beloved, what will be my triumph when I shall have corrected what Nature had left imperfect in her fairest work!"

"Be more explicit, pretentious Dr. Hamilton." Georgiana urged. "Do you wish tampering with and altering Nature's Will?"

"Even that wild Greek boar Pygmalion, when his sculptured woman statue assumed animated life, the impulsive asshole felt not greater ecstasy than mine will be when I successfully remove the grotesque black blemish. And then, I'll maniacally and adroitly squeeze all of the black pus and goo out of it. Afterwards, at *that* propitious and glorious moment, there will not be any damned *statutory* rape as in the case of Pygmalion, because you and me babe are already-hitched!"

"It is resolved, then to happen," Georgiana decided and declared, faintly smiling at her demented love-mate. "And Elmer, though you should find the abstract twin sister birthmark in my aching heart, spare its removal. I mean, please don't treat that suffering refuge in my chest as a blemish to also be excised! Otherwise, my crotch can't possibly pump, if first, my heart stops pumping! Got that action, Cowboy?"

Her husband tenderly kissed Georgiana's left cheek, but not the right one, which now bore the impression of the crimson and black hand crushing an erect penis.

* * * * * * * * * * * * *

The next day, Elmer Hamilton apprised his wife of a brilliant plan that his non-dynamic, unenviable cerebrum had formed. The couple was to seclude themselves in the extensive adjoining apartment, normally occupied by Elmer, and used as his secondary secret laboratory, and where, during his toilsome youth, while making am eighth-grade science fair project, the dreamer had made simpleton discoveries in the elemental powers of Nature, several of which had roused the admiration of a few senile professors belonging to various dunce and dolt societies over in Europe.

Seated calmly in that aforementioned adjoining laboratory, while simultaneously smoking three long marijuana joints, the pale young philosopher had investigated the significant medical and chemical secrets of the highest New England university campuses, and also, those clandestine secrets of the area's profoundest deep gold and silver mines, where naughty Elmer Hamilton had mastered how to give females (including Georgiana in the dark) the regal shaft, better known as the 'royal erect salami'.

In his intensive and extensive research pertaining to the facial mole operation, the zany experimenter had satisfied himself of the causes that kindled and kept alive the fires of the recent Hawaiian volcanoes, studying the matter while taking a healthy dump in his laboratory's *lava*tory. The aspiring genius had also explained the mystery of water fountains and of usable fountain pens, and how it is that they both gush forth (geysers and old geezers alike) in a similar matter as shooting sperm juice; some geysers so bright and pure, and others (old geezers) spewing semen with such rich medicinal curing properties, when amply swallowed by gullible horny women like Georgiana.

Here, too, at an earlier period of his unheralded life, the budding scientist had studied the wondrous flowers, and analyzed the human anatomy, focusing his prolific studies mostly upon tits and ass, pussy cracks, testicles, and super erections.

"You have no surgical skills or training!" Georgiana maintained. 'You possess no cutting-edge technology. Can't I just go and see a competent dermatologist for a second opinion?"

"Absolutely not," the nutcase marital loon prattled. "Quite frankly, I need not study such a simple and elementary facial operation for six additional years in all-too-expensive Harvard Medical School."

And next the crazed lunatic attempted to fathom the very process by which Nature assimilates all her precious influences from earth and air, and from the spiritual world, to create and foster man, *her* not-too-fantastic fucked-up masterpiece. During the latter pursuit, however, loony Elmer Hamilton had long laid aside (in stubborn unwilling recognition) that our great creative Mother, as she amuses and deceives us while apparently working in the broadest visible sunshine, is yet severely careful in keeping her own secrets secret. And in spite of her assumed pretended openness, Mother Nature shows us nothing but spectacular results, with only certain occasional dumb-ass defects like tiny tits, fat asses, impotent balls, and ugly facial moles being randomly discernible.

Nature permits us to mar, but seldom allows us to mend. And like a jealous patent owner, *she* is on no account liable to making amends to that which needs mending. Now, however, ambitious Elmer Hamilton preposterously resumed those half-forgotten investigations into the forbidden secrets of nature. But now, the incompetent experimenter was motivated and compelled to act and delve, because the quest involved much physiological truth, and lay in the path of his proposed scheme for the explicit treatment and cure of Georgiana's distressful facial condition.

'Will Mother Nature kick and punish my ass for me being too proud and arrogant, while trying to discover her well-guarded hidden secrets? I wonder: what calendar day is that prude Mother Nature going to have her' asshole monthly period? I don't want to fuck with her notorious, unpredictable disposition *that* goddamned lethal week!'

As the need-to-get-laid husband led his apprehensive wife over the threshold of the upstairs secret laboratory, Georgiana was cold and tremulous, as frigid as an Arctic iceberg, and as cold as a lesbian dead whore's tits. The 'orifice man' looked cheerfully into her face, eyes, ears, and mouth, with intent to reassure his spouse, but the junior scientist was so startled with the intense crimson glow of the hideous birthmark upon the whiteness of her cheek, which the charlatan surgeon could not restrain a strong convulsive shudder suddenly overwhelming him. The madman's petrified wife fainted from fright at looking at his flawed, madman's countenance.

"Aminadab! Aminadab!" Hamilton shouted, stamping his right foot violently upon the wood-planked floor. "Come here this instant, you retarded cripple, or else I'll sack your scrotum sac right off your abominable abdominal, leaving you with no intestinal fortitude!"

Forthwith, there issued from an inner apartment a limping modern Neanderthal man of low stature, having a huge thick skull, but of bulky frame, with shaggy hair hanging about his forehead, which was grimed with vapors that had directly emanated from the obsolete cellar furnace. This miniature Frankenstein personage had been Elmer Hamilton's worthless, lackadaisical assistant during the unemployed scientist's whole piss-poor research career, and the slow-learner was admirably fitted for that lowly office, simply by his great ability to do hardly anything helpful.

Aminadab, an imported former jihadist recently converted to Atheism before arriving to America as a merchant ship's stowaway, was truly incapable of comprehending a single basic principle, but incredibly, the distorted-looking nincompoop had faithfully executed all the amazing details of his master's experiments while not knowing what the fuck the fundamental studies either entailed or involved. With his vast strength, his shaggy hair, along with his smoky, dirty appearance, the ponderous-but-short lame Arab seemed to represent man's brutish physical nature; while in opposite contrast, Elmer's slender figure, and pale, intellectual face were no less apt to symbolize mankind's counterpart spiritual and intellectual properties.

"Throw open the door of the boudoir, Aminadab," the insane master ordered. "And burn a candle for adequate light without setting yourself on fire, you' awkward junior arsonist!"

"Yes, Master," the dim-witted assistant affirmatively complied, looking intently at the lifeless form of Georgiana barely breathing with her tight clothes hardly moving. And then, the miniature monster muttered to himself, "If she were my friggin' wife, I'd never part with that *natural* birthmark. My asshole boss thinks that his wife's ugly blemish is a blemish on his going-nowhere, fraudulent scientist reputation. My own theory is that Georgiana might be a damned Tory mole for the British Crown! The local gossipers, who are always bullshitting down in the village square, don't call her 'Lady Tory' for nothing! I mean, the British King George III had all of the Tories on his redcoat side except one: Vick Tory!"

When Georgiana slowly recovered general consciousness, the wife found herself' breathing an atmosphere of penetrating fragrance, and the almost-magical potency of which had marvelously summoned Hamilton's spouse from her recent deathlike faintness. The scene around her, to the wife's blurry bloodshot eyes, looked like sheer magical enchantment. 'I must be somewhere in Georgia,' gorgeous Georgiana first thought. 'But I don't see any damned Dixie cups filled with mint juleps anywhere! Maybe I'm lying on a table somewhere in Mississippi, instead?'

Sinister Elmer Hamilton had scrupulously converted those two upstairs smoky, dingy, somber rooms into his secret (off limits to Georgiana) investigative headquarters, where the lunatic amateur experimenter had spent his brightest years in academic pursuits that had accomplished positively nothing.

The two additional side chambers had been modified into beautiful locked apartments not unfit to be the secluded abode of a lovely sex-starved woman, just like his frustrated wife. The walls were hung with rich purple curtains, that imparted the combination of grandeur and grace that no other fabrics in the residence could ever achieve; and as the curtains fell, draping from the ceiling to the floor, their finite exquisite folds appeared to shut in the surgical scene from infinite space (whatever the hell *that* totally nebulous, fucked-up, convoluted phraseology actually means).

For what spaced-out and drugged Georgiana now knew, the ordinary, locked adjacent rooms might have been a wondrous pavilion floating among the wild blue yonder clouds. And Elmer, even excluding the "off-limits" chambers from cheery sunshine, which would have interfered with his secret-but-ineffective chemical processes, had supplied the dark and sinister place with cheap perfumed lamps, eerie objects emitting flames of various hues, but all uniting in a soft, purpled, entrancing radiance, especially near the mysterious dual apartment's entrancing entrance.

The born loser now knelt by his devoted siren wife's side, lustfully and earnestly watching her magnificent, solid breasts expanding and contracting, but without any *alarm* plaguing his intent, for that type of electrical house device had not yet been invented.

Now, the blundering fool was quite confident in performing his long-explored warped science, and the delusional fanatic felt that *he,* the perverted lunatic, could draw a magic circle around his experimental wife within which no (non-existent) evil might encroach and interfere.

"Where am I? Ah, I remember, in Mississippi," uttered hazy-minded Georgiana, speaking faintly, under the influence of recently administered drugs. And soon, the study's subject placed her right hand over her right cheek to hide the terrible expanding and contracting frightful birthmark from her nutcase husband's detection. "Am I now at the Pilgrim Beauty Academy, getting a deluxe three-penny facial done? Where's the damned mudpack? What the hell's that freak Aminadab doing inside the arcane Mississippi beauty shop?" the doped-up wife wondered.

"Fear not, my delusional dearest!" infatuated romantic Elmer Hamilton exclaimed, desperately needing to get laid. "My precious flower, do not shrink from me like a wilted violet! Holy molely, beloved Wife!" the pseudo-scientist gasped. "Believe me, Georgiana; I even rejoice in this single imperfection, since it'll be such a tremendous rapture for me to permanently remove the frightening defect with a scalpel. I can't wait to deeply dig-in with my surgical instrument, and also using my Cub Scout Puritan pen knife."

"Oh, spare me from your insanity!" the impostor doctor's scared-shitless, concerned wife uttered mumbled from her semi-conscious state. "Pray, do not look at the birthmark ever again. I never can forget *that* convulsive shudder shown upon your pallid face, which makes me become instantly constipated with excessive gas."

In order to further soothe well-built Georgiana's stress, and to release her beleaguered mind from the burden of harsh reality, the pathetic, self-appointed phony surgeon now put into practice some of the light and playful secrets which primitive kindergarten science had taught him among its more profound lore. Initiating his grand deception, airy figures, absolutely bodiless drifting ideas, and forms of unsubstantial beauty, came and danced before the horizontal lying patient's drugged eyes, imprinting their momentary footsteps on intangible beams of artificial light. And naïve, heavily drugged-up Georgiana actually believed that *this* contrived, mentally-suggested peculiar light show, really wholly represented a stupid-shit, realistic, beneficial experience about to happen.

Although the experimental wife had some indistinct idea of the obscure method behind those ongoing optical phenomena, still the ultimate envisioned illusion was almost perfect enough to warrant the belief that her impostor husband, disreputable, unemployed, and masquerading as a quack scientist, possessed a definite powerful sway over the very complicated spiritual world.

Then again, when Georgiana felt a wish to look forth from her potent hypnotic seclusion, immediately, as if her fleeting thoughts had been interpreted and fathomed by her operating room surgeon, a kaleidoscope of ever-changing, colorful images hypnotically flitted across a common wall, quite effectively communicating Dr. Elmer Hamilton's greenhorn chicanery.

"Are you Elmer Hamilton, or are you the magnificent Franz Mesmer?" the wholly mesmerized wife asked. "For all the hell I know, you might be Aminadab looking for a quicky; yes, a-mini-dab, in search of some sort of rapid perverted sex, so to speak!"

"No, Wife. I am not Aminadab, nor do I ever wish to be. Only my shrunken pecker is lame. And you're no spoiled-rotten Arabian princess, and I'm not fuckin' Alibaba, either!"

When wearied of *that* rather-meaningless dialogue, roguish "Dr. Elmer Hamilton" bade his deluded spouse to cast her eyes upon an ordinary-looking vessel containing a quantity of common earth elements. Half-alert Georgiana reluctantly did so, at first with little mundane interest in executing her action; but next, the cooperative wife was soon startled to perceive the germ of a plant shooting upward from the chemically-treated "magical soil". Then came the slender stalk mystically rising like a firm erection; the leaves gradually unfolded themselves; and amid their grandeur sprouted a perfect and lovely purple/crimson flower.

"It is truly magical!" Georgiana exclaimed. "I dare not touch the flower. Elmer; I think you should consider changing your accursed name to Bud!"

"Nay, pluck it, even though it lacks chicken feathers," the inspired husband prompted. "Pluck it, Baby Doll, and deeply inhale its brief perfume while you may. The miraculous flower will wither in a few short moments, and leave nothing, save its brown seed vessels. But it then briefly may perpetuate a race, a species just as ephemeral as itself. For I've learned and conquered how to blend man's science with the intricate elements of man's spiritual religion, and the realistic result is obviously some sort of fucked-up, inexplicable magic as had just been demonstrated with the ordinary plant seed!"

But Georgiana had no sooner touched the purple/crimson flower that the whole plant shockingly suffered a very terrible blight. Its verdant leaves slowly turned coal-black, as if negatively affected at its own accord, and not by the devastating influence of intrusive and contaminating fire and smoke.

"There was too powerful an external stimulus being exercised," realized and declared the novice unaccomplished scientist, with a trace of disappointment characterized and being evident in his vocal tone. "Another fucked-up abortive attempt at achieving scientific genius! Only I, Elmer Lucifer Hamilton, the Anonymous Wizard, shall foolishly endanger your precious life attempting to attain scientific fame and medical repute!"

To compensate for this most recent disrupted experiment, the quack scientist endeavored making *her* "perfect living portrait" by means of a novel experimental process of *his* own invention. The project was to be effected by rays of light striking upon a polished tin plate. Being still substantially drugged-up and semi-conscious, Georgiana reluctantly assented to passively participate in "Dr. Hamilton's" developing insanity. But upon again briefly looking at the now-decayed purple/crimson flower, the frightened patient was harried to the point of hysteria.

'I should've given her crack cocaine instead of lousy barbiturates,' the failed scientist selfishly complained to himself. 'So far, this bummer demonstration has been a real downer! My confidence is beginning to wane!'

Soon, however, the possessed madman forgot those mortifying past failures that a common idiot could have told him would not have succeeded from the outset. In the intervals of study and premeditated chemical experiment, the adamant loon again approached his still lying flat wife/patient, who was now emotionally flushed and exhausted after, in her imagined fantasy, mentally visiting Georgia and then Mississippi.

Invigorated by his spouse's presence, the rejuvenated risk-taker again spoke in glowing language of the resources of his advanced art, giving Georgiana an exaggerated biased history of the long dynasty of medieval alchemists, who had spent so many centuries in quest of the universal solvent by which the golden principle of "playing God with science" might be pragmatically elicited from all evil things vile, base, and forbidden.

"You might as well delude yourself into thinking you're Rumpelstiltskin having the ability of magically spinning straw into gold," the entranced woman, still lying horizontal upon the operating table, logically stated. "Pretentious dreamer! Artificial discoverer! Go dig a deep hole into the ground and imagine that you're a goddamned mole yourself! Merlin reincarnated, fake Dr. Hamilton, you most-certainly are not! By the way, Elmer. What is your middle name?"

Despite his realistic wife's disenchantment with his peculiar enchantment scenario, conniving Elmer appeared to believe that, by the plainest scientific methodology, it was altogether within the limits of possibility to discover *this* long-sought arcane healing medium. 'But,' the zealous fanatic haughtily hypothesized, 'a philosopher should go deep enough to acquire, using science, the secret powers of Almighty Nature. In the occult process I'm about to employ, me, the expert investigating scientist, would attain a lofty, transcendent wisdom, and significantly contribute to the advancement of both science and medicine.'

"You belong either in a prison dungeon or in a damned mental asylum," Georgiana evaluated and stated from her horizontal mild stupor. "In fact, I think I need immediate asylum from your demented craziness! Live in a damned straightjacket, for all the hell I care! I'm not any stupid-ass New Guinea guinea pig, ya' know!"

Not less singular were the incompetent scientist's opinions in regard to the newly-formulated elixir vitae. Quirky "Dr. Elmer Lucifer Hamilton" more than intimated that it had been his option to concoct a splendid chemical recipe that should and could prolong life for decades, perhaps interminably. But the ever-present caveat was that the new substance would produce a measurable discord within Nature, which all the world (and chiefly the drinker of the immortal elixir) would partake and immediately determine that the delicious flavor tasted exactly like Kentucky bourbon.

"Elmer, are you in earnest about this absurd removal of my huge facial mole?" Georgiana eerily inquired from her semi-trance, her bloodshot eyes looking-up at the obsessed fanatic with both amazement and fear. "It's terrible to possess such almighty power, or even to ever dream of possessing it. Why the hell didn't you, in your pathetic youth, matriculate your scrawny ass into a defunct dermatology school instead of enrolling in Philosophy at Harvard?"

"Oh, do not tremble, my love," Georgiana's mentally-unstable husband declared. "I would not wrong either you, or myself, by working such inharmonious effects upon our failure-oriented lives, even though only you might become the femme fatal victim. But I would have you consider how trifling, in comparison, is the skill requisite to first removing that little black fleshy hand, remarkably and presently 'changing its skin color'. That enigmatic part of the hideous black mole is still deeply embedded upon your otherwise beautiful face. Enough of this ineffectual conversational bull-shit! Let me get to work immediately upon that diabolical right cheek!"

At the mention of the grotesque birthmark, Georgiana, as usual, emotionally shrank-down upon the operating table as if a red-hot iron had touched and singed her delicate right cheek. "You might as well be the village blacksmith!" the wife sarcastically objected and chastised. "Why the hell don't you just put my lovely head on an anvil and start hammering away at the despicable black mole with a blazing mallet?"

* * * * * * * * * * * *

Again unfazed, the Impostor Chemist/Physician applied himself to his laboratory chores. Georgiana could hear his raspy voice in the cellar furnace room giving vague and incorrect directions to lazy Aminadab, whose harsh, uncouth, misshapen tones were hardly audible in response, the lame Arab sounding more like the grunt or growl of a prehistoric brute than a contemporary human articulating logical speech.

After hours of unnecessary absence and wasting of time, Elmer Hamilton reappeared (re-entered the designated operating room), and showed still-groggy Georgiana a small vile vial, remarking that the vessel contained a gentle yet most powerful fragrance, capable of impregnating all the breezes that randomly blow across a kingdom.

"And exactly what is this nonsensical fragrance bull-shit?" Georgiana dizzily asked, her right hand pointing to the small crystal globe containing a gold-colored liquid. "You' say that the shit in *that* vile will impregnate the damned air? Well now, *I'm* the one who has to be impregnated in order to have our first child!"

"In one sense, my dear wife, it's a gold crystal wholly incapable of enacting any mystical crystal-blue persuasion," Hamilton obtusely replied. "Or perhaps, rather, dearest Georgiana, it's the most excellent elixir of immortality, similar to the mythical nectar and ambrosia of the ancient Greek gods. Quite probably, it's the most precious compound that has ever been cleverly concocted in this heinous world that we both unfortunately inhabit, along with several billion mentally-challenged morons like that weirdo midget Aminadab."

"What particular purpose does the special concoction have?" the fearful wife asked out of her semi-trance-like state. "If it makes my tits any bigger, I won't be able to even stand-up, let alone walk around my boudoir."

"By its magical aid, I could easily extend the lifetime of any mortal at whom you might casually point your finger," the deranged junior scientist insisted. "The strength of the potion's dose would determine whether he or she would linger additional years, or instantaneously drop dead in the midst of a single prodigious breath. No imperial king sitting on his well-guarded throne could ever keep his life if I should deem that the welfare of millions justified me in depriving the royal prick from breathing."

"You're a power-hungry, stark-crazy bastard who needs to be institutionalized yesterday!" the newly-wed Mrs. Hamilton insisted. "Why do you keep such a terrible and highly dangerous drug?" Georgiana asked in horror. "Do you think you are God, emulating the Creator's genius? You're no Jesus Christ, and I'm no damned Mary Magdelene! Doom *yourself* to Hell, fraudulent Dr. Hamilton, but not my cherished butt!"

"Do not mistrust me, dearest," Elmer pleaded, slightly smiling all the while. "The marvelous elixir's potency is far greater than it is potentially harmful. But see! Here is a powerful cosmetic that's better than any plastic surgery ever devised. With a few drops of this cure-all, fix-all, carefully mixed with ordinary water," Quack Scientist Hamilton unpersuasively explained, "freckles and wens may be washed-away as easily as the hands are cleansed of everyday dog or cat feces. A stronger infusion would take the blood, sweat and zits right out of your right cheek, and then the excessive liquid would change the rosiest beauty into a pale ghost if you by chance accidentally overdose."

"Is it with that exotic formula that you intend to bathe my right cheek?" Georgiana anxiously asked. "Why the hell don't you rub and bathe my whole body with this magical crap, starting with my inactive clit button?"

"Oh, no, my dear Wife," suddenly replied her quixotic husband. "This is merely a superficial chemical compound I've mustered together. Your unique case demands a quality remedy that shall delve much deeper into your skin. Not into your magnificent love tunnel, mind you, but penetrate into your right cheek's poor pores."

"You really know how the hell to rub me the wrong way and get under my skin!" Georgiana bitched, even from her semi-trance-like state, while possessing a hazy frame of mind similar to Dracula's vampire victims roaming about at night on the Count's Transylvania haunting estate.

In his rambling and illogical interview with Georgiana, Quasi-Professor Hamilton generally made minute inquiries about her physical sensations, and whether or not the room's temperature agreed with her desire to later share her abundant feminine charms after the successful facial operation had been performed. Those inane and irrelevant questions had such a particular drift that Georgiana began conjecturing that she was being subjected to certain diabolical, metaphysical influences, currently being breathed-in with the fragrant air slowly enveloping her weakened horizontal presence.

Georgiana fancied that her body was experiencing a stirring-up of her formerly inactive reproductive system; a strange, indefinite pressure creeping through her veins, and thus tingling her usually dormant clitoris, half painfully, half pleasurably, and also then stimulating her now-surrendering heart. Still, whenever the obedient wife dared to look into the foreboding side wall mirror, there she beheld herself pale as a white rose, and the wife's perceptive eyes vaguely viewed her face, featuring the crimson/purple birthmark stamped upon her right cheek, without any damned accompanying United States Post Office seal.

"Ah, the secret potion is working,' observed and surmised the obsessed husband. 'Indeed, the sensational elixir is also a wonderful aphrodisiac!'

As Georgiana remained stationary upon the improvised operating table, her nebulous mind recalled how she had once found ten pages of Elmer's private notes that had been concealed inside a book on a shelf inside the home's dingy library. Scrutinizing the language of several old tomes, which the flustered wife had diligently read, but failed to fully comprehend, whimsical, poetic verses had depicted the subjects of romance and wonderful sex. The prosaic prose represented the inferior works of senile Middle Ages' philosophers, phony scurrilous sages such as Albertus Magnus Carta, Cornelius "Get a Grip" Agrippa, and the ancient psychopath, Paracelsus Post.

But to sweet Georgiana, the most engrossing discovered verses were written from her husband's own hand, in which Elmer had recorded every fucked-up experiment of his unimpressive, non-famous, scientific career, including each immaterial study's original questionable aim. The language, in truth, was a contrived history describing Elmer's ambitious, imaginative, fanciful-yet-impractical, laborious laboratory failures. Being a complete asshole, in fact the ultimate asshole of assholes, Elmer Lucifer Hamilton had never recognized the simple notion that science and spirituality never satisfactorily mixed, or ever satisfactorily blended together, into anything except fuckin' trouble.

In the psychotic experimenter's insane mental grasp, the dubious clod assumed that after the black mole would be excised, there would be a new stellar facet to his wife's face. Georgiana, as she recalled diligently reading in *his* implausible bull-shit notes, the naïve female lying upon the makeshift operating table suddenly reverenced, trusted, and loved Elmer more profoundly than ever before.

So deeply did the recollection of those poetic verses affect Georgiana that the patient burst into tears, the liquid from her eyes causing a wicked chemical reaction to occur inside the room. In that stunned condition, the wife was soon found by her mercurial-minded husband, who from her rambling words, immediately comprehended exactly what had happened.

"It's dangerous to read the contents of an inspired sorcerer's book," Elmer articulated with a forced smile, though his countenance was both uneasy and displeased, and the bungling shit-head momentarily contemplated committing sinful homicide. "Georgiana, there were pages in my personal notes which I can scarcely glance-over and still keep my senses. Take heed, lest my records prove as detrimental to you as you finding them are to me."

"Your wonderful verses have made me worship and trust you more than ever," Georgianna confessed, since she now felt a trifle guilty about inadvertently discovering the poems in the home's library.

"Ah, just wait for this one success I've been meticulously planning. Indeed, my first and only damned laboratory triumph ever," her fucked-up marital mate crazily rejoiced. "Then, dearest Wife, if you miraculously survive the non-medical operation, you shall worship me, if you will, as the Junior Creator. I shall deem myself hardly unworthy of your explicit admiration. But come," Elmer implored. "I have sought you for the luxury of your melodic voice. Sing to me, dearest Wife. But please try using a falsetto soprano tone rather than your customary bass or baritone."

So, subordinate good wife Georgiana, in her semi-hypnotic state, poured-out the liquid music of her voice to quench the never-ending thirst of the control-freak's hungry, possessive spirit. Elmer then took his leave with a boyish exuberance, assuring his prospective patient that her seclusion would endure but a little longer, and predicting that the optimal result was already certain. Scarcely, had the rabid fiend departed, hopping and skipping-down the dank dusty corridor, when Georgiana felt irresistibly compelled to rise from the table and slowly follow his gloomy hallway path.

The wife had forgotten to inform Surgeon Hamilton of a symptom which for two or three-hours past had begun to excite her attention. It was a queer (but not gay) sensation originating inside the fatal birthmark, not painful, but a feeling which induced a terrible restlessness throughout her circulatory, nervous, skeletal, digestive, respiratory, epidermal, and reproductive systems. Now hastening after her absent-minded husband, the weak and worried woman intruded (trespassed) for the first time into the portal of the "sacred laboratory", where a second furnace had recently been built.

The first observation that struck her eyes was the enormous furnace, that hot and feverish metal machine, demonstrating the intense glow of its fire, which by the quantities of soot clustered above it, seemed to have possibly been a convenient crematorium illegally burning corpses, or incinerating legal documents. There was also alongside the furnace an ominous-looking distilling apparatus in full operation, possibly, as Georgiana aptly speculated, 'was used for manufacturing moonshine whiskey'.

Around the formerly secret room were jars of chemical compounds, myriad test-tubes, cylinders, crucibles, and other various apparatus essential for chemical research. An electrical machine stood nearby, and apparently, the device was ready for immediate and incomprehensible deployment. The room's musty atmosphere felt oppressively close, and the air was tainted with gaseous odors that had been tormented-forth by the processes of *his* perverted science.

The severe and homely simplicity of the isolated laboratory apartment, with its naked walls and brick pavement, looked irregularly strange, accustomed as Georgiana had become to the low elegance of her mediocre-looking, lower middle-class, downstairs' boudoir. The wife mentally began piecing separate parts of the whole blurry puzzle together.

'So, Elmer makes his money distilling and selling illegal whiskey,' Georgiana surmised. 'I'm wondering where he ever got the money to pay our many bills!'

In the secret laboratory, the junior chemist/apothecary wannabe' appeared as pale as death, anxious and absorbed in his assiduous labor, and the pseudo-doctor/scientist's flaccid torso hung over the mammoth furnace as if its material sustenance depended upon his utmost watchfulness, regardless of whether the liquid liquor which it had been prolifically distilling should be the draught of immortal happiness, or the genesis of earthly misery. How different was that bull-shit tableau from the sanguine and joyous mien that the imbecile jerk-off had (in the beginning) assumed beneficial for Georgiana's encouragement and happiness!

"Carefully now, Aminadab! Cease thinking that you're back at the desert oasis eating your dates, both male and female, you bisexual fuck-head! Use your hands carefully, thou clumsy human machine; carefully, thou clumsy man of clay!" Quack Professor Hamilton loudly instructed his clumsy assistant in an unflattering manner, mumbling more to himself than to his encumbered, nearly-deaf, lame helper. "Now, if there be a thought too much, or too little, for your weak brain to understand, it is all over but the fuckin' shouting. Yes, yes! Harvard beats Yale at chess! Yes, yes! How marvelous!"

"Ho! ho!" Aminadab muttered like two-thirds of a chubby Santa Claus. "Look, to your left Master! Look over there! It's your encroaching cunt, er, I mean your wandering, busy-body wife! Curiosity killed the damned cat, my Master. Who knows what the hell it'll do to her goddamned pussy!"

Elmer Hamilton hastily raised his eyes, and at first his skin reddened, but then his flesh appeared growing paler than ever, upon his tired pupils presently beholding Georgiana. The incensed maniac rushed towards his weakened spouse, seizing her arm with a grip that left the print of his fingers (his fingerprints) imprinted upon her left shoulder.

"Why do you come hither? Have you no trust in your infallible husband?" impetuously shouted the livid fanatic. "Would you throw the blight of that fatal birthmark, and make it overshadow my dedicated labors? It is not well done. Go away, prying woman, go away! And I advise that you find a goddamned sturdy screwdriver if you sincerely wish to pry!"

"Nay, Elmer," Georgiana answered. "It is not you that have a right to bitch and complain. You dirty bastard! You mistrust your wife! You have concealed the anxiety with which you watch the development of this doomed, ill-fated, wild-notion, sinful experiment of yours. Think not so unworthily of little old me, my indefatigable Husband. Tell me all the risk and hazards we shall run, and fear not that I shall shrink like your flaccid dick does every dark night in the sack; for my share in it is far less than your own. After all," the neurotic wife concluded and affirmed, "for in your narrow mind, I'm but a commonplace colonial cottage woman, and am therefore expendable in your male-dominated cottage industry world."

"No, no, Georgiana!" Elmer impatiently disagreed. "It must not be as you've so inaccurately depicted. Don't fret even though you have no guitar to play! I'm not a warped undertaker looking to make your cremation a cottage industry! This furnace is a scientific machine and not a vile crematorium oven as you might've suspected!"

"I wholeheartedly submit to you my entire spirit and body, including my desirable brown fluffy bush," the wife emotionally replied. "And, Elmer, I don't give a shit anymore! I shall quaff-down whatever draught you bring me, because quite frankly, I don't care one iota whether I live or die in this fucked-up male-dominated world; but my voluntary participation will be on the same principle that would induce me to take a dose of poison if offered by your enticing, perfumed hand. Hemlock or arsenic, I just don't give a sister's shit anymore!"

"My devoted Wife," Elmer declared, deeply moved. "I haven't asked you to choose your poison. I knew not the height and depth of your exploited nature until now. I sincerely promise, nothing shall be concealed," pledged the wacky experimenter. "Know then, that this crimson hand, superficial as it seems, has clutched its grasp into your being with a strength of which I had no previous conception," the husband preposterously articulated like a nutcase crackpot. "I've already administered agents powerful enough to change your entire physical system, ass, breasts, clit, and ovaries all included, starting with permanently eliminating your rather putrid and disgusting menstrual cycle. Only one thing remains to be tried. If that prospect fails us, we are ruined."

"Why did you hesitate telling me this stupid nonsensical crap? I thought that you were only going to surgically remove my facial birthmark!" the insulted wife argued and wanted to know. "Begin your ludicrous and amateurish experiment as soon as possible; you'll then expeditiously kill me and get the whole damned thing over with!"

"Because realistically, dear Georgiana," the very concerned marital partner expressed in a low-toned voice. "There is imminent danger that I too might die during the procedure's enactment."

"Danger? There is but one dumb-ass danger, and *that* formidable factor being this horrible stigma shall be left upon my cheek after your dumb-ass procedure fails!" Georgiana protested and sobbed. "Tell me candidly the whole truth, my insane Husband. What fucked-up angel in Heaven would ever want to dare kiss me? Remove it; I say remove it, whatever be the cost, whether I live or die, or we shall both go mad on our speedy journey down to Hell!"

"Only apathetic Heaven knows if your derogatory words are true or false," Elmer sadly acknowledged. "And now, dearest, return to your private boudoir and powder your face. And please put about five layers of heavy talc on and around that horrendous-looking mole. I'll wager that *that* ungodly black birthmark must consist of billions upon billions of demonic mole-cules. In a little while, though, all will be tested and rectified."

The peeved wannabe' scientist soon conducted his doubting wife back to her boudoir, and took leave of her with a solemn silence, a queer quiet which spoke far more than his words of how much more stupid horse-crap was now at stake. After his swift departure, while still being under the influence of strong barbiturates, Georgiana's affected mind became rapt in odd fantasy musings. Her mental analysis considered Elmer's basic character and personality, and her stark contemplation most-accurately assessed her furtive husband's diminished integrity, more so now than at any previous moment in their volatile relationship.

The sound of her husband's heavy footsteps aroused Georgiana's senses just when the wife was attempting to masturbate to relieve the burden of her great anxiety. Elmer was carrying a crystal goblet containing a liquor as colorless as water, but bright enough to be Ponce de Leon's draught of immortality. The on-a-mission husband confidently entered the woman's boudoir.

"The concoction of this complex draught has been perfectly coordinated," the quack pseudo-scientist maintained in response to Georgiana's doubtful (for good reason) stare. "Unless all my science and rudimentary knowledge of astrology has deceived me, this experiment cannot fail. Georgiana, I'm tired of fuckin' failing over a thousand times without one minor success to advance my unknown name! My whole adult life's career is at stake right now!"

"Save your dunce excuses on your account, my dearest Elmer," observed and enunciated his dubious spouse. "I might wish to put-off this insidious birthmark of mortality by relinquishing mortality itself, in preference to any other mode of corporal or spiritual existence. Life is but a sad, melancholy possession to those who have attained precisely the degree of moral advancement of which I presently endure, you totally immoral, inferior, arrogant bastard! You have totally corrupted me! If I happened to be weaker and blinder than I am, then Husband, this dumb-ass experiment of yours' might be construed as being naïve, indeed a reckless poetic catastrophe. If I were to be stronger and miserable in actual context, then your laboratory madness might be hopefully survived. But, being what I find myself'," the wife paused, "methinks I am of all mortals, the most fit to die, and I shall gladly do so to get the fuck off this pathetic Earth that your grandiose ambition wishes to dominate."

"You are fit for Heaven without ever tasting death!" replied her intelligent-deficient, mentally-challenged husband. "But why do we speak of dying? Perhaps we should instead discuss dyeing your ugly mole? But dearest Georgiana," the addled phony chemist resumed his gibberish. "I've read my favorable horoscope for today, and I'm certain that the indispensable chemical draught that I've meticulously prepared cannot possibly falter or fail. Behold its effect upon that plant over yonder wall."

On the window sill, there had been placed a withered geranium, quite diseased with yellow blotches, which had overspread all its yellow and brown leaves. Crazed Elmer Hamilton slowly poured a small quantity of the anonymous liquid upon the soil in which the plant grew. In a short time, when the roots of the dying flower had absorbed and taken-up the moisture, the myriad, unsightly blotches upon the diseased plant began to amazingly become eradicated, occurring in a remarkable display of living verdure.

"There needed no proof," Georgiana quietly declared. "When is the Women's Rights Movement ever getting started in this accursed country?" the wife rhetorically asked. "Husband, give me the damned crystal goblet. I'll joyfully stake all my remaining breaths upon trusting the merits of your arbitrary words."

"Drink hardily, then, thou thirsty lofty woman!" Elmer exclaimed, with fervid admiration and zeal. "There is no taint of imperfection evident upon thy benevolent spirit. Thy sensible hourglass frame, too, shall soon be all perfect, once the right side of your face becomes comparably impeccable, even to a pecking crow or a ravenous raven. I must reveal that I don't have the guts to remove the despicable mole surgically, so therefore, Georgiana, I expect this exotic formula to easily do the fuckin' job for me, in place of me implementing my rusty scalpel."

The drugged-up spouse quickly quaffed-down the liquid potion, and then shakily returned the shiny crystal goblet to her marital companion's steady hand.

"It is grateful," Georgiana summarized with a placid smile. "Methinks it is like water from a heavenly fountain; for it contains, I know not, what unobtrusive fragrance and delectable aroma, but I believe it smells unlike any harsh methane odor ever-present in the community sewer. The elixir allays a feverish thirst that has parched my tongue for many moons, yes, full ugly moons that I've witnessed from your scrawny ass. Now, dearest Husband, I feel intoxicated, so let me sleep-off this annoying hangover. My earthly senses are closing over my spirit like the shrinking leaves surrounding the heart of a rose at sunset."

The afflicted woman spoke those critical last words with an obstinate reluctance, as if her speech required almost more energy than she could command in order to pronounce the faint and lingering final syllables. Scarcely had her odd utterance loitered through Georgiana's swollen lips that she was soon lost in total deep slumber. Elmer sat by her side, watching her pulsating face with the self-controlled emotions deemed proper to an ethical man.

While thus employed, and with his vexed mind immersed in serious fantasizing, Elmer Lucifer Hamilton did not neglect gazing often at the deeply-rooted, fatal facial black hand upon his subject's right cheek, and not without demonstrating a shivering series of involuntary shudders.

Yet but once, by a strange and unaccountable impulse, the dumb-fuck husband irresponsibly pressed his lips against the dreadful multi-colored mole. His aggressive spirit then recoiled, however, in the very completion of the dramatic act, and Georgiana, out of the midst of her deep sleep, moved uneasily about upon her chair, and the dazed woman murmured a series of indecipherable utterances as if in remorseful remonstrance. Again, Elmer resumed his vigilant watch and industrious note taking.

Nor was his vigil without uncanny actions to record. The accursed crimson hand, which at first had been strongly visible upon the marble paleness of Georgiana's right cheek, now grew more faintly outlined. Her face remained as pale as ever, but with each successive breath, the birthmark mysteriously came and went, expanding from her face down to her lovely firm breasts, and then contracting back up to her colorless cheeks. During the alternating process, the mobile mole was losing some of its former distinctness. Its presence had been awesomely awful; its gradual departure was more awful still. Watch the stain of the rainbow fading out the sky, and you will know how that deplorable symbol almost quite miraculously and eventually passed-away into empty oblivion.

"By Heaven! It is well-nigh gone, evaporated into infinity!" bewildered Elmer whispered to himself, in almost irrepressible ecstasy. "I can scarcely trace its existence now. Success! The sweet smell and taste of success! Success doesn't suck one iota! And now, the same area of concern is like the faintest rose color," the husband softly and insanely mumbled. "The lightest flush of blood across her cheek would certainly overcome it. But she is so pale, just like my untanned ass looks like in the large bedroom mirror!"

The befuddled examiner drew aside the window curtain, and his weary eyes suffered the light of natural day, its radiance harshly falling into the room and resting upon Georgiana's exposed right cheek. At the same time, the enthused scientist heard a gross, hoarse chuckle, which he had long known as his servant Aminadab's expression of pure (or perhaps impure) delight. The unsettled master then addressed his mischievous servant.

"Ah, you asinine Clod! Ah, earthly Asshole Pauper!" Elmer bellowed, laughing excessively in a sort of frenetic frenzy. "You have served me well! Matter and spirit; earth and heaven. You have had a mere cameo role in this fabulous tragic play! Laugh, you' obscene, grotesque-looking dreg! You've earned the right to laugh, you dumb-fuck, lowlife, midget shit-head."

Those loud exclamations instantly broke Georgiana's sleep. The "patient" slowly opened her big brown eyes, and gazed into the nearby mirror, which her husband had shrewdly arranged upon a close table for *that* specific purpose. A faint smile flitted-over her lips when the full-bodied wife recognized how barely perceptible was that crimson and black hand which had once formerly blazed forth with such ominous brilliancy, a cruel uninviting curse now scientifically erased-away. But then, the woman's fatigued eyes sought Elmer's pallid face, which had been exhibiting a dire, troubled and anxious expression that he could by no means account.

"My poor Elmer!" Georgianna weakly murmured. "Poor in your money accumulation, and yet remaining poorer in your spirit! You need to become a religiously divine Soul Brother, my very lacking, greedy Husband!"

"Poor? Nay Wife. I'm now richest, happiest, and most favored!" Elmer exclaimed. "I'm completely exhilarated! My peerless bride, my difficult experiment has been incredibly successful! You are now quite perfectly formed!"

"My oh-so-poor Elmer," the distraught "patient" repeated, with a more than human tenderness. "You have aimed too loftily; you have done nobly, despite your tiny mini-brain. Do not repent *that* truth with so high and pure a feeling; you've rejected the best the Earth could offer. True, I am now bodily perfectly formed, but thanks to your bull-shit experiment, my spirit is now imperfectly deformed! Elmer, dearest Elmer, can't your blind ambition see that I am dying!"

Alas! The devastating news was all too true! The fatal hand of man's science had precariously grappled with the mystery of life, and the tampering with Divine Knowledge was the bond by which an angelic spirit kept itself in stellar union with a mere mortal feminine frame. As the last crimson tint of the birthmark (that sole token of human imperfection) faded from Georgiana's right cheek, the parting breath of the now perfect woman passed into the atmosphere, and her soul, lingering a moment near her husband, promptly took its heavenward flight. Elmer's unwise exploration into the majestic forces of Nature had condemned his only precious love to death.

'I'm vividly imagining the village church-bells pealing to the lively refrain,' Aminadab lamely conjectured. 'Ding-dong; the witch is dead! The ugly witch is dead'! I think I'd like that catchy tune much better than the hackneyed erratic lyrics and melody belonging to 'Sweet Georgiana Brown!'

Then, a hoarse, raspy laugh was heard again, originating from a distance. The eerie chuckle sounded like the cackle of Aminadab, but the suspected supernatural intonation was apparently originating from the deepest depths of Hell. Yet, had Elmer finally reached a more profound wisdom plateau, in the final analysis, the enterprising numbskull had accidentally flung-away the greatest happiness, which would have woven his mortal life of the selfsame texture with the too-deep-to-comprehend celestial spirit.

The momentary circumstance was too strong a tragedy for the disconsolate amateur dabbler to fully comprehend; now the junior scientist/chemist had egregiously failed to look beyond the shadowy scope of time and, living but once in a small temporal space of eternity, the proud young narcissist endeavored to futilely search for the perfect future existence in the present New England Puritanical moral time dimension. Elmer Lucifer Hamilton's vile actions truly constituted a completely ignorant immoral enterprise.

'How wonderful is Nature's sweet revenge!' Aminadab lamely concluded inside his dingy room. 'Ever since Master Elmer made me into a eunuch, I can't screw anyone, even though I had the hots for lovely Georgiana. Oh well; why should I be the only one in this fucked-up house forced to suffer the pain of sexual denial?'

About the Author

Jay Dubya is author John Wiessner's initials (J.W.) and also his pen name. John is a retired New Jersey public school English teacher, having taught the subject for thirty-four years. John lives in southern New Jersey with wife Joanne and the couple has three grown sons.

Jay Dubya has written other adult literature besides *Thirteen Sick Tasteless Classics, Part III. So Ya' Wanna' Be A Teacher*, *The Wholly Book of Genesis'*, *Black Leather and Blue Denim, A '50s Novel* and its sequel, *The Great Teen Fruit War, A 1960' Novel* are humorous literary endeavors. *Frat Brats, A '60s Novel* completes Jay Dubya's coming-of-age action/adventure trilogy. *Pieces of Eight, Pieces of Eight, Part II, Pieces of Eight Part III and Pieces of Eight, Part IV* are short story/novella collections featuring science fiction, paranormal and humorous plots and themes. *Nine New Novellas, NNN, Part II, NNN, Part III* and *NNN, Part IV* are other sci-fi/paranormal story collections. *Two Baker's Dozen* is another collection of short fiction works.

Ron Coyote, Man of La Mangia is adult humor and a satire/parody on Miguel Cervantes' *Don Quixote*, published in 1605. *The Wholly Book of Exodus* is adult satirical humor. *Thirteen Sick Tasteless Classics, Thirteen Sick Tasteless Classics, Part II* and *TSTC, Part IV* are adult satirical rewrites of famous literary short fiction. Other satirical works are *Mauled Maimed Mangled Mutilated Mythology, Fractured Frazzled Folk Fables and Fairy Farces* and *FFFF & FF, Part II*.

John has also authored a trilogy of young adult fantasy novels, *Enchanta, Pot of Gold* and *Space Bugs, Earth Invasion. The Eighteen' Story Gingerbread House* is a new collection of eighteen diverse children's stories.

Jay Dubya likes '50s rock and roll music, and he also enjoys pop' songs by the Beach Boys', Fleetwood Mac, the Eagles, the Rolling Stones, *ELO*, John Mellencamp and by John Fogerty. When not writing or listening to music, Jay Dubya likes watching *76ers* basketball and *Phillies* and *Yankees* television baseball games.

Author Biography

Born in Hammonton, NJ in 1942, John Wiessner had attended St. Joseph School up to and including Grade 5. After his family moved from Hammonton to Levittown, Pa in 1954, John attended St. Mark School in Bristol, Pa. for Grade 6, St. Michael the Archangel School in Levittown for Grades 7 and 8 and then Immaculate Conception School, Levittown, Pa. for Grade 9. Bishop Egan High School, Levittown PA. was John's educational base for Grades 10 and 11, and later in 1960, the aspiring author graduated from Edgewood Regional High, Tansboro, NJ. John then next attended Glassboro State College, where he was an announcer for the school's baseball games and also read the nightly news and sports over WGLS, GSC's radio station.

John Wiessner had been primarily an English teacher in the Hammonton Public School System for 34 years, specializing in the instruction of middle school language arts. Mr. Wiessner was quite active in the Hammonton Education Association, serving in the capacities of Vice-President, building representative and finally, teachers' head negotiator for 7 years. During his lengthy teaching career, John had been nominated into "Who's Who among American Teachers" three times. He also was quite active giving professional workshops at schools around South Jersey on the subjects of creative writing and the use of movie videos to motivate students to organize their classroom theme compositions.

John Wiessner was very active in community service, being a past President of the Hammonton Lions Club, where he also functioned for many years as the club's Tail-Twister, Vice-President and Liontamer. John had been named Hammonton Lion of the Year in 1979 and in 2009 received the prestigious Melvin Jones Fellow Award, the highest honor a Lion can receive.

John also was a successful businessman, starting with being a Philadelphia Bulletin newspaper delivery boy for two-years in the late 1950s in Levittown, Pennsylvania. After his family moved back to New Jersey in 1959, John worked at his grandparents and his parents' farm markets, Square Deal Farm (now Ron's Gardens in Hammonton) and Pete's Farm Market in Elm, respectively. He later managed his wife's parents' farm market, White Horse Farms in Elm for three summers.

Also in a business capacity, for 16 summers starting in 1967 John Wiessner had co-owned Dealers Choice Amusement Arcade on the Ocean City, Maryland boardwalk and also co-owned the New Horizon Tee-Shirt Store for eight summers (1973-'81) on the Rehoboth Beach, Delaware boardwalk. In addition, "Jay Dubya" was a co-owner of Wheel and Deal Amusement Arcade, Missouri Avenue and Boardwalk, Atlantic

City. And then, for 18 summers beginning in 1986, John had been the Field Manager in charge of crew-leaders for Atlantic Blueberry Company (the world's largest cultivated blueberry farm), both the Weymouth and Mays Landing Divisions.

After retiring from teaching in 1999, writing under the pen name Jay Dubya (his initials), John Wiessner became the author of 62 books in the genre Action/Adventure Novels, Sci-Fi/Paranormal Story Collections, Adult Satire, Young Adult Fantasy Novels and also Non-Fiction Books. His books exist in hardcover, in paperback and in popular Kindle and Nook e-book formats.

In January of 2022, John Wiessner (Jay Dubya) was nominated into Marquis Who's Who in America, and in April of that same year, was one of nine distinguished Who's Who in America members honored with Lifetime Achievement Awards, all nine sharing an article of recognition appearing in the Wall Street Journal.

Google: Jay Dubya books